THE RING

Douglas Todd

Douglas Todd

Infinite appreciation to Misha Fletcher for edits and to Debby Levinson for edits, image wrangling, and listening to me gripe.

THE CASE of the LOCKED AIRSHAFT

"Slow cycle," the captain said, looking out the port—don't let any space crew hear you call it a window—at the Ring quickly enlarging at us.

Aren't they all? I thought, but I didn't say it aloud. I had been on board for eighty-six cycles and four Ring transits, and even those stopped being a change of pace by the third time, once I found that I no longer had to throw up. I'd spent a certain amount of time reviewing the Pergati that I'd been learning in my sleep, and a small amount of time learning Bak'ti the hard way from the storemaster (who I suspect was hoping it would lead me to thank him horizontally) ... and the vast bulk of my time sitting in my cabin burning through the store of books I had been hoping would last me at least six months on the Ring.

There are no outside time cues on a ship; no sun, no moon, no darkness or light you don't make yourself. A cycle is a little over three hours longer than an Earth day. It has thirty-two periods and those each have thirty-two sub-periods. For the first five or six cycles I couldn't stop myself from trying to convert into hours and minutes in my head. Then I couldn't make myself try. You go to sleep at thirty-one (in base eight, so it's actually twenty-five, just to make it complicated) because everybody else who isn't on third watch is going to bed then, and you get up at one, definitely no later than two, because you've been told that lying in your bunk for more than eight periods is a bad idea and will lead to your lying there all cycle and forgetting to eat. Meals, served at specific times, become the only focal points. None of this makes space travel any less numbingly dull, whether you're crew or just a landpig going off to a new job.

I was told that the Ring used ship time as well, so I might as well get used to it.

Anyway, I knew what the captain meant. The previous four Rings had all been surrounded by ships—every dock position on the Ring filled, and a cloud of other ships waiting their turns for transit, plus a handful of small craft shuttling people or cargo back and forth and trying not to collide with anything. This Ring had no ships waiting, and only one ship was docked to the Ring itself, rotating along with it.

"Is that normal?"

He shrugged. "I've seen it busy before. Get your gear together."

"How long until we dock?"

"We don't. You're the cargo. They're sending a shuttle. Ten to fifteen."

So they had no other business here. I wondered what I had cost to ship. I'd heard far more than I needed to hear from the captain about costs and cargo value and how damned hard it was to make a living in this business, especially with what Rings extorted for transits, so either I was conveniently on his way or someone had paid a lot to get me here. It certainly hadn't been me.

Ten to fifteen subs—a sub-period is about a minute and a half, and that's the last time I am ever going to convert, so use it well—was long enough for me to get my gear, though I guess it wouldn't have been long enough for most people uprooting a quarter of the way around the galaxy. When you spend years living in a virtual space, you don't accumulate physical objects. The shuttle came in nine subs, though, so I got a disapproving look as I arrived at the locks. From the captain. The other person waiting could not possibly have cared less.

This other person gave me a slight nod and gave the captain an even less energetic one, and ushered me into the lock. When it cycled, it opened directly onto the single cramped area that served as both bridge and passenger seating. It had a slight smell of stale sweat and the seat I was gestured to had a rip in its upholstery. There were no other occupants. The pilot looked back to make sure I had fastened my harness, turned to their console, and fell off the bigger ship and was accelerating toward the Ring before I'd had a chance to wonder how smooth the dismount was going to be.

A few subs later and we were close enough to the Ring that I couldn't see more than just a bit of it at top of frame as I looked out the front port. We had turned and matched spin, moving around the Ring in the same direction and speed it was rotating, and then I felt something strike us and we were tugged up, into the Ring itself, moving inside it. Apparently the shuttle had an enclosed bay. We stopped moving, and by the time the pilot had finished switching down their console, the red lights on the airlock had turned green.

After we had climbed a short airway to a dim corridor, the pilot said, "This is deck nine, on the outer circumference. Deck one is closest to core. You want to go up to deck two, spinward to sector forty. Director's office. Follow the numbers." Then they walked off, in the opposite direction from the one they'd pointed to, without another word.

§

Following the numbers wasn't hard, but the "find the closest ramp to go up one deck, then the next ramp up may be in the other direction" game took a little work. My first thought was, this would be a horrible mess in an evacuation, and then I realized I was being a landpig. Where would they evacuate to?

The door had nothing on it but DIRECTOR. I had already learned on the ship that knocking was a landpig thing. If you pressed the panel and the door didn't open, it would buzz in the room; and if no one on the other side responded to the buzz, go away. This one opened. A small room with a desk and a single spare chair, no other furniture, nothing on the walls. The woman sitting behind the desk was probably around fifty, brown hair just beginning to salt white, pinned up messily with a strand hanging nearly to her eye, with dark bags below her eyes and a few lines at the mouth but otherwise not showing many signs of age in the face. She looked up at me and I got the sensation, as she met my eyes, that a permanent image of me had just been stored in her brain. She did not smile. "Yes?"

"I'm here to see Catherine Worthington?"

"You're looking at her. You must be Jessica Gray. Sit down." She fussed with a machine on her desk. "Lean in and put your elbows on the desk. Rest your head in your hands. Yes, like that. Hold very still." Retinal scans. I'd had those before. She put down the scanning gun and checked the machine. "Good. I don't always get them on the first try ... I'm giving you Class 1 access. Don't abuse it. Your passcode is GRAY. I'll expect you to change it immediately when you get to your rooms."

"Just like that," I said.

She looked up from the machine to me and I saw one corner of her mouth turn up. Barely. "First, Clarkson reported your arrival when he docked. Second, anyone else walking in here would know me on sight. I've got an image of you around here somewhere, but I'm not going to bother to check it. Even if you were an impostor, that wouldn't relieve you of the obligation to do the job you're here for."

"Which is what exactly? 'Security officer' covers a lot."

"I'm not going to narrow it down. Keep the peace, essentially. We get visitors and transients who see the Ring as a place to let loose. We make a lot of money from them, so we won't discourage them from drinking and sexing and shouting, but our permanents come first. No one would live here if they didn't feel safe, so you make it clear that causing trouble for permanents is not allowed. Also, make it clear to visitors that they can't dodge their debts just by getting back on their ship and leaving. Problem is they usually *can*—once they leave we may never see them again—so you have to get them to pay for damages and so on before they go. Weapons discouraged; breachables prohibited. Ship's crew hate them as much as we do, but sometimes some idiot passenger brings one. How's your Pergati?"

"Good. I've been using sleep-impression."

She nodded. "You'll use it more often than Trade, so keep working on it. Bak'ti too if you haven't; we get crews in who need it." Something in the room made an electronic chirp, and she frowned. It chirped several more times and she ignored them all, not without effort, as she continued. "That reminds me—you'll need a feed—I think Alsop's is still in his rooms—your rooms, now. Alsop kept a lot of notes as well. I suggest you read them." The chirping continued and she growled. "I'm going to have to answer that. Your rooms are antispin from here, this deck, sector twelve. After you set up there, go find Max Tenbom, he'll likely be in five:thirty-one. Look for the door that says CUSTODY. He'll tell you more than I can." She picked up the small black rectangle that was doing the chirping, had a look at it, held it to her ear. "Director. Yes ... what? No, we've told them they can't do that. No, not even for a surcharge." She pushed her hand at me, palm out, in a "get out" gesture. I got out.

I hoped this Tenbom person was more useful.

§

It took me fifteen minutes—excuse me, ten subs—to walk the twenty-two sectors from Worthington's office to the door marked SECURITY OFFICER. I realize forty minus twelve isn't twenty-two. The sectors were also in base eight—the number before 40 was 37. I made two mental notes—first, to find out how many sectors there were so I could figure out how long it took to go the whole circumference, and second, to find out who had such a fetish for base eight and why.

It smelled musty inside, and was dark. I'd grown accustomed to automatic lighting aboard ship and it took me a while to find the panel, which wasn't just inside the door. The room was only marginally brighter with the lights on. Apparently the previous owner—whom I assumed had been this Alsop—had liked it cave-like. The ambient light was dim; three of the walls were painted a gray that looked even darker in shadows than it probably was, and the false curtains on the featureless rear wall were a subtle black herringbone pattern on brown. The only really bright area was the desk and data station at the back right corner, which had a task light shining straight down at it. The desk and its comfortable-looking chair were the only pieces of furniture that looked like someone had been choosy about what he wanted. There were two upholstered chairs, back near the curtain, and two straight chairs at the small table near the front of the room, and none of them matched, and none of them looked pleasant to sit on.

On the right, separated from the main room by a short wall with a bar top, was the kitchen. It had either never been used or had been very well cleaned after Alsop—quit? Died? I was surprised to find that there were still plates, glasses, utensils—although not many. Alsop could have had a friend over to dinner if they didn't use more than one plate each. And if they brought in food; there were no cooking implements, no pots, no pans.

The door on the left was the bedroom, and off that, the shower and toilet. The bed had another of those task lights, illuminating only the side with the small night table with a clock on it. The other side of the bed was pushed against a wall. If I'd needed any confirmation that Alsop lived alone, that was it. Lived alone, apparently left without taking his dishes or his clock ... or his clothes, I found as I opened the closet. He liked plaid.

I was beginning to be sure Alsop had not quit.

Back in the main room, I examined the small pile of objects I'd noticed on the table. One item was a clone of the little black rectangle Worthington had used. A thin cylinder turned out to be a small but very bright flashlight. Then there was a small pad of notepaper with a cover and a pen—a real surprise; that was the first paper and ink I'd seen since I left Earth. Even there, paper is for throwbacks and other eccentrics. Like me. There was a small strip which was the right size and shape to be a money transfer, assuming they used them and they looked like the ones on Earth, and a plastic box with compartments. In the long compartment were some tools—a probe that came to a point, long tweezers, a delicate-looking brush, and an elongated, thin magnifying lens. The smaller compartments had their own lids. They looked empty except for one that had a tiny amount of some dark crumbs or fragments in it.

I was positive now. Pity; I had started to like Alsop's personal style. He seemed like the kind of person to whom I could have said, "I have 'ere, Mr. Holmes, the contents of the victim's pockets," and not gotten a blank stare.

Alsop kept a lot of notes as well. I suggest you read them. Well, he hadn't kept them on paper. The notepad was blank but had many pages torn out. That had been short-term storage. I sat down at the desk and turned on the data station. The first thing that displayed after I entered my passcode was a message insisting I change it immediately, which I did, and then another informing me that ownership of 'Alsop, Peter Martin' file space was transferred to me by Class 1 user 'Worthington, C. E.' The E probably stood for Efficient.

Alsop had either been neurotically compulsive or very big on contingency planning or both. C. Efficient Worthington had been right; there *were* a lot of notes, a vast amount of notes that must have taken years to accumulate—and they were labelled, tagged, cross-referenced, catalogued, sorted, and probably indexed too. I looked up PERGATI and got an entry that wouldn't have been out of place in an anthropologist's reference books. Right again, boss; I was going to want to spend serious reading time with these. But at the moment, I wanted to be somewhere that didn't make me feel like I was sitting in the room with a ghost.

§

I found out later that the long circumferential corridors—one on every deck but the lowest—were called "concourses." I found them a little unsettling. Most of the other spaces in the Ring look like normal rooms and ramps and halls and stairs—mostly. But the concourses curve. And you can *see* them curve, especially in a slow cycle like that one, with no other people in the concourse blocking your view of the hallway curving up to an artificial horizon in either direction. It reminded you that you were not in a normal space. During my previous job, in the artificial world of the Vault, I'd realized how important it was for ninety percent of people there to maintain the illusion that they were in normal space, to have their virtual houses look just like real houses and their virtual streets look just like real streets. I was not part of that ninety percent, but it was still clear to me that the Ring was going to take some getting used to.

From my arrival on deck nine up to the locations on deck two, I had encountered a total of three other people (not counting Worthington). But on deck five, things were a little livelier, even during a slow cycle. Apparently deck five was where all the Things To Do were. The doors and storefronts reflected this: bars, dance halls, skin shows, and combinations of any of the three; shops carrying all sorts of merchandise, very little of it necessary or useful; food establishments at all levels of cost and formality; A/V booths, public data stations, game rooms, gambling houses. Any kind of business where a ship's crew could blow its accumulated pay was amply represented.

The sector numbers were hard to find amid all the glitz, and as I stopped walking to search for one to see if I'd somehow gone too far, something ran into me from behind and nearly knocked me over. I turned and had to look down; Pergati are not all that tall. This one had mahogany fur ranging to tan on the extremities. I apologized in Pergati, trying not to look like I was staring, but they didn't notice anyway. They growled at me and continued hurrying, almost-running, down the hall, kilt flapping. Some distance ahead, I saw them open a door and rush in.

I kept wandering past the dens of iniquity until I did almost miss it—a bare door, too unobtrusive among all the fun and games. Inside CUSTODY, facing the door so he could see anyone coming in, a round-bodied, round-faced man with very little hair, wrinkles around his eyes and mouth, and a nose one size too big for his face sat behind a desk, listening to the Pergat who'd run into me. To the right of the desk as you came in, along the back wall of the room, were five identical doors with little windows in them, evenly spaced. At the far end of the room were some shelves with what looked like housekeeping stock—towels and cleaning products and such—and a sink.

"Now you go back to your work, Prit-man," he was replying in Pergati. "I will examine. Can you work other places for now?"

"Yes, yes," said the Pergat impatiently. "But I want no blame for this—already bad enough delay—"

"Be calm. No blame will come."

The Pergat spun and stalked out, giving me what I took to be a suspicious glare. He was probably annoyed you can't slam a sliding door.

"May I help you?" the man asked me, switching to Trade.

"Are you Tenbom? I'm Jessica Gray."

"Ms. Gray!" He smiled broadly, which made his face scrunch up into a mass of wrinkles, and got up to shake my hand eagerly. "Sight for sore eyes. Welcome aboard." I suppose I was making a surprised face, because he added hastily, "Oh, sorry, forgive the 'Ms.' I'm a little too old to have really gotten used to this business of just last names, especially when you spend all day dealing with Pergati and they still use titles, you know, they're all 'Prit-man' and 'Shil-woman' if you're being formal, and you have to be formal with the important ones unless you want them to be even grumpier than they already are. You should call me 'Max'—I'll try to remember to call you just 'Gray,' unless you'd rather I call you 'Boss,' of course ..."

It was impossible not to smile. "Why don't you call me 'Jessica.' Just don't call me 'Jess' and we'll be fine. Am I actually your boss?"

"The Director didn't tell you? It figures. How'd you do with her, anyway? I hope she didn't spook you too much."

"No, should she have?"

He shrugged. "You didn't hear it from me, but she's got sort of a dragon-lady reputation. Runs Dispatch with an iron fist and all that. No complaints, myself, except maybe that it took her so long to fill your position; I'm not cut out to do your job and I don't care who knows it."

"Pretend I know absolutely nothing, Max. What exactly *is* your job, and where do you and I overlap?"

"Tell you what, can I explain on the way? It's a long walk. Plenty of time."

"On the way to what?"

"Oh! Well, that's what Prit was in here about, see. There's a body at the bottom of one of the core vent shafts. Probably been there a while. I probably know who it is. Might as well start your first cycle on the job off right, huh?"

§

"I'm really just supposed to run the custody rooms," Max said as we hustled along. He walked faster than you'd expect from his weight and build. "We put people there to, you know, cool down a little or if we want to make sure they don't run off for some reason. But they're not really a jail—the doors are a little special, but otherwise they're just regular rooms. So a while back Pete decided he wanted someone to keep an eye on them and he got me the job, which is good, because as you can see, I'm not really in shape to be a cargo beef any more. In fact, gotta say, if Pete hadn't talked me into it I'd probably have gone back to Earth to retire. Oh, I guess you don't know who 'Pete' is—"

"Alsop," I said. "Max, how did he die?"

"Who said he died?" Max replied, but he could only keep his poker face for a second. "Yeah, okay, I can see you're not the delicate kind. We think heart attack. He was found in a hall on deck six. Not a lot of traffic on three and six. He'd probably been there a couple of periods. No robbery and no injuries. Pete always pushed himself hard, poor guy. I figure he just wore himself out. We double back here; next ramp's the other way. You'll get used to the zigzag. Anyway so since Pete died I've kinda been trying to keep a lid on things, but like I say, I'm not too good at it, and I'm glad as hell you're here."

I wasn't sure I'd be too good at it either, but Max didn't need to know that. "Is it normal here to just leave someone's stuff after they die?"

"A lot of the time, yeah. Costs so much to ship it off, so we don't unless there's family somewhere else that really wants it. Though ... nah, she'd have taken anything she wanted. Never mind. If it's there it's yours now, do whatever you want with it."

What we'd been passing on deck seven looked like personal residences—names on the doors—but as we headed down a ramp to deck eight, suddenly things looked different. Darker, about half as bright as the deck above, and fewer doors. Despite not having stopped talking the whole time, Max saw me looking. "This is upper cargo. A lot of cargo storage is two decks high, and usually we load in from below on nine. Up here is just high load—if you have to take cargo from the top of the stack, get what I mean?—or crane operators moving stuff around below."

"Good place to get mugged," I remarked.

"Knifed is more likely. We don't get a lot of robbery; our problem is drunk visitors getting in fights, settling their grudges here where their captain can't prove anything and throw 'em out a lock."

"So these levels are 'enter at your own risk'?"

"Well ... permanents don't come down here except to work cargo."

"And we don't give a damn about anybody else?"

He just grinned. "Not much. Look, you wanna try to get someone to do patrols down here, be my guest. But I bet you the Director would tell you to jump out an airlock before she'd pay for it."

"No monitoring at all? Why not just put in some cameras?"

"We have door logs—we know who goes in and out of everything—but ..." He shook his head. "Well, hell, say we did keep all that. Who'd slog through the data? You wanna pay someone to sit in a room and watch a hundred displays all cycle just in case something happens? You couldn't pay me enough. Well, maybe you could, but it'd take a lot." He grinned again. "And if something nasty did happen what good would be finding out about it too late?"

"Might get a glimpse of whoever was putting the knife in somebody else's back," I said.

"And we'd find out it was a visitor and he shipped five subs later and is halfway to the ass end of the galaxy by now." He shrugged. "Now, you wanna hear about this body?" I nodded.

"So, we have these shafts. They go all the way from deck nine up to past deck one, right into the core. Some of them pump air in, from the pressure tanks out here on eight and nine; some of them let air come back out. I think three of each maybe? We have a guy who goes around to keep them all clean, and make sure everything's running right, and so on. Only the one guy, because he has to be able to fool around near the core and we don't let just anybody go there. OK, so, this is kind of embarrassing, but I guess nobody really checks on this guy much. We'd know if he wasn't doing his job, Prit says, because we'd start getting warning lights and alert messages and so on after a while, but it's not like he was checking in with anybody every cycle. Prit's his boss, but Prit knows the guy likes to be left alone, and as long as the work was getting done—see?"

"So he could have been dead for a while, is what you're leading to."

"Yeah. From what I could tell of Prit's techspeak, the alert was about too much crud where the air came out at the core end. For it to get that dirty, he figures maybe thirty, fifty cycles with nobody cleaning the filters or the shaft. Prit figures the guy is slacking; worst case, he's taken a kormor a little too long. Kormor— you know that one? Pergati hibernate, only not really. Every so often they decide they're fed up with everybody—not much of a stretch—and they eat a big meal and then go sleep in their rooms for a long time—cycles and cycles. I hear they send out announcements. 'Sincerely regret to inform you that I will be unavailable for twenty cycles because I need a nice long nap.' Funny stuff."

"Max—"

"Yeah, sorry, don't mind me. All over the place. Just yank me back to the point if I do that too much. Long story short, Prit goes over all the places this guy has been supposed to be working to see what's been neglected and he gets to this shaft and finds—well, he wasn't real clear about that, so let's see for ourselves. Definitely dead though. This is it, this little hall here."

The "little hall" was about one person wide and four people deep if they packed themselves in back to belly, and the unmarked door at the end of it was much shorter than usual—more than a meter and a half, but less than two. Max walked up to it, stopped, then turned around in the confined hall and made me back out. "What's the problem?"

"I don't have access, I guess," he said. "I knew they kept these tight, but—anyway, you open it."

"I don't know if I can either."

"Yeah, you can. You can open anything. The reader's not in the usual place so be sure you look right at it—see the black dot?" I went in and stared at the dot, and the door slid open.

The corridor beyond was the same height as the door. I could go in without crouching if I didn't mind my head brushing the ceiling. Max didn't have that problem; his issue was girth. "This is why they give these jobs to Pergati," he muttered as he squeezed in. "Go right."

Besides being claustrophobic, the lighting was very dim, and I wasn't thrilled when the door shut behind us and made it even darker. I hoped we could get back out. "Max, do all the doors on the Ring have retinal readers?"

"Yeah, they—Damn!" I heard him recoil a little and thought I heard a skittering noise. When I spun around, he was looking behind us into the dark hall at something. "Did you see it? I hate those things."

"No, what was it?"

"P-rat. Our only pest control problem. They get around in cable conduits. Director doesn't care because they don't like the taste of wiring, but they sure as hell like our food. We have a guy goes and hunts for them sometimes—no, keep going, I don't want to stand around—but they're on half the damn ships in the galaxy, so we just get more. You were asking about doors. Yeah. We used to use passcode pads for low-security ones but we had some trouble, so now it's readers for everybody. Amazed they paid for it but I guess they thought it was worth it to keep everybody quiet."

"What, somebody was robbing rooms?"

"Nah. Say you're seeing somebody and then you have a bad fight and she comes in next cycle because you gave her your code, and she trashes your rooms ... 'course it doesn't help any because now, you'd put her on your reader list, same problem—I guess this is it, huh?" The corridor dead-ended at another door. This one didn't have any security at all. In fact, I realized as I looked around for a panel, it wasn't even automatic. I was glad I had noticed before waiting too long for something to happen. I pulled the handle and was surprised how hard the door was to drag open.

The first thing was the smell. I won't try to describe it; I'll just say that I stepped back involuntarily and I heard Max make a noise that was somewhere between a gulp and a moan. I didn't ask him if he was going to throw up because discussing it might have made me need to throw up myself.

There was no lighting in the shaft. All four walls looked black, and the tiny amount of light coming in from the doorway barely helped. There was no ceiling; presumably somewhere far up there was the other end of the shaft, up in the core. I wished I had brought Alsop's flashlight. The shaft was only a meter squared in floor area, and nearly all of that was taken up by the body. It lay diagonally, and had just enough space to lie flat, face up.

Pergati look like teddy bears to me. Let's just get that stated and get it over with. Of course this was only the second one I'd ever seen in the flesh, but I'd thought this even when all I had were pictures. Their limbs are longer than a teddy bear's would be, and their faces, especially their muzzles, are shaped a little differently, but the ears and the eyes and the general roundness are dead-on. Teddy bears in kilts. Of course, if you said that to a Pergat—well, fortunately I don't think anyone's been brave enough to show them a teddy bear, so they probably wouldn't understand the reference. Otherwise you'd be missing a limb or two.

This one looked like a teddy bear that had been too-well-used and maybe even left out in the rain one day. It had big discolored bald patches where its fur was missing, and the rest of the fur was matted or stuck out in strange directions. Some parts were misshapen, bulging, as if stuffing had fallen out and then been packed back in badly; other parts looked moth-eaten. Yet it looked strangely peaceful. Its hands—if you prefer, upper paws—were clasped over its chest, as if someone had found a discarded toy and arranged it carefully, reverently, in repose. Waiting for its owner to claim it.

You may think all of that is a pretty strange reaction, but it's what saved me from throwing up. Bodies in the Vault didn't stink.

"Max. We can't do anything in here." I wasn't even sure I had enough room to stand in the shaft with the body without stepping on part of it. "We need to get it out."

I turned. He was still standing and staring and I wasn't sure he was even with me, until he blinked a couple of times. "Did you hear me?" I asked.

"Hmmm ... yeah. Get it out where?"

"Anywhere. We can't examine it here. Who's the medical examiner on the Ring? Or coroner?"

He crinkled up his face, but not smiling. "I don't think we have one. If Pete ever needed anything like that, he didn't tell me about it."

"What do you do when you need to certify death?"

"Well, I—"

"You've never needed an autopsy? No unexplained deaths? No violent crimes?"

"Well, come on, isn't that—I mean, yeah, we get deaths all the time, sometimes nasty ones, but—Oh, hey, wait! I know who you want. You want Dr. Kohl. This is right up his alley."

"I'll take your word for it. Where is Dr. Kohl?"

"Deck four. All medical stuff's on deck four."

I sighed. "I guess we can both carry it that far."

"You gotta be kidding—no, actually, wait, I have a better idea. We just need to go get something on this deck, not too far. Come on."

"Do we both need to get it?"

"Well, no, but—what, you're waiting in here?"

"Yes. I want to think about this a little more."

He gave me a look that I think was bewilderment, then shrugged and headed back down the corridor.

My eyes had adjusted to the light better now. I could see that the wall of the shaft opposite the door wasn't actually a wall, not the lowest meter or so of it. It was a grating. That was where air came in. It hadn't been one of the shafts flowing the opposite way; Prit had said so. Why wasn't I feeling wind from it? Someone must have turned it off. Probably Prit while investigating; I imagined turning off the shaft's air completely would send him all kinds of warnings, so it couldn't have been earlier.

"Damn it." Max had come back. "They really keep this place tight. Don't know why they think anybody would care."

"What's the problem?"

"You gotta let me out. Damned door needs access on *both* sides." I got in front of him, with a little difficulty, without stepping on anything, and led him back down and let him out the door, then came back to stare at the shaft.

I ran a finger along one wall. I had been expecting to see the fingertip completely black with dirt, but no—the walls were actually black, I mean colored black, and very smooth—in fact, slippery. Plastic, or some kind of coating. My finger had only a couple of small flakes of dirt. I tested another spot. This one was a little worse, a scattering of powdery particles not just on my fingertip but falling into my palm. Still, this was filthy enough to cause warnings? The core must be pretty picky about cleanliness.

Then something occurred to me about the color of those particles. I tried smelling my fingertip but there was no hope of that, not with the smell in the rest of the room drowning it out.

I stooped next to the body and tried the floor close to it, came away with fingers covered with the same stuff. Enough of it to be sure. It was so dry that I could remove it from my hand just by brushing it off. It occurred to me to wonder how much of it had made it all the way up into the core air intake.

Next question: Should I check the obvious place? Or wait for better light and so on? I admit part of it was not really wanting to get any closer to that smell, or touch the body, let alone rearrange it. It couldn't possibly hurt me, but the back of my mind was shouting NO NO UNCLEAN THING DON'T TOUCH. I sighed. Damned monkey brains. You'd think we'd have evolved past this.

A distant thumping sound startled me aware. What was that? Oh—it was Max. He couldn't get back in.

He'd come back with a sort of L-shaped cart, a pivoting upright shaft with a handle, attached to the end of a long flat tongue, so close to the ground that I couldn't see whether it was on wheels or rollers or what. "Cargo trolley," he said. He also had a folded tarp or something like that under his arm. "What's that for?" I asked.

Again he gave me that look like he had a problem he couldn't solve. "Well, see, I figured we might not want to haul a stinking body in plain sight up five decks ..."

"No, I suppose not. This cart isn't going to make that bend, is it? We'll need to drag it out here."

I'm not going to bother giving the details of that. It wasn't pleasant. "Max, it looks like this thing can be handled by one person—"

"Sure," he said. "That's the idea."

"Tell me where Dr. Kohl is, and I'll bring this up to him. I want you to go find Prit and tell him not to tell anybody about this. You don't either, OK? Also tell him he can turn that shaft back on if he wants, but he can't clean it yet."

"Four:twenty-seven. Why not?"

"Because there's blood all over the floor and I may want to go in again and look at it with a good light." He looked down at his shoes. "No, we left most of it in the access corridor," I said. "But you probably want to wash your hands."

He shot me another glance and headed off to find Prit.

§

The door to four:twenty-seven opened when I pressed the panel, but if Max was right and I could open anything, that meant nothing. "Is anyone here?"

"Hello? What?" a voice said from deep in the back of the room. I describe it that way because I couldn't see it; my view was blocked by several rows of high shelves that were so crowded with specimens, equipment, and plain old junk that visibility through them was impossible. Even with shelves in the middle and around the edges of the room, apparently some of the detritus didn't fit and was just piled in random places on the floor.

I wandered into the back half of the room—leaving the trolley by the door—and found the back half was less like a storeroom and more like a morgue. The only strong light was over a lab table covered with chemistry glassware, but in the shadows I could see a big metal-topped table with a drain and a rim—an autopsy table—and what certainly looked like drawers for cold storage built into the back wall.

The man who had not yet looked up from his work at the lab table was old, but not fragile. He was solidly built and you could definitely see biceps below his rolled-up sleeves when he moved his arms. He was bald except for a white fringe that seamlessly turned into sideburns and a well-trimmed white beard. He had bushy white eyebrows and, I saw as he looked up at me, piercing blue eyes.

"So she finally found a replacement, did she?" he said, and turned back down to his equipment.

I sifted through all possible replies rapidly. "I suppose there could have been other people besides me the door would open for."

"Yes, but none whom I wouldn't recognize. Frederic Kohl," he looked up again and nodded briefly as an introduction.

"Jessica Gray. I have a body I'd like you to look at."

"Do you now," he said. "One moment ... there! That's positive. Unsurprisingly." The test tube had a white liquid and a yellowish liquid, and a pink area had appeared at the point where they were trying to mix. He put the tube in a stand and stood up. "Well, I suppose I'll have to see it, then."

We walked out to the front and he sniffed and wrinkled his nose. "Fairly advanced, eh? Let's get this to the table before we unwrap it. There should be enough room down this side."

I pulled the body into the back and we lifted it onto the autopsy table. He went to some panels on the wall and turned on a pair of painfully bright lights over the table, and also what sounded like a powerful fan somewhere overhead. He removed the tarp and we both waited a minute for some of the smell to be lifted away.

"Pergat," he said, "adult," he lifted what was left of the kilt, "sprocket, well into decomposition ... body hair falling out and—" opening the mouth—"teeth loose so I'd say dead at least twenty-five cycles."

"When we found it," I said, "both hands were over the chest, like this. I think it was pressing a wound. Did you say 'sprocket'?"

"Yes, there's something here," he said. He leaned in close and began probing the chest wound with a metal pick. "'Male' and 'female' are sociological, not anatomical, terms, and not meaningful in all species," he said absently as he worked. "But all sentients so far encountered with two and only two anatomical sexes which engage in direct reproductive intercourse—as opposed to indirect fertilization—have one phenotype with recessed sex organs and the other with protruding sex organs. It just seems to be the optimal format for getting it done. Hand me that loupe."

While he dug into the wound carefully, his face as close to it as he could get, I opened the pouch that Pergati carry at their waist. They don't seem to believe in pockets. It was large—a working pouch, if you will, instead of a dress one—and contained, in addition to his ID and a money transfer, several rags in various stages of dirty, a couple of brushes, and an unlabeled bottle of a bleach-smelling liquid. Nothing unexpected—unless something had been removed, of course.

"On the Ring," Dr. Kohl continued, voice slightly muffled by his position, "to avoid having to have an anthropology discussion every time you're trying to figure out whether you want to have sex with someone, we frequently use the somewhat ludicrous terms 'socket' and 'sprocket.' This is a puncture wound," he concluded, standing upright. "Made by a sharply pointed object of a material which left no splinters or particles in the wound, about one centimeter at its widest, penetrating about four centimeters deep. Got a lung, but not the heart."

"That wouldn't have been fatal."

"Not quickly. Do you have reason to think it might have been?"

"Well, do you see anything else that would have killed him?"

"It's hard to visually locate wounds and contusions on Pergati even when they're not decomposing," he said, pushing aside fur in various places and feeling the body. "All the bones feel the way they should. Help me flip him over."

"There was a lot of blood," I said, "but I don't picture him lying there waiting to bleed out, not if he was conscious. He'd have gone to get help."

"Still, you imply he did most of his bleeding where the body was found. Did you find any suggestive objects in the area?"

"No." I had checked after we got the body onto the trolley. "We weren't the finders, but unless Prit picked something up ... actually Prit is the number-one candidate. Apparently there aren't many people allowed to go where the body was."

"Nothing obvious on this side. Unless it's extremely subtle, cause of death was not physical trauma."

"I suppose if it were something chemical there wouldn't be any sign of it left by now."

"Probably not, but there are a few things I can look for. It won't be fast," he said. "Come see me in a cycle. I may have something for you, or I may not."

"I'm sorry to interrupt your other work."

"I don't have other work," he said, not harshly. "I suppose you could call me the senior physician in residence. They can't do without me because I know too many useful things, so I get to stay here rather than being forcibly being retired to Earth. Sometimes I investigate deaths aboard ships—they have to get those certified. Last year I got to play epidemiologist a bit. Sometimes I do some chemical analysis." He gestured to the lab bench. "Mostly I sit and wait for someone to have a problem. So you don't need to act guilty."

I nodded.

"Wash your hands before you go," he said. "I should have made you put on gloves."

§

All right, suppose he had been drugged. Drug him, drag him into the airshaft where no one was likely to find him ... then stab him and let him bleed to death slowly, taking the risk that he might wake up too soon and crawl out? Probably not. Poison him? Maybe. If it was administered the right way. Best would be something very fast on the weapon itself. The wound wouldn't need to be fatal because the poison would be what got him. If you gave him something slower-acting, say in his food, you wouldn't be able to control where he was when he eventually kicked it ... then again, if you knew his habits, say, if you were his boss ... but then you don't have a reason to stab him in the airshaft, and it's just too hard to imagine that you stab him somewhere else and drag him there bleeding all the way ...

I was letting my brain run in circles. I counted backwards to when I had last eaten. I know my brain. Sure enough, it had been too long.

Max had mentioned that there were some parts of deck five which were more for the benefit of permanents, a little quieter and prices tending less toward the exploitative. On my way to search for restaurants, I realized I hadn't had a chance to confirm whether I had any money. My accounts were supposed to have traveled with me, in the ship's data packet, but I hadn't checked to see if they'd made it. I was pretty sure there'd be account stations on deck five—have to enable the visitors to spend money!—so I turned around and went to search for some back in the gaudy zone. On the way there I passed CUSTODY and decided to see if Max had come back to his desk.

"Boss! What's the news on the body?"

"Nothing much yet. What's a good place for a new permanent to have a quiet dinner?"

"You name it, we got it. What's your taste?"

"A sandwich and a cup of coffee would do. Does coffee cost a fortune here?"

"Eh, it's not bad, but it's not real coffee either. I can't taste the difference, myself." He started rattling off some places and recommendations and I half-listened; something else had occurred to me.

"Max, can you arrange for us to talk to Prit after dinner? Say, a couple of periods from now?"

"Sure, but not to sound lazy, that's gonna be off-duty time for him and it would carry more weight if you asked him."

"Probably, but he knows you and not me. He thinks I'm just this person he bumped into in the concourse. Also ... I haven't figured out how to use whatever it is everybody communicates with here yet." In fact I hadn't even brought it from my room.

He grinned. "Not a problem. Meet me back here after you eat. I'll warn Prit we're coming."

By the time I found an account station and confirmed my money was there and got a fresh transfer and started heading back into the quiet parts of the deck, my stomach had started to get annoyed at the delay. But even though I remember it fussing, I don't remember what I ate, or where, or whether I enjoyed it.

§

"What we must know," I said, wishing my Pergati hadn't gotten this well-tested quite this soon, "is of anyone who would want to kill Bral-past-man."

Pergati honorifics are probably the hardest thing about their syntax to translate. The closest I could come to that would be "Mr. Bral, may he rest in peace," but even then it wouldn't convey the implied hand-over-heart and downcast look. Pergati and Trade share the assumption that one speaks well of the dead. There's no polite way to say "Mr. Bral who got what he deserved." Not that I'm implying Bral deserved to die; just pointing out it's a little silly to suddenly become reverent about how you refer to someone just because he's dead.

Prit held up both palms in a gesture I was interpreting as a shrug or "how should I know?" I'd already seen it from him at least three times in our conversation so far. "Bral"—he gave up on the honors—"knew very few. Very to-himself kind."

"But you say he did good work."

"Until this, yes." He fixed me with his little dark eyes. "I am not a fool. You are trying to know if I killed him. I did not. I would be the fool, then, to kill him when so obvious, and to put him in a place so few others could reach! Yes?"

"Point taken," I said. Time to change the subject. "The airshaft—are there any other openings in it? Can it be entered from any other decks?"

"No." He considered it. "At core end, would need to drop spin so you could turn off some core machines, then unweld the grate."

"I guess dropping spin is a big thing?"

Even from a Pergat I could tell a "dumb landpig" look when I saw it. "Very big thing."

"No gravity," Max said. "Only do it when we really have to."

"Yeah, that'd get noticed." Damn it, I hated looking ignorant. "What about the grate at the bottom?"

"That has the impeller not far behind it—even harder way there, would have to turn off much air system, " said Prit.

"So it would only be those who could get to the door. Who are they?"

"You. Me. Bral-past. Top-big-woman. Maintenance-big-man." He meant the Director and the head of Maintenance. "Korm, also works for me." He thought a little more. "No others."

"Could Korm have killed Bral?"

He raised his hands. "I think they may never have met. Bral was very to-himself kind."

I gave up. At least I didn't have to warn him not to leave town unexpectedly.

§

"So, what are the odds?" Max asked, as we walked along the concourse. "No, wait, you're probably not a gambling type."

"I'm not, but it doesn't matter. If you said you were convinced Prit did it, I'd want you to show me a motive, and if you were sold anyone else did it, I'd want you to show me a reenactment." He chuckled.

The whole corridor begin to vibrate. Not in a way that shook you around, it didn't try to knock you over. More like a hum, a hum that you heard through your bones instead of your ears. Getting louder. It made you want to shout over it, even though you didn't need to. "What the hell is that?"

He laughed. "I guess business is starting up again. That's the Ring doing its thing."

"How much worse does it get?"

"You'll get so you barely notice. I'd say about three more subs. Keep walking, they say if it bothers you moving around is better."

We kept going and then, abruptly, the hum stopped, and I felt—it was very odd, sort of an energy rush, a charge, although clearly it was just the tension being lifted. Everything was instantly a little bit better. Then it passed. "How often does that happen?"

"Depends. Lots, if we're busy. Where are you going?" I'd turned around.

"I'm going to go look at the airshaft again."

"You've got to be kidding. Look, Boss, maybe I shouldn't say so, but you've gotta pace yourself. You've been running how long? When did you last sleep? It's your first cycle and you're already gonna overdo it."

"I'm not asking you to go," I said.

"Would you trust me on this? Go get some sleep. It'll all be there when you wake up. You'll just make yourself nuts. Pete was the same way."

He was actually concerned. I studied him a little, and smiled and said, "OK, Max. You're right, I haven't even unpacked. See you in the morning—sorry. I mean 'see you next cycle.'"

§

But when I got back to my rooms, I knew from long experience I wouldn't be able to sleep and I didn't try. I didn't even unpack; for one thing, I hadn't decided what to do about Alsop's clothes. Was there a place I could sell them? Should I just dump them into the garbage?

I started up the data station and fetched his personnel record. Looked like a quiet, inoffensive kind of person—the sort of face you see and then quickly forget. He'd been on the Ring—I had to convert a little because it was in cycles—damned near twenty years. No listed family, contacts, very little Earth history at all. My record probably looked very similar. I wondered what image they'd used for mine.

We have a door log—we know who goes in and out of everything.

OK, but how far back were the logs kept? Could I remember the location of the door? Even if I managed to figure out how to use that damned feed to contact Max and ask him, he'd fuss at me for not going to sleep.

I found the Ring schematics first. There were a lot of them but it wasn't so hard to find what I wanted. I was pretty clear on where we'd walked. The little access corridor only went two places; the shaft if you went right, or an unrelated electrical service area with absolutely no exits if you went left. So it was that door or nothing. And the log for that door said ...

The log for that door said that, other than this cycle's fun and games, no one—*no one*—had used that door except Something-or-another Bral (Pergati family names are long and impenetrable and even Pergati don't use them unless they need them) for many, many cycles, far more cycles than the twenty-five or so from Dr. Kohl's guess. *Hundreds* of cycles. Years.

No problem. Bral opened the door and brought someone in with him, that person killed him, then left. But no—I'd had to let Max out. The log for this cycle verified that—there was me going in, me letting Max out, me opening it for Max again, then opening it a final time when we were carrying out the corpse. So that was impossible; someone would have had to come in with Bral and then somehow get out without leaving a record.

OK, Bral killed himself. Never mind why for now. And then had time to push whatever it was he stabbed himself with into the grating nearby before collapsing.

I absently reached for a cup of coffee that didn't exist, then blinked a few times in surprise at my own brain. Right. Not the Vault, Jessica. If you want to foster bad habits here, you'll have to do it the hard way and get a coffee maker.

I stood up, telling myself a lie. The lie was "I wonder if there's any place I can get a cup of coffee right now." I knew it was a lie, because I put Alsop's flashlight and his little specimen case in my pockets.

§

I hadn't expected the shaft to be more intimidating with no corpse and a good light, but it was. I shone the light up the shaft—it just barely lit the grate up at the top enough to be visible—and told myself not to do that again. The forty-plus meters of dark, narrow space were nerve-wracking for some reason.

The grate was solid, no give at all when I shook it. I didn't see any bolts or fastenings, in fact not even a seam between it and the rest of the shaft wall. The mesh was coarse enough that I was able to light the space behind it pretty easily. It was less than a meter long, and at the end was an even finer mesh or porous surface of some kind that I assumed was part of the impeller. An object would either have stuck in that, bounced off it, or left a hole—depending on what that surface was made of—and I saw none of that. There was nothing at all in the small space but air and dust.

Maybe someone fired something from the core end. Sure, and first they told the victim to please cooperate and lie down so they could neatly penetrate the front of the chest. And whatever it was was on a string so they could pull it back up afterward. I *did* need sleep.

I scraped around on the floor and the wall in several places, and got three samples of dried blood in the little case. Then I went back to my rooms. On the way the Ring opened again and startled me just as much as it had the first time. I hoped Max was right about my getting used to it.

One cycle on the Ring and this is the first problem I get, I thought. What if I blow it? What if there's no answer? Max didn't seem to care, but Max didn't seem to care about a lot of things. I wondered what he'd been doing with murders while my job was empty. He certainly hadn't been bringing them for autopsy, not if he didn't know about Dr. Kohl's lab setup. Pushing the remains out a lock and asking no questions? That certainly seemed to fit with C. Efficient Worthington's attitude, what little I got of it. Strange place I had wandered into.

Eventually I managed to clear my mind enough to get some sleep, telling myself that I would figure everything out next cycle. For the record, I didn't. I didn't figure it out for nearly three hundred cycles, and when I did, it was almost by accident.

THE CASE of the HEADLESS BODY (in the TOPLESS BAR)

Time was even more meaningless on the Ring than it had been aboard ship. There, almost everyone slept at the same times and ate at the same times, and the only people awake between thirty-one and forty were the crew unlucky enough to draw night duty. On the Ring, ship arrivals happened when they happened, and so parts of the Ring—notably, medical on deck four, the tourist traps on deck five, and Dispatch—ran constantly. The security officer, I gathered, was permanently on call, although I suspected people were still mostly taking their problems to Max. I told Max to start telling them to talk to me instead, it was my job, but I suspected he had some idea about not bothering me except for the big stuff and was still seeing to minor peacekeeping himself. I couldn't really blame him; I wouldn't want to sit behind that desk in CUSTODY all the time twiddling my thumbs either.

All of which is explaining that I'm not sure how many cycles it had been between my arrival and when the boss (I had already begun thinking of her just as "the boss," probably picking up this bad habit from Max) first spoke to me about Kezar. Five or six? As many as ten? I'd broken up a few fights, talked a pair of lovers out of a quarrel that looked like it might draw blood, and dealt with a little fee dispute at one of the sex houses just before someone got hurt. Nothing noteworthy. I do know by then Max had shown me the ins and outs of the feed—which turned out to be some kind of wireless transmission system, but was *not* a telephone (apparently), and you didn't call people on it, you signaled them or hailed them or so on.

"OK, so it's more like two-way radio. But it handles a lot of conversations at the same time, right? And nobody can hear anybody else's conversations?"

"Well, they could, if they just changed the frequency and decoder a little, or at least that's what Pete always said. He liked to say it was no better than standing in the concourse and shouting your business—"

"Yes, OK, but my point is, why aren't they 'phones'? Who decided to call them 'feeds'?"

"Because they're just not, I guess. And they're not 'feeds.' It's all one feed. The feed, that's all there is." He shrugged.

Silliness. Still, I didn't want to sound any more like a landpig than I already did. One plays along.

The boss contacted me on the feed, using the verb of your choice, one cycle when I was eating what we might as well call breakfast, since I had woken up the period before. "Are you settled in?" she asked.

"Getting there," I said.

"Good. I want you to investigate Soei Kezar. You know where the files are."

"Anything in particular I should be looking for?"

"I want him off the Ring. I don't want to have to invent a reason. Find one."

She disconnected. I finished my breakfast.

§

In addition to the personnel files—we keep information on permanents and any long-term transients—Alsop had a file of his own on Kezar, which the ever-efficient boss had obviously known about. She could see Alsop's files, so she might even have read it.

The photo in the official file showed a man with slightly hollow cheeks, a high forehead, and a mustache. I have a theory about facial hair. A man with a mustache is putting on a character; the type of character varies, but he's always trying to present a face which covers up what he really is. I don't say that's automatically bad, but it means I'm likely to get impatient with him because I don't like having to try to dig past the false face. A man with a beard, on the other hand, is making a statement to the world about how much he doesn't give a damn about what the world thinks. That's often false too, though not always. Sometimes it just means he doesn't like to shave.

As for his bio, Kezar was the kind of person who begged to be labelled SUSPICIOUS CHARACTER. Alsop suspected him of rigged gambling, loansharking, and smuggling various kinds of contraband, with an implication that he'd try any other racket as well if it presented itself. The former was sufficient to ban him from the Ring if I could prove it—the cheating, not the gambling; gambling was fine. My personal philosophy on loan sharks is that if you were stupid enough to contract with one you deserved what you got; I wouldn't throw him out for that, and I wasn't sure the boss would either. As for the third—well, what did "contraband" mean on the Ring anyway? We had no illegal items I knew of, other than breachables—and there was no profit in smuggling guns onto the Ring and even less in smuggling them off.

"What do you think, Max?" I asked him later that cycle.

"Well," he said, leaning back and kicking his feet up onto the desk, which I couldn't very well complain about since I was sitting on a corner of it, just as rude, "there's all kinds of things he could smuggle, but qov is really the big one, and that's kinda funny because—"

"What is that—what was the word?"

"Qov. Or qoph. Or maybe more like khov." He shrugged. "I can't say it like the Pergati do, and it's their word. It's a plant. You dry it, and then you press it into little blocks or pellets or whatever, because whenever I've seen a Pergat use some that's what it's looked like. They put one in their mouths and then chew it for a while. I guess they spit it out eventually but not whenever I was looking. I don't think they swallow it. I'm pretty sure they don't."

I had learned by then that Max could spend all day talking about something and miss all the important points. "Is this a narcotic? Stimulant? What?"

"You know, I'm not sure. I hear it doesn't do a damned thing for humans, and Pergati don't like to talk about it, seeing as how they're not supposed to be using it."

"Wait—it's illegal?"

"For them, yeah. Illegal everywhere in Pergati space, any place they control, their ships, all of it. Go figure. Doesn't stop them from using it, and since their laws don't apply on the Ring, the ones here don't usually bother keeping it a secret. That's why it's funny—"

"Half the permanents on the Ring are Pergati! Their government just puts up with it?"

"Well, the Director doesn't give a damn, is what I heard. That's what's funny, like I keep trying to tell you."

I sighed. "Sorry. What's funny?"

"Well, say Kezar's smuggling qov, okay, he's been around for a while now, and he's been doing what he does since he got here. How come she asks you to drop the hammer on the guy now, all of a sudden? If it's qov how come she suddenly cares about that? See what I mean?"

"I don't know, Max. Maybe he's gotten worse. I guess I'll have to find out."

"Y'know, I'm just the hired help, but here's my crazy idea—why don't you *ask* her?"

"She wants me to figure it out," I said. "If she'd wanted to tell me, she'd have told me."

He rolled his eyes. I don't know if I had been intended to see it. "What?" I demanded.

"Aw, you two just—you deserve each other. I guess she picks 'em like that on purpose. Pete was the same way."

I shook my head. People say I'm blunt, but I don't go out of my way to make fights, and if I'd told Max the reply I had in my head, we'd have had one. Instead I said, "Let me know if anything explodes," and left.

Thing is, Max had a point, and it was a point that had already occurred to me. This wasn't new. Kezar had been running his gambling house for more than long enough for Alsop to make a file on him, amass suspicions, even go collect proof—if he or the boss had wanted to throw Kezar out earlier, they had more than enough opportunity. Alsop didn't strike me as having been a slouch, and the boss certainly wasn't. If they hadn't already busted him, it was because they didn't want to or didn't feel there was sufficient cause to.

This is what prevented me from doing something blatant, like barging into Kezar's place and confiscating some of his gambling equipment, or even being too overt about interviewing people he might have been squeezing. That was old ground. I decided the best bet was to follow his movements for a while and see what his usual orbits were like. It wasn't going to be fascinating, but it wasn't like I had anything else going on.

§

I spent five cycles doing nothing but watch Kezar's movements, and they were very boring cycles, so this is a good place to divert and say more about the body in the shaft. Two cycles after I brought it to Dr. Kohl, I hadn't heard anything from him, so I went to check. "Ah, there you are," he said. "I'm sorry to say I know what killed him."

"That doesn't sound promising."

"It's definite. Whether it's promising is up to you. The toxin I found was still present in the tissues because it was designed to be. It's the poison we use to kill P-rats. Has anyone told you about P-rats?" I nodded. "We've never found a way to trap them that works; they're very clever about bait. But there's a Pergat on the station who has amazing luck going after them with a sort of spear gun. He used to do it just as—I suppose you could call it a hobby. It wasn't an effective deterrent because he couldn't kill them often enough to make any difference. But at some point it occurred to him that if he could put some sort of long-term poison on the spear ... P-rats seem to be fond of meat, and they don't care if it's fresh. My theory is they're always somewhat protein-starved. We knew they'll eat their own, we've seen evidence of it. It was more than possible that if it stayed in the tissues of his kills long enough for others to ingest it ... as it turns out, this has been fairly successful."

"A little dangerous."

"Not really. I'd have been reluctant to recommend the use of poisons anywhere in or near our food supplies—too much danger of someone using the wrong box—and in a closed airsystem one has to be extremely cautious about fumigation. But inside the conduits where we can't go? I found a neurotoxin that is particularly prone to linger—"

"You?"

"Yes," he said. "That's why I'm sorry to learn this was the cause of death."

"But you didn't just hand this stuff out to anyone who wanted it."

"Oh, definitely not. Only this Pergat with the spear gun—Ferm is his name. And I believe he's been conscientious; certainly I tried to put the fear into him when I issued him the poison. But there are a number of people who have sufficient access to open the locker where he keeps it without his knowledge or consent. I suppose that would be where you begin investigating."

"Could his spear gun have made the wound?"

"I wondered if you'd ask," he said, smiling slightly. "Yes. I've seen the gun. It uses a long spike—not barbed, which would have made a different wound. I recall it being the right general size. Of course we have no way of knowing whether the poison entered the body through the wound. The residues were dispersed enough that I couldn't speculate on that. And if he'd been given, say, an injection, I would never find evidence of it, not in that stage of decomposition. Which reminds me. What would you like to do with the body?"

"What's the normal thing here?"

"Into the digesters. I'm told that there is a sort of memorial hall for permanents, where plaques with the names of the dead are placed. I've never gone to see it myself. Whether to place a plaque there for him is not up to me."

"Nor me. He didn't seem to have any friends on the Ring. I'll ask Prit about next of kin. But I guess we wouldn't ship a corpse out even if they asked?"

"I don't believe so. Possibly in extraordinary circumstances. The cost would be steep. At any rate Ring tradition is the digesters. Waste not, want not."

"Will the neurotoxin be an issue there?"

"No. It's not going back into the food, water or air. Metals and other salvageable durables are removed; the remaining organic waste is converted into power in a variety of ways."

"Then go ahead and digest it. If you can't learn anything else from it."

So it was definite, but it turned out it wasn't promising. The people who had access to Ferm's gun locker were all Maintenance crew, plus myself and the boss, and it didn't seem a likely list of killers. Ferm swore to me up and down that his gun was always either in the locker or with him on a hunting trip—and while he admitted he sometimes set it down to walk around looking for likely prospects, it was never out of his view when hunting for more than a few minutes at a time. I couldn't find evidence that anyone else had borrowed it. Certainly not any of the five still-living entities who could have accessed the shaft, one of whom was me.

I gave Dr. Kohl the blood samples and a cycle or so later, he confirmed they were the same type of blood as the corpse—which had been a needless precaution, as the idea of the blood on the floor coming from some other source than the corpse didn't stand up to Occam's Razor.

In case you're wondering about my delirious idea of someone shooting something from the core end and retrieving it, I should note that the spear—or, rather, spike—was indeed on a line so it could be pulled back, but the range on the thing was only about three meters. I had Ferm demonstrate it for me.

The body went into the digesters. Since the normal waste chutes weren't built to handle that sort of thing, I supposed the medical center had something special. I didn't ask. I also didn't ask whether Prit decided to put up a plaque to the memory of the dead, and I have never gone to look. Prit was permitted to finally clean the shaft, much to his relief, and we didn't discuss whether he was still a murder suspect.

Sometimes you just have to file things away as unfinished. I had other work to do.

§

As I say, I kept a close eye on Kezar's movements for five cycles. For four of those five cycles, the only things I learned were that he paid a lot of attention to his hair and his clothes, and that he didn't get out much. He went from his gambling house to his rooms and back. He did seem to be a very cautious person. I never saw him eat, so he either prepared his own food or he had someone he trusted cooking for him. He could have had a cook in his private offices at the back of the gambling house. I had access to the schematics and there was plenty of space back there. Not enough space for smuggled goods in bulk, though. If he was doing that, he was storing them somewhere else.

As for going into those offices, when he wasn't there the door was presumably locked (not locked to me, but I'd want a good excuse); when he was in, it was guarded by two large men who looked like they were identical twins. One on each side of the door. Though Kezar had a constant stream of visitors, it was clear from the actions of his door guards that there was a list of who was acceptable. Again, I'd wait to gatecrash until I had a good reason.

It was tricky. If I confiscated his gambling machinery to study it, I had better be right. Certainly I wasn't going to be able to tell just from watching the players whether the house was winning more often than it should. The gambling house never closed, so if I went into his private offices for any reason, at best someone would notice and tell him; at worst there would be a fight. If he was blackmailing or squeezing one of his many visitors, they wouldn't confess it to me. I could bug his rooms—and I would have done it without a qualm—but the door logs had already told me he lived alone and never had visitors. A recording taken there would be useless unless he talked aloud to himself a lot. His file space had absolutely nothing of interest.

On the fifth cycle, Kezar broke routine. When he left his rooms, he didn't go straight to his offices. Instead, he visited fifteen other businesses on deck five. Mostly bars, but also two A/V booth places, three skin shows, and two game rooms. He didn't linger in any of them; if he so much as had a drink in any of the bars he went into, he was a very fast drinker.

Following people without being noticed was not in the job requirements, and I don't claim I was ever any good at it. He saw me. I know he saw me because, not one full period after he had gotten back to his gambling house and I had taken a position inside it where I could see everything, he came to my table and sat down without being invited—which I suppose was his prerogative.

"Jessica Gray, I presume? We haven't met. Soei Kezar."

"I'm aware," I said.

"Yes, I'd imagine so. It seems like an awful lot of trouble. Wouldn't it be simpler just to talk to me face-to-face?"

"I doubt if I could ask you any questions you'd be willing to answer," I said.

"I don't know what you mean," he said, and I have to admit he did a very good job of looking like a person who couldn't possibly be up to anything. It would have been better if he'd had little shifty eyes instead of wide-open, warm, sincere ones. Still, there was that mustache. "I assume you have some reason to investigate me, and certainly I want to cooperate with Security—but honestly, I have no idea what the complaint is. You've seen my business; you've certainly spent enough time in it the last few cycles. I'm happy to clear up any possible confusion about my activities. Would you like to come inspect my offices?"

Which meant there was nothing in his offices I cared about. "If you're actually open to questions, then I'd like to know the purpose of that round of visits you did earlier."

"Oh, well, that's a little embarrassing—" he didn't actually stop meeting my gaze—"but if you insist, though it will put me in in a delicate position. The fact of the matter is—have you seen the rates the Ring management charges independent business operators for space here? No? Well, take my word for this much—they're ridiculous. Horrible. We have been getting together a little—well—I suppose you could call it a coalition of businessmen. We're not quite ready yet to confront the Director en masse about this. I don't suppose I could get you to keep quiet about it until we talk to her? After all, it's not *really* a Security matter, now is it?"

"I'll keep it to myself," I said, standing up, "if your story checks out. I trust you don't mind my asking some of them about it."

He shrugged. "As I say, it will be a bit embarrassing, but if you must ..." Seeing I was leaving, he stood up as well, and inclined his head to me politely as I walked out.

§

I didn't go to any of the businesses he had visited. Two reasons. First, I wanted him to wonder whether I believed him. I didn't think there was much chance that he thought I did, but you never know. Some men think all women are stupid. Second, he could get on the feed to them faster than I could walk there. If I'd gone into one of them and asked, of course it would have agreed with his story. No matter what he had them scared of—whether he was selling protection or blackmailing all of them or whatever—they certainly weren't going to admit it to me. No, if I wanted the truth out of one of them, I'd enter their rooms when they were sleeping some cycle and startle it out of them. The need for that had not arisen yet. Meanwhile, if the son of a bitch thought that little show was going to get me to stop following him, he was wrong. It wouldn't hurt to keep him on his toes.

The next three cycles were even more tedious than the first five. I didn't bother to try to be subtle any more. He knew I was watching him. I hope it was unnerving for him; it would have been some consolation for my troubles. You may wonder how I got any food or sleep myself. The answer is I just didn't watch him while he was in his room asleep—well, of course I don't know he was sleeping the whole time he was in his rooms. But I did know he was alone in there, and he didn't once try to slip out when I wasn't watching. I had set his door to record not just entrances but exits. The door wasn't high-security enough to have a reader on the inside, so it didn't record *who* had exited, but it told me when he came and went. After there was no mischief in his sleep hours the first two cycles, I stopped doing more than check the logs. It was where he went when he wasn't in his rooms that interested me. Also, of course, he had no idea whether I'd put some other watch on his rooms. All that said, I admit I was pushing my limits—I hadn't gotten more than four periods of sleep in a row since I started following him—and more than once I considered whether or not I should try to recruit some help.

On the ninth cycle, a little after twenty-five, he left the gambling house and headed spinward on the deck five concourse, same as usual, and I was not far behind him; not a full sector. Business was booming. We'd gotten in two large crews within the last twenty periods, one human, one Pergati, and it looked like they were all on deck five at the same time. Kezar walked past a particularly crowded bar, overflowing out onto the concourse, loud and rowdy—in fact it looked like a fight was ready to break out, and it did. As Kezar passed, one human lost his temper over something and shoved another, knocking the second guy back two meters straight into Kezar, who fell under him. The gent who had landed on him immediately picked himself up and dove in for revenge on the instigator, who by then was tangling with two of the victim's friends. At that point two of the first gent's friends also decided that honor was at stake, so then there were six, and by that time I was in the middle of it.

I don't fight clean. I shouted two warnings and nobody heard me and that's when I kicked the nearest brawler in the sprocket. He went down and I got another by the arm before he could react and twisted it way up and around behind him. About that time I could see a third one pulling back for a punch in my peripheral vision, so I spun with the one I had a hold on and he got the punch in his face instead. I could see that if I let him go he was going to stay down, distracted by his broken nose, so I dropped him and ducked another punch from the third one and slugged him twice in the stomach, putting my whole body into it. I had been telling them throughout this that I was the security officer—well, shouting it really—and by the time I was three down it had finally started to sink in. After that it was just a matter of sending Broken Nose to medical and telling the other five to go back to their ship—all six were from the same ship—and sleep it off and I'd better not hear another thing from them.

Of course Kezar was long gone. I'd known that was going to happen as soon as the fight started, but what else could I have done?

Part of me was relieved. If I'd lost him, I'd lost him, and I was sick of this game anyway. I'd just have to try something else. But I did check the door logs when I got back to my data station ... and found he'd gone to his rooms! He hadn't had enough time to do anything else on the way, either. A man with nothing to hide. I told myself to deliberately avoid thinking anything about Kezar for a while, and hit my bed with the intention of getting at least eight periods of solid rest to clear my brain.

It didn't work out that way. At thirty-one, when I had barely been in bed three periods, the feed chirped and it was Max. "Boss, we've got a little problem."

"Can't be that little," I said blearily. "Go ahead."

"There's a body in a back room at Tiny's. I'm trying to keep anyone from leaving. The owner is giving me trouble."

That woke me all the way up. "You don't mean natural causes."

"No clue, but even if it was, sometime after that she lost her head. Look, I gotta deal with Tiny, just come on down, okay?"

§

Tiny's was a skin club—nude dancers—and not one of the ones that tries to be elegant about it. The front part was arranged with bars along every wall but the back one, which had doors into a couple of halls and a curtained opening where dancers came onstage. The stage was a T-shaped platform extending from the middle of the back wall, with the crossbar in the center of the room. There were no seats. The back halls connected to dressing rooms, an office, and a storeroom, but mostly they connected to several small rooms where apparently dances could be had for an audience of one. Nothing more than that, the owner assured me frantically, his wattles shaking as he yammered. He smelled like a grease trap that needed cleanout, and one of his private rooms had a corpse in it.

The body was a female human (I should say "socket," otherwise I was leaping to conclusions based upon anatomy, which I was), and that was all we knew about the victim, because she was missing her head. Max had been telling the literal truth. And I'd established that the head wasn't anywhere in the club. I was having trouble getting beyond that. Max was out front trying to keep people from leaving, Tiny was trying to get me to either turn a blind eye to the whole thing or just let him get back to business, I couldn't tell which, and four of the dancers were trying to talk or ask me questions at the same time.

"EVERYBODY SHUT UP!"

Everybody shut up. I coughed. Hurts my throat to yell like that.

"OK, you. Tiny. Stop trying. I'll let you reopen as soon as I can, but you're not at the top of my priorities, you understand? And if you don't start doing it exactly my way, then I report that you were letting your dancers go a little too far with the customers and you'll be shut down."

"It's a lie! I'm telling you, we run a clean house—"

I held up a hand. "Listen again: I don't care. I think you were, because you're so nervous about it, but it doesn't matter. What matters is what I tell the Director.

That's all that matters to you. You *really* want me to not be angry with you right now. Is this sinking in?"

He nodded, eyes bulging a little. "Good, because I'm going to need you to use your brain now, and I don't want you to be distracted. Was the victim one of your employees?"

"Well, she's in here and she's not wearing any clothes—"

"Anybody can take off clothes, Tiny," I said. "Are you telling me you can't definitely identify her as one of your employees?"

"Well, y'see—"

It developed that Tiny didn't really keep close track of his dancers. Actually, even that was an understatement. I could report the conversation with him verbatim, but then you'd want to strangle him as badly as I did, so I condense: Tiny made most of his own cash from the bar sales. The dancers were all freelancers; they were what got the customers to the bar. Tiny paid them a fee for showing up, if they danced for a certain amount of time and did a decent job. Apparently the fees were variable "because some of 'em are better draws than others." If a dancer wanted to take a customer to a back room, she was welcome to do so as long as there were enough dancers up front to keep the crowd happy. Tiny charged the dancer a fee for the back room, so the dancers would charge for private dances accordingly. They were expected to not take too long in the rooms and "wipe down the chair" after they were done. No one was tracking who was in what room; the dancers just looked for an empty room and didn't go in one where the door was closed. Tiny was mostly back in the office and usually had no idea which dancers were working a given night. In other words, it was complete chaos.

I couldn't resist asking, "If you're not keeping track of who's where, how do you know who to pay? How do you know someone's not using a room and stiffing you on the fee?"

"Sure, that might happen sometimes, who cares? If one of them did it too much, the other girls would come gripe to me about it."

Trying to narrow down how long the body had been in the room was just as futile. One of the other dancers had found the body when she thought that the room had been in use "for an awfully long time." How long was an awfully long time? She wasn't sure. A quarter period? Half a period? No, those would have been normal. At least a period, she thought.

Another dancer had seen someone leave the room and was pretty sure he closed the door when he left—which wasn't unusual if the dancer was taking a minute to clean up. What did the someone look like? A man. Any particular kind of man? She wasn't sure. She thought she'd know him again if she saw him. Was he out in front right now? She went out for a look and came back and said she didn't think so.

"Besides, nobody out there has a bag."

"A bag?"

"This guy had a bag."

"How big a bag?" Could you possibly be any dumber, you little twit? Maybe with practice.

"Oh"—she indicated with her hands—"about like this."

"Uh-huh." I couldn't help myself. I had to do it. "You know what was in that bag?"

"No, what?"

"Her head. He cut off her head and put it in his bag and walked right past you with it."

"Oh, *ewu*!" It didn't make up for the frustration by any means, but it did help a little.

"OK, Tiny," I said, with what I hoped was not a malicious smile, "I've got good news and bad news for you. The good news is, you can reopen everything but this room, and as soon as I get this body out of here, you can have this room back too. You'd better clean it first. There's a lot of blood back in that dark corner." At that point He-Had-a-Bag turned pale and hurriedly left the scene of the crime. "The bad news is, you're going to put together a list of every dancer you've paid, even if they only turned up for one cycle, for the last one hundred cycles. I know you keep records of that, or we'd have already had your hide. You're going to get on the feed to every single one of them—you yourself, you don't get to farm this out—and you are going to note their status. All I want to know is whether they're alive and well. If they've left the Ring, note that. If you get anything strange, note that. I'm going to want this list sent to my files within two cycles, and that's not negotiable. If you don't do this, or if you try to cheat or cut any corners, I'm going to make six kinds of hell for you. Among other things, if I think you're cheating, you become murder suspect number one. I believe you're a slime, not a murderer, but I could change my mind. Understand me?"

I wouldn't want to guess what he had been about to say to me before he choked it back and nodded.

"Also. I realize running a sex house has a lot of rules, and of course you wouldn't want to bother with those. But that's too bad. If you want to run a sex house, follow the rules and run a sex house. If you want to run a skin club, then make sure your dancers stay in bounds from now on. I may come back for a surprise visit. See you around."

I went out front, leaving him to seethe behind me. Max was still blocking the door, and some of the customers were getting angry. "Boss, did you notice that Pergat over there in the corner? We should talk to him—"

"Forget it, Max. Whoever did this walked out with the head in a bag long before we got here. Would you go down and get a cargo trolley?"

"I—sure—but what about all these people? We just let 'em out?"

"We just let 'em out, Max," I said. "Trust me; what we want isn't here. Let's get this body out and go get some sleep."

§

"Max, why'd you tell me we should talk to the Pergat?"

It was thirty-three, thirty-four, somewhere in there. We'd finished getting the body out, waking up Dr. Kohl, telling him there was no point in an exam for now, we just needed a cold drawer to put the body in while we figured out what to do with it. We'd put back the cargo trolley and I'd said, "Max, do you drink?"

I think I nearly gave him heart failure. "Do *you?*"

"Sometimes. I need to get the taste of that place out of my mouth. Where can we go that's quiet?"

So we were in a little bar for permanents, far from the noise and the crews and Tiny, and the muscles in my neck were finally beginning to unclench.

"Oh, well, see, Pergati don't really get the whole skin club thing—"

I nodded. I'd never seen one wear any clothes but the kilt, yet they had two phenotypes and were mammals, so I'd figured "nude" was just not a big deal to them, or at least "topless" wasn't. Personally, I still couldn't make out which ones were which.

"—and they don't seem interested in humans. I mean, you know, *that* kind of interest. So he kinda stood out. I mean, I guess he could have been there just to see what it looked like ..."

"Are there any who like fooling around outside their species?" I asked. "I bet there are."

He shrugged. "Probably, but I don't want to know about it."

"I wonder if Tiny realizes the sex houses make more money," I said.

"How do you figure that? They've got to deal with all those shots, and the certificates—"

"And we charge them less rent for their troubles, and they charge their customers far more than he can possibly be getting out of his bar markup and his private-room fees. I've been trying to read up on the business of this place as much as I can."

"Well, so he's a lazy slob, which we knew. But think about it this way: Do you really want someone like him running a sex house?"

I managed a chuckle. "Good point." I finished my drink.

"Want another?" he asked.

"No, I need to go sleep. For a year. Max, this is personal, sorry—don't answer if you don't want—"

"Oh, this should be good."

"Just curious. Are you—I mean, is there anybody? You know—" I don't know why I asked, I don't know how I got there, but he took it in stride.

"I know." He shook his head. "There was. We were together a long time. She died. Every so often I think, Max, you should find somebody, this is a hell of a way to go into old age, but every time I look, I have the same problem: It's not her."

"I'm sorry."

"Nothing for you to be sorry about. Go on to sleep. No offense, but you look done in."

I left him there, sitting staring past his empty glass at a point far beyond the back wall of the bar.

§

"It's crazy," I said to Dr. Kohl the next cycle. "No fingerprints, no biometrics at all, just one image in their files that we got who knows where. Who'd expect to get to a station that punches holes in space and find they'd traveled back in time to the 1870s?"

He raised an eyebrow at me. "You're dating by Bertillon, then? Vucetich was two decades later."

I had to smile. "All right, so you read too. I'd deduced that already."

"I read statistics as well, and for my own I don't even need to do that. During Alsop's time, I saw twelve to fifteen cases of death caused by direct action of one sentient against another per year. Pardon my units; I dislike ship time for long durations. Thirty percent of those were outright accidents, or at the very least I'd say there was no malice aforethought. Just events that got out of control. Of the remainder, almost all are extremely clear-cut cases, with witnesses, motives, obvious weapons ... we're talking about drunk visitors here, not criminal masterminds. Tenbom hasn't even bothered to bring them to me, as you may have realized."

"This woman wasn't a visitor. Well, I assume not, if she actually did work at Tiny's—"

"No, and that's unusual. Permanents don't even die natural deaths here very often; they retire to some other place and die there. I may plan to die here with my boots on, as it were, but most don't."

"My point is, it can happen. Better identification would be useful as prevention—"

"There are seldom more than a thousand permanents," he said. "You do realize you could check on every single living being on the Ring in just a few cycles? Even if Tiny doesn't come through, how long do you think a missing person on the Ring can possibly stay missing?"

"Bral stayed missing for quite a while."

"And he was an extreme case, a hermit, and yet eventually was found in the normal course of affairs. I realize you're impatient, and I understand why. But this is, in essence, a tiny community where everyone knows each other. We like to believe we don't need fingerprints, that we don't need cameras. It's only the visitors who ever make any trouble. Or at least that's what we prefer to think."

"I can't tell whether you're agreeing with me or disagreeing," I said.

"Neither," he said. "Just stating facts."

§

The thing about people "just stating facts" is that they often seem to enjoy muddying the waters. I'm not saying Dr. Kohl was wrong—you won't find me ever betting against him, on anything—but "will be identified eventually" wasn't good enough here, not when delaying that identification had to have been the whole point of taking the head (and, presumably, tossing it down a waste chute, which I had realized too late to save it from the digesters).

It was also clear why he *only* took the head; he could get it out of the club without anyone noticing, whereas even at Tiny's I don't think he could have dragged a body out the front room. And Tiny's had no back door. But unless I was totally wrong and he was keeping the head as a trophy or something, there was only one reason to go to the trouble of removing it, especially since with the hand tool he had used (a fine-toothed saw of some kind, according to Dr. Kohl) it had to have been a gruesome, desperate job.

When I got the file from Tiny—nearly a cycle later, as near to the deadline I'd given him as he dared—there was one and only one missing person. A dancer named Britt Areese hadn't answered the feed, and (Tiny added in a note) while he couldn't get anybody to say for sure she'd been there at the time of the murder, he'd found her things in one of the communal dressing rooms. He even provided her room location. Either Tiny was being very cooperative, or he was deliberately trying to make her the victim. The thing about Tiny was, he was too apathetic for a crime of passion and too dumb for subtlety. Sure, I could have believed the scenario "she was sleeping with the boss and they had a fight and he killed her," but if he had been I'd have gotten a different feeling from him. I didn't believe his temper leaned physical either. Too much effort; he'd just shout at you and walk away. If he'd been the kind who hit people, I'd have known it from the attitudes of the other dancers, and probably would have castrated him on the spot. I was going to assume he was playing nice, at least for now. Also, he'd had no opportunity to remove the head from the club, and I was taking He-Had-a-Bag at face value because she was just too stupid to lie.

Areese's rooms were in Sugarland, which figured. People mostly live on decks two and seven. I don't want to sound elitist, so I'll just say that room rates are a lot higher on two. Not all of seven is bad; for example, a lot of the Pergati warrens are there and the ones I've been in are all pretty nice. But Sugarland is not a place anyone wants to live if they can avoid it. It's where the marginal workers live, the freelancers—the nude dancers and the cargo beefs, the ones who are just hoping to scrape together enough money here so that when they eventually go off somewhere else, they'll have enough saved up to get a foothold. Some of the residents of Sugarland, I'd been told, freelanced in more ways than one. Impossible to prove; someone takes someone else back to their personal rooms, you have to assume no money changed hands because you don't have a choice. Max had said that's how Sugarland got its nickname, but I wasn't sure whether I believed him.

It was a cramped place, meant for sleep and not much more. The shower, toilet and sink were only in a separate room in the sense that their alcove had a different kind of floor. There was no kitchen, and the room didn't have enough shelves so things were piled everywhere—no, wait, I was wrong. Her belongings weren't scattered for lack of space; they'd been tossed around. Either she'd thrown a temper tantrum, or someone had searched the room and hadn't bothered to be subtle about it.

That would do for a reason to obscure her identity for one or two cycles—just enough time to make sure no one came to check her room or claim her effects before someone could do the search. Unlikely that someone (me) would have gotten to her room that quickly anyway, but I could see someone taking the head just as a precaution. Of course there was no way to guess what they'd been looking for, or if they'd found it.

The next step was the door logs. Sugarland rooms don't have data stations. I went all the way back to my own rooms because public data stations bother me even though I'm assured they're secure. When I checked the logs, I hit a dead end. Oh, there were all kinds of door accesses ... including one two cycles ago at more or less the exact time Max was waking me up with news of her body ... but no record, in most cases including that one, of who the person opening the door *was*.

It took me longer than it should have to figure out. Britt Areese, who had either been very innocent or very dumb, just left her door unlocked a lot, including when she'd gone merrily off for her last cycle as a live human. The retinal reader is what records your identity. If you don't need to use it, we don't record who you are.

So it could have been anybody, that final access. A lover, a friend, an employer ... well, no, I didn't believe she'd have told Tiny anything. But that set me thinking.

Tiny had noted Areese "hadn't been coming around too long." Her personnel file didn't say a thing about her freelancing for Tiny, which figured ... but it did note formally that, ninety-some cycles before, she had been declared no longer an employee in any capacity of the Wandering Moon, known to all and sundry as Catalan's.

§

I had been hearing about Catalan's since my first cycle on the Ring. Apparently it was the sex house with the highest standards, or the best quality (how does one judge quality in that situation?) or the most class, or something. At one point in some rambling conversation or another, Max had commented how, "if you were going to go for that kind of thing, it was definitely the one you wanted to go to," and then he'd immediately gotten embarrassed at having said it.

Catalan's was at five:seventy-six, well away from the main tourist-trap zone, and its entrance was not gaudy. In fact you could have walked right past the door that said WANDERING MOON without realizing what you were passing ... although you might have noticed an absence of other doors in that part of the corridor, because Catalan's was a big place, whose employees lived on the premises, with its own kitchen staff and other amenities. (So I was told by Max, who had clearly been here a few times, and I don't mean for certificate inspections.)

The door opened to a short hall, which forced you to pass by a reception desk at the entrance to a large room, evenly but dimly lit, with a lot of comfortable chairs, sofas, several other exits, and a small bar on the far side. The room had six people in it. The person in an armchair with the black-haired woman perched on one of its arms was probably a customer. He (gender presumed) was the only one in the room who didn't scan me when I entered. Everyone else in the room clearly stopped to make an assessment—a fast and professional one—before going back to whatever they had been doing. All were humans except two—a bald blue-green biped species I didn't know but had seen occasionally around the Ring, and a Pergat. All of the humans read as "likely female" to me except the customer in the armchair and a slender person with long hair in the back corner, engaged in a lively conversation with the Pergat.

The woman behind the reception desk had a lot of unruly, kinked red hair, tied up loosely but attempting to escape, which is what caught my eye first. Also blue eyes, pale skin tending to red, and a solid, curvy build with a lot of hip and bust. Some people would have made comments about her weight, and I got the impression that she'd have just laughed at them, if she bothered to take notice at all. She smiled. "I don't think we've seen you before. What's your pleasure today? We have—"

I cut her off, I admit it, because I thought she was about to point out one of the people in the room and I really didn't want to find out if she were able to read me that easily. "I'm not a customer. My name is Jessica Gray. I'm the new security officer. I need to speak to Catalan."

She raised her eyebrows a little, and gestured toward one of the other doorways, which was a relief. If she'd said "I'm Catalan" the score would have been two-nothing for her. "Last door on the right. Knock first. Our doors don't have buzzers."

"Will I be disturbing anything?"

She smiled. "No, but she gets surly if you don't knock."

Catalan had that sort of skin with yellow undertones that some people call "olive," which has never made sense to me. Thirty years older than the women in the front room. Black shiny hair pinned back in a severe bun, black thick untrimmed eyebrows, and dark eyes which read me from top to bottom as I entered, then glared at me. "Who are you?"

"Jessica Gray. I'm the new security officer."

This piece of information made her even grumpier. "And?"

"I need to ask you about Britt Areese."

"She doesn't work here anymore."

"I know," I said. "I was hoping you could tell me a little about her."

"Why don't you go find her and ask her?"

OK, lady, you asked for it. "Because she's dead. Her decapitated body was found in a private room at the club where she worked."

I got just the tiniest sliver of a reaction—her eyes widened briefly, but then less than a second later they hardened again. "Where'd she end up? She was at Tiny's, right? Go talk to Tiny."

Someone told me once I had a short temper. I'd replied that it was only because I was such an optimist; I expected people to behave like they were part of a civilization. I looked for decency and politeness, I said, and only responded in kind once I didn't get it. As I recall, she laughed at me.

I walked over and sat down on her desk. "Are you about done? You know as well as I do that Tiny's a useless slug who doesn't know one of his dancers from another. His other dancers are no help either. If she had any friends I don't know how to find them. She was here for two years, and you're the kind of person who makes sure she knows everything about her employees. So you can drop the attitude, tell me what you know, and get rid of me, or you can keep acting this way and I'll keep asking you until you stop. I have plenty of time."

I didn't expect her reaction at all. She tossed back her head and laughed—a deep laugh, from the throat. Then she straightened up and put on her stone face again, but I thought maybe the glare wasn't as harsh as before.

"All right, so we agree on something," she said. "Nobody deserves to end up at Tiny's, but I'm not sorry I fired her either. She's only the third person I've ever fired; to me, if I fire somebody, it means I misjudged and shouldn't have hired them in the first place. Britt was a thief. I don't mean a borrow-things-from-the-other-girls-without-asking thief. I mean she'd go to shops sometimes and lift stuff because she got a thrill out of it. I ignored it for a while, even though nobody here liked her, because she had a couple of important regulars and I like happy customers. But then she stole from one of *them*. Something like that gets out, it drives away business. I told her to go get some mental help."

"I guess asking 'who do you think might have had a reason to kill her' is a waste of time, then. Sounds like she made enemies."

"Nobody here would have done that," she said. "Don't you go setting us up for that. We didn't like her, but it's a long way from that to wanting her dead. The girls got annoyed with her at first, then they thought she was pathetic, that she needed help. She did need help. I wish she hadn't ended up at Tiny's."

"Did she ever confide in anybody here that you know of? Did anyone here get to know her well enough for that, do you know?"

"I doubt it. How come?"

"After she was killed, someone searched her place. She had something somebody wanted. Would she have told anybody here about something like that?"

"Not likely. I hate to say it, but if she had something like that, she probably stole it. And if she stole it, she didn't tell anybody about it."

"Thanks. You can have your desk back now."

"Come back sometime when you're not on business," she said as I left the room.

The receptionist gave me a searching look as I left, and I thought she had a comment to make, but whatever it was, she didn't make it.

§

So Areese stole something important enough to mark her for death. Things like that were usually information, not valuables. Or maybe this was a theft that proved to someone she was a liability; maybe it wasn't what she stole, but the fact that she had the audacity to steal from that person at all. If she was actually a klepto and she also needed money then she probably had a fence; she certainly didn't keep a lot of stolen goods in that little room, especially if she didn't lock it. Did she steal something too hot for her fence? Did she steal *from* her fence?

The problem was that a lot of things pointed to Areese being a complete idiot, but the woman I'd just been talking to didn't seem like the type to hire those. OK. So tentatively assume Areese had some blind spots but wasn't dumb. But she was compulsive enough to steal from one of her customers at Catalan's ... I had to give up and admit all things were possible. All I could really be sure of was that her judgment was suspect and she'd gotten in over her head.

I had an idea. It was a really farfetched idea. But it was an idea that wasn't going away, and the only cure for those is to examine them and take them apart to reveal just how ridiculous they are. While I was getting some lunch—I'd found a place I liked a lot, a little counter with six stools and good coffee, even if it was fake—I turned over the numbers in my head.

It had been maybe five subs between when Kezar left the gambling house, a little after twenty-five, and when he got knocked down in the bar fight. Say that was 25:15. He'd opened his room door at 25:35 ... sixteen subs later, give or take. Twenty-four, maybe twenty-five minutes, for landpigs. (That time I did convert, to make sure of my math.) But—if I hadn't been so tired that night, after days of following him, and handling the fight, I'd have noticed; it didn't take sixteen subs to walk from the gambling house to his rooms. I'd made that walk. It took about seven if you really hurried; twelve or so if you didn't. And Tiny's was on his way; he'd have passed it on his way to the ramp up he always used.

It took a lot of stretching. I was willing to swallow someone not discovering the body for nearly three periods, in that madhouse. The part that was hard to believe was that he'd had enough time to duck in, find Areese, get her into a private room, kill her, *and cut off her head.* With a hand saw. With enough time to put on and take off the apron or whatever he must have used, because if he'd walked out with blood all over his clothing, someone would have noticed, even at Tiny's. Even if I allowed some wiggle room on when we left the gambling house, that still only bought a couple of extra sub-periods.

It would be easier, of course, if he'd already made plans to meet Areese and she was waiting there. Not implausible, especially since the fight had obviously been just for me—he'd certainly arranged it for *some* reason. Still, it was totally farfetched and I knew it. There was nothing connecting the events at all. It was just my desperation to get something on Kezar, that was all; it was affecting my thinking. There was only one thing that kept me from shrugging it off completely: Kezar had had a bag when he left the gambling house. That wasn't unusual, he often had one and it was the same one he always carried. But it was a bag. And though it would have looked kind of bulky, you could have fit a head in it.

It wasn't going to go away until I disproved it. I had two threads I could tug.

The *Fair Margaret*, the ship the brawlers had come from, was still docked. It was a merchant ship, so it was a little hard to find somebody who knew where to find anybody else—only military ships keep up any sort of protocol while in port, the merchants just lock up the valuables and let everyone unwind—but eventually I found somebody who admitted to being in the chain of command and I was able to dig up the crewman who had tossed another crewman on top of Kezar. There is always value to taking incident notes, and making sure you get people's names in them.

He was the one whose nose had been broken, and the way he reacted when he saw me was really something. I couldn't tell whether he was thinking about hitting me or running away or both, so I said, "Relax. You goofed, you paid, we're even." We sat down. "Mostly."

It was definitely panic, and I don't think it was all because of the broken nose. "Mostly?"

"Here's the thing. I don't want to cause you any more trouble." I was trying my hardest to be sweet and gentle. "But I'm trying to investigate a murder, and if you don't tell me the truth, it could be a problem. I wouldn't want to have to hold your ship because of something you did or didn't do, and I don't think your captain would like that either"—he really looked unhappy now—"so let's see if we can't clear this up." He nodded. Eager to cooperate. "Who paid you and your buddies to have that fight?"

It floored him. I had thought he'd been expecting it, but I guess not.

Of course it hadn't been Kezar who actually paid him and his friends, so it proved nothing. On the other hand, Kezar would have been too smart to have paid them himself, so it proved nothing. Wild theory still intact. I thanked him and reassured him that all debts were paid, and that I wouldn't hold his ship. Especially that I wouldn't hold his ship. Captains get very upset when they miss schedules.

Time to go back to Tiny's.

§

After I tugged on my second thread and the wild theory not only was still intact but looking better than ever, the next question was when to do it.

I could have waited until after twenty-six, when Kezar was sure to be in his rooms. Certainly it would have made more sense to do that. I don't always do things that make sense. I can offer two possible explanations, and you choose the one you like: either I wanted to show him up at his place of business, in front of his customers and employees, or I was nervous about waiting any longer because he was such a tricky son of a bitch. The correct answer could well be 'both.'

It did mean I would have to deal with the beef twins, though.

"Nobody goes in unless they're on the list," the left one said.

"Do you know what 'security officer' means?" I asked. They did; I saw them exchange a oh-man-are-we-sure-we're-paid-enough-for-this look, but I hadn't really expected it to break any ground. They were scared of Kezar; I was an unknown.

The right one did say, "Sorry, but he's real strict about that," and he actually looked sorry. He was going to be sorrier in a moment. I shrugged. "Play it your way." I pressed the panel and the door opened.

They both reacted at the same time. Tweedledum attempted to grab my left arm; Tweedledee, with no sense of symmetry but a better sense of tactics, tried to move in front of me to block the doorway instead. He was more than twice my weight, so I didn't plan on letting him play roadblock. As he came in, while twisting away from the other one's grasp, I hooked his leg out from under him.

Damned if Tweedledee didn't manage to right himself; he did it by half-landing on Tweedledum. I could easily have gotten him in the sprocket right then, but I felt a little bad for these two, so instead I kicked him hard in the stomach. I had taken the time to put on my kicking shoes. All his air exploded out of him and he ended up sitting down. He did this just as the other one was trying to get past him, and in trying not to trip over Tweedledee, Tweedledum turned enough that I had a clear shot to kick him in the ass, which I did, and he ended up face first on the carpet.

"Gentlemen," I said. "At this point I could go for your faces or your more sensitive areas, but I'm not because you're just doing your job and I'm in a good mood. Do we want to continue? Don't worry about your boss; he has other problems."

They looked at each other and decided to pass.

"Free advice," I said. "Be somewhere else quickly. This place is about to close." I headed down the hall. Along the way I pulled out my collapsible riot baton and un-collapsed it. I don't like using tools on people; makes it too easy to do more damage than you intend to. But unlike Tweedledum and Tweedledee, Kezar was likely to have and use a weapon, and I wanted the insurance.

As it turned out, it was needless. Whatever he had was in a desk drawer. I brought the baton down on his hand as he reached for it just to make a point, but I could have stopped him in that time with just my own self.

"You crazy bitch! You think you can just—" Actually it was a little more incoherent than that but you get the idea.

"That's right, I do. Now I'm going to pull your arm way back like this—yes, I know it hurts—and we're going to Custody, and if you try one damned thing on the way, you're going to get a lot more hurt than just a hand. After we get there, we can have a nice long talk."

"I have rights here—just because you're security officer doesn't mean you can just go dragging people off—ow!" Right down again on the hurt hand. I'm a big believer in behavioral modification.

As I led him out, I noticed Tweedledum and Tweedledee had taken my free advice. Good for them. "Everybody out! This place is closing, right now. The owner has had his license revoked. You!" I hailed a worried-looking casino employee. "I don't know who helps run this place, but go find him and tell him the security officer says he's out of business. When I come back, I expect to find this place shut, empty, and the lights off. Got it?"

"You can't—" Kezar growled. I yanked on his arm a little harder and he bit the sentence off. Slow learner.

§

We got stares all the way along deck five to Custody, including from Max when I came in. I opened the first of the custody rooms and pushed Kezar in, not gently. "I'll be a bit, Max. Can you see about arranging some dinner for our guest?"

Kezar hadn't tried to get up from where he had landed in the corner. "This room's soundproof," I said. "I mention that just for your information. Now let's talk about Britt Areese for a while."

"I don't know any Britt Areese."

"I think you must have known her pretty well, if you could ask her to meet you in a private room. Doesn't strike me as the kind of thing she'd do for a total stranger, don't you think? I bet sawing off her head was fun. Did you sweat a lot while you did it? Did you lose your grip anywhere in there and drop the saw? How was it, trying not to get stray blood on your suit and hoping no one outside could hear anything and worrying you were running out of precious time?"

I was figuring that a guy who never had a hair out of place and who wore the shiniest suits I'd yet seen on the Ring had probably been really unnerved by the butchery—not that anyone would be utterly calm about it, you understand—and I saw him give a little involuntary shake, and I saw his eyes, and I knew I had him.

"You're crazy," he said, but this time he said it without conviction.

"Sometimes," I said, "but not at the moment. Another dancer saw you come out of the room. You must have seen her see you. Of course by then you were in a real rush, you had to lose the head and get back to your room in time, but it was dark in the hall and it was a good risk. Besides, you'd never been there before; who could connect you to that place? But I showed her an image of you a couple of periods ago. She says yes. By the by, I noticed when I came to get you that your black bag you always carry wasn't in your office. Did you spill something on it? Oh, and I think you overpaid those crewmen. I talked to one of them earlier as well, and I think he probably would have started the fight for the price of a couple of drinks—"

"Enough!" he shouted.

I indicated eager interest in listening.

"Look, I want this clear, all right? Whatever else you think. Because it was even worse than you can imagine. In that little room—and I didn't even know her ... I do a lot of things, but I wouldn't have done that."

"I can't tell if you're admitting or denying," I said. "I don't have a lot of patience, Kezar."

"I'm trying to tell you! I had to do it—for somebody else. I didn't have a choice. You don't understand. I didn't want to do it, and now everything's shot to hell, just because of—" He caught himself.

"Who? Who told you to kill her?"

He shook his head, a little frantically. "No. I want to ship out. I want off the Ring. You don't get that until you get me out."

"You're pretty good at improvising a lie."

"It's the truth!" he said. "Give me a reason why I'd make this up—"

"What were you looking for in her rooms?"

"What?"

"Don't give me that. You searched her rooms. That's what you were buying time with, the trick with the head. What were you looking for?"

He looked surprised enough to be genuine. "But—I get it now ... that—!" Now he looked genuinely angry. "I never searched her rooms. But I know who did. And that's all you're getting from me until we make a deal."

When someone sets his face like that, it's time to find another tactic or take a break. "I'll consider it," I said, and left the room.

Max was sitting at the desk with an expression half curiosity, half bewilderment. "Make sure you check the window and be very careful when you bring him his dinner," I said. "He doesn't look like much, but he's a murderer and he's feeling a little desperate."

§

I hadn't actually been in the same room with the boss since the cycle I'd arrived. She didn't seem any more interested in seeing me than she had then. Nor pleased. Maybe she didn't ever get pleased.

I'd filled her in on all the details, and she had listened to all of it without saying a word. When I'd finished, she inhaled sharply through her nose, as a preamble.

"I realize that when I first briefed you it was cut a little short," she said, "and I'm willing to forgive your wasting my time—this time. But I want to make sure this is clear, because I don't want to have to explain it again. Part of your job is making sure I don't have to concern myself with your job. I have too many other things to think about. Except in very unusual circumstances, I'm not interested in the details of your work."

Yes, it *did* worry me that she apparently didn't consider these to be unusual circumstances.

"If you do something I don't like, believe me, I'll tell you. If at some point you have reason to want clarification, send me a file, or even use the feed, but I expect it to be to the point, and I expect it not to happen often. If you constantly suspect the soundness of your judgment, then I've hired the wrong person. For what it's worth, I don't think I have."

I wasn't sure I should thank her, so I kept silent.

"As for Kezar, I need to clarify that as well, and again, I attach no blame; I hadn't realized this situation would come up. I'm aware I told you I wanted him off the Ring, but that was before you had established that he had killed a permanent resident. We do not tolerate that. Eject him from an airlock."

"He says he was ordered to do it by someone else—"

"That wouldn't be a mitigating circumstance even if there were any. There will be no tolerance of killing permanents. I won't repeat it a third time. Extract what he knows if you like, but after you have it, eject him from an airlock. If you can't do that, then I'll have to find a new security officer."

§

I went to get some dinner first. I wasn't hungry; I was stalling.

If you think I was fretting about pushing Kezar into space, you misunderstand my morals. Kezar had killed and decapitated a woman who, no matter what her faults, had deserved far better than that. Pushing Kezar out a lock was probably a tamer fate than he deserved.

The problem was getting the information from him. I couldn't promise him amnesty and then push him out the airlock anyway. Again, if you don't understand why that would bother me and the actual execution wouldn't, you need to pay more attention. I had no lever to use on him, and I wanted very badly to find out who had him so scared he'd kill someone he didn't want to kill on their say-so. I didn't think that appealing to Kezar's better nature was going to work, since it didn't exist.

I hadn't come up with a good idea by the time I got to Custody. When I opened the door, I saw a foot on the desk and a dark puddle on the floor. Oh, hell, he got out, was my first thought—Max—oh Max—

The foot on the desk was Max's; it looked like he had been pushed backwards over his desk from the front side, taking his chair down with him. His throat had been cut. His skin was still a little warm. He had been slaughtered while I was fretting over my damned dinner.

How had Kezar gotten out? Had Max let him out for some reason and then let him get advantage? But then I looked through the window in the door to the custody room. Kezar hadn't gotten out.

Whoever it was—X—had walked right into Custody, because fool Max didn't make people buzz in when he was there. Max had gotten up from the desk to either talk to X or stop X and had gotten cut down. X had opened Kezar's door—anyone could open it from the outside—and Kezar had come to it, maybe to talk to X, maybe to escape? And his throat had been cut as well. The door had then closed on him. He hadn't gone quietly. There were bloody fist marks on the inside of the door where he'd pounded on it.

My eyes hurt. I was sitting on the floor just outside the door of the custody room. I didn't remember sitting down. I don't remember how long I sat. I don't remember what I was thinking. I don't remember when I got up. I don't remember the rest of that cycle at all.

THE CASE of the BLUE PLAGUE

You have to continue to function. Even when you want to never leave your bed again. Even when your brain is running a non-stop loop of how badly you've screwed up. There are always things that still have to get done.

There were three people who knew Kezar hadn't gone out an airlock: Dr. Kohl, me, and whoever killed him. I don't know how Dr. Kohl disposed of the body without anyone else seeing it, but he said he did, and that's good enough. I let the gossip spread that Kezar had been penalized appropriately for murdering a permanent. The boss wanted a deterrent. She didn't seem to want anything else, so I didn't tell her the truth.

You may have a problem with that, but here's the thing: even if I trusted the boss—and I wasn't sure I did—operating on a need-to-know basis cuts both ways. She didn't want to spell anything out for me, fine. Max had been right about that; I operated the same way. But as far as I was concerned that gave me equal freedom not to spell anything out for her. She'd said she wanted me to operate independently. If it turned out to be a problem later, I'd have learned just how much independence was actually permitted.

Max also went into the digesters. Several people asked about him; I told them I'd found him dead of natural causes. Once again, Dr. Kohl knew the truth, and so did Catalan, who surprised me by contacting me several cycles after his death and asking if he was okay. I didn't tell her about Kezar's death, but I felt she was entitled to know how Max had really died.

I didn't put up a plaque for Max. Maybe somebody else did. I don't do memorials.

I took to working in Custody during "business periods." I not only put the door on buzz-for-access even when I was there, I got a door camera installed so I could see who was buzzing. Tiny community maybe, but one member of that tiny community was not answering the door for a murderer if she could help it. I also had a data station installed at the desk. I heard no comment from the boss when I submitted the bills.

§

A couple of cycles after I spoke to Catalan about Max, my door buzzed. My personal door, not Custody. I'd just come back from eating dinner and was thinking about what I might do until time to sleep. "Read" and "stare at the walls" were looking like the top two choices.

It was the woman who'd been receptionist at Catalan's the day I was there, the redhead. "Hi," she said, as if there were nothing unusual about her turning up.

"Um, hello."

"We didn't exchange names before. I'm Meridian ... Catalan told me about Max. I'm sorry. We all liked him."

I think I was probably giving her a blank stare throughout this. I don't know. I wasn't trying to make her uncomfortable, but what did I say?

"She said—well, I just thought maybe you might want some company."

"I don't think I'm in the market for that kind of company right now," I said, "and if I were I probably couldn't afford it."

"Oh, I wasn't approaching you as a customer!" she said.

"How were you approaching me, then?"

She looked like she was looking for something to say and not finding it.

"Right," I said. "I appreciate the offer, though. Have a good night." I let the door shut.

§

Even if I didn't want that sort of contact—and I didn't—I knew I needed to make more connections. Max had been my sole source of information and gossip. If I waited for people to tell me things on their own, I would wish I had known about the situation sooner for half the tasks I got. I needed to be able to get the latest news about everything happening on the Ring *before* crises erupted.

One source was the businesses. Several of them seemed grateful that I had ousted Kezar, which was a good start. I noticed that these tended to be the same ones Kezar had visited on his tour, that cycle, but I didn't ask if they had been paying him extortion, and they didn't volunteer it. I didn't want to sour our relationship when it was just beginning. I wanted to be able to walk in at any time and have a pleasant conversation with the managers or owners about anything I happened to need to ask about. Even little things, like who was the hot A/V star these days, and what was that new energy drink they were selling so much of? I understand some people talk to friends to learn these kinds of things.

Another source came about because I happened to be on lower cargo—deck nine—one cycle when a ship disgorged some fifty bipeds in full-body veils, long black formless garments that concealed every bit of their bodies but their eyes and their hands (and the latter only because they were carrying bags). From the baggage, they looked like they were preparing for a long stay. Fifty transients, especially fifty transients whom I couldn't tell were human or what under all that, was definitely something I wanted to know about ... and if I hadn't been there at that time by sheer accident, who knows how long it would have taken me to find out about it. Finding out which ships were about to leave or port through the Ring was easy—there were displays with the queue (spelled "Q" on the Ring) all over deck five and other likely places, so crew could know when it was time to hurry back to their ships. But for tracking arrivals, the only source was Dispatch.

Dispatch has a vertical slice of the Ring. (Or "radial slice" if you prefer space crew ideas of up and down, which is to say, none.) The sixty-fourth sector would be sector 100 in the damned base eight, and would spoil the two-digit sector numbers on the walls—at least that's my theory for why the sectors were 00 to 77 (zero to sixty-three, in numbers that made sense). I still hadn't figured out why sectors and times were in base eight. Anyway, sector zero was Dispatch—all of sector zero, cutting straight down all decks, with its own ramps. It had its own dining facilities, its own living quarters, everything. Dispatch was a self-contained town within the Ring, and they very definitely ran the place. Which didn't intimidate me, but it did leave me at a loss for how or where to crack it.

As it turned out, no cracking was needed. The Dispatch main door on deck four respected me, and so did the receptionist/sentry/bouncer just inside it. When I said I was the security officer and wanted to look around, she looked at something on her data station (possibly my image) and nodded and said only to not disturb anyone who looked like they were talking to a ship or doing something delicate.

There wasn't much else to see on deck four. The part that is probably what you're picturing, the big control room with rows of people in headsets at data stations trying to coordinate complicated things, was on deck six and was two decks high. Deck five had a gallery, looking down at the room through a glass wall. I watched the activity for a while. It was a reasonably busy cycle, with the Ring opening at least twice a period. Large displays on the walls showed waiting ships in nearby space, from various angles. No one below seemed especially agitated or even hurried. There also weren't as many people in the room as I'd expected. A smooth, efficient operation. The boss must be proud.

Eventually I went down to deck six and went into the room, directly to a man at a desk near the back. He had very short brown hair, sticking straight up a few millimeters atop his head, and a disappear-into-the-crowd face that was distinguished only by the dark circles under his eyes and a sort of permanent wry smile, as if he had worn himself out keeping an eye on everything and he was unimpressed by all of it. I introduced myself.

"Bob Flanagan," he said. He couldn't bring himself to be rude to the security officer, but he was steeling himself to have his time wasted. "What can I do for you?"

"For a start, I'd like to know the story behind the group of people in veils who arrived earlier this cycle."

"They're members of a religion, or a cult, called Tanngrevers. Sounds like they're being sent off by the mother church to found a splinter colony. They're going way the hell out to nowhere to do it, where nobody has a reason to go, so they'll be waiting here for quite a while for their ride. We've given them some overflow space on deck six to live in. Say, what made you think I'd know anything about that?"

"I watched from the gallery for twenty subs," I said. "Every time anyone else in this room had something they couldn't figure out on their own, they came to you. You didn't take long to solve any of it either. You aren't talking to ships or doing any of the actual wrangling, so I think you're here just to solve any problems that come up. That means you know all kinds of things. Head troubleshooter."

He grinned. "No, that'd be you. They call me an 'Operations Supervisor.' Want a job?"

"I'm only just getting used to this one. Anything else I should know about those—what was it?"

"Tanngrevers. Named for the founder, Tanngreve. Feed is they're weird but harmless. They keep to themselves. All I have are rumors, which I offer with no guarantees. I've heard that you can't tell the sockets from the sprockets until you get absolutely all their clothes off, which apparently doesn't happen much. I also hear from several sources that they're unable to lie. Not sure how *that* works. That's all I've got."

One of the other people in the room had stood up and was approaching his desk, so that would do for now. "Thanks. I may need to come ask you about other things from time to time, if you don't mind."

"You'll come whether I mind or not," he said, "but I don't. Just be prepared— some cycles you may have to take a number and wait in line." He smiled his wry smile and I knew that I hadn't actually annoyed him at all.

§

The next addition to my arsenal came as a complete surprise. One cycle the door to Custody buzzed and on the other side I saw Tweedledum and Tweedledee from Kezar's gambling house. They looked more nervous than hostile, so I didn't get ready for trouble as I opened the door. Much.

It turned out their names were Rob and Don, and they were indeed twins, and they wanted a job.

"It's rough for beefs right now," Don, in the green shirt, said—to this day unless they're wearing different things I can't tell them apart—"not enough work for everybody."

"Ships have been cutting down lately—longer loadouts with fewer people," said Rob in the red shirt.

"We don't have a problem with, you know, the rough work, breaking up fights and things like that, but—"

"—we'd, well, we'd rather do it for—" They looked at each other; both seemed at a loss.

"You'd rather work on this side of the law?" They nodded. I wasn't completely sure that had actually been what they'd been embarrassed to say, but it didn't matter.

"We're better at it than it looked, that cycle when you—" Don began. His brother gave him a "shut up, idiot" face.

I smiled. "I know you are. If you hadn't been falling all over each other in a confined space you'd have done better. Look, what I do can get really nasty, and if you gents are working for me I may have to send you out at all periods. I understand if you also need to do beef work—I get slow times too—but if you don't come when I ask, right away, then you're no use to me. On the other hand, if I pull you away from a cargo job I'll make sure you're paid enough to be worth it. Clear?"

They both nodded, trying not to look too eager.

"All right. I'll give you a tryout. I don't know when I'll actually need you. Could be this cycle; I'm expecting some bar fights later." We had a Cleit ship in, which I was learning was always good for trouble, and a Pergati crew who hadn't had off-ship time in so long they were having to relearn how to get stinking drunk.

As it happened, there were several bad brawls over the next two cycles, and I fetched them out, and they did a fine job. They had more finesse than I would have expected for men so bulky, and seldom did any more physical damage than they absolutely had to. And it developed over time that they were still impressed by how easily I'd passed them at Kezar's—even if I had gotten lucky—and apparently that, plus the fact that I never skimped or weaseled on their pay, bought me a lot of loyalty.

So now I had muscle when I needed it.

§

Forty-two cycles after Max and Kezar were murdered. Every night I asked myself who killed them, and every night I concluded there was absolutely no way I could find out, and went to sleep frustrated. For a variation, when I got tired of kicking myself about that, I changed to kicking myself about Bral dead in the airshaft. I had no foothold on that either. Some security officer I was. I don't know which I was pondering that cycle as I strolled through lower cargo. I had no particular reason to be there; I could either fret in my room or fret while taking a walk, and I liked the exercise.

Deck nine, like deck eight, wasn't a place people went unless they had business there. It didn't really have any predictable "empty periods," but the flip side of that was that you couldn't predict what parts would be busy and what parts deserted. It had automatic lights like nearly every other public-access space in the Ring—they came on when someone was in the area and turned themselves off when they left—but apparently they hadn't felt it was necessary to light it as brightly as, say, deck two residences. It was a shadowy place with unmarked, enormous cargo doors and odd geography, with warehouse rooms squeezed in among infrastructure and around the three shuttle bays and airway access and so on. Lower cargo was the only deck that didn't have a concourse—you couldn't go around the Ring in a straight line; you had to turn corners and find your way. It was a good place to get jumped unexpectedly. Part of me would have welcomed an assault attempt; it would have given me a reason to beat the hell out of someone.

I was entering what amounted to a small alley between two warehouses when I heard a low moan or a cry up ahead, in shadows. The alley was not lit on its own, and light from the larger corridor at either end didn't quite seep into the middle. I ran in. It was a Clxl. They had been stabbed several times in the chest; I could see that much. They were having trouble breathing, and the wheezing was even more disturbing coming from all their spiracles at once.

"I'll get help," I think I said.

"True—" they said.

I thought for a moment they were trying to say yes. Translation sometimes does that. "No, don't move—"

"True. Free."

"I don't understand."

"True. Free ..." they gasped.

"Don't try to talk," I said, trying to see if I could do anything about the chest wounds that would possibly help, knowing that I couldn't. They trailed off into a choking noise. Then they were dead.

§

Clxl were the third most common species among the Ring permanents, but that wasn't saying a lot; the vast majority of us were human or Pergati. There were probably fifty Clxl on the station, tops, and had only increased to that number recently, when nine had arrived on the same ship. The blue-green biped I'd seen on my first visit to Catalan's was a Clxl. They did not seem to socialize with other species much, the one at Catalan's notwithstanding.

What surprised me—as I sat in my rooms, two periods later, reading Alsop's file on Clxl—is that what I had taken to be two different species from two different places were actually the same. During the visit of the recent Clxl ship, I'd seen a few bipeds who were the same colors all Clxl were—blue-green with occasional mottles of black or brown—but who looked like they were wearing built-in armor, face and head plates included. It was hard to recognize those hulking things as the same species as the slender, smooth-skinned ones who seemed to be the majority of the ones on the Ring. Most of the armor-plated ones left when the ship did.

Alsop's notes: "Clxl evolved from marine arthropods; apparently at some point their genetic line split, or was divided, or some other intervention (unknown), so that some still have plates which grow beneath their skin and eventually protrude, while others do not. This is not a sex-linked difference—there are sockets and sprockets of both types—but it is definitely a psychological one."

I wanted more on that, but most of the rest of Alsop's notes on Clxl were about their language, which was difficult for Pergati and humans alike and which he'd apparently had some working problems with. Even when the Clxl used our letters, they used them their way. For example, their collective name: The "cl" was a high click or cluck sound with the tongue, and the "xl" was a low click which they made by snapping together hard surfaces in their mouth, vestigial mandibles. You try saying it. Alsop noted some humans called them "tick-tocks," apparently from attempts at saying their name. It was better than calling them "crabs," which was about as accurate and as polite as calling humans "monkeys." Some humans called them that anyway. There had been some bad blood between humans and Clxl in the past—something about a moon they both wanted—and a few crabby people (pardon the phrase) had not entirely forgotten.

The victim had no identification and was wearing nothing but the shoulderless, cinched-waist dress they seemed to prefer. Learning their identity wouldn't be hard since there were so few Clxl, but I wasn't sure where to start. We didn't have anything like a by-species registry; I was still searching for a way to cross-reference or otherwise make my data station "show me all Clxl on the Ring" when I found it.

Trofri Assembly. Pronounced: true-free.

§

The Trofri Assembly had been started by some of the nine who had arrived recently, so it had been operating maybe thirty cycles. It was some sort of gathering spot for Clxl, but whether it was a church or a dance club or a revolutionary outpost, I could not learn. There was a cure for that.

It was in the seediest sectors of deck five, and even among those businesses it was notable for lack of exterior decor. Over the door it said "Trofri" in Pergati runes, or close enough, and just below that what was probably the same thing in their writing, which looked like a jumble of scratches and dots. That was it. There was a small info display by the side of the door which showed something that could have been a manifesto, or it could have been that cycle's dinner menu.

I buzzed at the door, turning my head to avoid the reader. (The problem with doors just opening for me when I tried to buzz was that no one on the Ring was attuned to the sound of knocking, or the doors muffled it, or both. I once knocked on a door for five subs, assumed no one was home, let the reader let me in, and scared the resident—who had been in the same room as the door the whole time—half to death.) I had to buzz twice. When the door opened, it revealed one of the armor-plated kind of Clxl. They were taller than I was, and I'm not short. They were in Rob and Don territory on both height and bulk, but meaner looking. They said something I didn't understand, a lot of consonants and clicks.

"I need to speak to the person in charge; there has been a death," I said in Pergati. I got another response I didn't understand. They didn't budge. I tried again in Bak'ti (translated roughly: "Need talk big person belong place on dead person.") Still nothing. They didn't look any happier and they weren't moving. I turned away and they shut the door.

I wasn't going to barge in; I didn't have reason, at least not yet, and anyway I wasn't going to try my odds against that brute without some backup. What I really needed was a translator.

I had somebody obvious in mind—but I didn't get there, because I hadn't walked two sectors down deck five when the feed chirped. It was Dr. Kohl—who had never before then used the feed of his own volition in any of my dealings with him.

"What can I do for you, doctor?"

"I'd like you to come to medical, as soon as you can. Not my rooms. Four:fourteen. Ask for me." And that was all.

Well, I owed him for waking him up to handle Britt Areese's corpse. Besides, I was intrigued. I hurried up to deck four.

§

"What do you think?" he asked.

"I think either this light is bad or these people are a color they're not supposed to be."

He snorted. "Well, what did you expect?" I said. "I'm a decent policeman, but a lousy pathologist."

What I was looking at were three unconscious patients in adjacent beds, all on some sort of ventilator or oxygen supply, all human, all fairly young, all—well, they were a faint blue-green. Not Clxl blue-green, and not throughout. All the parts which in a normal person might tint red/pink were instead this cyan color. They were very pale—every human on the Ring is pretty pale, no matter how much time we get in the sunrooms—but this wasn't a normal-looking pale.

"That color is cyanosis," Dr. Kohl said. "It's caused by a lack of oxygen in the blood. Two of these three self-reported—Dr. Wright, why don't you give the rundown. Lois Wright, Jessica Gray."

Dr. Wright smiled politely. She had gray hair in a neat bun, hazel eyes, and a face that was aging in the way of becoming more taut and rawboned, rather than sagging. "As Frederic says, two of them checked themselves in, complaining of muscular and especially abdominal cramps. One of them had diarrhea. Food poisoning would have been the first thought except for the cyanosis; on the other hand, their having no dizziness, disorientation or headache mostly ruled out the kinds of gas poisoning which could cause the cyanosis. We gave them gastric lavage—that is, we emptied their stomachs—and oxygen. The third patient had no interview because he was found unconscious on deck two, doubled over as if from abdominal cramps. Frederic analyzed blood samples and said all three should immediately be treated for methemoglobinemia—"

"—which we had to do the old-fashioned way, with methylene blue—"

"—and the oxygen supply in their blood appears to be returning to normal, or what passes for normal in this place—"

"Dr. Wright feels the atmosphere on the Ring leaves something to be desired," said Dr. Kohl.

"This is very interesting," I said, making a mental note to look up "methemoglobinemia" later, "but I'm not sure how I'm involved. They're recovering now, aren't they?"

"Yes," he replied, "but recovering from what? The methemoglobin, the cyanosis, these were in effect only symptoms of what poisoned them. Serious symptoms, obviously, but not the cause. On the Ring three people are enough to make a syndrome—or at least begin searching for one."

"Do you have any guesses? Anything I can use as a starting place? We've already seen that I'm out of my depth here."

"I'm not asking you to be the epidemiologist," he said. "I'll attempt to do that. What I need from you are eyes, hands, and legs. As for guesses, I need to do more analysis, but gas seems improbable; simply not enough opportunities for it in this controlled atmosphere. It could be something absorbed through the skin, but if I were playing the odds, I would look for something unusual they ate or drank first."

"So, something they all consumed ... in what timeframe? Earlier this cycle? Last cycle? Five cycles ago?"

"Not earlier this cycle," said Dr. Wright, "The two whose stomachs we pumped had nothing useful. Whatever they last ate or drank was mostly gone. As it is, it doesn't seem that they had any dinner."

"Heavy drinkers?"

"One of them," she said. "If the other was, he wasn't doing it this cycle."

"Hmm. Well, I'll do what I can," I said. "If you find any hints, let me know. I'll keep my eyes open for more blue people. Should be easy to spot."

"Funny thing, that," Dr. Wright said. "I interviewed them both myself, and both of them said nearly the same thing when I asked about their skin color ... 'Why? what's wrong with it?'"

§

By then I needed sleep, so I waited until the next cycle to go to Catalan's. Meanwhile, no one got on the feed to ask, "Have you seen a Clxl anywhere? We seem to be missing one." That in itself was suggestive; the problem is I wasn't sure which of several things it suggested.

When I got to Catalan's, she herself was in the "parlor," sitting back at the bar, reading files on a data pad. It was too early for many customers, and the room was empty; most of the staff were probably still asleep. She was in a good mood. "Well, if it isn't the house detective! Can I buy you a drink? Anything you like, as long as it's a real drink."

I smiled. "What qualifies as a real drink?"

"Oh, well, anything so long as it isn't mostly sugar water. Or that pink stuff."

"Pink stuff?"

"You know, that energy drink. I won't let that in here. I keep getting customers who want to cut it with vodka, and I ask them, 'why not just have the vodka?' Some people never do learn to drink properly. What can I do for you?"

I sat down. "Maybe I should buy *you* a drink. I need to ask a favor. I'd like to borrow one of your staff."

She raised her eyebrows. "We don't do house calls. No, no, I know you didn't mean that, I'm just being difficult. What's the problem?"

"You have a Clxl here, I remember. Do you think they'd be willing to play translator?"

"That's their decision. You can ask ... if they do, they'll expect compensation— but I don't have to tell you that, you seem like a quid-pro-quo type. How long?"

"If I'm lucky, just a period or two; but it could be longer. How much compensation, just so I have some idea?"

She named a figure. "Huh," I said. "Hope my boss doesn't kill me. Is that average?"

"On the higher end. Popular."

"I wouldn't have thought Clxl were much that type," I said.

"Oh, not with Clxl. I don't think I've ever seen one in here as a customer. Trixi doesn't associate with the rest of them. If you're trying to investigate something among the Clxl, that might be a disadvantage."

"It might. But for the same reason, they might be the only one I can trust."

"Do you want to ask them now? I'm watching the house, but ... oh, there. Meridian!"

Meridian, who was passing in one of the side halls, stepped in. "Hi," she said to me, not coldly.

"Can you find Trixi and ask them to come in here?"

(In case you are thinking "Trixie": No. "Tree" plus a high click. Catalan said it easily, but she'd had practice. It took me several cycles to even come close.)

As I got a good look at a live Clxl for the first time, I realized it wasn't as unlikely as I'd thought that humans might want to go to bed with them. Of course they had utterly no hair, but plenty of humans, especially space crews, go bald on purpose (it gets in the way) and not everyone was put off by that. The big impediment, I think, would be that they have no noses whatsoever, not even nostrils, not even a faint bump. I kept looking for something in the middle of the face that wasn't there. They did have what looked like very long, high eyebrows (no eyelashes), but at close range these were actually thin, feathery clusters of something that wasn't hair—sort of like short antennae. Their eyes had a green iris so dark it was difficult to make out where the pupil began, and no whites.

I couldn't see the spiracles across the shoulders and the back of the neck, because Trixi was facing me. They had no mammaries, but then, I was pretty sure Clxl weren't mammalian, so that proved nothing. They did have hips, but they also had broader shoulders than a human female usually would. I really needed to stop playing the socket/sprocket guessing game with non-humans, but I couldn't resist.

The other visible differences (besides the skin color, of course) were that their bare feet, instead of having toes, split into two asymmetric parts at the end, and they had three digits on each hand, one opposable, all three of them longer and thicker than ours and each tapering to a slightly rounded point.

Trixi looked at us, scratched the bandage on their upper arm absently, and said nothing, not even a greeting, until Catalan had finished explaining. They then said, to me, "You know the other Clxl on this station think I am—I don't remember the word—they don't like me."

"Immoral," Catalan provided.

"The Trofri ones may not think that yet," I said, "and anyway it's not important they like you, just whether you can translate accurately."

Trixi nodded. "Now?"

"Might as well," I said. "Maybe we can get you back here in time for the busy periods."

§

When we reached the Trofri door, Trixi's attention was drawn to the information on the display. "Anything interesting?" I said.

"These are the times when they let others in and the things they will talk about," they said.

"What sort of things? Is this a church? A political group?"

"It is—is there a word for it? These talks are about how to become better, how to improve self and life. How to keep outside things from making their lives worse. Like that."

"A Clxl motivational speaker. Well, conclude what you can, but keep it to yourself. I'll talk to you about it afterward." I buzzed.

A few tries later, the same goon answered. They gave me the same unimpressed look. The look they gave Trixi was more complex—I think it may have been curiosity, but that wasn't all of it. "Tell them we need to talk to whoever is in charge about the death of a Clxl."

They exchanged sounds. "They say they are closed and we should come back at the next open time."

"Is the person in charge on the premises right now?"

"... Yes."

"Then we want to come in right now. I would much rather speak to that person when they're not in session."

More sounds. "They don't want to allow that."

"I guessed. Ask if they know what the position of security officer on the Ring is. Explain that this is a murder investigation and is urgent."

Quite a bit more chatter, interrupted by a third Clxl voice, belonging to another one of the armored kind, walking up behind the door goon. Trixi immediately switched to addressing this third party directly, and after a bit of that, the goon reluctantly moved aside and we were allowed in.

The main room had several rows of backless benches and nothing else. At the open end where you'd expect a podium or dais, there were a couple of doors in the back wall, and the Clxl led us into a room with a few chairs, and a table with a data pad and some other items on it. The armored Clxl didn't seem to favor the dresses the other kind did; they just wore a sort of loincloth. Contrasting the bulk, the movement of the plates on their back and shoulders as it walked, with their light step and general grace was mentally dissonant. I expected them to stomp around more, bang into doorways, or break the chair when they sat down.

"This is Mratl," Trixi said. "They are the head of the assembly. They give the talks; they also seem to be the one whose idea this was. They've come to the Ring just to do this. They are very"—Trixi looked for a word—"enthusiastic about their goals here."

Mratl was still chattering. "They say we are welcome to attend one of the talks, but they feel the message is primarily for Clxl and would be of limited use to humans."

"Have they had much success with the Clxl already here on the Ring?" I asked.

"They admit the start has been slow," Trixi said after more chatter, "but they have a few regular attendees and are hopeful."

"Interesting," I said. "Ask them about this Clxl." I took out my data pad and displayed an image of the victim.

Mratl looked at the image and clicked rapidly several times—it was an exclamation, not a sentence. "Poor she," they said. Then I realized that was a name—Porshi.

"Was Porshi part of the staff here?"

"Yes—" Trixi was still listening. "Porshi was their assistant. They worked closely together. Porshi has been missing; Mratl has asked other Clxl and none had seen them. Mratl says they even would have asked among humans, but they were unsure who to appeal to. Mratl is very unhappy to learn Porshi is dead."

"Would you explain that, while I'm sympathetic to their loss, there are unpleasant questions I have to ask as part of my job?"

Trixi explained. Mratl replied. "They understand. What would you like to know?"

"How many work here, besides Mratl and Porshi? Is it the entire nine who arrived at that time?"

"... No. Beside those, only Chrl, who was at the door. Mratl says one of the others who was on the ship with them, Rit, helps out here during the talks, but Rit and the others have come to the Ring for their own reasons."

"Does Mratl know of any reason why anyone would want to kill Porshi?"

When Trixi asked this, it seemed to me like the sounds from Mratl were more hostile than they'd previously been. Trixi took a while to translate. "They say no, not among Clxl."

"You're leaving out something. They didn't like that question."

"They—they are assuming you meant among Clxl, which they find offensive. Mratl believes that the likely answer is that some human saw a Clxl and decided to kill them out of hatred."

"Charming. So they don't think very highly of humans, then."

I caught something extra in Trixi's look, but just then Mratl said something else; I got the impression they were deliberately trying to go back to being a good sport again. "They say of course they don't condemn all humans, but they have seen much—hostility—and that you must admit there are still many humans who would dislike a Clxl very much for no other reason than being Clxl."

"I concede that. Tell them I don't have any more questions right now, but I may need to ask more later."

§

"You didn't ask much," Trixi said, as we ate.

It had taken me a while to convince Trixi to have lunch with me. It developed that Trixi's diet was mostly raw protein, and they had learned that humans didn't like watching Clxl eat. I assured them that my stomach was made of iron. Frankly, I'm not sure I would have noticed. Between this and Dr. Kohl's syndrome, I didn't have enough brain free to pay attention to what either of us was eating.

"There was no point in asking anything else. Not then. Maybe later. Trixi, before I ask you some questions, I need to know. You don't seem to get along with the other Clxl much. Did you mean it when you said they thought you were immoral? No, wait, Catalan said that. Do you dislike other Clxl? Do they dislike you?"

"Which kind of Clxl do you mean?"

"Let's start with the ones who were already on the Ring."

"Clxl are very—traditional—about sex," they said. "Just what I do would be enough for most of them not to want to talk to me. They also know, because there are so few of us here and all of them are a close group, they know that who I have sex with are not Clxl."

"And that shocks them?"

"Shocks, no, that's wrong. They just don't understand it. That's the softshells—"

"Softshells, really? That sounds like what a rude human would say."

"But that's what our word for it means. The hardshells are different. The hardshells would think I was—I need the word—"

"Obscene?"

"No ... well, yes, but—betrayal, that's the word."

"A betrayal of what? Of the Clxl?" They nodded. "Are all hardshells xeno like that?"

"Some hide it more. You don't know about Clxl past, I think. We don't tell others much, especially not humans." They gave me an intent look.

"Should I promise to keep it secret?"

They considered. "No, but take care who you tell. Humans who hate us shouldn't hear. A long time ago, we all were hardshells. We were hostile, harsh people; we fought with anyone who came near, and when no one came near, we fought with each other. One day some of us decided that this was a way of life they didn't like. They left our home and went off to try to live on another planet.

"When they did, after a time, they noticed that we weren't growing the hard plates on our bodies. There's something on our home world—later a scientist learned what it was—that makes us form them. So any Clxl who were born and grew up anywhere but our home world are softshells. But more than that, it is political. Hardshells think Clxl should be fighters; they are usually soldiers and nothing else. Softshells think Clxl should be peaceful and stay out of trouble. Mostly.

"Sometimes people leave our home world just so their children will be softshells. Most are born softshells now; we have spread far and most Clxl are no longer born on our home world. But it's easier to go the other way. You can take the chemical that makes the plates and become a hardshell. It takes many cycles. When a softshell does this—"

"Can you go back—become a softshell again?"

"No, not really. You can stop taking it, and the plates get smaller, but unless you didn't take it for very long they won't go away completely. But also—I had a friend, back where I was born. Their—what is your word for another child of same parent?"

"Brother? Sister? Sibling?"

"Sibling. Their sibling became a hardshell when still just barely an adult. My friend, and their family, have never spoken to them again. To softshells it is abandoning everything they stand for."

I pondered all this. "So was it unusual for Mratl to have a softshell as an assistant?"

"More than that," Trixi said. "It is unusual for Mratl to be doing what they are doing at all."

"Mratl hates humans more than they let on, don't they?"

Trixi nodded. "I think so. You were asking about me because you want to know whether I don't trust Mratl because I am a softshell, or whether I don't trust them because they are not to be trusted. How can I be sure? But I know I don't trust them. They hate you, I know that. You wouldn't have been able to tell from the sound."

"I hadn't realized they hated me in particular, but they seemed pretty clear how they felt about humans in general. Under the sweet talk. How possible is it that Mratl killed Porshi? I'm not asking you how likely that is, just whether Mratl would be capable of doing it."

"They would be capable. Hardshells are—well, I am a softshell, so my opinion ... I will say, no matter how valuable an assistant they were, Mratl wouldn't have thought twice about killing Porshi if they felt they had reason. Porshi was only a softshell, you see."

"Yes, I very much see. Was Mratl—could Porshi have been more than just an assistant to Mratl?"

"Do you mean sex?"

"Well, a relationship that—yes, I guess I do mean sex."

It was amused. "Oh, no. Mratl is a socket and so was Porshi, and Clxl are *very* traditional. Also, Mratl wouldn't with a softshell."

"They could be a deviant," I said. Trixi didn't know that word. "Perverted. Obscene."

"No, not even then. It would be a matter of pride. If you're searching for that kind of reason, I would say Mratl is with Chrl. If anyone."

I thought some more. "Trixi, when you were talking to Mratl, how did you play it? Were you a filthy human-sympathizer, or were you just the innocent translator whom I roped into this, maybe unwillingly?"

"More of the second. The other way would have made them angry."

"Well done. I need to ask you a big favor ... there's no way I'm going to learn anything useful about that place, with or without you present. But Mratl has to be preaching to softshells; there aren't any other hardshells here to preach to. If you presented yourself as 'oh, I was so impressed and intrigued by what you said, I just had to come hear some of your speeches to find out more about it'— not that blatant, obviously, but you get the idea—do you think it would work?"

They looked, I think, horrified. "Must I?"

"No, you don't have to. That's why it's a favor. I'm not too happy about having to ask it, either. But I have to find out what's really going on there. Mratl is very invested in whatever they're really doing. They wouldn't want to endanger that with a murder investigation, yet they knew Porshi would immediately be traced there. Either Mratl lost their temper—badly—or they had to kill Porshi because of something Porshi knew, or threatened to do, or both. I don't favor the temper-tantrum theory. Do you?"

Trixi shook their head. "They are very careful. They smell of hate and lies. Would I be in danger?"

"I don't think so. If I did, I wouldn't ask. Mratl may see through you and kick you out, but they won't hurt you; they know if they did, that would make my suspicions definite and I would come with my helpers and throw them out an airlock."

"You're sure they killed Porshi, though. You walk around it but you think so. Why not just throw Mratl out an airlock now?"

"Partly because I can't make myself do that if there's a chance I'm wrong, but consider this: We have to provide proof for everyone else. Do you have any evidence that Mratl killed Porshi other than how they sounded and smelled?" They shook their head again. "Nor do I. Just a feeling. That's not good enough. If I push Mratl into space, and we can't give anyone else a real reason why, what will Clxl think of humans after that? How will other militant hardshells react when they find out?"

They nodded. "I will try. Once. I promise nothing after that."

§

The next assembly wasn't until the next cycle, so I let Trixi get back to their real job, and I went to follow up on my other case.

I'll spare the jury's time. I had the names and rooms and close contacts of three patients, and I spent the rest of that cycle—until I gave up and went back to my rooms to sleep—and part of the next one following that information. I got nothing. One of them had been out drinking before ending up in medical, and she apparently did that most cycles after work—the drinking, I mean, not ending up in medical, although from one piece of information I got on her alcohol consumption, that was a small miracle. The second had gone out that particular cycle but had had one drink. Neither of them seemed to have eaten or drunk anywhere in common, at least not recently. The third patient—the one who hadn't come in under his own power—was a health nut, never drank alcohol or any other bad habits, and cooked all of his meals himself, always. Two of them lived on deck seven, not near each other; the third lived on deck two. And so forth. I couldn't find any common link anywhere.

After I ate some lunch, I went to find Dr. Kohl, who was, unsurprisingly, at his lab table. He looked up at me inquiringly. "Nothing so far," I said, "though not from lack of trying. I think I've run out of data."

"Then have some more," he said, handing me a piece of paper. Of course he would have actual paper. There were five names and rooms written aligned with the left margin; interspersed with those, indented, were several other names and rooms. "Oh," I said. "More blue patients?"

"Five new ones within the last cycle," he said. "The other names are next-of-kin or other close contacts here on the station, for the ones we've managed to speak to coherently."

"So this is an actual epidemic now. Wonderful. Anything new I should know on the medical side?"

"Actually, yes. Whatever is causing this is depositing alkali-metal compounds in the tissues. The most immediate issue is sodium nitrite, which is what's causing the methemoglobinemia, but others are present in places they aren't supposed to be. The patients will continue to have muscular pain and joint stiffness for quite a while, although obviously that's not as serious a problem as the blood oxygen."

"Obviously. Anything else?"

He raised an eyebrow at my wry tone. "You look tired. Have you been remembering to sleep?"

"Yes," I said, "but having two mysteries at the same time puts me at least one over quota. Sorry about the tone."

"As it happens, the nitrite finding is important, but it won't help your mystery quota, I'm afraid. The few cases I can find of sodium nitrite toxicity indicate that its onset is very rapid and the dose needed is fairly small. So whatever they consumed, they should have succumbed to it almost immediately ... so fast, in fact, that it seems to me some of it should have been in their stomachs, or some other evidence of the vehicle should be in their bodies. But from what we've been able to collect so far, there's been none."

"You're describing an impossible situation, then."

"Not necessarily. If some substances were slowly dissolving or recombining to form these compounds over time ... I describe that poorly because I'm not sure of it myself. The point is, if there were some sort of timed-release factor here, there could be something in their bodies we don't know what to look for yet that is slowly causing these unwanted chemicals to accrete. Once those chemicals reach a certain concentration—"

"They turn blue, fall over, and end up in medical. I get it. Remember what Dr. Wright said? If they were getting this gradually, they might not notice they were turning blue. Critical mass could sneak up on them. But what kind of substance would the timed-release stuff be?"

"That's the problem," he said. "I have no idea."

§

Another two cycles elapsed, or maybe it was three, and I missed an opportunity to talk to Trixi somewhere in there because I was so busy drawing a blank on all Dr. Kohl's new data, but I eventually met up with them at Catalan's.

"How was your first Trofri meeting?" I asked.

"I have been to two," they replied.

"I guess that means they decided to buy your story, then."

"They were skeptical. This Rit has been their recruiter among the Clxl here. Rit is also a softshell. Mratl knows if a hardshell were to ask local Clxl to attend, they would not be as willing. But Rit has not seen me among the local Clxl and was suspicious."

"What sort of turnout has Rit been drumming up?"

"What do you—Oh, I see. Not many. Four besides me at the first meeting; three besides me—a different three—at the second one. Not counting Rit or Chrl. I think Mratl took that as proof of my sincerity. You will pay me well for having to listen to them talk."

"I can imagine. And I will. How suspicious were the talks?"

"Not at all. They were exactly as said on the display. Very innocent. But they were trying to test me, I think. After the talk there are questions, conversation. They asked me how I felt about humans. But carefully. I think Mratl's ideas of self-improvement have much to do with what they think Clxl should be doing to humans."

"Very likely. I assume you've been telling Mratl what they want to hear."

Trixi nodded. "Mratl has a weakness. They believe what they say is so obviously the best view that they don't question agreement. Unless they are—playing with me? Is that right?"

"Yes. They could be stringing you along. Do you think so?"

"No. That would smell different. I have been invited to another assembly next cycle. One not shown on the display. Apparently I have passed a test."

"Hmm. Well, I still don't think there's a high risk of danger, but be careful. You know how to reach me in a hurry."

They nodded.

"Say," I said as I stood up, "wasn't that bandage on your other arm the last time I saw you?"

They looked at their arm, as if they had forgotten the bandage was there. "Oh. Yes, that one is finished now. I try to make them—what is it? the same on both sides."

"Symmetrical. Make what?"

They made a word not in Pergati. "I don't know how—here. Touch." They pointed to a spot on their other arm, where I thought the bandage had been before. I touched it. Under the skin, not visible, I felt a tiny hard bump—and one or two others nearby.

"I put the—" another untranslatable—"in with a needle, like—for medicine ..."

"An injection?"

"That. Then I must keep this over it—" the bandage—"soaked with—" untranslatable—"for a few cycles. That makes the—" they repeated the original word. "I have many."

"This is the same material hardshell plates are formed of?"

They nodded. "But be careful what Clxl you say that to."

"Is there a purpose?"

"I don't understand."

"I mean, is it something people do like tattoos or hairstyles, just to change the way their bodies are, or is there some other reason you do it?"

"The first."

"But why do it if no one can see it?"

"It isn't meant to be seen," they replied. "Those aren't who it is for."

"Oh," I said, and my face was a little warm. I'm not usually that slow. I decided I should probably leave.

I think they were amused.

§

It was nice to be able to think there was progress on that case—even if, strictly speaking, it wasn't my progress—because the other one was making me want to tear out my hair. I had this sinking feeling there was something obvious I was missing, and I just couldn't see it.

Two of them were utter non-drinkers; the others ranged from occasional consumption to heavy. Three of them cooked at home, the rest ate in a range of restaurants wide enough that the idea of sampling all those places for contamination gave me the fidgets. From what I was able to get them to remember of their recent meals, the only common links were things *so* common—like the water supply—that if the problem had been there, everyone on the Ring would have been lying in the hospital, blue. Was there anything they had been consuming more of lately than usual? The three I had asked that so far didn't think so.

Very early in the cycle after I spoke to Trixi, about four or five, Dr. Kohl hailed me on the feed—a bad sign. I think he sounded disappointed in me, or maybe that was just my conscience talking. After having to tell him I was still nowhere, he dropped his bomb. "We have a repeater."

"What?"

"One of the patients from the first three is back in. Worse than before."

"Rescuable, I hope."

"She'll recover, but if we let her out and she relapses a third time—"

"She must have gone right back to eating or drinking whatever it was, if we're still working on the ingestion idea. This was the heavy drinker."

"Yes, and we had told her to avoid that, at least during recovery."

"Is she awake? When can I talk to her?"

The recidivist—whom I might as well call by her name, Sue—didn't pull it together enough to interview until several periods later. Sue swore she had followed orders about the booze. She'd had some trouble finding appetite in her weakened condition—I suspected withdrawal/hangover had something to do with that—so she had a very good idea what she'd eaten since being released the first time.

Douglas Todd

Armed with that list, I went out to trace the food chain. We had a definite time frame and a definite list of sources. Something in there must surely be enough to solve this.

§

Sometimes you get blocked on everything, and you're about to jump out an airlock from sheer frustration, and then all of a sudden everything falls away at once.

I had gotten most of the way down Sue's list. I'd gone into restaurants, interviewed, taken samples ... and even before analysis I could see that none of it looked promising. Since leaving the hospital Sue had apparently been a saint. Yet she relapsed somehow ... it had already occurred to me that Sue might not have been entirely honest, no matter how sincere she sounded; she was verging on alcoholism if not there already, and alcoholics lie. So I decided, just for the sake of thoroughness, to go take a look at her rooms.

It was already late when I started heading that way; well after dinner and into the periods when the "day shift" types were heading off to bed. Twenty-seven or thirty, thereabouts. On my way to Sugarland (I trust no one is surprised Sue lived in Sugarland) my feed chirped. It was Catalan. "You need to come over," she said. "Trixi's very upset and I think you need to talk to them."

I don't know if Clxl actually cry. They don't have eyelashes and for all I know they don't have tear ducts either. But Trixi looked like they had been crying. Their eyesockets were a darker color than usual, and they were visibly shaky.

"I'm sorry," they said. "I've ruined your plan—I couldn't do it—"

"Couldn't do what? It's all right. Tell me. Did they ask you to do something? Another test?"

"They drink ibiri," Trixi said. "They wanted me to drink it. They said it was the path to true strength—they said we could only truly face the humans if we were all strong again—"

I was pretty sure "ibiri" had been one of the words they used when I asked about the bandage. "Ibiri is what makes a hardshell?"

They nodded. "To do so, to take that drink with them—I could not! And now they know. I cannot go back."

"Relax," I said. "I don't blame you a bit. I wouldn't have expected you to drink that. And no, don't try to go back. We'll find some other way."

I sat down and rubbed the bridge of my nose and closed my eyes and tried to come up with some new options. I was on the verge of thinking Trixi had been right and I should just raid the place. If nothing else, they'd established that they were not wanted on the Ring—but could I throw someone out just for preaching nastiness against humans?

"I've made everything more difficult," they said, watching me. "You look so tired. Should you sleep? ... It's the wrong thing to say right now, I know," they added, "but you need trofri."

I opened one eye. "I don't recall," I said, "that you've ever actually told me what 'trofri' means."

"Trofri ... trofri is—When you are tired or sad and you go and rest, and then you wake up and everything seems better, that's trofri. It was a good name for what they pretended to be about ... or for what they were actually about, if you see the world as Mratl does."

"What does ibiri look like?"

"... You mean the drink itself? Pink. Cloudy. It smells like—I don't have words. Not like any other drinks I know. I don't know how it tastes. Why?"

I stood up suddenly. "If you're still feeling guilty, don't. I think you've just solved everything. Tell you later."

I rushed to Sugarland, hoping Sue was a slob.

§

I'm afraid I woke up Dr. Kohl yet again, but I was sure this time he wouldn't mind.

"What is this?" he asked, rubbing his eyes with his free hand, trying to focus on the bottle I'd handed him.

"It's an energy drink," I said, "called ReCharge. It hasn't been on the Ring very long and it's become very popular in a short time. It's the latest bar fad. People have been drinking it cut with vodka, probably because it tastes horrible on its own—I tried a tiny bit. It's supposed to be really good for your stamina if you're going to go on a carousing marathon. Sure, some of the patients didn't ever go to bars, but there's no reason why you couldn't drink this without alcohol. You might even get used to the taste. It'd be right up our health nut's alley. Sue didn't lie about the booze, but she already suspected she was drinking a little too much of this stuff, and she left that part out. Her room had a whole lot of empty ReCharge bottles."

He was already getting out the equipment he'd need to analyze it. "If this is what you think it is, you're postulating some diabolical master chemist who has some very strange motivations."

"If it's what I think it is, yes on the motivations, no on the master chemist. The person I have in mind would not have needed to invent it. If I'm right, it was already available."

"Go," he said, waving me off. "I see you want to chase that down, and this will take a long time."

§

"This is going to be rough," I said to Rob and Don. I had my riot baton out and they both had long pry rods they'd swiped from cargo. There were two armored Clxl to deal with, and we were taking no chances. Actually, I reflected, we were taking a lot of chances. In addition to our big sticks, we also had some restraint ties, which I wasn't sure whether Clxl could break. It didn't fill one with confidence.

Chrl slept on two of the benches, pushed together. They woke up as soon as I opened the door and started to make loud noises, which of course would wake Mratl up immediately. Don went for Chrl and just about got knocked halfway across the room. When Chrl turned to face Rob, Rob was ready and hit them across the stomach with the pry rod—which was two centimeters wide and designed to relay a whole lot of force without bending. Chrl went down onto their rear with a whoomph, but didn't seem hurt at all, and bounced back up. Meanwhile, Rob was testing his hand like he'd struck something that was a lot harder than he expected.

Don was still getting up, and right then Mratl charged out of the back room wearing some sort of sharp-looking blade over one hand, a metal glove with about a half-meter of sword extending from the top, over the fingers. "Move, Don!" Don got out of the way of the blade just as Mratl was reaching him. The blade hit the wall where Don had been, and recoiled off, putting Mratl slightly off-balance. I brought my baton down over their spiracles, thinking those couldn't possibly be armored. This worked better than I could have hoped—Mratl went down to their knees, and Don, who had decided all bets were now off, gave them a pry bar square across the eyes. Mratl howled and lashed out ... but not with the sword arm, thankfully, or Don might have been in two pieces. Instead they just knocked Don backwards, hard, far enough that Don collided with a wall headfirst at the end of his slide.

Chrl and Rob had been feinting at one another, not doing much but knocking over benches, but seeing Mratl down brought Chrl rushing immediately to Mratl's aid. (I wondered if Trixi's speculation was true.) I spun, remembered Chrl was a sprocket, and went for broke. They swung at me, and while ducking that, I brought my baton up between their legs. I couldn't have hit very hard—see how much force you can put behind an upswing in those circumstances—but it definitely worked. Chrl flailed backward. Unfortunately, as they did, they backed into Rob, and they both went over.

I made a judgment error then. I wasn't sure whether to see to Rob, who had Chrl on top of him, or Don, who was having some trouble getting back upright again, and either choice would have been wrong anyway. I went over to Don, because I was worried Mratl would try to gore him while he was still down—and Mratl took that moment to break for the door. I was surprised they could *see* the door. I wasn't anywhere near; they made it out. Rob had rolled Chrl off him and was now in a position of advantage, Don was recovering, and I cursed and rushed out into the corridor. Mratl was gone. They must have run like hell.

"Damn," I said, coming back in. "Is Chrl under control?"

Rob nodded. "I think we want to use a whole lot of these ties though."

"You do that," I said. I didn't have to look through the other rooms too long to find the large case containing a lot of little bottles with pink liquid in them—clear bottles, not ReCharge bottles. I grabbed a couple. "Are we ready to walk them?" I asked, coming back out. "Watch for ambushes. I have no idea where Mratl is. If we have another fight, look out for Mratl's knife, and go for the eyes, across the shoulders, or in Chrl's case, the sprocket. They're too mean for clean fighting."

§

We got Chrl into Custody without incident, although I looked around nervously a lot, especially since Chrl was so placid on the way that I assumed they were expecting a rescue. Once we got Chrl in, I calmed down a little. I was pretty confident the walls and door of the custody room could take anything they dished out.

"Rob, take these to Dr. Kohl; don't worry, he's already awake. Tell him to compare them to the other sample I brought him. He'll know what that means. Don, get that skull checked ... no, don't argue. I know you have a hard head, but I saw how long it took you to get back up and a concussion is no joke. Then be ready; I may need you again shortly. We can't sleep until we get Mratl too, or who knows what'll happen."

As they headed to deck four, I sat at the data station, checked the logs to make sure they hadn't snuck back in, then locked Mratl and everyone else out of the Trofri rooms. Not that I expected them to go back there, but I was already over my quota of bad judgments for the cycle.

Now, where would Mratl go? They wouldn't stay in the corridors if they could avoid it. A hardshell with a big knife on its hand running around would inspire comment, even during that period when the place was relatively empty. They wouldn't go to where most of the Clxl lived; they'd freak out even more. Mratl lived in the Trofri rooms, so a personal room somewhere else was out. But a question had occurred to me earlier ... ReCharge was selling through like crazy. No one had run out yet. Mratl had to have a big stock of it somewhere, right?

I started cross-checking door logs on decks eight and nine and found what I wanted. Mratl had entered a storeroom on nine about when we had been tying up Chrl, and unless that room had a secret door, they hadn't come out; the door hadn't opened since then. I locked everyone off that door but me, or tried to. I wasn't sure if I could override Mratl being able to leave, because the door system in cargo is a little hard to figure out, but even if I hadn't it would keep them from getting back in to their supply of poison. I got on the feed. "Rob— how are we doing?"

"Don's okay but they say they want him to sit and be quiet for a while. Dr. Kohl wants to know what you know."

"Meet me there. Just yourself. Let Don sit. Bring that pry rod."

§

"They call it ibiri. It's what causes those plates to build up under their skin. Most of the ones here on the Ring don't believe in taking it. Call it a philosophical dispute. The ones who do take it tend to like to fight, and humans are not their favorite people."

"Apparently not, if they were trying to addict us all to this," Dr. Kohl said.

"Addict? Is it habit-forming, too?"

"Chemically, I don't know yet. I may be analyzing this for cycles. Psychologically, quite possibly; the energy rush and the euphoria would be very strong, as strong as several other drugs I've seen people abuse—and those had many more barriers to acquisition. What led you to make the connection?"

"Partly what you said about alkali metals; if it caused mineral deposits one way in one species ... also, a remark Catalan made about not allowing 'that pink stuff' in her bar. If Catalan had it lying around, it's possible Trixi would have been the person to make the connection. She says it has a distinctive smell."

"Is there a lot more of this stuff lying around?" Rob asked. He'd been listening to the whole thing, but I hadn't realized until then he'd been paying attention. "I mean, could this Myrtle make more trouble with it?"

I hire good help. "That's what we're going to look into right now. Got your pry rod?"

§

"Remember, they're probably still in here," I said to Rob, not whispering. I had thought about trying for stealth and then decided, no, Mratl would just hear the door or our footsteps anyway.

The room on deck nine was piled floor-to-ceiling with rows of identical crates, everywhere except the shorter stacks at the front of the rows closest to the door, where it had been using up stock. The lighting wasn't very good, and the crates blocked a lot of it, making shadows I didn't like. One crate not far from the door was open and half-full. I lifted a bottle of ReCharge out of it to show Rob, put it back down.

"If they're not in here they can't get back in," I said, "but we have to check. Row by row, stay together, be ready—" I did lean in close to him for this part—"and listen for movement elsewhere in the room as we go."

It was nerve-wracking. We hesitated, listening, at every step. We had finished two rows, front to back, around the end, back to front, around the end—and at the point where we were down the third row far enough that we were between the high stacks, I noticed something wrong with the shadows out of the corner of my eye and shouted, "Move!" before all of my brain had even processed it.

I got out of the way; Rob tried. Mratl had been lying atop the high crates, squeezed into a space between them and the ceiling I wouldn't have thought they could fit into. They rolled over and took the dead drop, about three meters, straight down with their blade extended below them. I don't know what they thought would happen to that blade if it met the floor perpendicular like that. But Mratl didn't hit the floor. They landed partially on Rob, who yelped— had he just been speared, or was it the impact?

Mratl hadn't even had the air knocked out of them. They stood up, and as they withdrew the blade, I saw it had gone into Rob's thigh. I couldn't see more of Rob's condition, because Mratl charged me and I had to run.

Mratl was more affected by the drop than I'd thought—slower, maybe even limping a little. I got a good lead, made it all the way around the U-turn into the next row and toward the door end before I realized running in circles wasn't going to help me. I couldn't leave; Mratl would go back and kill Rob. I started climbing the stacks of crates, working my way up from the short stacks, hopefully without giving myself away by sound. I made it a little more than two meters up—well over its height—and then had to stop because Mratl was too close. They had definitely been banged up a bit. Their breathing—the multi-part breathing from the spiracles, several sounds at the same time—was rough, labored. It was also coming from right below me.

"I knew I could wait and you would come," they rasped, in Pergati. I was unsurprised; I had suspected they understood me during the interview. "You are almost a warrior. It is sad that you are soft. The soft will always disappoint."

Their voice didn't move. I wondered if they knew I was above it, and were playing with me.

"I thought Porshi understood, though they were soft. I was a fool. They grew scared. I had to use another, after all the time I had spent teaching Porshi the truth. If I had not made Rit see some of the truth while we traveled, my plans would have been ruined—ruined by a soft one! I have learned. No soft one will stand in the way of my truth again."

I was trying hard to work my baton under the edge of a crate silently. It was no pry rod. If I wasn't careful I would break it.

"You humans are a plague. The galaxy will be better when you are all gone."

I tipped the crate over and it fell onto Mratl's head.

I didn't jump down after it—with my luck I'd have broken a leg. I climbed down the crates as fast as I could. Mratl was trying to get up, and I lashed them across the spiracles with the baton over and over and over until they were lying flat. When they tried to get up I kicked them in the head, but they didn't stop trying to get up and I beat them until they were flat again, and that time they didn't get up because they were out cold and I was standing there wondering why I was having so much trouble breathing.

Rob!—but as I ran over to his row, I saw he was sitting up and had twisted his shirt around his leg to keep pressure on his wound. He was sweating heavily and his color wasn't great, but alive was good enough for me. "Are you sure they're down?" he asked.

"Yes, but I need to get ties on them fast. Are you stable?"

"I'll hold a while. Handle that thing first."

I went for the ties, which I'd dropped nearby when Mratl had attacked. As I was picking them up, we heard a soft, brief, unpleasant noise. Somewhere between a grunt and a cry. I ran to the other row.

Mratl hadn't been fully unconscious, or had recovered *very* fast. They had sat up, taken the sword-glove off their hand, and worked the point of it carefully into the narrow gap between their frontal plates. Then they had pushed it in with both hands, and pulled it upward, groin to neck. Dark things were seeping out.

"I am weak," they whispered. "You should not have heard." Then they closed their eyes.

§

In crime stories, I notice, they seldom talk about the cleanup. They don't talk about what happens afterward. But what happens afterward is the hard part. It's easy while your brain and your heart are running at top speed. Then it's over and you still have a huge mess and what you really want to do is go sleep forever, or until your head stops hurting, whichever comes first.

Rob had to go to medical. On a trolley because I didn't want him to try to move under his own power. The blade had gone into his leg at a bad angle and he'd also fractured a bone, and he would need help walking for a while. The corpse had to come out, also on a trolley, and someone had to get recruited for cleaning up vital fluids various beings, alive and dead, had left on the warehouse floor. The stock of ReCharge had to be destroyed, and merchants needed to be told to destroy any stock of it they had. The Trofri rooms had to be cleaned out. We had to figure out what we were doing with Chrl, and for that matter what was to be done about Rit. We had to explain the situation both to the local Clxl and to the Clxl government, in a way that hopefully did as little permanent damage as possible. I would probably need to write an official report because this would be of concern outside the Ring, and even if I didn't, there were notes I needed to make for my own future use. And I didn't want to do a single damned bit of it.

Two cycles later, I was still putting off the less urgent parts as I walked into Catalan's just before the start of the busy periods. I think I might have planned to fill Trixi in. Or maybe I was just wandering in for no good reason.

Meridian was working reception again. She studied me. "Are you all right?"

I thought about the polite fiction, then decided she was actually asking. I shook my head. "Not really."

"Would you like to go have dinner or something? Catalan owes me a night off. I could get someone else to work the front."

"You know what?" I said. "That'd be nice."

§

"You still use 'day' and 'night'," I said.

"I use 'week' and 'month' too," she said. She took another long sip of her drink. "I don't know how people do without them."

"I have trouble too; I have to keep remembering to correct myself."

"Why correct yourself? If people think it's strange, so what? I'm not from here, nobody is. I'm allowed to stick to my customs a little. It's about the only thing from home I've wanted to keep."

"How long have you been off Earth?"

"I'm not from Earth," she said. "I'm from a place called Eire Nua. Fifteen years, I think? Not all of it here. Would you like to talk about what happened?"

"What do you mean?"

"You don't understand small talk," she said. "I mean, it's sweet that you're trying, but you're not really there. You've been through something that's still taking up most of your head. Want to tell me about it?"

"It might be a little inappropriate for dinner conversation."

"Eh," she said, smiling, "you know what I do for a living; I'm hard to shock."

So, as we worked our way through an excellent dinner I barely tasted, I told her.

She had declined dessert and accepted a cup of coffee and had sampled it for temperature before she said, "It's a really strange plan, though, wasn't it? Only the heavy users were affected; it could have taken ages—even with no treatment!—to even get all the humans on this Ring, and that's such a tiny number ..."

"I think this was a testbed. I think Mratl wasn't absolutely sure that ibiri would do what it did to people. If the plan had succeeded well here, they would have moved to, I don't know, some more efficient way of getting it into us. Why this Ring? Maybe because of the Clxl here that they needed as a cover. Maybe we just got lucky."

"Just our luck," she said. She sipped her coffee. "Why the suicide?"

"So we wouldn't be able to answer these kinds of questions, I think. They didn't want to be interrogated or judged. Chrl might know, but they've told us nothing and I don't think they ever will. Actually—"

She waited patiently, watching me.

"—I killed Mratl. Or as good as. Because I had beaten them—a lone human, a soft thing—and that was unbearable. If I could beat them, other humans like me could, and they didn't want to live to contemplate that."

"It's a good thing they didn't realize there weren't many other humans like you," she said.

I deliberately focused on my coffee cup.

"Would you like me to come back to your rooms with you?" she asked, after a moment.

I nodded. "I think I would."

THE CASE of the BRIAR PATCH

Early one cycle, I was looking at some files and I saw my arrival date, and I did some subtraction and saw I had been on the Ring just over eighty-eight cycles, and just for the fun of it I did some more math and found that was exactly, or nearly exactly, one hundred Earth days.

This called for an anniversary celebration. So I finally dealt with Alsop's clothes.

I hadn't been letting them sit around due to sentiment, nor exhaustion, nor laziness. It's a little more embarrassing than that. In the Vault, clothes were not an issue. My physical body didn't need them and my virtual body could have whatever clothes I wanted. During the job I briefly held between the Vault and the Ring, I wore a uniform when I was on duty, and didn't really go anywhere or see anybody when I was off-duty. Long story short, I'd come to the Ring with only about eight cycles' worth of clothing—and some of that I'd bought especially for the trip.

Many of Alsop's clothes suited me. A lot of them fit me. He'd had shorter legs and no hips, so his pants were out, but most of his shirts were just fine if they were short-sleeved. But I worried that if I wore any of it outside my rooms, someone would say, "Hey, wasn't that shirt Alsop's?" and people probably thought I was strange enough already.

(It's not like Alsop had any use for them now! But humans are odd about the dead.)

Even if I decided not to wear any of them, throwing out clothes on the Ring wasn't something people did unless they were absolutely rags, and maybe even then you reused the rags for something. It's not that people on the Ring were all that frugal, or anti-waste—though the latter was encouraged—it's that new goods cost so damned much to be shipped in. On the Ring there was absolutely no stigma in having second-hand furniture and so forth. Everybody was always using everybody else's cast-offs.

So my plan was to go to the used-goods shops and sell them Alsop's clothes. Then, later, if I happened to buy some of it back again, I could say to that hypothetical critic, "Oh, this? I have no idea who it belonged to."

I can be a little neurotic.

Douglas Todd

§

I acquired two unexpected things on my expedition to Secondhand Row.

On my way around deck five, I got caught in a place you want to try never to be: between two angry fumwah. I didn't intend to; it was purely poor timing.

Cleit, like Clxl, come in two kinds. Unlike Clxl, they are two very different species who happened to originate on the same world: ahpesh and fumwah. Ahpesh we didn't see much of, except when bringing a fumwah back to confine it to its ship, which happened depressingly often. I'll describe ahpesh later.

Cleit never stayed on the Ring for any length of time; they were always visitors. But they visited a lot—spacefaring labor-for-hire passing through—and fumwah were not allowed to drink while aboard ship. So when they were on the Ring, they drank a lot. Their other favorite hobbies were fighting and breaking things. We'd have banned them long ago if they weren't such steady business.

Fumwah look like warthogs but are uglier, not especially tall but weigh a lot and are very strong, have thick skin, thicker skulls, and have tiny sharp little tusks at the corners of their mouths which can easily cut you open in a close-up fight. Fortunately, when they're in bar fights they're usually not out for blood. But they're none too smart, and they get carried away easily. And you can't even kick them in the sprocket. I'd tried and it didn't seem to have any effect.

We tell the bar owners not to serve them if they're drunk, but even the ones who were conscientious wouldn't refuse to serve an angry fumwah who was about to smash through their bar. The ahpesh were also supposed to help out— when you could find one. By the time you got back to the Cleit ship and called an ahpesh out to intervene, an angry drunk fumwah or two could destroy a whole business.

In this case, a fumwah charged another one—they like to lead with their heads— and I had walked into their path. They couldn't stop in time even if they'd wanted to, and I'd been taken by surprise so my response wasn't optimal. Instead of moving aside, I crouched ... and they tripped over me, went flying, crashed into the other one, then landed on their head. Which was a shame, because that meant they'd get right back up.

With fumwah logic, *both* of them seemed to blame me for having spoiled the fun, and now #2 charged me. I'd gotten pretty good at matador after many fumwah fights, and I managed to pull aside at the last minute so they went straight into a wall. Our walls are built tougher than fumwah. But that would only keep them busy a moment, and #1 had gotten up and looked to be starting another charge.

As I was getting ready to try for the veronica a second time, and not liking my odds, a black ball came flying through the air—seriously, that's what it looked like. It hit the standing fumwah squarely in the middle and knocked them flat on their back. The black ball unfolded; it was a Pergat. Glossy black, no highlights in their fur, bright excited eyes. They leaped onto the fumwah by me that was still trying to recover, and grabbed the neck in a peculiar way for a few seconds. The fumwah stopped trying to move and collapsed back onto the ground. Out cold.

"Watch it, the other's up," I said. The fumwah charged. I managed the dodge—the bouncy little Pergat of course had no difficulty—and when we got that one down, the Pergat did the same thing they had done to the other, and that was that.

"That's a useful trick," I said. "Now where did you press again?"

"Side of the neck, here, hard. Two or three subs. Works well—if you can get to their neck for two or three subs. Gray-woman you must be. I am Sul. Good fortune!"

"Certainly good fortune for me," I said.

"Is a pleasure. You need more fumwah knocked out, maybe do something else, you let me know." They showed teeth, which is a grin for Pergati too but for them always means "mischief." "Lots of free time."

So that was my first unexpected acquisition. The other was a hat.

I don't know what this hat was doing on the Ring, sitting alone and dusty atop a coat stand in Sal's Rag Trade. No one—except those veiled Tanngrevers—wore headgear on the Ring that I had ever seen except the protective kind. Even on Earth it was nearly impossible to find anyone any more who ever bought or wore a hat like this—an old-school, broad-banded, chocolate-brown felt fedora, just battered enough to show that someone had actually worn it and loved it.

I would have traded Sal everything I'd brought for that hat, but I didn't tell her that. After I'd finished selling Alsop's things, and had picked out a small stack of items I thought I could wear, I added, as if an afterthought, "How much for that old hat?"

I dashed back to my rooms with it like I'd found lost treasure, which was doubly ridiculous since it was unlikely I'd ever wear it anywhere. I dusted it off, and put it in a place in the main room where I could see it whenever I cared to look at it.

It's difficult to explain.

§

Peak bar periods later that cycle were busy, as they always are when Cleit are in. Fumwah didn't go to the sex houses, they didn't gamble, they didn't shop, they didn't seem to be interested in other entertainments like A/V booths; they liked to drink, and they liked to fight, and that was it.

At about thirty or thirty-one, I was overdue for sleep, exhausted, and my patience was running out, so you can imagine how thrilled I was when Rob got on the feed and said he had a dead fumwah.

It was in one of the infamous back rooms of Corphon's bar. Corphon was the kind of proprietor who didn't even try to follow the rules about not serving drunks, and fumwah liked his place because of its atmosphere. They especially liked his back rooms, where—for the right price—they could set up a pit fight or pretty much whatever else they wanted to do, and no one would catch on unless it went very badly.

This wasn't a pit fight gone badly, though. As I said, fumwah don't use their tusks if they're fighting for entertainment, and they never use weapons even if they're fighting for blood. This one had been slashed on the neck—a cut three centimeters long straight up that crucial, semi-exposed artery in the neck Sul had shown me. If pressing on that for a few seconds could knock out a fumwah, I figured this one had passed out before they had bled out. There were no other obvious marks or wounds.

"Rob, get Don here."

"He's already here. I hailed him. He's out front making sure nobody leaves."

"I'm raising your pay. Go help him. Keep an eye on the back door, too."

If it had been human customers, I'd have had one of them watch the doors and the other haul out the body while I interviewed people. But not with fumwah, and I couldn't wait long to do the interviews or the fumwah would get antsy and then we'd have real problems. I didn't want to summon Dr. Kohl unless it was something extraordinary. The body was just going to have to stay there a while. It wasn't going to get any deader.

I examined the mess with my flashlight; the room had a dark floor and was inadequately lit. There was a strange wide blood smear leading out of the room, like someone had dragged something out. Had there been another body? If there were two kills, why leave only one behind?

The back hall was clearer than I'd hoped. The room with the body was the last on the left before the back door; the smear continued out the back door without too many people having the chance to step in it and track it around. They wouldn't have noticed if they had. The hall was just as badly lit as the private room. The back door opened to a corridor that ran behind Corphon's and three other businesses. I headed "outside" and realized I was having increasing difficulty following the blood. The swath was growing fainter the further away I got from Corphon's. By the end of the corridor, where it turned and reconnected via a narrow alley to the concourse, there was nothing.

As I turned back to Corphon's, my light caught something that gleamed. The bars used this back-alley hall to pile up crates of empty bottles and other things which didn't go into the waste chutes. A crate had not quite been pushed to the wall, and the gleam was on the ground behind it. I reached in for whatever it was—and got sticky on my fingers. Blood! Not mine—I checked my fingers, I wasn't cut, and the color of the blood looked a little wrong anyway. Carefully, I reached in and pulled out a fat-bladed gold knife, or dagger, with an elaborate hilt, colored stones. It was fairly dull and probably meant to be ornamental, but was sharp enough that you could poke in and rip open an artery with it.

As I went back into the bar, Corphon was waiting for me by the room with the corpse. I didn't let him start. "Not a word. The body is staying there until I choose to move it and your doors are shut until I'm done, and if I hear anything from you about it, I'm closing you for twenty cycles. Find me a clean cloth. I want to wrap this in something." He snapped his gaping mouth shut and waddled off hurriedly.

Interviewing a fumwah is painful. Their own language is unintelligible to everyone else and would give you a sore throat if you tried it. They do speak Bak'ti, but Bak'ti isn't suitable for complex questions. I persevered, but I'm going to spare you the transcript. I talked to twenty fumwah and almost none of what I got is worth telling. Some of them knew the corpse—whose identification tags said Lu Cush—but none of them knew when Lu Cush had gone into the back room or why, or could remember when they'd last seen them alive. I got only one useful piece of information: one fumwah said they had seen an ahpesh leave earlier by the back door.

Ahpesh are snake from the waist down. Well, actually they're all snake, but I mean they have arms and a reasonably humanoid head and torso. No hair, scale colors vary widely, eyes anywhere from green to yellow with vertical pupils. I've never wanted to study them any more closely than that. Below the waist is what would probably be over four meters of tapering tail if they lay down on the floor and stretched it out straight, but since they hold the first meter of it upright, putting their heads at about average human height, and the rest of it tends to be in any configuration but straight, it's hard to tell. Their tails are muscular and very flexible—I don't know how they do it, what they use instead of a spinal cord, but I've seen them wrap the ends of their tails around objects and lift those objects into the air, or drag them away.

They move by undulating over the ground ... and if an ahpesh had gotten their tail in the mess and then left the room, the broad streak of bloodstain was exactly what they would leave behind. By the end of that back corridor the blood would have been all wiped off or dried on or both.

I ended up taking the body to Dr. Kohl's myself; I let Rob and Don go home after they'd fetched a trolley. Then I went for some sleep. There was no hurry; the Cleit ship wasn't slated to leave for another three cycles.

§

I'd never been aboard a Cleit ship before, and the ahpesh made it pretty clear that, in their opinion, once was too many. When I finally convinced them they had better let me aboard, and got an audience with the captain, the first thing they said was "Please explain why this intrusion is necessary?"

"A fumwah, Lu Cush, was killed a few periods ago. Evidence suggests that an ahpesh killed it."

I shouldn't have expected any sort of facial reaction. "Ridiculous," they said in their sibilant, over-enunciated Pergati. "Why are you attempting to start hostility? What do you seek to gain?"

"Interesting that you jump straight to that idea," I said. "Tell me why you instantly think an ahpesh couldn't have done it."

"You fail to understand," they said. "If an ahpesh had killed fumwah, they would have done here, on our ship, where it would be not your concern."

Charming. "Ahpesh seem fond of ornamentation," I said. "Those armbands you're wearing, for example. Every time I've seen an ahpesh it's been wearing two or three pieces of body jewelry. Now take this—" I unwrapped the dagger. "It's not much good as a dagger, I think, but it would make a fine display sidearm, just something for looks. Has anyone in your crew misplaced one of these?"

The captain exhaled sharply. You could call it a hiss. "That is mine," they said. "How did you get it?" They got up—ahpesh don't sit on chairs, but they do have a resting posture where they sit propped on their own tails—and went to a cabinet at the back of the room to check. "Who took it from here? Who gave it to you? This is outrageous!"

"Anyone else on the ship have one like this?" Rigid silence. "Captain, I don't actually suspect you right now, but if you don't cooperate, I'm going to start. Does anyone else on the ship have a dagger like this?"

"No," they said. "It is a symbol of rank."

"When did you last see it—in that cabinet, or anywhere?"

"Many cycles ago. I wear it only seldom."

"And the cabinet doesn't appear to be kept locked—yes?—so anyone could have taken it any time."

"No—" they began and stopped.

"Go on," I said.

"Not anyone. Only ahpesh are allowed here. Fumwah would be prevented." They knew they had lost ground, so they returned to outrage. "I will have my dagger now."

"No. It's evidence. It was found at the scene of the crime with blood on it the same type as the victim's. And the wound matches."

"I tell you it is unthinkable! It is not the way an ahpesh would do it!"

"Let me make sure," I said, trying to keep my voice level, "let me make absolutely sure I understand your position clearly. You don't deny one of your crew could have killed a fumwah, and you don't sound very concerned whether they did. You merely say that if they had done, they wouldn't have done it in a public place on the Ring, leaving evidence behind. Is that right?"

"Yes," they said.

"I will want to speak to many members of your crew."

"Why? They won't tell you anything." They shook their head. "I understand you now, I see what you are. You assume things. But you have seen fumwah when off-ship. You know how they behave. Sometimes they behave so badly they must die for it. Sometimes they die because they do stupid things. They die many ways. You talk of concern. There are only six hands of ahpesh on this ship." They meant thirty. "Fumwah ten times that. We can barely keep them from destroying the ship. If we let them, the idiots would kill us all and be left adrift to die." The captain unholstered and showed me a gun of some kind that was clearly *not* ornamental. "We walk in caution at all times. It exhausts us. How much concern do you think we have available?"

We both didn't do anything but glare at one another for a bit. They had said their big speech, and I was trying to get back to level again.

"Look," I said, "Assume for a moment that I think you have a point. Just for argument. But even so, a fumwah was killed on property where I'm responsible for keeping everyone feeling safe. A murder, especially an unsolved one, doesn't keep anyone feeling safe. The people who live on the Ring and visit it don't care whether the victim was a fumwah; they just know that someone was apparently out having a good time and got killed. I can't say 'I won't bother to investigate this, they were just a fumwah' even if I wanted to. I wouldn't be doing my job."

They made a noise I might record as "feh" or "pft." "You think fumwah are an annoyance. Your Ring tolerates them only to sell them alcohol. Then you send them back to us, as if what you have allowed them to do is our fault."

I wasn't going to admit I agreed with them there. "So fumwah shouldn't be allowed to have any fun?"

"You say that when you, more than anyone, see what happens when they are?"

I moved to leave. "I'm tired of philosophy chat," I said. "This murder is going to be investigated. And since it's either an ahpesh that did it or someone trying very hard to make it look like one, some of that investigation is going to happen on this ship. If you don't think your crew will talk to me, fine—*you* talk to them. But there will be some answers from somebody."

"I have no reason to cooperate with this," they said.

"You'd like your ship to be able to leave at its scheduled time, wouldn't you?"

They made the "pft" sound again. "We are returning to our home world, after many cycles of work. This crew has no new business waiting. All you do is allow the fumwah you have so much concern for more time to squander their saved wages in your bars."

"Since you feel that way," I said pleasantly, "you're blocked. Congratulations. Your ship will be released when I have a murderer. Your dagger too. I suggest you start with motive. Someone killed Lu Cush for a reason. Who would have a reason? Ponder it."

§

I don't like blocking ships. It makes Dispatch crazy. I don't pretend to understand the math, but I know that if a ship doesn't make its window of opportunity it might not make it again for many cycles, and we wouldn't be able to let it stay docked—we don't have enough slots—so it would have to hang around near us waiting for its next opportunity. Or try to reach someplace the long way. But the long way is *long*.

It would be better for all concerned if I could solve it before the ship was scheduled to leave anyway—in something less than two cycles—but I didn't have any decent place to start. I would do well to follow my own advice and look for a motive. But motive was exactly the problem. Putting aside my anger at the way ahpesh treated them, who had any reason to kill a fumwah?

Leaving out ahpesh for the moment ... fumwah didn't kill each other except by accident, and that one had been no accident. Their drinking and brawling was fierce, but at heart, and when sober, they all treated each other like buddies. More than once I'd seen two of them spend ten subs tossing each other to hell and gone, and then get up and go off together to have a friendly drink.

I couldn't think of a reason a Ring resident, permanent or otherwise, would want to kill one even if a fumwah had trashed their business; they'd just make them pay for the damage. The general sentiment was that you couldn't really be too angry at a fumwah; it would be like staying angry at a dog. Maybe if one of them had killed a permanent—but that had never happened. That I knew of.

I went back to my room to check Alsop's files.

Alsop on Cleit wasn't very useful. His notes were good, but I'd seen enough Cleit that they didn't tell me much I didn't already know. I did learn that Cleit wandered the galaxy as labor-for-hire because it was basically all they had to offer, and also their home world, which had been devastated by a series of brutal wars, didn't sound like a great place to be. I also learned that kicking them in the sprocket didn't work (assuming you were kicking a sprocket—Alsop said he couldn't tell them apart either) because the fumwah who travelled as labor were required to be reversibly chemically neutered, and a side-effect was numbing of the genitals. (I wondered how Alsop had managed to get *that* information.) The tight leash of the ahpesh looked tighter and tighter.

As I moved back to the file lists, mulling that, I noticed a subject area: COR. I'd spent some time in the C's, what with Cleit and Clxl, but I hadn't noticed that before. I wondered if he'd misspelled CORE. I certainly didn't know of any species called Cor.

I opened the subject, and was prompted for a password. I'd never been given any kind of password.

The system didn't have individual protections on files that I knew of; your personal level of access controlled what you could and couldn't see. I wasn't sure how Alsop had pulled this trick, but he'd had something he didn't want anyone else to see. I tried two or three guesses, not expecting any of them to work because they were all things he was far too smart for. Then I filed it in my head on my growing list of Unsolved Mysteries.

§

I was having lunch, that same cycle, when the boss hailed me on the feed. "We have an unscheduled sub-eight contacting us for permission to dock. Cleit. It was vague, but seems to be investigating a crime."

"Must be quite a crime."

"Meet it at arrival. If it isn't prepared to be more specific about why it's here, I don't intend to let it stay."

Seemed the boss didn't like investigators on the Ring unless they were me. I gulped the rest of my lunch and got moving.

A few things were implied in those three sentences. Ship hulls have standard length limits. They're named for how many can physically dock at the Ring at the same time. Fours must be "no longer than the tangent segment length of eighty-eight degrees of arc." I don't care to look up the exact number of meters. We can handle four fours at once—remember ships dock in the same plane as the Ring, crossways is impossible to do—or eight eights. Every so often we'd see a ship bigger than a four; I'm not sure one has ever physically docked. (Ships that big have their own shuttles anyway. The last one I remember was a military fleet carrier.) The thing is, ships smaller than an eight are impractical for cargo. The cost of running the ship wouldn't be offset by the tiny amount you could fit in it. A sub-eight tends to have either Very Important News or Very Important People—or at least very rich people; we did get private vessels once in a while. Also, an unscheduled ship was coming from a nearby system, the hard way. If it had come through the Ring it wouldn't be unscheduled. Whatever it was, it was not going to be something ordinary.

This sub-eight was quite tiny. I could tell because the airlock area was directly adjacent to the bridge. The three crew I saw might have been the only crew. All three were ahpesh. When I explained my identity, I was told that Inspector Kalmas was not aboard ship at present and they knew nothing about their task here.

"Weren't you instructed that the inspector was not to be permitted to leave the ship until we spoke?" They exchanged looks. It's funny how well that particular look translates among disparate species.

"The inspector didn't take the message well and headed off anyway, eh? Don't worry, I won't hold a grudge—if you can tell me where they went." No, the inspector hadn't told them where they were going. "Were they investigating Cleit?" Yes, they were sure about that.

"If they come back before I do, tell them to contact me immediately. This is urgent. You are blocked from departure until I speak with them."

The inspector would be going to the Cleit work ship. There weren't any other Cleit on the Ring. They would want to speak to the ahpesh from that ship, and none of them had left it. I got there and this time, they either remembered I was someone to let in, or they were too frazzled to cause trouble. Certainly when I got in it seemed like someone had set off a commotion. All the ahpesh were very agitated. I couldn't get clear answers from any of them until the captain saw me.

"You!" they said. "Did you send this to us? No, you could not have. I don't have time to talk about your fumwah now. Go away."

"What's got everybody in a panic?"

"Why do you—never mind, I'll tell you, if you go. An inspector is on our ship. They want to speak to everyone in my crew. Do you understand, an inspector? They can ask anything they want, do anything they like. On our ship!"

"Hide all the dirty towels, eh? Interesting they come in and you hop, I come in with equal authority and you freeze me out. Oh, no, don't bother explaining, I know why. I need to talk to this inspector."

"No! You cannot! You will just make them angry—"

"Actually, captain, they have made *me* angry. They disobeyed our instructions. I came to tell them how displeased we are." I figured the captain would enjoy seeing that.

The captain grabbed another ahpesh as they passed. "Herash! Where is the inspector now?"

"They are with Sovesh," that one replied.

Another slithered around a corner. "Who is with me?"

"Sovesh! Where is the inspector?"

"You asked me to take them to a room where they could speak with people privately. I have done."

"Take me to them," I told Sovesh. They looked at the captain for approval, then led me down a hall to a door not far from the ship's bridge. The captain came along.

I opened the door. "Well, that's not going to be helpful," I said.

Inspector Kalmas was dead. They were wearing a neck chain, fine links of some sort of reddish metal, and had been strangled with it. The chain had cut deeply enough into their neck to remain in place, tightly in front, slack in the back where someone had been pulling on it. In a few places I could see blood under it where the skin had broken. It had taken a strong necklace and a determined attacker. The captain looked like they were about to have a heart attack; they were making sibilants which probably weren't words even in ahpesh-speak. I turned to Sovesh.

"I didn't do it!" Sovesh said. "The inspector was alive when I left!"

"You got them settled in, and then where did you go?"

"You saw—I was just returning from that."

"We didn't walk down this hall for more than a sub. Are you saying that you left here, came directly back to where we were, and yet someone managed to enter the room and strangle a struggling ahpesh with their own jewelry and get out before we came back, all in that time?"

"I did not come directly."

"Aha. Where did you go?"

Sovesh pointed to one of the doors we had passed along the way. "I stopped at that door to speak to Daeres within. Two, maybe three subs."

"Did you actually go into the room where Daeres was?"

"No, only the doorway."

"Who walked past you in the hall while you were in the doorway?"

"No one. But if someone had come from the bridge ..."

"Thank you, yes, I got that on my own."

The captain may or may not have heard any of that. They was leaning on a wall and still muttering hissing sounds. I think they were seeing visions of career flameout. I eventually got their attention. "This is horrible, horrible," they said.

"I'd like to talk to you in here," I said.

"In there? With—"

"They're dead. They won't bite you. Sovesh, wait outside the door. If you step away, for so much as a second, you'll be very sorry later. Let no one in. If someone passes by and asks, you know nothing."

The door closed. The captain was trying to be as far from the body as possible in the little room.

"Still think an ahpesh couldn't have murdered Lu Cush?"

"That has no relation to this! The inspector could not have known about that!"

"I agree, they were after something else. But they were undeniably killed by an ahpesh. No fumwah can get into this area, as you yourself said. I'm the only other species on this ship and I didn't do it. I'm just saying, you have at least one ahpesh on this ship who is capable of murder. If you're right about these being unrelated deaths, you have at least two."

"You must solve this! If I return home and there are no answers—"

"Right. Now that an ahpesh is dead it's important suddenly."

"This is not just any ahpesh!" I decided I shouldn't twist the knife anymore; the captain really did look about to keel over.

"What was the inspector here for? Did they give you any idea?"

"No," the captain said. "They came, took charge, and asked for a place to work."

"All right. Listen. You're the only ahpesh on this ship I'm sure of. The main suspect is Sovesh; I'm not sure they're telling me the truth. Did you hear any of our conversation? If Sovesh is lying about stopping to talk, they're the only one who had enough time to do it. Even if they're telling the truth it was barely long enough. We have little time before the murderer gets any other bright ideas, and I might not be able to scare or coerce your crew into talking to me. You can. If you want me to solve this and save your tail, you'll have to help."

There was utterly no defiance left in the captain. "What must I do?"

"First, I want you to tell your door patrol not to let any ahpesh off this ship. On your way to that, I want you to send Daeres in to me without letting them talk to

Sovesh. In fact, it would be good if we kept Sovesh from talking to anybody." I opened the door. I was relieved to find Sovesh still there. "Sovesh. The captain is going to be leading people in and out of this room. We need you to guard the door and keep the hall clear. Tell no one anything. Captain, can you keep everyone at their posts or whatever unless you fetch them yourself?"

The captain had only one remark. "You are going to talk in here while—?" They pointed to the corpse.

"Sure, why not?" I said. "It'll make an impression. There's nothing like a dead body to make everyone realize we're serious."

§

Actually, I'd been thinking leaving the body in the interview room was a cruel thing to do. But by the time I staggered out of the ship I'd lost any remorse. There was not a single chair anywhere in the ahpesh portions of the ship, I was told the fumwah furnishings were all permanently mounted in place, and I couldn't sit on my tail like ahpesh could. Six periods is a long time to do anything without sitting down.

The first thing I'd done was talk briefly to Daeres. Of course it meant nothing if Sovesh had managed to reach Daeres long enough to get them to agree on a story, but they said that Sovesh had indeed stopped to talk. They weren't sure how long. I wasn't buying Sovesh's estimate.

Then I'd had the captain keep everything together for a few minutes while I ran to the sub-eight. It wasn't just to break the bad news to that crew. "I need to see the inspector's data."

They didn't think there was any. We went to the inspector's cabin. No data pad, no papers, nothing but personal effects. There was no data station in the room and they hadn't seen the inspector use one aboard ship. I made them check anyway, and could find no files the inspector might have put there. I couldn't make myself believe that the inspector had been on a case with no notes or information of any kind. I also didn't think this crew was lying to me. "Did the inspector have anything with them when they left the ship?" They said maybe. It came out that the inspector had been a very prickly, high-and-mighty type, and the crew had taken to minding their own business and leaving the inspector alone whenever possible, to avoid confrontation.

The body had one of the sort of purse/packs ahpesh use, but there hadn't been a data pad in it or anything else useful. Nor in the room. "Captain," I asked when I got back to the work ship, "I need some ahpesh you can trust reasonably well. Some who weren't anywhere near this area during the death and can prove it. We need to search the ship—your crew, the fumwah, your supplies, your trash, all of it." I explained the situation and they went to go scare up a search party. Since I could barely tell one ahpesh from another, I waited for the captain to get back from that, already wishing by then I had something to sit on.

If any of the ahpesh we interviewed over the next several periods were shocked or thrown off balance by being interviewed in a room next to a corpse of their own species, they hid it well. I got nothing, except tired legs from standing up so long. Any number of ahpesh had opportunity; none of them would admit to the slightest glimmer of a motive for either killing. I did end up convinced that, no matter how little they thought of fumwah, ahpesh wouldn't just randomly kill one, especially since the fumwah were the ones who earned the money that kept them all running. The idea that an ahpesh would kill an inspector—apparently inspectors were feared and hated by all—was even wilder.

We had talked for a long time to every ahpesh who might possibly be relevant, I was on the verge of giving up for the cycle, and the captain was on the verge of despair, when one of the search party brought us a data pad with a badly cracked surface that they had found in the waste hold.

"Someone tried to smash this," I said. "Those cracks were made with an object. See where it struck?"

"We might get something," the captain said, slightly reenergized. "Come."

They led me to the data station in their quarters and I watched—I couldn't read any of the displays, of course—while they tried to access files from the data pad.

"Most of this has bad damage," they said after looking at several things. "Perhaps an expert—we have none such on ship ... Na Shae?"

"Who is Na Shae?"

"That is my question. The name seems to be in these notes many times. I can't read enough of anything to find out why, but there is even a file with that name."

"Sounds like a fumwah name."

"Indeed yes, which is why I wonder at it. Was the inspector looking for a fumwah?"

"Do you have a Na Shae on board?"

They switched to examining a different file, not from the data pad. Fumwah roster. "No. Are you now going to want to ask everyone about this Na Shae?"

I smiled. "I'm tired too. Let's ask them all at once."

We assembled the ahpesh in the crew mess and asked them if they had seen, or heard, of a fumwah named Na Shae. Nobody. I was unsurprised.

"Captain, I'm going to want to hold onto that data pad for a while. Also, I'll be back in a sub with a trolley, but I'll need some help getting the body to the airlock."

When I got off-ship—possibly inspired by air that didn't smell like ahpesh—a thought came to me. Someone had killed the inspector in an awful hurry. They'd gotten lucky when they did (assuming it wasn't Sovesh); that was a busy hall. It would have made much more sense to wait, maybe until they were being interviewed by the inspector. They could just step out of the room and say later "they were alive when I left" and no one would have fetched the next person and it could have gone undetected for a long while. Why had it been so urgent? To prevent the inspector from revealing what they were doing there. A name had been dropped now, but a name wasn't dangerous enough in itself. To keep breaking that chain, who would the killer want next? I looked down at the broken data pad under my arm. Probably me. But there were others at risk.

I went to the sub-eight—good thing it wasn't docked far away—and warned them not to let anybody in. The killer didn't know they didn't know anything. Then I had another thought and got on the feed to Sul, hoping their offer had been sincere.

Back at the ship, trolley waiting outside, the captain surprised me by offering to help move the body. I guess all the time in a room with me had improved its tolerance. That tolerance got sorely tested (mine as well); the corpse's tail, long and limp and trying to flop everywhere except where you needed it to go, would have taken four or five people to lift and carry. We eventually had to drag it to the lock by the armpits, and of course we had to hook it to a cargo hoist to get it up the airway. If I'd been an ahpesh, I'd have found it offensive too.

"Captain," I said as we recovered, "be careful." I explained my worries. They agreed with me, said they would watch their back, and returned to their ship.

I looked around the dim angles of the dock area. "Sul, are you lurking?"

Invoked, Sul appeared, not far away. "Gray-woman has a good eye."

"I had no idea where you were," I said, "just that you were there. Actually that tells me my idea was right. Sul, would you be able to stay on duty for, I don't know, eight or nine periods? If it's going to be longer than that I'll get someone else to relieve you. I'll pay well for your pain."

"No trouble. Am I to watch this lock?"

"More than that. I have an idea an ahpesh may come out this lock. I'm no good at following without being seen, and Rob and Don are worse. I think you are probably better at it."

They grinned and nodded. "Might not be any fun," I said. "You might sit here all night for nothing. But if an ahpesh does come out—I don't care about fumwah—follow them to see what they do. If they do anything interesting, get on the feed and let me know."

In addition to getting the inspector into cold storage—Dr. Kohl and I had to sort of fold the body up to fit it in a drawer—and returning the trolley, I made two other stops before going home. One was for dinner, which I needed urgently. The other was the arms locker.

The arms locker is a door down from Custody. I don't like using weapons except my baton, so I tended only to open it when placing a confiscated weapon into it, and I seldom needed to confiscate a weapon. Most people knew better, even visitors, so weapons tended to be improvised if they were used at all—things like broken bottles, which I didn't keep, I just trashed. Every so often someone had a real weapon, and if they promised to behave, I'd have it sent to their ship (it was always visitors) so they could have it back after they left. The confiscated ones came from the people who'd pissed me off too much for me to do that.

Even I wasn't going to break the rule about breachables, but I found a neural gun that I was pretty sure would work on anything that had a nervous system. Nonlethal, just caused a whole lot of hurt. It didn't have much charge left, and I didn't have equipment to recharge it, but I wouldn't need to use it more than once. Ideally I wouldn't need to use it at all.

§

I'd been sitting in my room for about a period, theoretically reading but really falling half-asleep in a chair, when my door buzzed and startled me fully awake. To give you an idea where my brain was, my first thought was, "It's killed Sul." Because Sul hadn't warned me something was coming, see.

I got the gun ready and stepped back from the door as it opened in case something tried to rush me ... and it was Meridian. I exhaled.

"Expecting someone else?" she asked, looking at the gun.

I put it on the table and gestured her in. "Sorry."

Since the end of the Clxl business, Meridian had taken to coming over every few cycles. I wasn't sure what to make of it. She didn't warn me, she always just turned up at the door, and we'd go to bed almost immediately after she got here. We didn't talk, not really, just a few lines of casual conversation that meant nothing, and then straight to the sex. Then, in the early periods of the next cycle, she'd leave. It wasn't cold—I didn't get a sense of, "OK, all done here, gotta dash"—but, for example, we didn't ever go eat breakfast together or anything like that. I knew she didn't keep visiting because I was fabulous in bed—for one thing, sex had never been a big motivator for me and I'd never gotten very good at it, and also, the woman was a professional. On the other hand, if she was interested in my companionship, my sparkling personality, then why didn't we talk, or do something besides sex?

I wasn't going to turn her away, obviously, but I couldn't figure out exactly what was going on.

This time she didn't try to lead me to the bed. I think the gun had shaken her. She sat down in a chair and didn't give me the lazy I-know-something-you-don't smile that I'd come to realize was just the way she smiled, like she always had an interesting secret. Instead she looked at me, searching me. I thought she was preparing to have a Serious Discussion—part of me might have welcomed it— then she appeared to change her mind and instead cast her eyes around the room, aimless and neutral.

"Hey!" she said. "I like the hat."

"Oh—" I said, embarrassed. "I got that when I was out looking for some clothes the other cycle." Last cycle, in fact. It felt like much longer. She stood and went over to get it, then came back and put it on my head. I took it off.

"I want to see how it looks on you!"

"It's—I'm sure it looks ridiculous."

"Come on, let me see." She put it back on. "Oh, I like it." She adjusted it so it tilted a little to one side. I felt my face get warm. I tore it off and flung it across the room. It landed on the table.

"Damn, I'm sorry," she said, annoyed. "I guess I thought if someone buys a hat, they plan to wear it."

"I didn't buy it to wear. I mean, I did, but not really."

"You did but not really. What does that mean?"

"I bought it because I like it, but I can't actually wear it."

"Why not? If you like it, why not wear it?"

"Because people like that don't exist anymore. Because I don't need more people looking at me and pointing out how bizarre I am."

"Do you actually think people do that?" she said. "I haven't heard anyone do that. Catalan respected you immediately, and that's unusual."

"Oh, I'm respected. People think I know what I'm doing. But that's not what I'm talking about—"

"No, you're talking about some idea of fitting in with some kind of standard that you've got inside your head. You know what? Nobody else really cares. I think you should work in a sex house for a while, then you'd know for a fact that nobody gives a damn except if it affects whether they get off. Why don't you believe that? Why can't you just go ahead and be what you like to be?"

I didn't shut her down. I don't know why I didn't; she wasn't entitled to say things like that to me, not then. I can think of a few reasons why I didn't, in hindsight, but you work those out on your own. I do know that I was surprised to hear myself giving her the straight answer.

"Because nobody wants the thing I want to be," I said. "I mean, I appreciate that you come to see me anyway, but—"

"Stop." Her voice was icy. "You think this is *charity?* You think I come see you because I feel *sorry* for you?"

Damage already done. What the hell. "I'm happy for it, but ... I honestly have no idea why you keep coming to see me."

She stared at me. Then she left.

§

My feed chirped at thirty-three. I'd like to be able to say it woke me up, but I was lying in bed staring at the ceiling. It was Sul.

"Gray-woman, you guessed right. Ahpesh came out."

"Can you tell where they're going yet?"

"No, but is at two:fifteen now so—"

"Yeah, heading for me. Thanks for the warning. Would you mind staying nearby until I let you know?"

The buzz at my door was not long after that. Ahpesh can move pretty fast, for things with no legs. I got the gun ready and opened it. As I say, I have trouble telling ahpesh apart—but I'd seen a lot of that particular one.

"You're supposed to be confined to your ship, you know," I said. "What's the story, Sovesh?"

"I wish to put myself in custody for your judgment," they said. "I killed the fumwah Lu Cush."

§

A little less than a period later, I was wondering what I could do to make my eyes stop hurting. Other than go to sleep, which seemed unlikely. I was sitting in Custody. Sovesh was locked in a custody room. Sul was leaning against a wall, looking unreadable. I couldn't tell if they were actually interested or listening out of courtesy.

"The thing is, they either did kill Lu Cush or have information from the killer. They know things they wouldn't know otherwise. But although I'm mostly interested in who killed Lu Cush, it's not that simple any more. The captain doesn't care about Lu Cush, and Sovesh's confession doesn't help us with the inspector's death."

"Sovesh killed both," Sul said.

"I think so too, but do you have anything for that besides your opinion?" They shook their head.

Sovesh's story was that they had killed Lu Cush because Lu Cush had built up some kind of permanent grudge against Sovesh while they were in transit—Sovesh claimed to have no idea what had originally ticked Lu Cush off—and after what Sovesh believed was an attempt on their life just before arrival, Sovesh decided they had to take matters into their own hands. They said they were confessing to this now after it became clear that many of their crewmates were assuming both killers were the same person. Sovesh insisted they had not killed the inspector, had no idea who had, and did not plan to be blamed for it.

Unspoken: They figured they would get lenient treatment for killing a fumwah, but killing an ahpesh—let alone an inspector—was something else entirely.

My instincts told me to believe little or none of it. But it definitely looked like Sovesh killed Lu Cush. They knew about the dagger, which we'd been holding back. I didn't think the captain had let it slip. If Sovesh didn't kill Lu Cush for the reasons they gave, then why?

I sighed. "Go home, Sul. Sleep. There's nothing else you can do for me right now."

"You should sleep too, Gray-woman."

I appreciated the concern. "I hope to try."

I walked back to my rooms slowly. The problem was my brain kept dragging me back to Meridian when I should have been thinking about idiot Cleit. I didn't blame my brain, but it wasn't being helpful.

I had undressed and was back in bed before it hit me: The problem was that I had been spending too much time talking to the wrong people. Suddenly it all opened up. I still didn't have an answer, but my path lay exposed before me. I knew what I needed to do next.

That was enough to let me get a few periods of sleep.

§

"This is a very bad idea," the captain said.

"They won't talk if you're around," I replied.

"At least take this." They handed me their gun, the one they had shown me in my first talk with them.

"I don't want to kill any of them!" I said.

"It doesn't kill. It is a synaptic pistol. It knocks them out."

"Oh, those." I'd seen ahpesh use them a couple of times when we'd managed to get them out of their ship to help break up fumwah fights. "No. If I go in with a weapon they'll think I'm assuming hostility and I'm not. Relax, captain. I'll be fine."

They muttered something in their own tongue—probably "it's your funeral"—and gestured for me to be let into the fumwah area of the ship.

The fumwah had free access to the airlock when docked, so they could come and go to party as they pleased—but since the command area of the ship and many ahpesh areas were always off-limits, the door was guarded even then. If I understood right, during actual travel the whole fumwah area was kept under lockdown, more or less, with only the ahpesh on what was essentially prison guard duty allowed in. It was a hell of a way to run things. If I were a fumwah I probably would have rioted just on the principle of it.

But, as I expected, the fumwah who were in their quarters didn't look very riotous. It was still early in the cycle and many of them were asleep in their bunks. Fumwah snore. Some were having breakfast in the mess, where other fumwah, under ahpesh supervision, were acting as cooks and food servers. I saw one watching something on a data pad—there went that stereotype. A few were just sitting squealing conversation at one another. (Sorry, but their language sounds like something that would come from a particularly unhappy pig.)

I approached one who seemed approachable and introduced myself in Bak'ti. They seemed a little worried when I told them who I was, but calmed down when I said I wasn't here to make trouble for fumwah, I was trying to solve something else and thought one of them might be able to help. We talked a little more and when they seemed ready, I asked them: Who is Na Shae?

Five conversations with fumwah later, I walked out, and asked the surprised captain—I think they had genuinely expected me to be torn limb from limb—"Did any of your crew sign up at the last minute? Just before you left home?"

They considered. "Yes, I think. I don't take care of that directly, but I remember we had a new one very late. I can check."

"Please do."

So many stupid people, dancing around the answers in the dark. I did not exclude myself.

§

Sovesh gave me a suspicious look when I entered the custody room and sat down, but then they remembered they were trying to be cooperative and friendly. I couldn't have cared less. "Let's talk," I said, "about a fumwah named Na Shae."

"You have asked me that before," they replied. "I do not know the name."

"That's what you've said, yes. All right. Let me tell you a story. I want you to listen to it quietly, though. If you get excited, say if you decide to rush me, I'm going to shoot you and it will hurt. Also, my helpers are outside and they don't like noise. Understand?

"Once upon a time there was a fumwah named Na Shae. They weren't a normal fumwah. Some fumwah have always been smarter than others, and most of them are smarter than ahpesh like to believe, but Na Shae was unusual. Na Shae was smart enough to realize that the fumwah were getting a bad deal. Most of them were happy with what they made for travelling all over the galaxy doing hard-labor jobs, but that was because their expectations were low. Meanwhile, the ahpesh, who ran everything because they insisted the fumwah weren't smart enough to, took a big cut of those wages for being the people who flew the ships and ran everything, and Na Shae thought they were taking too much.

"Na Shae began to teach other fumwah. They not only taught them things like Pergati, which they didn't admit to ahpesh they were learning, but they also taught them to be dissatisfied and to group together to show that they were not happy with the ahpesh. Am I telling this in simple enough words for you?—Good. In short, Na Shae was a bona fide labor agitator, and they had enough success at it that some ahpesh in high places had to sit up and listen. Now, the ahpesh in power weren't complete monsters and furthermore they knew where their money was coming from. So it didn't actually take much for them to be willing to meet with Na Shae and their team and start renegotiating the ahpesh-fumwah relationship.

"But there were some ahpesh who weren't happy about this, because those ahpesh believed that fumwah were barely sentient and had no rights to speak of. Some of them believed that the arrangement was already far too generous to fumwah, that fumwah should be slave labor, that all the money should go to ahpesh. One of them got a little excited one day and decided they needed to kill Na Shae. That would put a stop to this crazy negotiation idea. And they did kill Na Shae, and that did halt the negotiations.

"But they didn't expect that there would be an outcry among so many ahpesh in high places, because they were kind of an idiot and didn't realize the last thing the government wanted was some flashpoint that could start outright war between fumwah and ahpesh. So instead of being a hero, this ahpesh found that they were suddenly the most wanted criminal on the planet.

"The ahpesh did the only thing they could think of to do—they signed on as crew with a work ship that was just leaving. It left soon enough that the word didn't spread to that ship, and it would be out on the work run for quite a long time, and hopefully by the time it came home again, the whole thing would have died down. But then that ship docked at this Ring on its way back, and the ahpesh was able to catch up with Cleit news, and the fuss hadn't died down. And home was the next stop.

"So the ahpesh did something desperate. They killed a fumwah, deliberately being sloppy so that it was clear to even a stupid human that an ahpesh had done it. They then waited for the crime to catch up with them. The *only* reason they killed the fumwah was so they would be detained, possibly indefinitely, and wouldn't have to go back to their home world.

"Incidentally, Sovesh, that was the only place where your thinking truly baffles me. You assumed that I didn't care any more about the death of a fumwah than you did, that I wouldn't care enough to have you killed. But you can't have it both ways. Either I cared enough about the murder to throw you out an airlock, or I didn't care very much at all and would just send you on with your ship, which was no good to you. What did you think I would do, just say, 'Oh, I'll keep you here in custody on the Ring forever?' Can you explain that to me? Were you planning to stow away on some other ship or something?—no comment? Oh well.

"It doesn't matter, because the arrival of that fast sub-eight to catch you—I assume the idea was to get you before you could try something tricky here—completely shot your plans to hell. If it emerged that you had killed Na Shae, you might not have survived on your ship to make it home, not if the fumwah got you. Every single fumwah I talked to this morning knew who Na Shae was. Na Shae was their hero. If any ahpesh on that ship ever bothered to talk to fumwah they'd have known it. You had to get the inspector before they could tell anybody why they were here.

"I don't know if you realize how lucky you are. You were lucky that your government was withholding Na Shae's name, so that the Cleit news drop and the sub-eight crew had most of the story but missed that key piece. That helped you, but your *real* luck was that the inspector was such a headstrong type, not bothering to wait for my clearance or confer with me or tell any of their crew what they were doing. They rushed right over to apprehend you without backup, stupidly revealing this when they were alone with you, and you killed them the only way that was handy.

"After that, though, your risk was even worse. If we pinned the inspector's death on you, the captain would make sure you got home to be tried. Even if we didn't, if you got home, none of it mattered, you were doomed. And my focus had changed from Lu Cush to the inspector. Your best remaining hope was to come to me, confess to the crime you *wanted* to be caught for, and throw yourself at my mercy. The thing is, I don't really care about you killing that ass of an inspector—I realize I probably should—but your killing a fumwah like a disposable tool, a useful object, really upsets me. I know you'll probably never understand that, but do believe it: That's what I'm punishing you for. That, and Na Shae."

"You are a filthy lover of animals," Sovesh hissed—well, that's approximately what they said—"and you can prove none of this."

"Not yet, although with the help of a data rescue expert I think I can get enough from that data pad to make it absolute. All I need to get from it is your name. But it doesn't matter, Sovesh. I don't *need* proof; ask my boss. I just need to be sure of it myself, and I am. And your captain doesn't need proof either; they just want enough of a solution that they don't get blamed for the inspector's death, and enough reason to keep you in confinement under guard all the way home. By the way, the sub-eight crew have volunteered to take you home faster, for your convenience, but I'm not convinced they can guard you well enough, and I'm not handing you a fast ship to hijack. I want you to go home—alive—and get the welcome you deserve."

§

That was the end of it as far as my notes were concerned, but you may be interested in a little denouement.

The work ship had cold storage. The sub-eight did not; too small. So the inspector rode home on the big ship. The sub-eight crew requested that the body go back. Lu Cush went into the digesters. As I've said, I'm not the sort to give any dead a ceremony, but I did send a few apologetic thoughts their way. They had deserved better.

Many cycles later—space communication being what it is—we got a news drop that said labor negotiations had been renewed between fumwah and ahpesh. A line in one of the news items commented that it probably would not have been possible to repair them if the lunatic who killed Na Shae had not been caught and executed. I'm still waiting for my commendation from the Cleit government.

I met with the captain again before they shipped, to give them back their dagger. Their parting comments to me were the closest to friendliness I've ever gotten from an ahpesh before or since. I suppose that's commendation enough, in its way.

Douglas Todd

THE CASE of the SURFACE EVIDENCE

It hadn't taken me long to realize that I couldn't care about every ship that
docked and probably didn't want to. Conversely, it had taken me quite a while
to realize there were some ships I did want to keep my eyes on at all times.
Worst of these were probably the soldiers. Any species.

The problem with soldiers wasn't their bullheadedness, nor their tendency
toward the "when the ship leaves, all debts are paid" philosophy—it was their
attitude of moral superiority about it. Soldiers, in my experience, are people
who don't think anything they've ever done is wrong and if they did they'd never
admit it. Certainly not to a civilian. Soldiers think anyone not in uniform is their
inferior, and while they will listen to their commanders, their commanders feel
that way too, and so are rarely ever willing to impose justice. It was always a huge
surprise to them when they learned that while they were on the Ring, the civilian
woman in the pants outranked them. I'll admit here and now that I enjoyed
teaching them that probably more than I should have. On the other hand, they
often caused me a lot of trouble, and I felt justified in a little revenge.

The human military transport had docked at one of the "big docks." I watched
from above, standing on a crane operator's balcony on deck eight, as three
airways were attached to the ship and three different locks opened. As the
crowd began to climb out, I wasn't filled with optimism. Thick necks and low
foreheads all.

§

"Harsh," was Meridian's judgment, ten periods later, after I described my
reaction to the soldiers.

"Me?"

"You're the one who thinks people judge by looks too often."

I considered trying to explain why I thought the two situations were different,
but decided I'd better not. I was lucky she was there at all.

Five cycles after Meridian walked out of my rooms, I went to apologize to her. It
hadn't taken me five cycles to decide to apologize; it had taken me that long to
figure out how I could apologize without revealing that I still didn't have any idea
what I was apologizing for. I'd told her the truth—I was grateful for her visits and

her tolerance—and it still seemed to have been a mistake, and I knew it was a mistake I should try to fix, but it's hard to fix something if you're not sure what you did. If she hadn't been coming over because she felt sorry for me, as she put it, then why had she been?

I'm not utterly without self-awareness. I knew I was no prize. I also knew that I wanted her to keep wanting to see me. So it was selfish, you see.

She'd accepted the apology even though I don't think I fooled her, and we'd parted calmly, but we also hadn't seen each other again after that, for twenty or so cycles. I was afraid to ask, especially since every time she'd turned up before it had been her decision.

Then Azu C's ship docked. Azu C was a Kroy bard, a specimen of actual high culture. We don't get a lot of that on the Ring, and permanents in particular are perpetually starved for entertainment. We've read all the books and seen all the A/V and when we do get new stuff in a drop, we devour it immediately. We do have a theatre; it holds about three hundred. When a clever person in Dispatch got the idea of talking Azu C into doing two performances while their ship was waiting to leave anyway, they ended up having to do a lottery for theatre seats. Everybody wanted to go, if only for the change of pace.

I cheated. I pulled rank and managed to get two tickets from the supply before the lottery took place. The gent in Dispatch was surprised I even wanted them. Word on me had long since spread by then, and I think everybody in Dispatch except Flanagan thought I was a robot.

And that's how I came to be seated next to Meridian, wearing what I thought was a very sharp-looking pinstripe suit I had gotten on Secondhand Row the previous cycle, her in a black dress that was cut just short of scandalous, waiting for the lights to go down.

The only Kroy I have ever seen and am likely to ever see are Azu C and their entourage, so if they were atypical, I apologize to the Kroy ... but my first impression of one was to wonder when they had last eaten and whether they were going to fall over, or break in half at the first strong breeze. Azu C had mammaries (still no guarantee they were a socket) and those were the only bumps in their stick-figure anatomy. Their three skinny legs were a tripod, so maybe they wouldn't fall over, but they still looked like they might pass out at any minute. I grant I may have been biased by their skin tone—dead white, and since they were wearing no clothing it was easy to see they were that pallor all over.

They looked out at the audience, scanned us slowly left to right through eyes almost shut, readied the thin stringed instrument they had carried onstage, and without any introduction began to play and sing.

They sang happy things. The singing was gibberish to us, but we were happy. We laughed hard, the kind of laughing where you have to stop because your sides hurt and you're still giggling while you gasp for breath, and as soon as you catch your breath you're off roaring again. As we laughed, our laughter swirled over Azu C and their skin colored, ripples of red-orange spreading slowly over them like dripping paint into a beaker of water.

When they had completely changed color, they began to strum in a different rhythm, and we cut off the laughter. Some of us sighed. There was the sound of the first few people breaking into tears, quietly, trying not to make a disturbance. Then everyone was bawling, as purple and blue blotches passed over Azu C's skin like clouds.

The next song dried our eyes, a heat of anger and passion and rage and a bilious yellow that darkened into filthy brown. And then, before we realized, the melody had changed again and we felt something more subtle than the other songs—quiet, peaceful, hopeful, green and light blue.

It was over. I looked at my feed to check the time. Had it really been two periods?

Meridian sat, staring straight ahead. I waved a hand in front of her face and she blinked a few times. Testing.

"I don't think I want to go to one of these again," she said slowly.

"You're not likely to get a chance," I said. I stood up, surprised to find my legs shaky.

She was shaky too; she clutched my hand as we made our way to the exits. The crowd wasn't clearing out very fast and there seemed to be some kind of traffic jam near the doors. As we got closer, we heard a commotion—shouting outside, some kind of fight. I gave her an apologetic look.

"Go on," she said. "I'll see you later."

"Security!" I shouted. "Security! Let me through, please!" It worked pretty well since the crowd was mostly permanents. Permanents know anybody who'd make a false claim to my job is either crazy or stupid. As I was actually getting out into the hall, my feed chirped. "There's a major disturbance at five:fifteen," said the boss.

"I'm in it now," I said. "Or trying to be."

"Good," she replied, and disconnected. I don't know how she finds out the things she finds out.

Twenty or more humans—those damned soldiers—were in it with maybe ten Pergati. Bad odds—for the soldiers. Most of the crowd coming from the show were just trying to get out of the way, but few of them could. The theatre was in a major traffic area, one of the few places where deck five businesses overflow down to deck six, and the convenient ramps were by the theatre itself since it had exits on both decks, so the area was already packed and people had nowhere to move to. Bystanders were getting sucked into the fight. I got on the feed to Rob and Don and told them to hustle.

I had just finished doing that when I saw one of the humans pull out a gun. A bullet gun. I wasted valuable time not believing my eyes—then I ran, and I threw myself at him before he could fire the damned thing. He tried to shake me without seeing me, the way you do in a close-quarters fight when you just want to lose whatever's riding you. We rolled over a couple of times, just about knocking my breath out under his weight. I hit him in the belly. Didn't do much, he was hard as a rock there, so next I tried a knee in the sprocket. That got his attention. I pushed him off me while he clutched his crotch with one hand. I stomped on the other and it let go of the gun, which I picked up.

I was getting ready to tear into him—verbally, I mean—when a human screamed. My first thought was Meridian, but no, wrong location. I pocketed the gun and made my way down the ramp into the emptier bits, on deck six. Around a corner to a narrow hall behind the theatre. The screamer was between me and a dead Pergat, face-down. There was enough purple-black blood pooling around it that I didn't need to check for vital signs, but I did anyway. I hitched up my pants legs first. I'm not fussy, but I had just bought this suit.

The human was still making noises and I wished she'd shut up. Off in the distance the fight was still raging, but I heard Rob and Don shouting over the crowd, so that was something. I suddenly felt completely exhausted. I sighed, told the woman not to go anywhere, and got on the feed to Dr. Kohl.

§

"I'm not sure I know what to conclude from the increase in violent deaths since you've arrived," Dr. Kohl said.

"You said you got an average of a death a month, as I recall. I'm not over quota."

"Bar fight deaths," he said. "Not throats cut or heads sawed off or Clxl stabbings in dark alleys."

"I wish you hadn't said that."

He looked up from the corpse and studied me. "I didn't mean it as a personal slight."

"No, no, I'm just—I haven't figured out Max or Kezar or Bral in the damned airshaft, and you're right, things seem to get worse on my watch. I've started wondering how long it'll be before the boss fires me."

He shook his head. "I doubt that would happen."

"I wish I had your confidence."

"Is that all of it?" he asked, still looking at me with penetrating eyes.

"No. Since you ask. I was trying to repair ... a relationship ... tonight. And this happened."

"Mmm. Well, yours is a difficult position in that respect to begin with." He straightened from the exam table with a grunt, reached to massage his back, then remembered the state of his hands at the last moment. "At least your patients never complain about the quality of their medical service," he added, pulling off his gloves with a sticky noise.

The Pergat had turned out to be a sprocket. I'm not shy, but something about the exposed genitals bothered me—made the corpse seem more like an object without dignity. The genitals had no fur, and given how little of a Pergat is furless—tip of the muzzle, palms and soles, and the insides of the ears are the only other bits—it made them look ridiculous, as if they'd wandered into a place they didn't belong. I considered asking Dr. Kohl for a sheet, but instead turned my attention to the open chest, which strangely bothered me less.

"You didn't need to do all that cutting for cause-of-death, did you?"

"I presumed you'd want me to retrieve this," he replied, handing me a small chunk of metal.

"So he *was* shot." I examined it. "Small caliber." A lot of a Pergat looks like fat but is solid muscle. I wouldn't have bet against one walking away from a bullet this tiny.

"About five millimeters. But he was shot at very close range and in a very good place. Or a very bad place. Depending on your point of view. Do you want more specifics?"

"That it was a breachable gun is enough for now." I sighed. "I've already confiscated one this cycle. Actually—" The gun was still in my pocket. I managed to get a bullet out of the clip without killing myself. "What do you think?"

"I'm not a ballistics expert," he said. "All I can say is it seems the right caliber and—" he looked at the fired and unfired bullets side-by-side—"composition. If we fire another from this and I compare them under a lens, I might possibly be able to say whether they were fired by the same weapon."

"Oh, it wouldn't have been this weapon," I said. I had likely been wrestling its owner for it while the Pergat was being shot. "But this is a dress sidearm—look how well-polished it is." I showed him the military insignia on the grip. "We've got a whole shipful of soldiers with these. Half of whom probably took them off the ship despite being warned not to."

"Not a fan of the military, I take it," he said. I scowled and he chuckled. He moved to his lab table. "I took some images for you. I assumed you'd want to try to identify him. Unless he was carrying ID? He didn't have his pouch when I got him."

"No. It was missing, and I've never seen a Pergat go anywhere without one, have you?" He'd taken three angles of clear face shots. "Doctor, I don't know what I'd do without you."

"You'd figure something out. Shall I freeze him for now?"

"Please do."

§

The facts suggested I had found the Pergat only a few subs after death and that the screaming woman—who'd had nothing useful to say, by the way—had just missed the killer running out of the hall. The gunshot had happened during the fighting, when it would be hard to hear. Of course we couldn't have detained everyone at the scene, even if we'd thought to, and it wouldn't have done any good if we had. There was no guarantee the murder had anything to do with the fight at all.

Sure, the screaming woman could have been a really good liar and she could have magically found a place to conceal a gun in a featureless stretch of hall, with only one door a short distance behind the corpse which opened only for a handful of theatre staff who were all accounted for elsewhere, and a huge crowd fighting just around the near corner. And I am the Lost Heir of Phobos. Occam's Razor is your friend.

My feed chirped. "We're done with the cleanup, boss," Rob said. "We didn't find anything—"

"Right. Dr. Kohl found a bullet. The gun is probably one of hundreds. When you busted all those soldiers, how many of them had little shiny guns?"

"Uh, three or four. I can get a count if you want; Don has the names. We took the guns too. Weren't we supposed to?"

"Absolutely. No, don't bother counting. I'll get the guns from you later. Get Don to send those names to my file space, and go home. Good job as usual."

I really, really did not want to board that ship and interview an entire load of hostile soldiers. I couldn't send Rob and Don; I only let them ask questions if I gave them a script, and I wouldn't know what questions to tell them to ask. Sending Sul seemed like a bad idea, under the circumstances.

I checked with Dispatch. The military transport would be here for five more cycles. I sighed.

I know it's a strange thing for someone in my job to say, but I absolutely hate procedure. It's not the interviews, it's the legwork, the sheer amount of time spent hustling around trying to find people and facts. I'd love it if I could just sit in my office and have them come to me.

Be careful what you wish for. I had to pass by Custody to put the little gun in the arms locker, and a human in uniform and a Pergat were trying to shout each other to death outside the Custody door.

"Gray-woman!" shouted the Pergat. He was hopping mad. I mean that almost literally; he was so angry he was nearly bouncing up and down. I recognized him as I got close. His name was Xin Rath, and he considered himself the liaison-to-humans of the Pergati permanents. I'd never checked whether that was official, but a double first name among Pergati meant they were pretty high status, official or not.

"You cannot let this stand!" he said. "These miserable, stinking human warriors—they have gone too far! Dirty, rotten, foul, nasty, ill-tempered beasts—"

This is the kind of thing where trying to translate Pergati in a way that still preserves all of the flavor begins to break down. Human profanity is light-years behind Pergati, and this is the best I can do. But Xin Rath was not using the normal, everyday sort of Pergati profanity. He was genuinely upset and angry. Word had spread; other Pergati had seen the body being carried out.

"Wait," I said. "be calm. I am only learning the facts myself. This crime will not go unpunished." I retrieved Dr. Kohl's images. "Tell me, can you find out who the unfortunate was? Will you ask?"

"Will I ask? Will I ask? Do you have no idea? That unfortunate, as you say, is Kir Erek himself! Murdered in a back hall like a lowlife!"

Oh.

If Xin Rath was the informal liaison, Kir Erek was the real deal—the big boss of the Pergati on the Ring, and an official, duly enshrined representative of the Pergati government. This was not news I wanted to hear.

"If you've finished jabbering to the plush toy—" the human said in Trade.

I'd been up since four. It was now somewhere around thirty and I'd had a lot of bad news since then and no dinner. I didn't bother with a verbal correction. I spun and got my fingers into his windpipe. He outweighed me by a fair bit, but I caught him off-guard. I shoved him hard into a wall and put my other hand on his sprocket and applied a not-gentle grip.

"Pay attention, you peabrained side of beef," I said. "First, the next time you call a Pergat a 'plush toy' I won't need to break your neck; I'll just translate for them and they'll do it for me. They don't lose their tempers often because nobody with a brain gives them reason to, but that would probably do it. Second, although I plan to investigate this fairly, that doesn't mean I'm impartial. Stupid roughneck human soldiers who don't have enough sense to obey a clearly stated weapons policy, let alone not start fights with species meaner than they are, are definitely at the top of my suspect list. With a bullet. A small-caliber bullet fired from a dress sidearm that should not have been on this station in the first place. Do I make myself clear?"

He opened and closed his mouth a few times experimentally. "Do I make myself clear?" I asked again.

"Yes, ma'am."

"Just 'yes' will do here. Are you liaison?" He nodded. "Good. Next cycle I'm coming aboard and asking questions. I expect access to everyone, including command. I also expect every human on your ship to remain confined aboard until I say so. If I see a soldier wandering this station, they'll be in custody so fast their head will spin. If your superiors give you trouble about this, assure them that I'm quite serious, and remind them that can I block your ship five cycles from now, and will if I'm not satisfied. If you want to make your departure, you will create a spirit of cooperation. Also clear?"

He nodded.

"Then get moving," I said. He vanished in a hurry.

I think watching that improved Xin Rath's mood. I was pretty sure he spoke Trade, but I wasn't going to let on if he wasn't. I switched back to Pergati and said, "I apologize many times for this shame. I'll find the killer, but for now I must rest. I will tell you as soon as I know anything worth telling." He nodded and waddled off without saying anything else.

§

I'd managed to get some food and get back to my rooms and was peeling off my clothes preparatory to falling into a coma when the feed chirped. "No, no, no!" I said, but it was Sul, and since they weren't on a job for me just then, it was probably important.

"Apologies, Gray-woman, but you want to be at nine:twenty-four. Right now, and do not be seen."

"Can I have a hint?"

"Qov."

"That's a good hint," I said, and disconnected to collect my clothes.

I'd learned a little more about qov since briefly discussing it with Max, back when. It was a mild narcotic, and addictive but not in a consequential way. I mean, it didn't eventually kill you or anything. It had to be pretty mild because I've seen Pergati chew it all day long and not seem affected by it. Never has been clear to me why the Pergati government banned it, but they had, and I didn't imagine they were thrilled at the hands-off Ring policy.

I was mostly there out of a desire to know what was going on. I couldn't do much else. Docked ships are not Ring property; it would have been tricky to confiscate cargo from one even if it were actual contraband, and I still wasn't sure whether there was anything the Ring considered contraband. Even breachables—I couldn't enter a ship and seize those; only if someone brought them onto the Ring itself.

I watched from a shadowed corner as many large bundles—about as large as it was possible to hoist up the airways—were lifted to the deck and grabbed with cargo tongs by a number of beefs who then carried them off and returned for more. I counted how long it took the same faces to come back. Wherever they were taking it wasn't too far.

By taking back ways and cutting up to deck eight and back down, I was able to get to the destination without having to cross the path of the beefs. The ship whose dock area was accumulating stacks of bundles waiting to be hoisted down was cleaner and newer than the one they'd come from, but not bigger. In fact it was small enough that I wasn't sure where it was going to fit all those bundles. On the other hand, they were clearly pretty light; cargo tongs are exactly what their name says, they give you a better grip and allow you to hoist the load over your back easily, but you're still moving it with nothing but muscle power. If the bundles were just loose vegetable matter, maybe they were compressible as well? Right, of course they were—Pergati used it in compressed pellets. Max had said that.

All the beefs seemed to be clustered at the other ship. I snuck around behind some of the bundles and tore off the wrapping in one spot. Up next to the pile the peculiar odor of the dry leaves was very strong and made me a little queasy. I pulled off a leaf, rubbed it between my fingers, pocketed it, for no good reason except I wanted to be able to identify it if I ran into it again.

There didn't seem to be anything else I could do, and I wondered why Sul had fetched me. It was useful to know about, but hardly a crisis. I hadn't seen Sul anywhere and hoped they hadn't gotten into trouble. I noted the registration and location of the smaller ship, and went back to my rooms.

Of course I couldn't go to sleep without looking up the ship. When I did, I got a surprise: The *Prith Praj*, Kroy registry. Azu C's ship, wait period fifteen cycles from arrival, of which seven remained.

The other ship was a Pergati cargo eight whose name I don't remember. I don't think I even bothered remembering it at the time. It had been the *Prith Praj* that Sul wanted me to see.

I lay awake for a while considering what it meant.

§

I did manage to get some sleep, so I was able to look reasonably together (I hoped) when boarding the military transport the next cycle. I was met by some serious-looking older men I took to be the brass, and the liaison, who looked nervous.

"Ms. Gray," said one of the muckamucks—I've never bothered to learn rank insignia. "So you're the one who's keeping my men from their last leave before duty posting? Do you have any idea how—"

"Er, what the colonel means is—" began the liaison.

"I know what he means," I interjected, before the colonel could tell the liaison off for interrupting him. "Look, I understand this might be their last chance to get out of this can before a long trip to someplace rotten. But this Pergat who's dead was not just anybody. A visitor killing any resident would cause a fuss—my standing orders for a visitor who's killed a permanent are to throw him out an airlock—and the one you killed was a diplomat, the official representative of their government—"

"The one *we* killed?" an officer with a round, red face said. "That's gall! You have no proof—"

"I have this," I said, setting the sidearm on the table in front of them. "Now, if that'll keep you quiet for a minute, I'll explain. Projectile guns—or any other kind of weapon which could possibly breach our hull—are banned on this station. You were warned about this by Dispatch before you docked, and it's not exactly news, nor is this your first Ring. You had a responsibility to pass that warning to your soldiers and make sure they took it seriously. Yet a group of them brought their sidearms onto the station anyway. This is an established fact. A group of them—some with guns—were involved in a fight with Pergati, just around the corner from the murder site and at the same time. This is also a fact. And they were not above using those guns in the heat of the moment"—I raised my voice over their protests—"as is evidenced by the fact that I took this from one of your men as he was preparing to fire it!"

Silence. "Now, as it happens, he's not the murderer; none of the ones who were fighting could have been, because they were visibly busy elsewhere at the time. The point is, these little dress guns are not just the right caliber for the bullet that killed Kir Erek, they may very well be the only source of bullets on the Ring right now. I don't even use breachables myself. So even if one of your people didn't kill Kir Erek, it's extremely likely one of your guns did. Clear?"

No argument.

"I'm providing you with a list of the soldiers from whom we confiscated guns. They're confined to the ship for the duration of your stay. If I see them on the station I'll either put them in custody or send them back to you broken, depending on my mood. If you think I can't take on any of your soldiers and win, you haven't seen me fight. I expect you to talk to all of them and find out who is missing a sidearm that isn't on my list. I don't say that person's a murderer but I'll want to—Colonel, you look like you've stepped in something unpleasant. What?"

"Dress sidearms are for parade use," he said slowly. "They won't need them until we get where we're going. We inspect them occasionally to make sure they're being kept in good condition, but they're supposed to be kept stowed for the entire trip."

"So any number of these guns are sitting around in, what, lockers or something? Where anyone could—"

He nodded. "And the theft could have been any time since last inspection. If we find one of our men is missing one, he may be able to say honestly that he has no idea when it was taken."

"Wonderful," I said, "just great. Pretty cavalier about firearms, aren't you?"

"We are trained soldiers!" sputtered the red-faced man, whom I'd had about enough of.

"But apparently not trained in public behavior!" I shouted back. "Or in following rules!" I picked up the gun and moved to leave. "I want those soldiers confined. Once you do that, everyone else can come out and play. On their good behavior and *without their guns*. And I would appreciate any further information or assistance you can provide."

"What about the weapons you've taken?" someone had the nerve to ask.

"I may decide to return them to you just before you depart. If I let you depart," I said, walking out.

§

Of course I couldn't really make good on that, and I didn't plan to. I didn't actually think a soldier had shot Kir Erek. For one thing there was a question of motive. I'd have bet my hat Kir Erek hadn't been involved in the brawl, and unless in the heat of the moment, why would one of those soldiers have shot him?

The feed chirped. To my surprise it was Meridian, who didn't seem to like the feed any more than Dr. Kohl did.

"Sorry I haven't spoken," I said, "I've been running around on this—"

"I know. You go until you're finished, or you drop. The Pergati here can't talk about anything else but who might have done it. Actually I wanted to know if you've heard anything about Azu C. Catalan's having a fit."

"What's Azu C got to do with Catalan?"

"Azu C cancelled its other show. Catalan had a ticket for it. I was wondering if you knew why."

"Huh. First I've heard of it, but thank you!"

"Why? Did I say something useful?"

"Maybe. Talk to you later."

"I want a reward."

"That can be arranged," I said, and disconnected.

§

Whatever it is Kroy speak, I don't think anyone but them speaks it. And the one I tried to get to let me into their ship didn't seem to recognize Pergati, nor even Bak'ti, which is the closest thing to a universal language in the galaxy, and can be mastered by a small child.

I knew better than to try Trade, but I knew someone must have been able to communicate with them some way, so I persisted in not being understood until a different, haughtier voice got on the airlock intercom and addressed me in Pergati.

"The Azu has suffered an emotional upset," said the voice, "and must not be disturbed under any circumstances."

"I am saddened by this news," I said, "but this is official business of great importance and must take place."

"I tell you it cannot be done."

But it could be done, with a certain amount of arm-twisting. I was greeted inside the airlock by the tall Kroy to whom the snotty voice belonged. Their manner matched the voice. They seemed to be in charge of the place. This majordomo led me into Azu C's private suite and showed no intention of leaving. When I said I wanted a private chat, they said they would be needed to translate. Swell.

Azu C made their grand entrance from an adjoining room through a set of gauze curtains. The entrance was spoiled, though, by their appearance. They looked like they had been badly beaten. Their chalk-white skin was covered in large bruises, blue-black marks fading to a nasty purplish brown around their edges.

They mumbled something. "The Azu trusts you see why they cannot perform," said the majordomo.

"Who did this? I asked. Upon translation, Azu C just bowed their head.

"A Pergat has been killed. I am trying to learn who did it—" Azu C cut me off with a string of urgent syllables. Majordomo: "The Azu knows of the crime." Indeed. Without waiting for a translation. "They say they regretfully have nothing to offer you."

I tried a few more questions, but that was clearly the end of the interview.

§

So Azu C had seen something they shouldn't have, and had been convinced to keep quiet. Who had beaten them? The majordomo, or someone else? And what about the qov? Did Azu C know what their ship was carrying?

The problem was that "something they shouldn't have" was too vague. I had no good reason to believe that my murder, Azu C, and the qov were at all related. On the other hand, I might as well look into the qov, because otherwise I had no line of attack whatsoever.

"What is my brain being picked about this cycle?" Flanagan asked when I wandered into Dispatch.

"Suppose," I said, "just theoretically, a Kroy ship were smuggling qov. Is there any reason the Pergati patrols would handle them differently than anyone else?"

"How should I know?"

"Well, you've seen what the patrols do and don't do."

"Sure, but"—he pulled up some information on his data station—"just as I thought. There hasn't been a Kroy ship through here before. Only the performers circulate, and there aren't many of those—"

"And they cover so much ground we might never see one again. Right."

"But if we're theorizing about this particular one, it won't get stopped."

"Why not?"

"No cargo. Performer, crew, entourage, nothing else."

"So if I saw, say, a hundred large bundles of uncompressed qov being loaded onto that ship—"

He grunted and retrieved a set of ship schematics. "This is why we make them post these with their manifests. They hate doing it and we love it. Look—this thing's a speedboat. There's nothing but an enormous engine, consumables, and the minimal space its crew and passengers need. There is no way any cargo would be loaded in except restock. You sure about what you saw?"

"I didn't actually say I'd seen anything."

"Uh-huh. Well, if you had seen it, I'd say to get your eyes checked."

§

I didn't doubt my eyes. Smugglers are tricky. But this got me no further.

You may wonder why I hadn't contacted Sul and pressed them for more information. It was because I'd figured out what Sul's behavior meant. Sul had wanted me to see something without their being openly involved, or they would have shown up in lower cargo. If I hailed Sul and asked about the conversation from the previous cycle, they would say "what conversation?" And that'd be all I got. The message was clear. The Pergati wanted a smuggler. They probably also wanted a murderer. I might be able to get away with handing them only one. I wouldn't be able to get away with handing them neither, and neither was what I had so far. I couldn't just wander into Azu C's ship and confiscate cargo, especially if it wasn't even possible for it to be there. As for the murder, no matter what my suspicions, as far as proof went it could have been anyone.

I counted off when I'd last eaten, grabbed what we'll call lunch, and went back to my rooms to think. I didn't want to sit in Custody right then.

Not half a period after I'd settled into a chair, the door buzzed. It was Meridian. I have no idea how she knew I was there.

"I came to collect my reward," she said.

Unfathomable.

§

"You confuse me," I said. Later. Afterward.

"Not surprised," she replied. She stretched and yawned. "Did you find out anything about Azu C?"

"Actually, I did. They had been beaten. Bruises all over. Wouldn't tell me anything else."

"Oh, do they bruise?" She curled up around me.

"Why wouldn't they? Have you ever seen a species that didn't?"

"Once. Lobsters."

"What?"

"They reminded me of lobsters. Eyestalks. But they weren't hard. They got hard if you hit them."

"I think," I said, "that was almost supposed to make sense."

"They weren't, you know, hard-shelled like lobsters. Except where you hit them. If you hit them, that part of their skin would get hard."

"Interesting. Defense mechanism?"

"Suppose. We got one who wanted us to beat him so he'd harden up all over. He'd get so he couldn't move. That was what he liked." She shrugged.

My feed chirped and Meridian groaned. An unidentified contact.

"Security," I answered. It was the liaison from the troop ship. "We have a soldier you should talk to. When can you come down?"

"Right away." Meridian rolled her eyes. "Sorry," I told her. "But it's business periods."

"Not for me, not yet," she said, "but I guess I'll go find some soldier to play with."

She meant the comment to be light, even if she *was* going to find a soldier to play with, and I kissed her on the head to show I knew what spirit she meant it in. "Let me know if you find the murderer. Maybe he talks in the heat of passion."

"Nobody talks in the heat of passion," she replied, getting up. "They make noises, but you couldn't call any of it actual talking."

§

"They jumped us," said the soldier, who looked like her superiors had been giving her a very rough time. "Ask any of us. We didn't start it. We knew if we started anything, our sergeant would tear us new ones. Beg pardon, ma'am."

Being called "ma'am" would have hit me odd from anybody, but more so from a female. I wondered why that was, but filed it for later. "All the others confirm that," said the liaison. "The Pergati seem to have deliberately instigated the fight."

"Unless you're all covering up together," I said.

"No, ma'am!" The soldier looked genuinely shocked. I decided to buy it.

"All right, then. You had something else to tell me?"

She looked down at the table. "Some of us had our dress arms—"

"Despite orders. Yes. I'm aware."

"They fit in pockets, out of sight," she said. "Sometimes we go rough places—"

"I'm not interested in the excuses," I said. "Go on."

"When I got back to the ship, mine was missing."

"Had you fired it?"

"I'd never taken it out of my pocket. It must have fallen out during the fight."

"Do you believe that?"

She looked at the table again. "No, ma'am."

"Neither do I. For your honesty, you can have your leave privileges back, if your superiors allow it. Don't get in any more fights, and don't bring weapons onto my station."

"Yes, ma'am. Thank you, ma'am."

"May I ask—?" began the liaison.

"I'll be in touch. Thank you, this was very useful."

Taking the soldiers out of the equation was a relief, but didn't get me closer to an answer. I still had a murder—a murder I was now prepared to bet was one Pergat killing another—but even given that it was a Pergat, who? And what was the motive?

For some reason, the back of my brain kept hearing Meridian saying, "Oh, do they bruise?" About the fiftieth time my brain repeated it, I got what it was trying to tell me. It was bizarre, but I was sure it was the answer.

Getting it resolved was going to take a little preparation, though. I got on the feed to Flanagan.

"You know, some of us have work to do," he said.

"That Kroy ship. Tell me there are Pergati on board."

Pause as he checked data. "Yeah. All of the crew. Everyone but Azu C and company. This part of that qov hallucination?"

"I owe you a drink," I said, and disconnected.

Now to call out some reinforcements.

§

"I must protest!" said the Kroy majordomo. "This is unspeakable! I will make a complaint!"

"Complain all you like; my superior is the station director and she is fully informed of my actions," I said. The second half of that was a lie.

Azu C came in. Their bruises were fading somewhat. They gibbered worriedly to the majordomo, who responded in kind.

"This is extremely important," I said to the majordomo. "Your departure and your well-being depend on it. So you will translate what I say exactly, and you will translate the Azu's responses exactly as well. At present your ship is blocked. Do you understand what that means? We will not allow it to pass through the Ring, and will fire upon it if necessary." That last part wasn't just a lie, it was ridiculous; the Ring had fired its defensive guns once in its history and that was because it was being attacked. But I needed to scare the majordomo into behaving.

"An outrage!" the majordomo translated, once they had conveyed all that to Azu C. But Azu C hadn't actually sounded all that upset. I wished I could talk to them directly.

"We don't do anything without a good reason," I said. "Your ship contains a great deal of qov, narcotic plant matter, which is illegal where you will be travelling."

"This must be a mistake," Azu C said, via go-between. "This ship is not even equipped for cargo. Examine it yourself if you like."

"I might, but first things first. I assure you I've seen qov being loaded onto this vessel. Either you're both aware of this, or you aren't. If you aren't, then you've been deceived by your crew. If you are, I should warn you that if I am not allowed to leave this ship safely within a period, my superior will destroy it." Lies are best in threes.

"I suspect you're unaware," I continued, "because I've noticed that Kroy don't concern themselves with the details of travel, or commerce, or much of anything beyond their own activities. I haven't decided if you're aloof, naive, or both."

The majordomo didn't want to translate that at first.

"Why do you tell us this, then?" Azu C asked eventually. "If you believe there is qov on this ship, then take it, or destroy it, and go."

"Because I'm interested in solving my murder, and you're an important piece of evidence."

"I have told you, I have witnessed nothing."

"Not a witness. Evidence. Your skin is the evidence. The murder happened just outside your dressing room in the theatre. You absorbed the emotions. You felt it happen. Those are the marks on your skin, not bruises. I'm right, aren't I?"

They pondered and then inclined their head. "Yes."

"And you decided to hide in your ship instead of telling anybody."

"I could not ... I knew that I had caused the crime."

"You didn't kill him."

"No!" They looked as shocked as I'd have expected. I couldn't imagine them committing a murder; the emotional strain would have crippled them. Fragile thing! "I should not have agreed to play. You are not prepared. You were affected."

"Oh, I see. Forget that," I said. "You didn't incite this. Your song may have stirred somebody up, but they didn't do anything they weren't planning to do already. This murder was premeditated. The fight outside the theatre was started deliberately, as cover. The use of that particular weapon was opportunistic, but the murder was not. It was planned either by you—which I now strongly doubt—or a member of your crew. It was planned because the victim found out this ship was going to smuggle out qov, and as a member of the Pergati government, was trying to stop it."

"I assure you I know nothing of it."

"Then help me. If you are legitimate, you'll help me because you've been misused by your crew. If you're in on it, then you'll help me because you want to leave. But until I have that murderer, I won't let you leave this station."

"What would you have me do?" Azu C asked.

§

Because this foolish creature wandered the universe without bothering to learn a common tongue, the majordomo had to deliver the speech to the crew instead of Azu C. Pity. I felt this spoiled the effect.

There were ten Pergati—presumably the same ten Pergati who had started the fight with the soldiers. There were five Kroy altogether, but I figured that one

Pergat could handle about seventy-five Kroy without breaking a sweat. I hoped Azu C's idea worked. I was keeping out of sight, and so was my backup.

"The Azu," the majordomo said, "was sadly in the vicinity of an unfortunate crime last cycle—a killing. They have been affected by this, as you can see. The Azu is greatly shamed to say that the one who has done this is among their trusted crew. They feel they have no choice but to deliver that one to the station authorities. The Azu would prefer it, though, if that one were to come forward and confess their deeds, as is only proper and honorable."

I couldn't see, but I expected there was a lot of glancing around. I didn't hear anyone saying anything. Then I heard a yell, and movement, and I shouted "Now!" and covered my ears. All the Kroy began wailing. I could hear it even through my hands, and it made me fall to my knees. I think I was screaming; I couldn't hear my own voice through all the pain and the noise.

And then it stopped, and there was a different commotion as Rob and Don and Sul rushed into the room and started to put ties on the nearly-incapacitated Pergati. I wiped tears from my eyes and stood up.

Originally my plan had been to have Sul recruit a small force, because even the best humans can only take on one Pergat at a time. But that would have been a messy fight, and Azu C had explained that Kroy aren't as defenseless as they look, even the ones who don't perform. I liked their idea better.

Azu C was standing over one Pergat, looking mournful. I said, "I take it this is the one?" but the majordomo was nowhere nearby to translate, and it didn't need to be said anyway. I could see Azu C's skin beginning to color at the ends of their legs, purple-blue-black washing over them from where the Pergat lay writhing on the floor.

§

"Sul," I said, once the chaos had died down and the last of the Pergati crew had been led away. "A word or two in private?"

We wandered over to a corner. I signaled Rob to go ahead and finish up without me, and he nodded.

"Would have been simpler," Sul said, "to get murderer with Azu C alone."

"Couldn't. They didn't actually know who did it. They had felt the murder without seeing the killer. They were only sure after the majordomo's little speech, once the killer started to broadcast guilt and rage and whatever. But it doesn't matter; we'd have to take them all sooner or later anyway. They were all in on it. The ones who didn't fire the gun conspired to help the one who did."

"Kroy are idiots."

"I'd prefer to think of them as naive, but you have a point. I wonder what kind of lies they've been buying from their crew to cover up the fact that their engines are a lot smaller than the schematics say. I bet they've been accepting whatever travel times or 'maintenance stops' they've been told. Azu C just wants to perform and not have to worry about any of that. I hope we can find a temporary crew to get them off the Ring. Sul, I'm leaving the disposition of these criminals and the qov to the local Pergati."

They studied me. "Will Director-woman complain?"

"The boss doesn't give a damn about qov, you know that. That cuts both ways. Last cycle I got a mysterious communication about the movements of this qov. Of course you know nothing about that, but as far as I'm concerned, that makes this job—the qov part of it—a Pergati request. The murder investigation was already a Pergati request, from Xin Rath. If it's a Pergati request, then the Pergati can decide how to clean it up. Of course I'll implement your decision, although I would prefer not to push anyone besides the actual killer out an airlock. Let me know. I can hold all ten of them for a while, but not too long."

They nodded. "I will tell Xin Rath."

"One more thing, Sul. You know as well as I do that this isn't as far as this goes. Someone on the Ring helped arrange this qov deal. Kir Erek found out who it was. These guys are the hired help; he wasn't after them. That information may have died with him. If it didn't, and you or Xin Rath find out—I want in on it."

They nodded again.

"And until then—tell Xin Rath to be very, very careful."

"I would tell you the same," Sul said.

Douglas Todd

THE CASE of the FALSE VEIL

Sooner or later anyone who lives on the Ring for a long period of time has to deal with the maintenance problem. I don't mean Ring maintenance. I mean personal maintenance.

Vitamin D supplements are a given. We have two "sun rooms" (one for Pergati, who need it as much as we do but want a cooler room—they already think humans keep the Ring too warm) but since they're also the Ring's only public green spaces (hydroponics are restricted access), they're always very crowded, and who has the time to spend as many periods strolling around them as you'd need? Private sunboxes are too expensive and most people don't have space for them. So everyone takes vitamins and puts up with being pale and feeling listless. If you asked most other permanents, that would probably be the main health problem they complained about, but it wasn't mine.

I not only needed to keep in shape for my job, I needed to keep in training. It wasn't weight, which has never bothered me, but muscle and fighting reflexes I was worried about. In cycles where I did a lot of crowd-control or a lot of walking around, it wasn't an issue. But not long after the Kroy business, we entered a long slow time (for me at least) where not much of anything happened, and somewhere in there I started feeling the need to give my body the workout it wasn't getting.

The Ring had a gym, but I don't like exercising in front of other people. (I don't like exercising at all, except for sparring.) I sold both of the armchairs—I preferred the desk chair anyway—and rigged up some bars and a bag in the space where they'd been. But for my legs, there was nothing I could do but run, or at least walk a lot. Walking or running an entire concourse was something fast enough that I could manage to put up with it every cycle, and I tended to pick deck three to do it because three was so empty; even if I took my walk/run during peak periods, I usually wouldn't see any other people.

Actually, it didn't take long before a single orbit of deck three brought diminishing returns, and I moved up to circling it twice and then three times, and I was thinking about trying for four on the cycle when I ran past a room and noticed it had a red light above its doorway. This meant "don't go in," but there was no way for me to tell why, and I certainly didn't want to open the door and let poisonous fumes into the concourse, or be burned to a crisp. Shouldn't there be alarms or something?

It then occurred to me that there might very well be alarms, but they'd be ringing in Maintenance. I got on the feed and spoke to a bored-sounding Pergat whose name I didn't catch. "Yes," they said, "is a fire."

"A fire? Er—shouldn't someone be putting it out?"

"Is being put out. Automatic systems are working. Room is empty, no danger to anyone. Leave alone until finished."

Well, that was awfully cold-blooded, I thought, as the Pergat disconnected. I hoped they'd have felt more urgency if there'd actually been anything in the room. On the other hand, it made sense; the system was designed to keep fires from spreading. Better to close it off in one room and not let it get out.

As I was considering this, the light above the door turned off. The door didn't feel hot, and I was curious, so I opened it. The rooms were the basic midsize single residence, the same as mine but unequipped; the half-wall between the main room and the kitchen area didn't have a bar top, and no cabinets or appliances were installed in the kitchen. But there had been *something* in the room—the floor was piled inches deep in ash, some of it still smoking. It definitely wasn't something that had burned off the floor or walls; those were bare and fireproof and anyway there was far too much ash for that.

I'd been standing in the doorway, holding the door open, not wanting to step in the ash. This made a slight draft into the concourse, and a small amount of smoke washed over me. Not enough to make me cough—but there was something peculiar/familiar about the smell of the smoke. It took me a second to get it; it was different from the unburned smell, but I was at least seventy percent sure this was qov. Or, rather, had once been qov.

Well, if this room had really been used to store qov, would any of the other rooms in the same area have some as well? I checked the adjacent doors on either side, and the three across from those on the other side of the concourse. Four of the five doors I checked revealed utterly empty unfinished rooms. The door on the same side as the fire room, spinward of it, did something odd. When I tried to go in, the red light above the door blinked at me a few times. The door didn't open. Nothing else happened. I tried it again, and then a third time. Same response; light blinked, nothing else.

The thing is, if it were a door I couldn't open—and I hadn't thought there were any of those—then it just wouldn't open; there wouldn't be a light. The red light never meant anything but "don't come in here, it isn't safe," and I could see a door not opening to me if conditions inside weren't safe, but then it should have *stayed* on, like the fire room.

I resolved to ask Maintenance about it later. You might well wonder why I didn't get on the feed and ask them about it then and there, and the answer is, I didn't want to call further attention to the fact that I'd been looking at the room. Any of these rooms.

This wasn't the first time I'd wondered about the amount of empty space on the Ring. I'd done a bit of math one day and decided that if the Ring contained nothing but living space, based on the average size of living quarters, it could handle just under 18,000 people. Of course that number was useless, since more than two-thirds of that was occupied by all the things on the Ring that weren't living quarters—the businesses, the storage, the air and water supplies and equipment, the hydroponics, conduits, docks, halls, and so on. But even a quarter of the total or less would mean the Ring actually had living space for 4000 or so people ... and my guess on the average size of a residential space was probably high; rooms tended to be small. There were never more than half that many people on the Ring, and a third of those were visitors, who slept on their ships. So were the Rings designed for a larger population because they'd overestimated the number of permanents needed to function? Deliberately building them too big didn't strike me as the kind of thing the bottom-line-conscious Ring management would have done.

It hadn't occurred to me before that the situation would be ideal for smugglers, mostly because, again, what is contraband on the Ring? (We wouldn't even confiscate breachables if they were packed up and safe from actually being fired.) Why bother to hide it? Just use the warehouses. But assuming you *did* need to hide it for some reason ... You could get all kinds of things into and out of empty rooms on deck three in particular without anyone noticing. Assuming you had access to the rooms, but that didn't strike me as a big deal, because why would anyone care much about who had access to unused rooms?

I was already more than beginning to think that there were some things going on at high levels in Ring management, and I wasn't sure what I was going to do about them if anything, but I was sure that making loud noises at that point was not going to do me any favors. Of course, I also didn't know how I was actually going to proceed.

If you were going to store illicit qov, why would you then burn it? Had someone else burned it?

I returned to the fire room and took a big handful of the ashes—for analysis, perhaps, but really because I'm compulsive. I didn't have any sort of carrying case with me, so I went back to my rooms to deposit them in something.

It would have been a good time to keep looking into that, or looking into my other unfinished business. The problem was, I had no strings to tug on for any of it. "It is a capital mistake to theorize before one has data."

§

My slow cycles had started before everyone else's, but now we'd hit a long stretch where there wasn't much ship traffic and it was slow for everyone. Once or twice I went to Catalan's for no good reason except to sit in the parlor and listen to the staff tell me war stories. I think they had a betting pool to see who could shock me.

On one of those visits, the conversation had turned to customers who had definite preferences for a particular staffer, and why. "Usually they just have a kink for some little thing," said Lee, the black-haired woman I'd seen on my first day there. "Like, some ask for Meridian because she's our only redhead."

"But some do get attached," Meridian said. "Some regulars start off by trying a lot of different people and then they settle on one they like."

"Do you accommodate that?" I said.

"If we can," Catalan said from the bar. It was unusual for her to participate, but she didn't seem to mind the chatter as long as there were no customers listening or being neglected. "And at the staff's discretion."

"She means sometimes they're creepy and we can say no, pick somebody else," Lee said.

"Sometimes their reasons are a little crazy," Meridian added.

"Like the one who asks for you because he won the sweepstakes," Lee said.

"That's a good reason! Just a little superstitious."

"Just a little?"

"Are you using a meaning of 'won the sweepstakes' I don't know?" I asked. Catalan chuckled and Lee grinned.

"Well, you know Ring hum," Meridian said. "Sometimes if we're in bed with somebody when the Ring opens we try to, y'know, hold it ... if you can come right when the Ring closes and you get that boost, that's winning the sweepstakes. He's hoping one of these days we can do it again."

Catalan suddenly got up and moved near my chair. I couldn't tell if she was going to intercept someone or trying to block my view of something, but either way she didn't make it. I got a glimpse of someone swathed head to toe in black, leaving.

"Was that a Tanngrever?"

"Yes, it was," she said, "and I'll ask you not to mention you saw them."

"Right," I said. "Doesn't seem like something they'd approve of." No one had seen much of the Tanngrevers since their arrival, but the few encounters had given me, and others, the impression that any interaction with us heathens— "heathens" being anyone not a Tanngrever—was something they did only when forced. "Have you gotten many?"

"I wouldn't say 'many,' but it's been a steady stream," she said, "and before you ask, yes, they have sockets and sprockets."

"I wasn't even sure they were human."

"They're human, but they've got to be modded," she said. "Hormones at the very least."

"Why?"

"The sprockets look just like the sockets," Meridian said. "Except that bit."

"They sound like them too," Lee said.

Catalan scowled at them both. "Don't worry, my lips are sealed," I said. "I'm just curious. Their peculiarities are none of my business."

Of course, if you make a statement like that, fate will prove you wrong.

§

Early one cycle, four or maybe five cycles after that conversation, Dr. Wright got on the feed to me. Out of the blue; I hadn't had any contact with her since the Clxl business. "A person named Yur contacted us," she said. "One of the Tanngrevers—possibly their leader. Someone in their group has died, and they wanted to know what the procedure on the Ring was."

"Suspicious circumstances?"

"I gather he—they—thought not, but I felt that disposal without even determining cause of death was a bit much, and I told them I was referring the matter to you. I'm afraid he—damn it, they—didn't take that well."

"I gather you can't say for certain they're a male," I said.

"I don't even know if 'male' is meaningful there," she replied. "Forgive me. It's complete sexism and unjustified."

"Why do you say that?"

"Because of their manner. I mean, I'm making an unfair judgment based on their manner."

"Oh. I understand exactly what you mean."

"I thought you might," she replied.

I had already formed the impression that there was only one male on the Ring Dr. Wright had any regard for. I wondered if he reciprocated.

§

"This is an outrage," Yur said, but the impact was blunted by the calm, affectless tone in which they said it.

"I hear that a lot," I replied.

I'd been on edge ever since entering the Tanngrever area. Being scanned by all those disembodied pairs of eyes—obviously not really disembodied, but the black blobs barely registered as people—was unnerving. Strangely, I didn't feel unwelcome; if it had been coldness, I think, they would have refused to look, would have turned their backs after a moment. Mostly what I felt was unabashed curiosity. But being an object of curiosity is only slightly less off-putting than being a pariah.

If Yur actually was a sprocket they gave no physical evidence of it I could see, which meant precious little. All I had was the general shape—they had mammaries, not especially prominent ones—and the voice, which was contralto.

"I resent your implication that the circumstances of Mik's death were suspicious," they said. "We are utterly opposed to violence in all forms. Mik was not found in any attitude that suggested foul play. To subject us to an inquisition—"

"First, I've implied nothing," I said. "In fact I hope you're right. I would love to find out that Mik died peacefully in their sleep. It would make my life much easier. But you understand that we have to make sure of this?"

It was surprisingly difficult to communicate with someone who had no tone of voice and no facial expressions. I wasn't sure whether the silence was anger or contemplation. I did have a feeling they liked keeping me guessing.

"Look," I said. "I take it you're the leader here?" They nodded. "As leader, then, wouldn't you be relieved to know there was absolutely no doubt in anyone's mind how Mik died?"

"We don't care in the slightest what outsiders think," they replied. "I mean that without offense. It's simply not a concern of ours."

"I wasn't talking about what outsiders think," I said. "I should think you would want there to be no whispers within your own group."

That time I knew I'd hit, because Yur narrowed their eyes and inhaled sharply. "Very well," they said. "Investigate as you must, but I must ask you to respect our rules and customs."

"I'll do my best," I said. "Where is the body? I'll arrange to have it taken to medical immediately—"

"No!" they said, and then immediately, "I'm sorry. I shouldn't have shouted." I wouldn't have called it a shout. "We can't allow an outsider to—I assume they would have to—"

"You're going to have to be blunt, I'm afraid," I said.

"We—" They sighed. "You aren't aware of the history of the Tanngrevers."

"From what I understand, few people are."

"Our doctrine was begun by Arv Tanngreve. I'm one of the founders—the original five who joined with them. Arv believed that unless humanity changed, we would obliterate ourselves. The problem lay in our violence. What, Arv thought, was the cause of our violence? They found two causes. First, deceit, the fact that humans compulsively lied to one another, for reasons that were sometimes well-intentioned but nonetheless misguided. Second, the physical differences between humans and especially between male and female humans. So many thousands of years of evolution—the hard-wired impulses and desires and hates—were difficult to overcome, but Arv felt we had no choice if we were to survive for many more thousands of years."

"That's interesting, but—"

"We can only do so much with chemicals," they said. "To fully obscure our differences, we must conceal our forms. We can't allow an outsider—it would be a violation—don't you understand?"

"A medical examination would have to remove Mik's clothes? Is that what you're trying to say?"

"You think we're prudes."

"I wouldn't go that far," I said. "But I don't think the dead care about what they're wearing."

To my surprise, they shrugged. "That's not the point. This isn't about the dead. The living members of our group would consider it offensive."

"Would they consider it offensive if one of their own did the examination?"

"What do you mean?"

"You're going off to form a colony, right? You must have a doctor among you. If you don't, you're fools."

"We—I—" They considered. "That would be more acceptable—"

"Of course, I'll insist on being present as an impartial observer. Wait—before you start sputtering again," I said, holding up a hand. "If there were foul play within your community and only one of your own certified death, I'd look like a complete idiot. You must see that. Sneak me in, keep it to yourself, make whatever arrangements you like, but there will be an examination, and I will be present. I've offered you all I've got. It would be to no one's advantage if I called my assistants and removed this body by force."

They sighed. "When would you want to do this?"

"As soon as is convenient. Now, if you like."

§

Glor was definitely ill at ease. They looked sideways at both me and Yur repeatedly while the situation was discussed. I was relieved when Yur didn't insist on attending. I was pretty sure Glor was too.

"Is this your first post-mortem?" I asked. They nodded.

"You can talk, you know," I said. "I don't bite and I don't tell secrets."

They ignored me and began removing the corpse's head coverings, revealing long straight black hair and what I would otherwise have read as a female face, probably attractive when alive—although, again, I had no idea what the relative standards were. Maybe they were all attractive.

"Do you identify the victim?" I said.

"Oh!" It was the first noise Glor had made. "Am I supposed to?"

"Well, it would be nice to get confirmation," I said.

"But—"

"You can't." Glor nodded. "I guess you wouldn't have ever seen Mik with the veil off, then ... What? Go ahead, tell me. I won't tell Yur if you don't want."

"I can't—I don't know if I've ever seen Mik at all," they stammered.

"How is that possible? There are only about fifty of you."

"We don't speak!" Their level tone was starting to disintegrate. "There are three or four here I talk to often. Some of the rest, I've never known their names or anything about them."

"Who else could identify Mik? Anyone besides Yur?"

"I'm not sure," Glor said.

I felt a headache coming on. "All right, let's put the matter of identification aside for the moment. Keep going."

Glor continued to unwrap Mik, unfastening the dress-robe-thing as far down as the mammaries. They stopped, and made a sharp noise. Mik had dark angry marks all over their neck. I almost thought I could make out the shapes of fingers. I looked closer and I could see the swelling at the throat, and the blood spots below their eyes I'd thought were just tiredness circles.

Mik had not died peacefully in their sleep.

§

Surprisingly, Yur didn't throw a fit. When told that Mik's death had been by violence and there would be an investigation, they seemed more angry that anyone would dare do such a thing to one of its flock than anything else. The only point where we had some friction was when I explained I was taking the body.

"I'm not going to do anything you wouldn't approve of," I said. "Glor has reclothed it and it will stay clothed. But we have to keep the body on hand for now. We may need to examine it again. And there's only one place on the Ring where the body can be stored without becoming very unpleasant. Do you want to leave it here to decay? What would your people think of that?"

I called Rob and Don and they carted the body off to Dr. Kohl. Most of the Tanngrevers turned out to watch them go.

"Not sure there's a point in interviewing everyone," I said, mostly thinking aloud. "Everyone here knows now. Spotting the liar will be impossible."

"The liar—" I'd confused Yur, but I wasn't sure why.

"Yes, the liar. You don't think the murderer is just going to say, 'oh, sure, I strangled Mik,' do you?"

"We can't lie. You didn't know this?"

I remembered what Flanagan had told me about the rumors. "I'd heard something about that, but I don't believe it. I realize you're deeply opposed to the idea of lying, but that's not the same as not being able to, and when people are—"

"No, no, you don't understand. Listen." Their patience with me was wearing thin and the disaffect was beginning to seriously crack. "We can't lie. Every Tanngrever receives many cycles of mental conditioning. They must, to become one of us. It's a requirement. Tanngrevers are incapable of lying. We literally cannot do it."

"I don't believe you."

"Try it! Take one of us. Pick someone at random. Try to get them to lie about something. Find something obvious and ask them to deliberately tell an untruth about it."

"That wouldn't prove a damned thing and you know it. If you've decided that lying is a sin, then you wouldn't lie about something easy, especially if you knew an outsider was testing you. I'm not disputing that you think lying is bad. The question is what someone would say under pressure when trying to save their own skin."

"I don't know what I can do or say to convince you," Yur said.

"Tell you what," I said. "I'll interview all of you. It's not going to be a long interview—one question each. If I get through every one of you and someone says they killed Mik, I'll believe you can't lie. If no one says they did, then I'm going to continue to believe one of you is lying, and then we're going to try a different line of attack."

"You assume a Tanngrever did it."

"I was waiting to see if you'd try that one," I said. "You come to the Ring and from then on aren't seen by anyone else unless you have to go out to buy more food. There are probably plenty of people on the Ring who don't even know you're here. You keep to yourselves, no one else has anything to do with you, and you want me to think an outsider had a motive to do this, *and* could enter this area and kill someone without being seen by one of your people—who are very curious about strangers. No."

Of course, that didn't cover the ones who snuck off to Catalan's or other places, but I was holding that in reserve.

"Begin your questioning," they said, icily.

"I'll start with you. Did you kill Mik?"

"Of course not," they said.

"Great. That's one checked off. Line everybody up."

§

Even allowing that I asked everyone but Yur two questions each instead of one, getting all forty-seven (Yur included; I counted) to enter a room one at a time to be asked took longer than I expected. The meal I ate afterward might have been lunch, but it was a pretty late one.

None of them admitted to killing Mik, which was not a surprise. None of them admitted to knowing Mik, which *was* a surprise. I was going to follow up on that later, but in order to do it I was going to have to make sure I shook Yur off somehow. It wasn't that I suspected Yur; I just felt they were an inhibiting influence on their flock. Could Mik have really been in the colony and not known anyone? I supposed it was possible; a colony of True Believers was probably going to have one or two who were interested in the doctrine and not in social contact.

I wandered into Dr. Kohl's. "I haven't had a chance to look at your new patient yet," he said.

"I promised them you wouldn't, actually. I said to their leader that you would not undress the body or otherwise sully their beliefs."

"So you don't want me to examine it?" One corner of his mouth turned up.

"I just want you to be aware you're an accomplice to breach of promise if you do," I said.

He nodded and went to the cold drawers. "I've done worse."

"Actually I just want a second opinion on cause of death. Although I don't think it's in any doubt."

"Not if you have eyes," he said, having already exposed Mik's top half, without removing the body from the drawer. "Unless you know something else, I see no need for a further exam."

"How much force was needed to do that, would you say?"

"If you're trying to decide if a male or female did it," he replied, "or a Tanngrever—no verdict. The killer was strong, but a lot of people are strong. I can tell you that the victim did not go quietly. There are several sets of marks. The killer had a grip, the victim managed to break free, and the killer gripped again in a slightly different place. Possibly more than once." He closed the drawer and I sighed and turned to leave.

"You haven't asked me what I know about Tanngrevers," he said, sitting back at his lab table.

I turned back around. "I would be fascinated to know what you know about Tanngrevers. I'd be even more interested to know how you know anything about them."

"A colleague had an opportunity to examine some of them. His notes on them have been informally circulated." He smiled. "That means they've been passed under the table; he doesn't dare publish, and officially you know none of this, by the way."

"Understood."

"You know epidemiology is an interest of mine. There was an outbreak of Garba fever on the world where they originated, Marvin Tanngreve's home world—"

"Marvin?"

"Ah. That was a lapse on my part, forgive me. Tanngrevers alter their names when they are inducted to make them less obviously male or female. One should respect that, regardless of one's other opinions on the matter. Several Tanngrevers contracted Garba fever and ended up in the infirmary that had been set up for the epidemic along with many of with the general populace. It may have been the last time an outside doctor had the opportunity to do any sort of exam on Tanngrevers."

"Didn't the patients object?"

"One of the symptoms of acute Garba fever is coma. They were in no position to. But, yes, this is one reason the information remains illicit."

"Go on."

"He saw five Tanngrevers, all human, three whom I'll call male for simplicity, two female. The male Tanngrevers showed development of breast and adipose tissue, muscular changes, body hair loss, et cetera consistent with the type of chemical treatments given for sexual reallocation therapy. But they had not had genital surgery. They had male genitals which appeared to be properly formed. External exam only, of course, so we don't know if they were functional. They had traces of the likely chemicals—I'll spare you the specifics—in their tissues, indicating that not only had they taken a full course of the chemicals, but they were still taking the supplements that would be needed. Lifetime commitment." I nodded.

"All three of these male Tanngrevers had breasts which the doctor felt were on the abnormal end of what chemical therapy alone would create—not necessarily large, you understand, but out of the ordinary for the circumstances. Unfortunately, the state of the art with thixotropic injectables now makes it impossible to tell without biopsy—no scars, nothing to palpate for—but he was willing to speculate that they had had their breasts augmented. Now the fun part. The two females showed no signs their bodies had been altered chemically or surgically in any way."

"Huh. So they decided to try for uniformity by making all the males look female rather than the other way around?"

He nodded. "Which might indicate that they were trying to give everyone roughly the same veiled silhouette and decided augmentation was less offensive to their tastes than mastectomy. Or it might suggest things about the biases of their founders, who were all male."

"But the founders took the same course of alterations! Or at least Yur certainly has."

"Perhaps the others did. Tanngreve didn't. Do as I say, not as I do. Of course, he was—I suppose I should say 'they were'—close to eighty when they founded the group, so they may just have thought it was too late to bother."

"What do you know about their alleged inability to lie?"

"No one's ever proven or disproven it, but it's clear they themselves believe they can't. I don't know why they would admit to mental conditioning, which has caused them trouble, if they didn't believe in the justifiability of it. But that may not be saying much."

"What kind of trouble?"

"Their origin world considered it brainwashing and arrested Tanngreve. That was when they decided they didn't want to be around other people anymore and moved their whole group to a world which tolerated their practices. Eventually, depending on who you ask, they either decided they couldn't put all their eggs in one basket any longer, or the remaining founders had a spat. One way or another, they split into five groups; one stayed where it was, one is here, and I haven't gotten word of where the other three are. Trying to find suitably remote homes, I suppose."

"What happened to Tanngreve? They seem to be in past tense."

"They died in prison." He glanced at the cold drawer. "Natural causes."

§

A crime is composed of opportunity and motive. As far as I was concerned, opportunity was an open book for the Tanngrevers. It would have been an utter waste of my time to try to figure out who was where during what period and who could have killed Mik unseen.

Their rooms weren't organized like other rooms on the Ring; the space we'd given them on deck six wasn't intended to be residential. They had a series of large common rooms connected together, with access to the concourse at either end of the chain, plus some side rooms in various places along the way which were used for storage or other purposes. Glor and I had examined Mik's body in one. Yur had the only private personal room; the rest slept barracks-style (although the sleeping rooms were sub-partitioned with curtains) and dined communally. Mik had been found in bed, but clearly had been moved there. Mik had probably been killed late the previous cycle, when most of them were asleep if they were on the typical Ring schedule, but I couldn't see anyone strangling Mik in the sleeping rooms without waking everyone else up. On the other hand, if Mik had been killed in one of the side rooms, it wasn't out of the question that no one had heard even if they didn't go quietly; Ring walls are built to be fairly soundproof so we don't all make each other crazy. Doors weren't a factor; every door in their complex opened for any of them.

With opportunity a wash, I concentrated on motive, but found to my annoyance that this was just as much a dead end. During the next few periods after talking to Dr. Kohl, I commandeered one of those side rooms and interviewed several Tanngrevers in depth, but got nothing. No hates, no grudges, no loves, no rivalries. Some had groups of three or four people they talked to, as Glor had said, but seemed to have no interest in interacting with anyone outside that group. This crowd was going to be a self-sufficient colony?

After the third interview I started asking more aggressive questions out of sheer irritation, just to see what they'd do. I asked a couple of them for specifics about their sex lives, figuring they'd say "Why is that relevant?" or something similar. No. They just answered, in the same tone of voice they'd use to tell me what they'd had for lunch. I started to wonder if it wasn't that they couldn't lie, it was just that they couldn't possibly be bothered to.

I did get an interesting response to the sex question from one of them. "These rooms aren't a good place for that," they said.

"Well, yes, I suppose they're not very private. What about on the trip here? You had individual cabins on that ship, didn't you?"

They shook their head. "That would have been a bad idea."

"Why? Yur doesn't approve?"

"Oh, no, I think Yur would be pleased—" They cut off.

"Go on. If not because of Yur, why not?"

"We have no secrets," they said. And they would go no further on that topic. I'd already discovered that when a Tanngrever didn't want to talk about something, they just stopped saying anything. I guess if you can't/won't lie and are too polite to walk away, that's the only way to shut someone down.

By the time I gave up in disgust, I'd decided it was completely plausible that Mik could have died a stranger to them all. Might even have been voluntary; I didn't want to get to know any of these people either, and I'd been around them for less than a cycle.

In case I need to clarify this, the gender stuff didn't bother me. (I was pretty sure it bothered Dr. Kohl, but his approach was purely anatomical.) I had seen all kinds of approaches to gender, both in the Vault and on the Ring, and as far as I was concerned, that was an area where everyone was entitled to do what they damned well pleased. Certainly if anyone ever gave me grief about my personal choices—and it had happened, once or twice—they'd either get a freezeout or a punch in the nose, depending on my mood and the amount of energy I cared to burn on them. OK, I felt maybe the Tanngrever approach was a little naive, if that's the word I want, but that wasn't what bothered me about them, I was sure of it. The problem was, I couldn't quite figure out what *did* itch me about them. But it certainly did itch. More so the longer I spent around them.

§

I'd eaten dinner and had been in my rooms for about a period, staring at the ceiling, when Meridian buzzed. She'd returned to her pattern of dropping by every few cycles, and nothing had been said about the discussion we'd had—it was too short to call a fight—that had ended with her walking out. It hovered; not enough to keep us from going to bed together, but I had the sensation of an unresolved piece of music; sooner or later we would be returning to the theme.

"I was hoping you'd come tonight," I said.

"Bad day?"

"I wouldn't say bad ... just—look, do you mind if we—well, no, I can't say 'we.' Can I just talk for a while?"

She gave me a look I completely couldn't interpret, and pulled over one of the "dining room" chairs and straddled it backward. "Of course."

I was still trying to figure out where to begin, and she was watching me patiently, when the door buzzed.

"Who—? Hold on." I went to open it, deciding not to get my baton because that would alarm Meridian, and thinking for about the thirtieth time that I needed to get a camera put in this door like the one in Custody.

It was a Tanngrever. "I'm sorry," they said hurriedly. "I had to wait until I knew you would be in your rooms—if I'd gone to your other place someone might see—" I gestured them in and they saw Meridian. "Oh! I know you—from the sex house—"

"And I know you, Glor," I said. "What's wrong?" They were extremely upset or nervous or both, I couldn't tell which. Probably both.

"You recognized me?"

"Relax. If I hadn't examined a body with you I probably wouldn't have remembered. It was mostly your voice. Meridian is a friend, you can trust her. What's the trouble?"

"If I—if I told you I had killed Mik, what would happen to me?"

I tried to keep my face unreadable. "I suppose I would have to put you in custody. After that, I don't know. One Tanngrever killing another isn't a huge concern to us, or that's what my boss would say anyway—I guess the proper thing to do would be to let Yur decide what to do with you."

"Oh," they said. Not the answer they were hoping for.

"Doesn't matter anyway. Did you kill Mik?"

A long hesitation. "... No."

"And I'm not even going to touch the question of whether you actually can't lie. You didn't do it. You aren't the kind of person who could have examined that body, if you'd done it, without coming apart at the seams. Why don't you tell me what you really want?"

They stared at me for a while, eyes wide. I sighed. "Tell you what. I'll do it for you: you're looking for a reason to get held on the Ring. The ship finally comes to take you all away in two cycles and you don't want to be on it. Why don't you just tell Yur you've decided you don't want to go? Scared they'll throw a fit?"

"No ... I don't think they would. Another left us once, and I'm told that one and Yur had been very close ... if Yur let that one leave without a fight, they wouldn't care if I do, yes?"

I shrugged. I wasn't going to make any assumptions about the inside of Yur's head.

"—but I have no money, nothing, and I don't know how long I would have to stay before I could find another ship ... You could take me! I can cook, I can do things ... I could—" They glanced at Meridian.

"Stop," I said. "Before you make an offer that you'd regret and I'd find offensive."

"I'm sorry—I thought—"

"Meridian isn't here in that way. Never mind. If you want to stay on the Ring, by all means, stay. We'll figure something out." I didn't think they were reassured. "I promise."

"Oh, thank you!" They hugged me, which caught me by surprise or I'd have stopped them.

"You probably don't want to discuss this with your comrades," I said once I could reclaim my ribs. "We'll arrange something before your ship leaves."

I showed them out.

"Good to hear I'm a friend," Meridian said. "I had been wondering."

"Now, look—" I shook my head and went back to the desk chair. "What would you like me to call you? Which answer isn't wrong?"

"I didn't mean it like that," she said.

After a long pause, she added, "They could be here for a while. Glor. Are you going to pay their bills?"

"I may not have to. Glor is a doctor. I might be able to find them a job in medical. But—yes. If I have to."

Another long pause. Some silences are good; some are very unpleasant.

"Before I came to the Ring," I said, "I worked for close to ten years in a place on Earth called the Vault. You weren't born on Earth, so you don't know. Earth isn't a great place to live. A lot of people have left. Some of the ones who can't or won't leave, if they can afford it, they go live in the Vault. The Vault's a virtual space. You can have any kind of home you want there, live any lifestyle you want, eat any kind of food you want—if you can afford the buy-in. They put your body in a holding tank, hook up the wires to your brain and the tubes to keep you alive, and from then on your world is whatever you want. There are a lot of people in the Vault. Like I said, Earth isn't a great place.

"I was a little different. I worked for the people who ran the Vault. They needed—well, sometimes things went wrong. They needed a person on the inside. A policeman, I guess, although really it was more like a coroner. Or an insurance investigator. For a long time I thought it was my dream job. I got to dress up like a detective from an old A/V—" I pointed to the hat—"and pretend I was something. For a long time it was fun even when the work was depressing."

I hadn't lost her attention. "What changed?" she asked.

"It's too long—maybe I'll tell you all of it some time. But I think I'd have gotten impatient with it anyway. Because what I started to see, all these people in the Vault, they were alone. They didn't connect. I'd go days and I'd be just about the only person in the public parts. Even in places where there were multiple people, they weren't really noticing each other. I think they'd forgotten how. And I said, wait, I don't want to be that, and then I realized I couldn't work in the Vault any more.

"I don't think many of the Tanngrevers chose to be alone. They thought it sounded like a good idea, like the people in the Vault, and now they're stuck in it too deep to get out of it. Or maybe some of them actually like it, I don't know. But a couple of years ago being a Tanngrever would have sounded like a pretty compelling idea to me. Now—well, now I can't say to someone who wants out, 'No, I'm sorry, I have to throw you back in.'"

"It'd be cutting off your own foot."

"I was hoping you'd get it."

She got up and moved over to my chair, put her arms around me from behind. Her touch was warm. "Do you really think most of them aren't happy?"

"Vault residents or Tanngrevers?"

"Either. Both."

"Well ... the thing is, the buy-in's so big. People on Earth would sell everything they owned to make the cost, because, why did they care, they were going to paradise and never coming out again—if they did come out, what would there be for them? And these Tanngrevers, all they go through, the conditioning and the changes, and if they try to go back to the normal world it'll be hard for them. Also, I don't think anybody likes to admit their dream has failed them—"

"What?" I guess I had frozen. She leaned over and looked at my face. "You've solved it, haven't you? I can tell. You've got the answer. Do you want me to leave?"

I pulled myself out of my thoughts. "I'd rather you didn't."

"Are you sure? I'm not offended. I've seen how you get when you're onto something."

I shook my head. "I can't do anything until next cycle anyway."

"Next cycle's not as far away as you think ... I do know some ways to keep busy in the meantime."

I smiled. "Let me check something first, and then we can look into that."

§

Of course you could only get so much from the eyes, but I was pretty sure Yur wasn't happy to see me. Maybe it was the way I had come in. I'd found them in the side room they used as a kitchen, supervising something or another, and I'd told everyone else in the room to get out. They'd gotten out.

"When I questioned everyone in your colony last cycle," I said, "were all your people present for questioning?"

"I don't know why they wouldn't have been," they said. "We rarely leave this area—"

"You leave this area all the time. Possibly no one acknowledges it. How many people are in this colony? The exact number please."

They thought for a moment. "Forty-eight."

"Are you sure about that count?"

"I'd be a poor leader if I didn't know how many were here," Yur said.

"I agree," I said. "You would be. Here's a manifest from the captain of the ship that dropped you off. It enumerates the Tanngrevers separately. There are forty-seven names in that section. Including you. Which matches my mental count the other day when I was interviewing everyone."

"The captain must have left someone off."

"Captains don't make mistakes like that. We'd make them pay for it if they did. But you're right; there's someone missing. Mik. Because they were never there. The victim was not a member of your colony."

They moved, agitated, and I pulled out my baton. "I think it would be better for both of us if you stayed where you are," I said.

"You've overstepped," they replied. "This is ludicrous and insulting. I will complain directly—"

"Yes, yes, you'll tell my boss. I've heard that before. Why couldn't you wait another two cycles? If you'd killed Mik just a little bit later, if you'd been able to wait a little longer, you'd have gotten your wish, you realize that? I'd have been unable to solve it in time and your ship would have gone and Mik would have gone into the digesters."

"I did not kill Mik!"

"This," I said, displaying an image on my data pad, "is Miko Yaruta. There are several people in a position to confirm this is the same person presently lying in a cold drawer. She had what we call 'no visible means of support.' She didn't have a permanent residence. One of the occasional ones who slips through the cracks. She spent her nights with various friends—I wouldn't call her a sex worker, there's no evidence she ever charged any of them. She liked to sleep with them and they paid for her needs. You must have learned at least some of this, because how else could you have realized that when you killed her she wouldn't be missed for a long time because none of her friends could swear she wasn't with her other friends?"

Yur stammered a little bit and then sat down heavily on a kitchen stool. First serious hit and I already had them on the ropes. Made the amount of searching I'd had to do worth the effort. I'd initially thought I was going to have to check the whole Ring for a missing person, which would have been hard to do before the ship came for the Tanngrevers. Fortunately, Mik hadn't changed her name to something else; just reverted it.

"I didn't kill her!"

"Yur." I could afford to be gentle. "No one else here had the slightest idea who she was. You were the origin of the name; the only person who knew it."

"I've told you, we can't lie—"

"The others can't lie, maybe. But you're a founder. Did you even take the mental conditioning? Tanngreve didn't take the gender reassignment drugs. Founders have a tendency to grant themselves exceptions to the rules."

That was the end of the defiance. They put their head in their hands. Time to twist the knife.

"Seeing her here must have really upset you, if you couldn't hold back. Why did she leave you and the Tanngrevers, back on your home world?"

"How do you—"

"Some of your people know the story. They just never knew her name."

"We had been together for a long time," Yur said. "Before Tanngreve."

I waited.

"She joined us—she was with us for years—but then she said that our cause was a failure and a lie and she couldn't wait any more for me to see that it was."

"And she made her way eventually to our Ring, where she fit in the only way that appealed to her now that you'd stomped all over her brain. And you saw her one day here, while you were out getting supplies or something, recognized her, and decided you had to kill her."

"It wasn't like that! We talked—"

"Did you kill her because you were still angry she left you? Or did you kill her because you had realized she was right?"

"She wasn't right!"

"See, Yur, now I know you can lie, because I don't think you're stupid, nor blind. Of course she was right. Your experiment is a failure. You're surrounded by people who are scared to have anything to do with one another; scared to talk to each other for what they might say; scared to try to show interest in each other, much less become intimate with one another, because sooner or later they'd have to tell the truth and they fear the consequences. Tanngreve thought doing away with lies would open doors, but actually it closes them. Sometimes lies are necessary lubricants. You've got a group of people who can't tell who they are, have no idea who they're living in close quarters with; you hid their identities and then, to add insult to injury, took away the verbal tools they'd have needed to discover them.

"Sure, they're peaceful. I never saw such placid people. They're also badly damaged, and you know it. You keep hoping they'll get past it. One of them hinted you'd be delighted if they showed more interest in each other. Your flock has disappointed you, Yur, and you're too smart not to know why. Why did the founders split up? Was it because you were all at each other's throats over the reasons your big experiment had failed?"

"We were flawed," they said, very quietly. "We founders. We knew we were. We assumed they would be better than we were. We didn't pass on our own faults. And the next generation would have been even better."

"You can only get so far if it's the underlying idea that's flawed."

"What are you going to do with me?" they said eventually.

"You killed a permanent resident, or as near as makes no difference. I see two choices," I said. "I can take you into custody and eventually push you out an airlock. Or I can stand on the other side of this kitchen door and leave you alone in here for ten sub-periods."

They lifted their head and looked at me. Even with the face covered, I knew what I saw in that look. I nodded.

I stepped outside and waited at the door, baton ready in case Yur changed their mind and got tricky. It was a very, very long ten subs, and when they had elapsed, I didn't want to go back in. But I had to.

Yur had used a carving knife. It must have taken some effort. They had taken off their robes first, folded them carefully, and put them on a counter. To keep them clean.

I sighed and got on the feed to Don to ask if he would please bring up a cargo trolley.

§

Two cycles later, I was standing on deck nine, watching Tanngrevers help the ship's crew lower their belongings down the airways. Glor was next to me. They were no longer wearing head coverings, although they still had to wear the robes; they had no other clothes. About a third of the others had chosen to uncover their heads as well.

"You're sure you're making the right decision?" I asked.

"Where else can we go?" Glor replied. "What else can we do? We have to make the best of what we have. I think it can be different now, with Yur gone. We aren't Tanngrevers any more ... If I stay, I'll think for the rest of my life that I didn't change something I could have changed. Besides, they have no other doctor."

I was watching two Tanngrevers—former Tanngrevers—no longer in headcloths making hesitant eye contact with one another. "Be patient with them," I said. "They aren't as strong as you were."

"I know," they said. "Thank you. For everything you've done."

"You're welcome," I said, but by then they were climbing down the airway and I don't think they heard me.

Douglas Todd

THE CASE of the MISSING PIECE

In my two hundred tenth cycle on the Ring, I met a species I had never met before. That wouldn't have been noteworthy; even after all that time I was still encountering species that didn't pass our way very often. What made these special is that no one else on the Ring had seen them before either.

The boss wasn't going to turn anyone away who had money to spend, but her tone as she sent me down to lower cargo to meet the ship made it clear that I was to proceed with great caution, and why not? They could like to eat humans for dinner. They could belch cyanide. Anything was possible.

That was the first (and to date only) time I ever saw the kickers active while the airways were connected. I saw a Dispatch employee up on the crane balcony, watching cautiously. I wondered if anyone on the ship realized that at the first sign of any trouble he would shove their ship away from the Ring—and if they had an airlock fully open, as they probably did while unloading, too bad for them. (The airway would seal automatically on our side, so nothing more than a brief fuss for us.) Sometimes you become painfully aware how fragile a system you live in.

They didn't look dangerous, not that that meant anything. Lanky bipeds, in the vicinity of two meters tall, skins varying shades of gray. Hairless everywhere I could see except for wispy, white cotton-candy hair on their heads. Some had theirs trimmed into various shapes; others just let it stick out all over the place. Dark eyes with no whites, and like the Clxl they had absolutely no noses, but to compensate for this they had two mouths, one directly above the other. The top mouth was smaller than the bottom one, which made them look solemn or frowning—of course, maybe they were actually solemn; they didn't seem to be talking as they unloaded. Their faces were delicate and well-shaped, at least to my eyes. A human might have considered them beautiful, if they could get past the two-mouths issue. Gender or genders unclear. They favored very loose, unbelted caftans, which didn't help tell.

Most of them were looking around in what I thought might be nervousness or uncertainty. Not really surprising. We had four people from Dispatch, counting the one on the balcony; I'd brought out Rob and Don, who are visually intimidating; and one of the Dispatch people had three cargo beefs standing by just in case. I'm not saying we all looked hostile, but we weren't exactly a welcoming committee either.

Well, they weren't burping cyanide and they didn't look like they planned to eat anyone immediately. I stepped forward. "Do any of you speak Pergati?" No response.

"I speak for them all," said a voice at the back of their crowd. The speaker pushed through. They had a blue mark on their forehead. What was interesting was that they addressed me in Trade, which is common among Rings and other human-populated places, but otherwise is not bothered with unless some species is trying to score points with humans. Pergati is regarded as a saner language, and certainly a more widely spoken one. The Pergati get around.

"Are you the only one who speaks Trade or Pergati?"

"I am."

"How do they expect to communicate with other species while they're here?"

"All speak Bak'ti somewhat. Most speak it well."

"Bak'ti isn't good enough to tell them the rules. That means it'll be your responsibility to make sure they all know them before I grant access."

"I have done this. We received the information from you before docking."

"If they break the rules, or it becomes clear they have not understood the rules, they're subject to Ring discipline and if they get angry at that, it will come back to you. Is that clear?"

"Completely," they said—I thought perhaps a touch drily.

"All right," I said. "Welcome aboard." I gestured to the other watchers to stand down.

Just before disappearing into the throng again they turned back to me and said, "Do you always greet your visitors this ... thoroughly?" They didn't wait for an answer. That time the tone had been unmistakable.

§

"You," Flanagan said as I wandered into Dispatch, "want to know about our new visitors."

"No points for that," I replied. "Doesn't everyone?"

"Pretty much," he said. "They're called Mephenes, from a place called Mephin, and they've come a long way. This will be their seventh Ring. Two cycles in dock, and they're off for P space"—he meant Pergati-controlled—"and I have just told you everything official I know."

"Good. Now tell me the unofficial parts."

"Their cargo is listed as 'medicinal compounds,'" which we all think means qov. Unless it's immortality drugs, no medicine is worth shoving through that many Rings. A four full of qov might be—barely."

"A four?" I hadn't noticed the size of the ship before. "They'll drop the bottom out of the market."

"Your business sense needs work. Assuming they get through the patrols somehow, they're not going to sell to someone who dumps it all at once. Someone will trickle it out, keep a handle on the supply. If they get through the patrols. Which we're betting heavily they won't."

"Hm. I wonder if they have a human contact? Their liaison knows Trade."

"They list ten languages on their manifest. More likely they want to be prepared for everything."

"That's really all we've got?"

"We haven't gotten any data drops from the other Rings; they've stayed ahead of the news. You're lucky it's not first contact and you're not being called upon to be a diplomat."

"Yes, that'd be bad," I said. "I think I've already annoyed them."

§

As I walked back to Custody, I considered what he'd said in light of my own mysteries. If you were doing timed-release of qov to avoid bottoming out the market, and smuggling out little batches one by one, then storing it in those little batches made sense—say, in empty rooms on the Ring. You could tell someone to grab what was in a particular room and they'd never know about any of the others. But it still didn't finesse the secrecy question. Again, you could just keep it in a warehouse here and set up a queue and dole it out and as far as I knew, the boss wouldn't say boo. Or would she? I needed to find out exactly what her policy on qov really was. The problem was I didn't know how to get that without asking her directly, which seemed inadvisable if she was a suspect.

I took my time passing by businesses on deck five. I didn't realize what the back part of my brain had been doing until after I'd gotten to the desk and sat down: It had been checking for Mephenes. Waiting for something to happen.

The feed chirped. Catalan. "What have you brought me this time?" she said, in her usual perpetually-annoyed-but-not-really tone.

"They brought themselves. What's the matter, they don't bathe enough?"

"You've brought me a shipload of lesbian aliens, is what's the matter. All my sprockets are disappointed; we've been all these cycles with barely any business and now they find out they're still out of luck."

"'Lesbian' is unprovable and probably inapplicable—"

"You know what I mean. Every last one of them is a socket and they only want other innies."

"Interesting. Take notes—you might be breaking new research ground here." Her reply was a noise—half half-chuckle, half-grunt.

Of course Catalan just wanted to see if it would startle me, but it was definitely gossip worth having. I'm no more an anthropologist than she is, but I certainly had never heard of a dual-sex species with a dominant same-sex preference—highest ratio I've ever been told of is about half—and neither had she, or she'd have mentioned it.

Of course, it could also be that Mephenes deliberately picked such people for ship crews. Single-sex crews were common, for various reasons which you can probably guess, and it was only a short step from there. Stranger criteria have been used.

This was only fourteen cycles after Glor and the other former Tanngrevers had left, so it's possible some topics were in my brain a little more prominently than they otherwise would have been. Even at the docks, the "oh, another group of people who are dressing to conceal their gender" idea had sprung up—and I had promptly stomped it back down. Anybody can prefer loose clothing.

"Do they seem secretive or touchy about it?" I asked.

"Maybe. It's hard to tell if that's a sore subject, because they don't talk."

"They can talk."

"Sure, they can talk. They talk when they say what they want; they talk when they pay. But they don't say a word when their clothes are off."

"That sounds to me like it's a sore subject. Well, don't push, not that you would. But let me know if you find out anything else interesting."

She disconnected. I accessed the data station, created a new MEPHENES file, and started to take some notes.

§

I wandered around deck five for a while, still feeling like the other shoe was going to drop at any moment, but if Mephenes drank or brawled or even shopped, they weren't doing it where I could see or hear them. Eventually I gave up and went to have dinner. I'd have gone to poke around Catalan's, but I tried not to bother them when they were busy.

After dinner I ended up having to deal with a minor fight in Sugarland—not Mephenes—which ended up in my taking a permanent to Custody to spend until next cycle cooling down, and by the time I had finished that up I was thinking of heading home for some sleep, since whatever excitement the Mephenes had brought didn't seem to be touching me. I was making my way up to deck two when Catalan got on the feed.

"I've got a dead Mephene."

It was a relief, in a way, to no longer be waiting for it. "Violence?"

"Looks like it from here. I'm not touching anything."

"Good. Keep everyone from doing that and keep anyone from leaving. I'll be right there with some help."

Rob and Don made double time; maybe they'd been bored too. I walk fast and had contacted them while I was in motion, but we all got to Catalan's at the same time. The parlor was full of noise and it wasn't pleasant conversation. Lee was working the door. "Unhappy customers," I remarked.

"A Dispatch bigwig is stirring them all up," she said to me in a half-whisper. "The big one over by the bar."

They were all beginning to notice I was there—or maybe they noticed Rob and Don. "Quiet! Quiet, please. Everybody be quiet ... *everybody shut up or you can all sleep here!"*

Silence.

"That's better. In case you don't know me, I'm Jessica Gray, the security officer. Rob and Don act on my behalf. Right now they're going to need to detain everybody a short while until we figure out what's going on. I'll try to make it as quick as possible. In the meantime, if you could please stay in this room and keep it down to a low roar—"

The bigwig lumbered up to me. Lee had not meant "tall" when she said "big." "Do you know who I am?"

"Michael McGregor, Assistant Director of Dispatch," I said. "Is this a test?"

"I can't just stand around in this place all night. I have very important business to perform at six next cycle and I need sleep! Is there no way you can expedite this process?"

"For you in particular? No. If you manage to convince everyone in this room, including my men, that you should be first in line when we interview all of you, then more power to you. You should all be out of here by thirty-two or thirty-three anyway."

"By thirty-three! That's outrageous."

I sighed. "Then you should let me get on with my job and maybe we can make it sooner." He wasn't budging. "Look," I said, lowering my voice for just him. "You report directly to the Director. So do I. That puts us on the same tier. You'll get to go home at thirty-three and get some sleep. I likely won't. If we both have to report to the boss at roughly the same time next cycle, which of us is going to be in better condition and which of us deserves more sympathy? Now go sit down, or I'm going to consider you suspicious and you'll be the last one to leave."

Catalan entered the room. "There you are," I said. "Don, watch the door. Rob, take down the usual info for everyone here; I'll let you know shortly if anyone needs to stay." I gestured to McGregor. "If his lordship here tries to pressure you, tell him you work for me." I said it loudly enough for McGregor to hear it.

Yes, it was probably bad politics to deliberately puncture one of the boss's three seconds-in-command, the man who basically ran Dispatch. But I can't stand it when people try to pull rank, especially in situations where it doesn't apply. A baron has just as much chance of being a murderer as a peasant, and often more opportunity.

Catalan led me to the last door on the right of one of the back halls. Paul, one of her staff, was standing in front of it. At a look from Catalan, he left the area, and I opened the door. I'd been in Catalan's many times by then, but had never actually seen the inside of a work room before. It was a fairly nice bedroom—interchangeable decor, nothing you'd remember five minutes after you saw it, but there'd been effort to make it look like a place you'd actually want to fool around. Not clinical.

Of course, the effect was spoiled by the long gray corpse on the floor by the bed. It lay facedown, in the middle of what I took to be a black outline on the rug for just a moment, until I realized the black stain had come from the body. From something on the other side of the body.

"No visible cause on this side," Dr. Kohl's voice said behind me. Perfect timing. He pulled on gloves and crouched beside the corpse. "With your permission—"

"Go ahead," I said. I had expected him to fuss when I asked him to come to the scene, and he hadn't. Another one who might have been bored.

He turned the body over. Now it was on its back; the limbs fell in odd positions. The eyes had gone cloudy and both mouths were open. Catalan made either a low growl or a moan. Of course, it was Catalan, so for all I know she was only reacting to her ruined carpet.

There was a small wound in the upper torso, but Dr. Kohl was devoting his attention and his lens to the gaping wound, the same black as the stain on the rug, where the Mephene's genitalia had been removed. Completely excised. Not cleanly. An enormous black gash between the legs.

"Their blood clots very quickly, even under pressure," he muttered. "The vessels have closed themselves. Unless perhaps this body was moved—"

Douglas Todd

Catalan shook her head. "This is the room they went into."

"Then that settles it. Even if there hadn't been evidence that this wound was administered post-mortem, they didn't die of this. I realize it doesn't look it, but trust me. This wouldn't have bled out fast enough. They would have been able to get help."

"What's the other evidence it was done post-mortem?" I asked.

"These cuts wouldn't have looked the same if the victim had given any kind of resistance. This wound wouldn't have killed them, but it certainly would have been painful. If it wasn't post-mortem, then the victim was surely at least unconscious."

"Right. Implement?"

"That's an excellent question. Have you searched this room yet? A blade, but with a jagged edge, I think. This wound looks more like something had sawed through it. I'm going to want to do a real autopsy. Given the political circumstances, we might want to ask permission."

"Permission for what?" asked a bland voice from the hall. I turned. It was the Mephene speaker.

"Did Don let you in? I'll have to fuss at him."

"No," Catalan said. "They were in the next room at the time."

The speaker nodded. "I heard the events clearly."

"Don!" Don ran up. "Has Rob finished taking names? He can do that and keep an eye on the door too. When he's got them all, tell him he can let them go home. No interviews. Tell him to make sure they don't take anything out with them that isn't theirs. You take this to an unoccupied room and guard them. Be careful; they're meaner than they look. I'll take them to Custody when I'm done."

I expected the speaker to protest, but they said nothing, nor did they give the least struggle as Don led them off.

"Doctor, would you oblige me by giving this room a quick search? You won't find anything, but we have to make sure." I turned to Catalan. "Who was with

178

the Mephene in this room?" The back of my brain already knew what she was going to say; it had detected someone obvious missing from the scene.

"Meridian," she said.

"Where is Meridian?"

I would love to know, knowing everything I did later, how many different answers passed through her mind before she said the one she finally said.

"Safe."

I locked eyes with her for all of a sub, then broke away. "I guess there's not really anywhere she can go. No luck, Dr. Kohl? Thought not." I got out the feed. "Is this the head of sanitation? Good. Security. The digesters run fairly late in the cycle, right? Excellent. Don't run them this cycle. Don't run them again until I give you the okay. Yes, that's official ... you can check it with the Director if you like, but cancel the run first and check it later. This is very important. Make sure your people get the word. Thank you."

Next. "Dispatch? Security. Do you have any traffic for the next several periods? Good. I'm freezing all transit. Yes, that's what I said. I am prepared to have that verified. Ideally it won't affect you at all; I hope to have what I want by the end of your slow period anyway. Thank you."

I had never expected to ever be able to impress Catalan. "I didn't know you could do that," she said.

"I wouldn't want to do it often."

"Either you're jumping the gun a bit," Dr. Kohl said, "or you're far ahead of me."

"I'll have to explain in full later," I said, "but just this for now: There's a weapon and a ... severed item somewhere on this Ring. The killer removed them from this room. Not just anybody can open an unused airway or airlock, and not without alerting Dispatch. So they're not out in space. These items are either hidden somewhere on the Ring, or hidden somewhere on a docked ship, or have been thrown down a waste chute. Really, I'm just being paranoid about the first two because none of the Mephenes on the premises at the time had a chance to leave, and Rob won't let them out carrying anything like that. So they're either on the premises, or in the waste system. Catalan has a waste chute in her kitchen. Doctor, I'm afraid I'm going to have to ask for your help searching the place; I have another job for Rob and Don."

"I'll help as well," Catalan said.

"I'd rather you didn't," I replied. "Officially, one of your workers is a murder suspect. I know damned well you're trustworthy, but it would look bad. Bad enough she's not here."

"You know she didn't do it."

"What I know and what I can prove may not have much to do with one another. How many other Mephenes were customers at the time? How many in this stretch of hall?"

"I'd have to check the desk record; they've been coming in all day like crazy. But this stretch of hall, none but those two. They were overflow. I was sending most of them into the antispinward rooms."

I nodded. "Doctor, I'll join you in a moment. I'd check the room the speaker was in first. I have to go talk to Rob and Don about something unpleasant."

§

I got home earlier than expected. I'd arrived at Catalan's near thirty; my saying "thirty-two or thirty-three" to McGregor was based on how long it would have taken to interview everyone. Deciding not to interview cut that time back a lot, but we'd still spent most of two periods searching Catalan's—not helped by the fact that I had to detour to take the speaker to Custody when I wanted to send Rob and Don elsewhere. (Mental note: It was probably past time to give one or both of them access to the Custody door.) Then there'd been the time spent getting the body back to Dr. Kohl's. (Made faster, though, when I learned that he'd gone several decks out of his way to bring a cargo trolley with him. It was a shame I didn't pay Dr. Kohl myself; I'd have given him a bonus.)

Of course the people who were definitely getting bonuses—hazard-pay bonuses—were poor Rob and Don, who were presumably walking through piles of Ring waste in protective suits at that very moment.

All in all it was probably close to my original estimate—somewhere between thirty-two and thirty-three—when I entered my rooms, dead tired, stripping out of my clothes on my beeline for the bedroom ... and found there was someone in my bed.

Meridian woke up when I turned on the light, rolled over to look up at me, squinting. "Hi."

"How did you get in?"

"Catalan let me in. I guess you never took her off the door."

"I didn't know she was *on* the door. Why would Catalan have had access to ... huh. Really?"

"I thought you knew. They were very close. The joke was the only time Catalan ever left the shop was to come visit Pete."

"I had no idea." All of a sudden I had a flashback to Max saying about Alsop's belongings, "Nah, she'd have taken anything she wanted." With unexpected clarity, like he was standing next to me. I'm so sorry I blew it, Max. "So that's where she'd disappeared to when I got there." I sat down on the bed. "You know she's put me in a difficult place, hiding you here."

"I didn't kill him!" She was more upset than she looked, I realized. I hadn't expected it because I'd never seen Meridian seriously rattled before. I crawled into bed next to her and turned out the light. She put her arms around me and we just lay there for a while.

"You're going to have to tell me about it," I said.

"We had just finished." Her voice was cold, but steady. "About to get dressed. He said something to me, but it was in his own language, I didn't understand it. He didn't look or sound upset or threatening, he was like—well, like customers are afterward, calm, sorta slow-moving. But then the door opened and another one came in. They had a blue mark on their head. That one was upset, very upset. They said to me in Trade to get out right now. I thought they might have gone a little nuts. They had been in the next room with Rose, so I went in to see if she was okay; she was still in bed, she was startled they'd had run out on her but she was fine. So I went back to my room, and mine was—on the floor—" She shook a little then, and I let her grip me tighter.

"Where was the speaker then? I mean the one with the blue mark."

"They'd left. I didn't see where they went. I went to find Catalan—"

"Why did Catalan take you here? You could have just stayed and told me what happened when I got there. The speaker didn't run and you did. That looks bad."

"Catalan. When I told her about it she said, 'We need to get you somewhere safe,' and she took me here."

"I may need to have a little talk with Catalan about conduct during murder investigations," I said.

"Oh, don't! You know Catalan—you know she thinks we're all her kids. She was just trying to keep me out of trouble."

"Well, she might have put you in it instead."

I lay for a while not saying anything, until she took me by the chin and turned my head to face hers.

"I'm telling you the truth," she said.

"I know," I said. "Even if I thought you weren't, I can't think of a single motive for you unless your customer attacked you. No, it was either the speaker, or some other Mephene ran in and out to do it. But why? And what do we do about it?"

"I'm sorry I made a mess."

"You didn't make it," I said, kissing her forehead. "Go back to sleep."

I had nearly drifted off myself when the back of my brain signaled me. The back of my brain seemed to be doing most of the heavy lifting that cycle. "Meridian?"

"Mmmm?"

"You called the Mephene 'he.'"

"Mm. Yeah. Shoulda said 'they.' Sorry. Sprocket."

"You did just say they were a sprocket?"

"Uh-huh."

I let her go back to sleep. Either she'd been too sleepy to realize that was strange or Catalan hadn't told her. My brain wasn't sure what to do with that information yet, but I was too tired to churn it much just then.

§

I hadn't actually had to report to the boss at six—I just said that for McGregor's benefit. But she hailed me around six anyway. "Boss," I said, rubbing my eyes. "Sorry to have stirred up the nest." Right after I said that I realized I wasn't sure whether I'd ever called her "Boss" to her face before.

Of course even if it annoyed her she gave no sign of it. "You don't do things without a reason. But if you're going through the waste, do it fast. Maintenance says they can't accommodate more than another few periods of buildup."

"I have people on it, since late last cycle," I said.

"Also, McGregor has complained to me that you've overstepped your authority in freezing all transit—"

"McGregor was at the scene of the crime last cycle and is nursing a grudge because I refused to give him a free pass," I said. "I don't expect to have to maintain freeze beyond another period or two, and there's no traffic right now anyway."

"Which is fortunate. Although I don't agree with McGregor that you've overstepped your authority, we cannot delay transit schedules any significant amount except in dire circumstances. Do what you need to do before the slack period ends. One final item. The captain of the Mephene vessel is indignant that their speaker has been placed in Custody without cause—they say. I replied that I found their assertion difficult to believe."

"Oh, there's cause. The speaker isn't just the number-one suspect; they're pretty much the whole list. Of course the investigation would go faster if I could be assured they wouldn't make a fuss over our performing an autopsy on the victim ..."

"I'm sure they would be willing to accept that, if they were led to believe their departure depended on it. If they don't accept it, do it anyway if you need to. But get this straightened out quickly."

She disconnected. I lay back and thought about Alsop and Catalan, and wondered if the boss had some kind of relationship I didn't know about. I hoped it wasn't with McGregor.

The feed chirped again. This time it was Rob. "Boss, we got it."

"Got which?"

"Both. The knife, definitely, and what we're pretty sure is the, um, item."

I sat up. "That was fast work."

"We figured it went in from Catalan's, right? So Don went to Maintenance and found out which waste tanks were closest to that."

"Genius. You've earned yourselves a drink on top of the danger money. One more favor for me. Bring the stuff to Dr. Kohl. Then you're off-duty."

"The stuff?" Meridian said, sitting up as I disconnected.

"Less I tell you the better."

She made a face. "Unfair."

"How do I make this clear? You are a murder suspect. One who is getting unusually good treatment at the hands of the investigator."

"Not that good," she said, with an evil smile. "We didn't even get to do anything last night."

"I'm serious," I said. "I'm going to get up and go interview the speaker in a few subs, and the first thing they're going to say is, 'So, where's the human suspect? Of course that's one of your race and not some filthy alien like us, so it's no less than we'd expect from human justice.' The captain's already making noises about my detaining the speaker at all."

"Oh." She stopped smiling. "If that's the way it is, shouldn't you go ahead and put me in Custody too? I mean, it sounds like I'm making it worse if I stay here."

"Are you volunteering to be taken into custody?"

"If you think it would be better. Do I deny that we, you know, see each other?"

"I think too many people know about that to deny it. Anyway, no one will be asking you any questions but me. A better point is, what do I say when the speaker asks why it took me so long to haul you in?"

"I've been hiding somewhere. I got a temporary room or holed up with friends or something."

I moved to the shower. "It's up to you. If you do come out, you're committed. If you don't, I'll try to remember to bring you some food later."

"Hey!" She got up and came over. "What is it? You're not really mad at me, I can tell. What's the problem?"

I sighed. "I think this is going to end up with me sending the speaker back to their ship. And I can't think of any reason why I shouldn't do that. One Mephene killing another for unknown reasons, no one else affected—we should let them settle that, it's not really our problem. But I need to know. And if I can't figure it out very quickly I'm never going to find out."

"Let me clean up too. You can take me with you to Custody."

"All right."

"At least that way I know you have to feed me," she said. "How you manage to live here with absolutely no food, I don't know."

§

On the way down I spoke to Dr. Kohl and told him to cut if he needed to, and spoke to Dispatch and Maintenance to formally open everything again. I was beginning to get pretty good at using the feed while walking.

After stopping for breakfast, and locking Meridian into a custody room with hers, I entered the speaker's room. They showed utterly no sign of being interested in me or the tray of food I set beside them.

"I don't have information about Mephene dietary requirements," I said. "If none of that is acceptable, give me some specifics and I'll go get something else."

No sale.

I sat down. "Do you understand that you're under suspicion of murder?"

"Yes. I am uncertain why, but I suppose it is always simpler to blame the alien."

"Being a suspect isn't the same as being blamed," I said, controlling my wince, "and there are other suspects."

"Is she here? Have you even attempted to look for her?"

"She is, and that's not your concern right now. Tell me what happened."

They rocked their head from side to side. I couldn't tell what the gesture was supposed to mean.

"I went with others to your sex house. I had sexual activity with a human. Afterward my assigned partner and I were in bed when there was the sound of some violent activity in the next room. I recognized one of the voices as one of my crewmates, and as you yourself said, I am responsible for their behavior, so I went in. I found the body of my crewmate. No one else was in the room. I did not disturb the body. I went to go find the woman in charge of the house, and by the time I did, you had arrived with your others. You know the rest."

"Did your crewmate carry a knife or blade of any kind?"

They nodded, unsurprised. "All do. Except myself. Those of my role are not permitted."

"Would they have had the knife with them at the time?"

"'They' meaning my crewmate? She would have had it with her at all times, even there."

"Why 'she'?"

"I don't understand."

"We were under the impression you had only one sex. In the languages here, generally when a species has only a single sex, we use 'they.'"

"Of course, you would have learned that from the people at the sex house. Why would you call the ones we partnered with 'she' and not call us 'she' as well?"

"Whichever you prefer," I said. "So you do only have one sex, then?"

"Why do you ask this? Can this in any way be important to this death?" She was talking with her lower mouth while simultaneously breathing through her upper mouth, a disconcerting habit I wouldn't have noticed if her breathing hadn't begun to get louder and more obvious. I couldn't decide if it was stress or annoyance.

"The victim's genitals were cut off. Probably with their own knife. So it could be pertinent, yes."

"'Her' own knife."

"So you have only one sex, then?" I repeated.

"—Yes." It was definitely annoyance. Or she was trying to make it look like annoyance.

"So if I have a report that says the victim was of the opposite sex ..."

"'Opposite sex' meaning what?"

"Protruding genitals instead of crevice. Sprocket instead of socket."

"Not possible," it said.

"Thank you," I said, standing up. "This interview has been very helpful."

"That is all you ask? What about the other suspect? Do you ask her irrelevant, rude questions and then leave? This is a farce!"

"Oh, don't worry," I said, "I haven't nearly finished asking you questions. Do let me know if none of the food is edible. I don't want you to starve."

§

"Your timing is good," Dr. Kohl said when I entered. "I'd just finished."

"Actual cause of death?"

"We'll have to say 'heart failure.' Your heart does fail when it's been cut open, after all."

"Through that little hole?"

"Oh, you noticed that before? You didn't remark on it at the time. Still, you were preoccupied. Personally, I was too distracted by the large wound. Yes, the knife was pushed in and rotated in place and sawed around without notably broadening the entrance wound. It partially severed what I take to be the aorta—their heart is not quite the same shape as ours, but it's clearly the primary artery—and tore two chambers of the heart. The killer was practiced or lucky. Their self-sealing mechanism is remarkable; they essentially can't bleed out ... but the same mechanism works against them for this sort of injury. The heart remnants filled with clotted blood immediately; even if the heart had still been attempting to function, that would have stopped it. They must have died almost instantly."

"She."

"Pardon?"

"I'm informed," I said, "that the correct pronoun for all Mephenes, including dead ones, is 'she.'"

"So they use 'she' for sprockets, then?"

"No, for sockets. Were you able to identify what Rob and Don found?"

"I not only could identify it, I could practically match it bend for bend with the wound. I hope you pay those two well." He went to the drawer with the corpse and removed two sealed bags. One had the knife—a thin, flexible blade, sawtoothed in decreasing width on both sides, coming to a point. The other had a blackish object in it which I would never have been able to identify on its own, but when Dr. Kohl laid the bag atop the wound a certain way it became evident. "Furthermore this knife is exactly the sort of weapon to have done the job. Both jobs."

"More than that—unless we've gone very wrong, it was the actual weapon. It was the victim's own, by the way. Doctor, we have a riddle. We have an entire staff at Catalan's who insist that every Mephene they've taken to bed is a socket—which is apparently quite a few of them. We have a Mephene who insists that their species has only one physical sex, and that's socket. And then we have Meridian, who insists that she had gone to bed with a sprocket just before they died, and we have a chunk of anatomy to prove her right. How would you proceed?"

He scratched his ear. "I can't speculate based on their internal anatomy. Their heart was obviously a heart. Their lungs are obviously lungs. That's about as far as I'd want to go. They're mammalian, and this one has mammaries, which proves nothing. Their reproductive system apart from that is ... I can't call it 'odd' only because I don't recognize enough of it to be able to use that word."

"I know we've never seen them before, but Dispatch says we're not first contact— is there *any* literature? Any knowledge of them you can dig up? Anything we can find out would help."

"I'll look," he said. "If a human doctor or scientist encountered them at any point, they probably published a paper fifteen minutes later. The question will be whether our medical library has it."

"Do what you can. I'll go wander where I'm not wanted."

§

I had to speak Bak'ti to some flunky to get through the airlock and into the ship, but when the Mephene captain tried to speak Bak'ti to me, I'd had enough. I made it clear I wanted a private chat, and when the two of us were alone in her ready room, I said, "I know you speak Pergati. You'd have had a hard time complaining about me to Dispatch in Bak'ti." And it was much more likely than Trade, for a captain.

She exhaled loudly through her upper mouth. Then she said, in Pergati, "I speak to you this way only because you waited until we are alone."

"I take it no one but the speaker is supposed to seriously interact with outsiders."

She nodded. "It is ... I suppose you would call it a professional restriction."

"Union rules. I get it. I won't tell."

"When are you going to release my speaker?"

"Your speaker is the only plausible suspect for the murder of another Mephene," I said. "Under the circumstances, the question is less 'when' I will release her and more 'whether' I will release her."

"Even if she has, it is not your concern! Return her to us! I promise you she will be punished appropriately."

"Not happy to try to get through Pergati space without her? I don't know why not. Your Pergati is excellent."

"Your humor is unwelcome. I will make sure your government knows of this offense against us."

"No, you won't. Because if we mention to the Pergati government how you brought a full shipload of qov to this station, your government will have greater things to worry about."

"We have brought no contraband to this station."

"See, your command of nuance is perfect! It's true—you haven't brought contraband to this station. We don't consider it contraband. As soon as you jump through the Ring, though, you're in Pergati space and then it does become contraband, and they won't like you having brought it here in the first place."

"I tell you that we are bringing no contraband into Pergati space."

"Fine," I said. "Have it your way. It's not important. Let's try another approach. We don't like murders being committed on the Ring even if they're someone else's business. If I want to hold your speaker, and I make a good case for it, I'll be allowed to. If I want to push your speaker out an airlock and I make a sufficient case, I'll be allowed to. My boss likes making examples. If you'd like your speaker back—and I make no guarantees—the best hope you have is cooperating with me, and answering my questions. Including the ones you don't want to answer."

Her breathing was becoming annoyed. "Ask, then."

"Tell me about the other kind of Mephenes."

I knew she was lying immediately because she didn't look confused by the question; like the Speaker, she had gone straight to stonewalling. "There is no other kind of Mephene."

OK, I'd play along. "Do you understand the term 'genitalia'?"

Glare. "Of course."

"Are there not Mephenes whose genitalia are different from yours?" I presumed she was also a socket, but I phrased it so that no matter what she personally had under the caftan, the question was meaningful.

She exhaled loudly through her upper mouth again. "I suppose your sex women have been telling you things not theirs to say. Your information is wrong. We have only one anatomy. And this is not business for aliens."

"Alien" is considered a mildly xeno rudeness on the Ring. Sometimes people are joking around when they use it, like Catalan had. The way the captain said it was no joke. If they all felt like that, I wondered, why did so many of them rush off to go have sex with women of other species as soon as they arrived?

"It's become my business. We have testimony that the slain Mephene was of a different sex."

"Impossible," she replied firmly.

"Captain," I said, "I don't plan to drag your species' personal secrets into public view. I don't care about them. I'm just trying to solve a murder. I have evidence that says you have two physical sexes. You and your speaker both say you have only one. Someone is lying."

"Your evidence is wrong," she said. "Did you want to ask any other questions?" She was so visibly upset that I couldn't bring myself to keep trying.

"Yes. How common is it for members of your species to commit crimes of violence against one another?"

She closed her eyes.

"Has it happened? What's the murder rate like on Mephin?"

"Seldom," she said. "But it has been known to happen. If you have no better questions, please leave."

§

I checked in on Meridian. "How are you doing?"

"Bored to tears. At least bring me a data pad or something."

"Like this one?" I held it up.

"Oh! All is forgiven. Or nearly all. Hey—this is mine!"

"Mm-hm. Stopped by Catalan's. Have fun."

I didn't expect my next interview to be as entertaining, although there was a possibility it would be as brief. The speaker hadn't eaten any breakfast. "A hunger strike will do you no good," I said, "and if you're thinking that you won't eat until you get back to your ship, I urge you to reconsider."

"You are going to keep me from leaving?"

"I'm certainly thinking about it. I'm tired of getting blocked on all fronts. You're going to have to give me something concrete if you want to get out of here, and you're going to have to do it fast." I sat down. "Look. It is undeniable that the dead Mephene was a different gender from you. We have found the knife and the part you cut off."

That hit her. I thought her upper mouth was going to choke. "You could not have—"

"You'd be amazed what you can do if you search the garbage quickly enough," I said. "Now, is there any information you'd like to volunteer?"

That was the first time since meeting her that I'd actually felt sympathy. She *almost* managed it. There was very clearly something she wanted to say, if she didn't have heart failure first. That upper mouth was better than a lie detector. But she repaired the wall and shook her head.

"I can keep secrets," I said. "I know you don't believe that, but I can. If you tell me about the other Mephene sex, and it's a state secret, it won't have to leave this room."

"We. Have. Only. One. Sex."

I shrugged. "OK. I'll go try to pressure your captain again—"

"No!"

I gave her a look.

She tilted her head from side to side, in that gesture she'd used before, and this time I was pretty sure I knew it for what it was: *Whatever, what the hell.* "Talk to her if you like. It doesn't matter."

She looked away and ignored me. I got the feeling she'd just given up completely on something, like admitting defeat. But I had no idea what.

"Is there some lunch food you'd like better?"

No reply.

§

In practice, I wasn't completely sure I could make the speaker miss her ship. I'd certainly need some better reason than my unfulfilled sense of justice to convince my boss, or the Mephenes. I didn't want to give McGregor any further cause to say I was overstepping.

There was something I just wasn't getting. I felt like a bad detective because I hadn't even tried for any other motives, but the back of my brain kept telling me not to bother—this was the only road that led anywhere. I'd have liked to interrogate the back of my brain and ask how it could be so sure.

Why cut it off? Even if the speaker had been, say, an angry ex-lover who saw an opportunity while off-ship, why cut it off and make the crime from something relatively run-of-the-mill into something strange enough that even stupid humans couldn't possibly help noticing? Revenge for a past sexual assault was the only thing I could come up with. But while a rape victim might certainly be so traumatized/ashamed of the assault as to deny it ever happened, that didn't explain the statements from the captain—and it wasn't really the best fit for the speaker's denials either.

Cut it off just to keep people from knowing there were Mephenes with sockets? If so, that clearly wasn't well thought-out. Then again, how many crimes were?

Catalan hailed me on the feed. "How long are you going to be keeping my best employee?"

"Is she your best employee? You got her in a lot of trouble, you know. Why'd you put her in my room—that I didn't know you could get into?"

"Yes, I knew you didn't know when the door still worked. I thought someone would have told you by now."

"Never mind that. I'm sorry he's gone. I wish I'd met him. But why take her away at all? It would have been much better to ride it out there. She was never going to be a serious suspect."

"I thought, that Mephene might want to kill the others who were there, you see? Witnesses. Meridian didn't see anything but maybe the Mephene didn't know that. So I got someone here to watch Rose, but Meridian—"

"You thought that was the safest place to put her."

"If it let me in, yes. I figured, anything that would get her would have to go through you—I'm sorry I didn't warn you."

"Don't apologize," I said. "I'm flattered. As for Meridian, don't worry. She's enjoying the vacation. This will be over in a cycle one way or another."

§

"The upper one isn't really a mouth," Dr. Kohl was saying. "It's a nose. They inhale through it to breathe and smell things. They can actually breathe through both mouths, but they prefer the upper, especially when they're excited or upset or what-have-you."

"So I've noticed. Sorry, Doctor, didn't mean to spoil your fun. Too much close-quarters field observation of angry Mephenes. Carry on."

Dr. Kohl was owed a drink. Several drinks. He'd gone above and beyond the call of duty searching old, mostly unindexed data to find any traces of information on Mephenes.

"Ah, but the interesting thing," he continued, "is that they also *exhale* smells through that upper mouth. Different odors depending on mood. One smell for angry, one for excited, so on. Very pungent, says the paper, in terms of parts per million exhaled, but we can't tell at all. Our noses don't seem to be able to receive those frequencies."

"Fascinating," I said, politely. He shot me a look.

"It's powerful enough for a group effect," he said. "One Mephene having a bad day and suddenly the whole office is unhappy."

"Wait. So they can sense—not just sense, actually absorb—agitation in each other? Would that be strong enough to carry between rooms at Catalan's?"

"Finally. I was wondering how far in I'd have to go to get you to pay attention."

"I'm sorry; I shouldn't have doubted you. Is there anything else I should know?"

"Yes. But it's not nearly as definite, I'm afraid. Remember I said their reproductive system was beyond odd? One of these papers has a theory that could explain the problems you're having ..."

§

"I've brought you lunch," I said to the speaker. "I'm sorry it's a little late. I had some other business to attend to." I set it down, and I sat down too.

"Your ship is leaving early next cycle," I said. "I've already made the decision to let it leave. I haven't yet made the decision whether you'll be on it."

No response.

"I need to tell you a few things, because we need to both be clear where we stand. First, Meridian. The only reason I'm not releasing her right now is to prevent other Mephenes from possibly deciding she needs to die. I'm letting her out as soon as your ship leaves. For all your fuss, you know perfectly well there has never been any conceivable motive why a human on this Ring would want to kill a member of a species none of us had ever encountered two cycles ago. If you suggest we're all alien-haters here, I'll slap you and hand you a mirror. And no other Mephene was in a position to do it. So if you're still hoping the idea someone else murdered that Mephene still has a chance, forget it.

"Second. I've learned that you exhale pheromones—like smells—when in the grip of some strong mood, and when you do it affects others of you in the area. I suppose that makes some things in life very difficult. It might even explain why such xeno creatures were all so eager to rush off and go have sex with another species, if I worked at it enough. Armed with this information and other facts, I have a pretty good idea what happened late last cycle.

"Third. I don't actually have any particular reason to want to get you into trouble. I'm annoyed that you tried to frame a human, but that was never going to stick anyway. I don't want to get you hurt, or killed. So I'm going to ask you: Knowing everything you know, knowing everything your captain knows, all things considered, should I send you back to your ship or should I keep you here?"

Nothing. She stared at me. She looked like she was prepared to stare at me for the rest of the cycle.

"So it is my decision after all, then," I said, and got up. "Eat some lunch."

§

I was not received well in the Mephene ship.

"You're cleared to depart on schedule, Captain," I said when the two of us were alone. "But there are a few things I'm going to tell you first. You're not going to like them. In fact, you're going to dislike them so much that I have brought a weapon with me in case you decide to get violent"—I showed her my baton—"and I have two men outside who are going to take certain actions if I don't emerge from here alive and well in fifteen subs. So listen, because this will have to be fast."

§

I entered Custody at ten the next cycle and opened Meridian's room. "About time," she said. "The meal service in this place is horrible." She was making light, but I could see she hadn't slept well. Jail is no fun even if you're not really a prisoner.

"No more meals on the house for you," I said. "You're out. Hit the streets. Find a shower and your own breakfast. I'd have let you go earlier but I was waiting on something."

She gave me a hug. "How did it come out?"

"It's not done coming out yet," I said. "Go do your thing. I'll fill you in later. By the way," I said, "I've changed my door list. It doesn't let Catalan in any more. But it does let you in. Don't ambush me in my sleep."

"Never," she said, smiling. "You'd probably throw me through a wall."

The speaker had said nothing when I brought her dinner the previous cycle, and I had said nothing to her. She hadn't eaten any of that either, and I wasn't sure she had slept the whole time she was in Custody. Her hair was sort of matted in clumps and she looked absolutely miserable. "I didn't bring you any food this time," I said, "because I thought you would like to find your own. Your ship went through the Ring half a period ago. I'm releasing you."

She said something I couldn't hear. "What was that?"

"I said, it doesn't matter. They will kill me anyway."

"No, they won't," I said, "and I'll be happy to tell you why, if for once we can actually speak with some kind of honesty. You know, I now realize why it's in the nature of your species to clamp down when things go wrong, but it's not always a very good strategy."

She sat up straight, and began to run her fingers through her hair to untangle it. But she didn't say anything.

"I guess I have to go first again," I said. "One last time. All right. I think you and your captain weren't lying. I think you were telling the truth when you said Mephenes have one sex, because to you it is one sex. It's just that it's one sex that can change forms. The doctor found a paper which suggested retractable erectile tissue ... eh, you know, let's skip the details. The point is, sometimes you're a socket and sometimes a sprocket. But usually you're a socket. I don't know if switching to the other is seasonal, hormonal, voluntary ..."

"Voluntary," she said. "But very wrong."

"Yes, I figured out that part. You use the sprocket form only for breeding? And the places and times that's allowed to happen are very restricted. And a big secret. So big a secret that you never, never discuss it. Possibly even under penalty of death."

"There is no 'possibly.' I have already passed the point where any of my people who knew what I had said or done would have to kill me on sight. You don't understand how seriously this is taken. They will come back for me and kill me!"

"No, they won't. The only person who has anything to uphold is the captain. All of my conversations with her were strictly private, because she didn't want to admit to anyone that she speaks Pergati. You folks do love your secrets. And the captain is not going to pursue the matter because I'm blackmailing her."

"You are—what?"

"You understand 'blackmail,' yes? If she causes any trouble, I will have it spread that *she* told us the secret of your genders. I've left a trail of false information—all locked well, unless she does something rash, like trying to kill you or me or Meridian or one of several other things. The captain is upset at losing her speaker, and she takes her customs seriously—but captains are practical people first and foremost, I've noticed, and she doesn't want to risk her commerce or her skin. You'll be fine. You could probably even go back to your planet, if you wanted. There are four humans on this Ring who even have an inkling of the Mephene secret, and none of them is going to say a word. The body goes in the digesters. My boss thinks it was a crime of self-defense and you're being allowed to stay here because Mephene justice is far too harsh. She thinks I'm a little soft-hearted, but she doesn't really care so long as it's cleaned up."

"Why would you do this for me?"

"No. Your turn again first. Tell me what actually happened at Catalan's."

"It is ... a known problem. But never discussed. It is wrong to even admit the problem is there."

"The victim was a sexual deviant, by your species' standards. They liked doing it as a sprocket." She nodded. "And you could smell it, in a manner of speaking, when they did."

"Smell, yes, but that is not enough word. We ... we enjoy being near each other when ... when aroused; if one is, others around us are too. But that smell is different. It is impossible to ignore. It was unexpected."

"Are you saying you might have killed them just because the smell drove you to it?"

"Killed? No ..." I deciphered her expression. She was embarrassed!

"I'm sorry; I realize this is hard—"

"... I would have needed to breed with her. Immediately."

"Oh."

She nodded, seeing I understood. "But when I entered, she was already finished and she was saying threatening things to the woman. The woman couldn't understand them, of course. She would have needed to kill her. No one could be allowed to know."

"Meridian didn't even realize it was a threat," I said. "She didn't think they looked angry. She thought you were the threatening one. When she came back from checking on your bedmate, you were gone. Dropping the evidence down the waste chute. Why did you stay around Catalan's? You could have made it out and gone back to your ship. It might not have gotten you out of trouble; Meridian could ID you, she saw your mark. But your odds would have been better."

"I was not thinking as if I was here," she said. "There were other Mephenes there; I thought it would be enough to rejoin them ... at home, if a body were found like that, everyone would know why, even though they would say nothing ... and though they would be obliged to kill whoever had seen the intact body as well, if that person were among others, if they could say they had no idea who had done it ..."

"Plausible deniability. Pardon my saying so, but you have a very messed-up system. And that's my answer to your question, by the way. When I told my boss I was keeping you here because the punishment was too harsh for the crime, it wasn't a lie. I can't send someone to their death for breaking a code that's so fundamentally stupid. All you did was defend yourself from ... well, sexual assault, in a way. Oh, and saved the life of a human whose involvement was absolutely accidental—who also happens to be someone important to me. So I'm supposed to let you be killed as your good conduct reward?"

"We would not see it that way," she said.

"I know. And if your guilt or whatever is so strong you can't stand it and you need to jump out an airlock, so be it. But I wish you wouldn't. I tell you, it's a stupid set of rules, and you shouldn't die for them. Do you need a loan? Money to get somewhere temporary to live?"

"No, I have that," she said. "I don't know what I will do now—"

"You speak ten languages," I said. "I'm sure you'll find something. Right now, I suggest you start by finding some breakfast. I would hate to save your life only to have you die of starvation."

And she made another gesture I hadn't realized Mephenes had in common with humans, because up to that point I had never seen a single one of them do it.

She smiled.

THE CASE of the HARD KICK

Twenty cycles after the Mephenes left—hopefully seldom, if ever, to return—I got summoned to upper cargo by Flanagan, of all people. "Bryant is down there running a crane," he said, "and he says you really ought to come have a look."

I got the sector number and went to have a look. Bryant's instincts were sound.

I haven't made this explicit before, but to enter the Ring from a docked ship, you climb up. If you think about the position ships dock in, relative to the Ring's rotation, you'll see why this has to be. Ships have airlocks on multiple sides, so they can deal with a variety of docking situations, but it doesn't matter which side of their ship they try to mate with the Ring ... as soon as they match spin with us, the side that's adjacent to the Ring becomes "up." So they always have to use an overhead port, with a ladder that lowers so you can climb up into it. On the other side of the port there's a ladder in our airway. (The airway also has its own pressure doors at the top, which are usually left open for convenience, but which close automatically if the ship is accidentally or deliberately thrown loose, as I've already noted.)

We have a couple of methods to get cargo up the airways. There are small portable hoists for the lighter stuff, which we can roll to the airway, like the one we had to use on the unfortunate ahpesh inspector. For larger, heavier things there are the cranes. But I had never before seen someone using a crane to lift living sentients out of their ship, one by one. Even the ahpesh manage to pull themselves up them somehow.

"Centaurs? Really?" I said to Bryant. He was one of five or six interchangeable Dispatch juniors—all young, tired, and ambitious. They did all the tedious jobs too Dispatch-y to give to other departments and too skilled to hire out to beefs.

"What's a 'centaur'?" he asked.

"Old mythology," I said. "Don't worry about it. What do they call themselves?"

"Humans, I guess," he said. "They're from a planet called Barl."

"Ah. Modders."

He nodded, concentrating on keeping the crane load from hitting the sides of the airway.

"Well, they'll find it nice and accessible," I said. There wasn't a staircase anywhere in the Ring. "I hope they don't have trouble using our toilets."

You may think I wasn't treating the Barlians or Barlites or Barlings or whatever they were with respect, and you'd be right. Bipeds, nature had already decided, were the best format for sentients unless you lived in the ocean. Evidence: the number of completely different species that had evolved to be bipeds, in parallel and with no connection to one another. To take a superior form and deliberately mod it back to a much more unwieldy one struck me as a project fairly worthy of ridicule.

Also, it surely meant that somewhere during their stay they were going to complain about something that hadn't been designed for them, and I was going to have to find a polite way to tell them to go to hell, so I might as well make jokes to myself while I could.

§

Alsop had encountered Barlings before. His notes didn't tell me much I couldn't already guess, though. Barl had been colonized by an anti-technology movement; it was deliberately kept mostly agrarian, very little urbanization or motorized transportation. Nine-tenths of all Barlings were farmers. This meant they had a food surplus, most of which wasn't worth the cost of shipping off-planet. In recent times they'd switched much of their production to crops which were either high-value enough to export or could be processed into something that was, so their presence in space was increasing slowly.

I wondered if there were any other unprocessed crops of sufficiently high value besides qov. Then again, it had only been a short while since the Mephenes, so I was probably imagining qov even in places I had no business suspecting it. I would have given a fair amount to know whether the Mephenes made it through the Pergati patrols, and if so, how.

I still wasn't sure where I stood on qov. It certainly looked like the Pergati restrictions on it were idiotic. On the other hand, rules are rules, even idiotic ones, and I liked staying friends with the Pergati. It wasn't a case of having to choose a side, because cracking down on qov wasn't going to annoy any humans except smugglers, and you can guess how little I cared about them. On the third hand, most Pergati on the ring seemed to use qov and disregard their own laws, so if I cracked down, would I be angering more of them than I was pleasing?

I wondered where Alsop had stood on the matter. He'd been here for a long time, so surely he'd reached his own conclusions. The problem was that Alsop tended to keep anything like personal opinion out of his notes. I wished he hadn't.

It did occur to me, though, that there was someone he might have discussed these things with. Also, while I was thinking about it, she might be able to help clear up another mystery.

§

"We never talked about work," Catalan said. "It was a rule. Everything else. Where we came from, what we were going to do when we both got too old for the Ring ..." Her eyes went distant.

"I'm sorry."

She shook her head. "It was only a dream and we knew it. Neither of us would stop. If we stopped we'd die. Imagine me a wife in a little retirement cottage somewhere. Counting off time. I'd either kill myself or kill him. Probably both. He'd have been the same. You're the same."

I nodded. I wasn't about to say something and interrupt the flow—but she cut herself off.

"Anyway, no, I can't tell you anything about that."

"How do *you* feel about qov?"

She shrugged. "I've seen worse. Do they still smoke tobacco on Earth?"

"I'm not the right person to ask. I think so. Probably."

"It's about like smoking, except you don't smell up the air around you and you don't die of cancer, so big deal. Just so long as they don't spit it out on the floor. Some of my staff say it makes their breath smell funny, but Pergati aren't kissers anyway. Their faces aren't built for it."

"Is there ... do you get a lot of, um, cross-species traffic with Pergati? I know, none of my business."

"Eh. Some. But only one way. We get a few human customers who want to try it with a Pergat. Pergati don't seem interested in humans. Pergati like to tussle. Dor says she has to remind herself to go gentle with the humans." She gave me one of her penetrating looks, from under those eyebrows. "What was the other thing you wanted to ask me that you're not asking me?"

"I think Alsop may have left something in his files for you." It had occurred to me the moment I'd realized they had been close, but I'd been worried about how to approach it.

"Show me."

I accessed Alsop's files on her data station and showed her the COR file. "It's encrypted on its own—it needs a password I don't have. Any idea what the password might be?"

Her eyes were distant again. She said something in a language I didn't know, then came back to the world. "Do I get more than one guess?"

"I've tried a few and it hasn't locked up yet." I stepped away. If it was really a message just for her, I didn't want to look.

She made a little noise. "First try, Pete," she said quietly. She started reading whatever it was. Not more than a sub later, she looked up.

"This isn't for me. It might be for you."

"For me?"

"Come read."

It was one file—not very long—divided into several entries with date and time indications, like a diary. There were eight entries over a period of about fifty cycles. The gist was that Alsop had gotten intrigued with the question of empty space on the Ring and had started poking around. He'd found some of the same things I'd found, especially the doors that blinked and wouldn't open. He'd found a lot of those.

I've finally found a contact in Maintenance I believe I can trust absolutely. His name is Parn. He's going to do the monitoring I need. If there is a pattern here— when the highest number of rooms are in this condition vs when lowest—I'll need more data to find it.

He'd never found any qov, or at least didn't write about it if he had, but he clearly thought the rooms were used to hide something, because the final entry said in part

Blink rooms have been on a decrease for several cycles now. Next cycle I should have the spare time to go into some rooms which were blinking a few cycles back and look for samples.

He didn't say what he was sampling.

"That was written two cycles before he died," Catalan said. I startled a little. I'd almost forgotten she was there.

"I hate to ask this," I said, "but do you have any reason to suspect—"

"If someone killed him," she said, "no one knows how they did it. Maybe he really did have a heart attack. He didn't exercise like you do—though he wasn't in bad condition—and he worked very hard."

"Hm. What was that you said, that wasn't in Trade?"

"Must you know?"

"No. I'd like to, that's all."

"*De sobte encara em pren aquell vent o l'amor.* It's from a poem." She gave me a fierce look. "I don't break," she said, "and I won't have anyone walking around saying that I do."

"You know me better than that by now."

"I don't think anyone knows you. But who am I to talk? It means 'Suddenly that wind, or love, continues to hold me.' No, 'hold' isn't strong enough. Clutches. Grabs. Trade is a horrible language for poetry. 'Cor' is Catalan for heart. I don't want to talk about him more now."

"I understand," I said, rising.

"If he was killed," she said as I left, "I will want to know who did it."

§

Douglas Todd

Back in my rooms. I looked up "Catalan" because I wanted to see where on Earth the language had come from. I'm not sure why I looked; none of the history surrounding it was the least bit meaningful to me, all names of dead places. I had that problem sometimes when reading very old books, but usually I could get past it. Once I'd had to look up "Bohemia" and learned that it was a dead nation that was later absorbed into another dead nation that was later absorbed into a third dead nation. After that I stopped bothering unless knowing the politics was important to understanding the story.

I had no reason to suspect that Alsop had been killed, and there was no reason to dredge up trouble by suggesting to anyone else that he had. But it did worry me that he had felt there was a reason to encrypt that file, especially given how few people could get into his file space in the first place ...

Now that was an interesting question. I had Class 1 access and presumably Alsop had too. The boss obviously had Class 1 access or better. Hell, I didn't know how many classes there were; it was clear I wasn't at the bottom of the food chain, not if I could open every door on the Ring, but for all I knew everyone in Dispatch could do that too. Okay, then. Was Class 1 access good enough to allow me to find out who else had Class 1 access?

Worthington, C. E.
Gray, Jessica Louise

Seriously?

You might think it was really stupid of me not to look into that, say, the cycle I arrived, but give me a break. First, I'd been a little preoccupied. Second, why should I have cared? I knew I could read anything I wanted to read and open anything I wanted to open; there was no reason to consider who else might have those rights until considering issues of concealment. (And if you're wondering about the Mystery Doors, I'd already confirmed my idea that the list of people who could mess with those was far too broad to be useful to me.)

Although you'd think the boss could have bothered to mention that I was one of the only two people with the highest level of access on the whole damned Ring. (Unless, of course, the boss had a Class Zero.)

Not for the first time I wondered who had vouched for me and what they had said. C. Efficient Worthington didn't make mistakes, but she had taken even more of a risk hiring me unseen than I first thought. What if I'd turned out to be a psychopath? No, I realized, it wouldn't have mattered, because the first time I pulled something insane, she'd have come to my rooms and killed me in my sleep and that would have been that.

She had trusted me with the keys to the place and it felt like betrayal to add even more to my pile of suspicions, but with those two names sitting in front of me, what choice did I have? Perhaps Alsop had believed she was behind the qov smuggling and perhaps he hadn't, but he'd hidden his notes from her, and that was definite; there was no other reason to encrypt them, no one else he'd have needed to hide them from. Unless he'd been worried about someone hacking the file system, which seemed unlikely. (If he'd been worried about that he'd have kept notes on a data pad or some other independent file space. Or on paper, hidden somewhere.)

I didn't want to go down this road, especially not on insufficient evidence. That sounds more charitable than "no evidence," which is what I had apart from a handful of burned qov. Alsop hadn't left anything either, except for— Samples. He'd mentioned samples. There'd been something in his sample case when I found it among his possessions. I'd used some of the other compartments since then, but not that one. Instinct, caution, or maybe just dumb luck.

Of course I was predisposed, I thought, examining the dark crumbs. I smelled them again. No. It was definitely not my brain trying to fit facts to theories. The smell was faint after all these cycles, but it was undeniably qov.

It was consoling to know that Alsop had taken measures to investigate this. It finally pushed me off the fence I'd been on. I still wasn't sure that I would or should *do* anything about whatever I found, but I no longer felt it would be a waste of my time to try to get to the bottom of it, not if he hadn't. It was still possible that I was acting on boredom or whim or curiosity alone, but if he'd seen fit to chase it, that was all the justification I needed.

But now, how to proceed? This was going to call for caution, and help from a sympathetic source. I got on the feed to Sul, to arrange a meeting.

§

The meeting was set for a very late period. I had some periods to kill after dinner, and there didn't seem to be any crises, so I decided to go check a few doors.

I hadn't been making the systematic checks that Alsop had been doing, but every so often since the fire, when I felt like taking my exercise at a walk instead of a run, I'd gone through some empty parts trying doors at random. I'd found about one door in three was a "blink room," as Alsop had put it. Sometimes I'd found two together, but not always. I hadn't found any qov, or anything else, in an empty room ... but I had gone back to the fire room, just before the Mephenes arrived, and had found that someone had very carefully removed every single bit of ash from it.

Of course I didn't dare follow up. If I checked the door log, it would tell me someone from Maintenance had come in. If I looked into that, I'd just get told they'd done a routine check to see if cleanup was needed after a fire—which might even have been the truth—and anyone with their ear on Maintenance would then know I was more interested in the matter than I was supposed to be.

I hadn't felt inclined to do any door checks since then, but that cycle I thought I might hit a few. Maybe it was instinct again. I found qov on my third try.

A lot of it. I wasn't in a mood to try to do the calculations, but the room was packed floor to ceiling with bundles, stuffed full—you couldn't actually walk into the room at all. It was difficult to believe someone could pack this room this full without being seen, and of course they'd eventually have to move it all out ... but then, deck three was so empty, and there was a ramp not far away. In fact, I'd come up it. Cargo trollies on three were uncommon, but on four and below they were not. Just cover the contents, get on and off deck three as fast as possible, don't send your trollies too close together, do it when most people were asleep ...

There were markings on the bundle wrappings—a language I didn't know—that looked familiar. I'd seen them somewhere before, I was sure, but I couldn't remember where.

Of course, if I were trying to conceal my surveillance of empty rooms, I'd just blown that. Whoever was hiding qov in this room wouldn't forget to check the door logs. On the other hand, if I were going to continue seriously investigating this empty room business, it would only have been a matter of time before I'd have been unable to hide it anyway. Let them wonder.

It did strike me, though, that I had probably better not linger at this door. And that I needed to stop postponing getting a camera for the door to my personal rooms.

§

I have nothing against Pergati—I like them better than humans, in some ways—but Pergati dens are not for me.

I'm not short, and I'm at least fifteen centimeters taller than the tallest Pergat. Thirty centimeters taller than the average one. The problem is Pergati like their dens with low ceilings and tight spaces. They cover all the surfaces with some fuzzy material—I wouldn't exactly call it carpet—and they seem to like it best when their head just barely brushes the ceiling wherever they stand up, and their shoulders brush the walls in connecting halls. I'm told it's common for a Pergat to add more padding below that fuzzy stuff until their personal rooms are just the size they want. A Pergati sleeping alcove doesn't have a bed, just more padding under the fuzz, and it's just big enough for one or two Pergati to occupy lying down and stretched out straight. I couldn't occupy a Pergati alcove without curling up, and I can't walk through most Pergati spaces upright.

They also like it dark—at least to human eyesight—but fortunately Sul had waited outside to lead me through the warren.

I lied when I said earlier there were no stairs anywhere in the Ring. I had forgotten about the warrens. Although some Pergati lived in rooms structured like the human ones, Pergati often form extended families—clans—who like to live together. Some of the Pergati on the Ring had taken large spaces, mostly on deck seven, and subdivided them themselves into little mazes of housing. Since in general that deck is twice as high as the average Pergat, in some places they had divided the space into two levels. To get to the upper level, they used stairs—not enough spare space for ramps. I hadn't realized how unaccustomed I'd grown to stairs until Sul led me up a flight of them in near-darkness. I forgot to duck as I climbed them and the ceiling came closer, and of course Sul wouldn't have thought to warn me; Sul was short even for a Pergat. I was glad for the padding beneath that furry ceiling.

When we arrived, I was so ready to sit down that I didn't wait for an invitation. "My apologies," I said to the seated Pergat across from me. "I'm the wrong shape for your rooms. Sul, don't leave. You're in on this too."

"I was closing the door," Sul said, coming back and sitting down.

"We can't be heard here?"

"Possibly by one of my clan if they listened outside," said Xin Rath, turning up the light beside him. "Is that better? I know humans find it dark in our dens."

"Yes, thank you."

"But they would not listen," he continued. "I trust them. How long have you known?"

"Since Sul called me late one cycle to be sure I saw qov being loaded onto a Kroy vessel," I said. "Sul was acting for someone; it was likely someone involved with the Pergati government since—you will forgive me—many Pergati here seem not to be as concerned as their government is. It was either Kir Erek or you or both. By the by, congratulations on your promotion."

He nodded in thanks. "Yes, what you say—those of us on the Ring don't think it serious, and in truth if not for my position I would chew it myself. It is harmless. Our government's reasons for the ban are political and economic, not medical."

"I'd like to hear more about those reasons, if you don't mind sharing them."

"Is no secret," he said. "First, there is a group in our politics that believe qov makes us—you know qov is calming, yes? We can be very angry; qov relaxes us. This group thinks it relaxes us too much, makes us lazy, complacent. This group is strong enough that anyone who wants to stay in power for long must appease it—you see? So it is an easy way to keep them happy, this ban."

"I see. And the economic reason?"

"Qov has always been difficult to grow. Although there are worlds that grow it easily, they are not ours. The supply is always scarce and the people who sell it keep it that way. Even if it were not illegal it would still be expensive. Some say our government fears that people would buy qov before food, that they would break themselves trying to pay for it."

"Of course there are others—" Sul said.

"Yes, there are always those who whisper of people in high places who profit by its being illegal. I can't say whether to believe that; I don't claim our leaders are always honest. But I am!" he added. "And I do not like to watch while this Ring is used as a base for qov smuggling on a large scale, as it has been for cycles of cycles of cycles of cycles now." He meant "years."

"You know this to be true?"

"Of course," he said. "As did Kir Erek. As do you, if you are honest. The Kroy ship. The Mephene ship. This ship this cycle, the horse-men."

"I'd been wondering about that one. But, you know, a ship docking here full of qov isn't the same as the Ring being complicit in the smuggling—"

He made a dismissive wave with his hand. "Before we talk more of that—you have heard where I sit. Now talk of where you sit."

"Well ... I can't confiscate qov. Officially the Ring doesn't ban qov, and I can only confiscate contraband. Unofficially ... I don't like smuggling. I don't like someone getting away with it under my nose. And if some of my theories are right, people have been killed on this Ring by someone trying to cover it up. I'm definitely not happy about that. I can't stop qov from moving past the Ring, but—"

"What if qov is moved not past it but into it? Have you wondered how that Mephene ship was to get past our patrols?"

"Only about ten thousand times."

"It was stopped. This has not been in a news drop yet and likely will not be. It had no qov. In fact it had no cargo. Even if we did not know it was full of qov when it got here, would it have—"

"Right. No way it would have deadheaded through that many Rings—" I stopped. I'd just realized why I'd recognized the wrapping on the qov bundles. I'd seen that particular style of writing on labels and consoles while aboard the Mephene ship. The captain had been right: they had brought no contraband into Pergati space.

"Something has occurred to you?" Xin Rath said, watching my face and knowing damned well something had.

"All right. I concede that qov is being taken off ships in bulk and stored here until it can be smuggled into Pergati space a little at a time. But even then—even if I can justify destroying any I find on the Ring, I won't find all of it, I can't spend all cycle every cycle looking for it, and once it's on a ship I usually can't touch it. That's not the way. Finding the person or people behind all of this is. That won't stop the smuggling but it will certainly turn it down, at least for a while."

"I agree." He leaned back and crossed his paws over his stomach in a satisfied way. "Now, what help can we give you?"

"First, how likely is it that a Pergat is behind all this? Remember, qov doesn't do anything for humans. And we know some Pergati were behind the Kroy shipment."

"A truth," he said, still leaning back and completely unperturbed. "And likely some here are involved at lower levels. But do you agree the one in charge must be someone in a high position of control, surely in Dispatch?"

"Yes—oh. I see what you mean."

"While Pergati are most welcome in other areas of Ring operation," he said, "they have never, I think, been allowed into Dispatch. We do not have to discuss why; it might be offensive."

I shrugged. "They didn't ask for my opinion on their hiring practices. As it happens, your suspicions match mine; I just wanted your reasons. You realize, if this is at the very top, even having this conversation is dangerous."

"Of course. Which is why we did not have it." He grinned.

"As for what cooperation you can give me—I need someone in Maintenance who can work secretly, whom you trust, with a fairly high level of access to data. I have to monitor certain things and no one else can know they are being monitored, or it will be bad for both me and the person doing the monitoring."

He looked to Sul. "Parn," Sul said. Xin Rath looked back at me. "If Sul says Parn is the one, it is a truth."

"I don't dispute it." And wouldn't have even if Alsop hadn't picked the same person. "Sul, can you set up a meeting between us in secret?"

"Of course," Sul said. "And others as you need them. It is already known I work for you. Of course, you will still call me sometimes when you need fighting—"

I had to smile. "I wouldn't think of leaving you out of the fighting."

We didn't get to work out any details. Just after I said that, two things happened at the same time—someone knocked on the door to the room asking for Xin Rath, and my feed chirped. "Security."

It was a Pergat, a very upset one. "You come to seven:fifty-three! There is a death here! Murder!"

"I'll be right there. Don't touch anything and don't let anybody else touch anything."

I disconnected and Xin Rath, standing next to a member of his clan at the doorway, exchanged a look with me. "Same news?"

"That's not far from here. I might need help, Sul. Xin Rath, if you come, you may want to come separately, so we aren't leaving here together."

He shook his head. "I will wait to hear."

§

Seven:fifty-three was at the far end of the Pergati warrens. There were a group of Pergati in the hall chattering about it. Pergati spread gossip among themselves even faster than humans do, which is saying something. When we got into the warren itself, Sul took deep sniffs of the air several times.

"Something wrong?"

"This warren is not used. Has not been for a while. But there are fresh smells here. Not all are Pergati."

"Human?"

"No—or maybe."

We wandered through a couple of dim rooms. Even my nose could tell they smelled stale. At the back of the first set of rooms was a stairway. At the bottom sat a Pergat, their head in their paws, shaking a little. They stood when we approached, shakily, and pointed up the stairs. I ascended, remembering to duck this time.

At the top of the stairs, not far into the room, lay a dead Pergat, face up, limbs splayed. The face had been smashed, struck repeatedly with such force that it was no longer possible to make out the shape of the muzzle or any other features. I looked away deliberately and went back down.

"Was it you on the feed?" I asked the Pergat. They nodded. "Do you know who the victim is?" They stammered something. Pergati don't cry, that I know of, but if they did, this one would have been.

"I'm sorry, but I do need to know."

"That horse-man! I told Gar not to—" The rest was growling, not really understandable. Pergati don't cry because their usual reaction to bad emotions is to find whatever caused them and kill it.

"What horse-man?"

I'll spare you the rest. Here's the condensed version.

The Pergat, whose name was Bis, was Gar's (the corpse's) ... well, let's say "significant other" because Pergati relationships are simultaneously loose and complex. They were important to one another, put it that way. This Barling ship had been here before, many cycles ago. The last time it had been here, one of the Barlings, named Hart, had tried to pick trouble with Gar. Gar had complained to Alsop (politely sparing Hart's life, Bis implied) and Alsop had confined Hart to his ship. This time around, Hart had arranged a meeting with Gar, supposedly to apologize and make peace. Bis hadn't trusted Hart and warned Gar not to go. Gar went anyway, and when he didn't come back after a while, Bis went to this place, the place arranged for the meeting, and found Gar's body.

It seemed pretty clear, especially since Sul said that the not-quite-human smell could have been a Barling. There was only one problem.

"Bis ... why did you move the body?"

"Move the body? I did not! I spoke to you when I found it. You said not to touch it."

I looked at her closely. It's a lot harder for me to tell when Pergati are lying than humans; I can't read their faces well and they're very good at it. (They're the best traders in the galaxy for a reason.) But I didn't think Bis was capable of much subtlety; the person I'd just spent most of a period trying to cajole out of near-incoherence because of her rage and grief was either painfully open and sincere, or would have to be a hell of an actress.

But if she hadn't moved the body, how could a Barling have killed Gar?

I said my apologies again to Bis and told her to go home, there was nothing else sitting there distraught could accomplish. She didn't want to go, but I eventually convinced her she didn't want to see us take the body out.

"Sul," I said, after she left. "I don't think a Barling could get up those stairs. And they certainly couldn't have dragged a body up them."

"Had help maybe?"

"It'd have to be a lot of help. I don't think either of us could get that body up those steps alone. As it is we're going to have a fun time getting it down. Do I go fetch the trolley or do you?"

§

That was the first time I'd had to investigate a murder on the Ring that my mind wasn't invested in. I wanted to talk to this Parn and find out about empty rooms. But I know my duty. Besides, the meeting with Parn hadn't been arranged yet. So after getting not-quite-enough periods of sleep and a late breakfast, I headed off to the temporary Barling quarters.

The Ring doesn't have a hotel per se. Visitors sleep on their ships; that's what makes them visitors. Transients, people waiting until their ship comes or until their luck changes, have to arrange for rooms and pay the rent like everyone else. But we do have some rooms on deck seven that are better than Sugarland for roughly the same cost, and it's understood that these are reserved for very transient transients who want decent accommodations. Also, they come pre-furnished, which no other rooms on the Ring do (unless you happen to have inherited the furniture of the former security officer, along with his clothes), and we clean them after "guests" leave. All of these rooms were taken by the Barlings, who apparently didn't want to have to go up and down in a cargo crane several times a cycle—or pay for what Dispatch would have charged them to keep a crane operator on hand their whole stay. There is no free lunch on the Ring.

Dispatch acted as "hotel clerk" since, strangely, room assignments were their responsibility. I guess they couldn't find anyone else to do it. I had to check their records to see who'd been put in what room. I hadn't encountered Barling surnames before; they didn't do much for my sympathies. Silliness like Blacktree and Earthheart and Palewater, all which had to have been picked just for the way they sounded. I hate phonies.

Down on seven, I buzzed Hart's door and Brindi, the other person listed as being in that room, answered it. At least, I assumed so because Bis had said Hart was a male, and this one very much was not.

Maybe you're like Bryant and don't do old mythology, so here's the general idea. From the waist up, Brindi was a human, with sun-browned skin, short-cropped hair (all of them had very short hair, maybe it got in the way of field work or something), maybe a little more hair on the arms and torso than I'd have expected, but nothing unusual. Well, her breasts were large enough that I wondered whether they caused her back pain, but you know what I mean. She didn't have three eyes or anything like that.

From just below the navel, she was a horse. Starting at the lower stomach, her body hair thickened gradually and by the time your eye caught on to what was happening as it scanned downward, you were looking at the front legs of a horse, hooves and all. Not, I thought, a large horse. Overall, head to hoof, she was a little shorter than I was. I had never seen any horses in person but I was pretty sure they ran bigger than that. So maybe they were centaur-ponies. Her fur was reddish-brown with vertical blonde streaks, and I noticed the hair on her head was the same color. Stood to reason, I supposed.

She wore no clothing whatsoever, although that didn't match what I'd seen when I was on lower cargo, so maybe I'd caught her just coming out of the shower. I wondered if she had to shower in stages.

"What do you want?" she said.

"I'm the security officer. My name is Jessica Gray. I'm looking for Hart Blacktree."

"He's not here." She let the door close.

I counted to twenty. In fact, just to slow myself down, I counted to twenty in base eight, which means I counted to twenty-four. Then I let myself in.

She was in the sleeping area. She had a brush with a long handle and was using it on the fur on the back half of her body she couldn't otherwise reach. She yelped when she saw me and ran at me, waving the brush like a club. She had a lot of speed and probably would have hit very hard, but it was easy to see her coming. I dodged and she couldn't stop, and she collided with the far wall of the main room. A few centimeters to the left and she'd have tangled with a chair on the way and probably broken a couple of legs.

"Before you seriously hurt yourself," I said, "let's talk about what happens if you give the security officer a hard time. Would you like to be confined to your ship? Would you like to be placed in Custody?"

"I don't know where he is!"

"For some reason I don't believe you. Look, we can do this the hard way. I can drag a cargo hoist up here and get my beefs to hold you still while I strap you to it. I'll take you back to Custody kicking in mid-air if I need to."

"Okay, okay. Let me get dressed."

"Just tell me where he is."

"If you go without me, they won't let you in, and I'll either get blamed for killing you or for getting them hurt."

Getting dressed mostly seemed to be a matter of taking a long thin red cord and coiling it around her waist in a series of dangling loops, each a little smaller than the previous one. When she had made about thirty loops, she fastened them together at the back with the remaining length of the cord.

"It's called a silla," she said, "and I don't want to hear your jokes."

She also pulled on a top of sorts, just a stretchy band of tight fabric, which was either meant to be a shirt or a bra, or both. Then she put on her shoes, which were interesting. They were designed so she could step into them; they stood upright when not worn. There was a sticky closure at the top, which she could fasten shut by brushing it with the opposite hoof. She could do this on her back feet without looking. Such useless ingenuity.

"Why wear shoes at all?" I asked.

"Your floors hurt my feet," she said. "Let's go."

She led me four doors down. All that trouble. "Wait," I said, before she buzzed. "You go on in. I'm going to stand over here. You can have five subs to send Hart out. No more. I don't want to talk to him with a crowd around. Don't you come out either. You can wait until I'm done. Warn him that if he misbehaves, I'm going to be annoyed. I'm about to fetch some help, and if we have to go in, I'm going to be even more annoyed. I might not be able to take two or three of you all by myself but my team certainly can. They'll have weapons. Leg-breaking weapons."

She was wide-eyed. "What the hell has he done? We're not criminals. Is this always how you treat guests?"

"Try not to be funny, you're not good at it," I said. "If he doesn't know something is up, why was he hiding down here? What did he say to you last cycle before he told you he was coming down here to sleep on his friend's floor? ... Actually, I guess you all sleep on the floor, don't you? Can't see how you'd get on and off a bed."

"You're not very funny either," she said.

"Five subs. No more."

She went in and I got on the feed to Rob and Don and told them to rush. They weren't there when Hart came out, but he didn't look like he was preparing to kill me, so I decided to start without them. They'd really been summoned in case I had to go in the room.

He wore only the silla. His was red as well. Male Barlings didn't bother with shirts, I'd already seen, and he didn't have shoes on, which could have meant several things, none of them especially important. He looked like the kind of person built for heavy lifting and not brains. I might not have been able to make my hands meet around his neck if I tried to strangle him. His fur was gray-brown. He had a fresh, deep scratch all the way across his right cheek.

"This better be good," he said.

"Drop it. She's already warned you. I let her. Tell me about last cycle. Specifically, tell me what happened when you went down to the Pergati warrens."

"I never—" He caught himself.

"Uh-huh," I said. "I was getting ready to break your nose if you took that line. That was the whole point of the warning. Try again."

"I went down there to meet a bear named Gar. Last time I was here he made hell for me. He said he wanted to apologize. I went to the ass-end of their fucking caves, ran into walls, couldn't stand up, and then the fucker never showed up. After a while I gave up and came back here."

"Right. Why were you hiding, then?"

"Because a friend of mine came in right after I did and said he'd heard in a bar that Gar was dead. A lot of people know what happened last time. I knew I was gonna get blamed for it, just like last time. I was just trying to hold it off long enough to get some sleep."

"What else did your friend tell you about Gar's death?"

"Nothing. Just that he was dead."

"You don't know anything else about Gar's death? What made you so sure you were going to get blamed for it? He could have been killed in a bar fight for all you know."

"Don't matter." His ears were getting red. "That fucking bear nearly ruined me before and now he's trying to finish the job! He's gonna ruin me even now he's dead! And you people love them bears and you won't hear a fucking word we say about them! We know you hate us. So you can go to hell. Do whatever you're going to do. I don't give a fuck anymore."

I've given my best guess at how to translate his favorite profanity. The actual word he used was unknown to me.

Rob and Don were coming up the concourse.

"These gents are going to put you in custody. Notice what big sticks they're carrying. If you give them any trouble you'll be hoisted into custody with broken legs. Behave and maybe I'll bring you a big lunch. I bet you eat a lot." To Rob and Don I said, "Watch his feet. He may have kicked someone to death with them last cycle."

§

Still no word on the meeting with Parn, I wanted Hart to stew for a while before I tackled him again, I didn't have a single thing I wanted to say to any of his friends, Bis was useless, and it was way too early for lunch, especially after my late breakfast. I wondered if Dr. Kohl had looked at the body yet.

He wasn't in his lab, but he'd left a note on the lab table. JESSICA—ASK FOR ME IN MEDICAL. I found him in a room with Dr. Wright; they were studying big images on displays on the wall—of what was left of my victim's face. "Exactly the right time," Dr. Kohl said.

"He was worried he'd have to use the feed," Dr. Wright said, deadpan.

I smiled. "Not that it's unwelcome, but what's special enough about this one that you're both in on it?"

"We have been discussing," he said, "whether a centaur could strike with sufficient force to shatter the face in this way. Dr. Wright had an unpleasant case a while back involving a Pergat and a hydraulic arm. Accidental, I hasten to add."

"What's the verdict?"

"Yes," Dr. Wright said, "but only two ways. Either an all-out backward kick with one of the hind legs, or a straight-down stomp on a face lying on the ground. The complication with the former is that the victim couldn't have been standing—face would be too high, the angle would be wrong—but if the victim had been kneeling or sitting I'm not sure the impact would have looked the same. So I favor lying down."

"If a centaur did do it," Dr. Kohl added carefully.

For the record: I hadn't told Dr. Kohl any details of the situation the previous cycle. I had just dropped off the body.

"Could something else have made the same effect?"

"The problem is," he said, "there are so many facial strikes here they've obliterated their own outlines. We can't tell if the blunt instrument was hoof-shaped; we can't even tell how many strikes there were. We think more than twenty."

"Somebody was very upset," I said.

"It could be any hard object with a striking surface that approximate diameter. It wouldn't have been a club or an iron bar, swung from the side; these are straight-on impacts. Do you see what I mean? A ramming, end-first motion."

"But wider than, say, the end of a pry rod."

"Definitely. Also, there's the question of force again. Suppose I had a rod with a blunt end of the equivalent shape. A false hoof, if you will. I'm not sure I could wield it with sufficient power. Certainly not sideways—" he made a battering-ram motion—"and possibly not straight down either." He acted as if thumping the ground with a pole. "I don't think even many Pergati are strong enough. There's one way that might be possible for more people, but it verges on ridiculous."

"Something heavy strapped onto a shoe."

"Exactly. That would bring it within the ability of an average human, I think."

"I'll consider that if Occam's Razor fails me."

"Sensible. I think this one looks like a duck and quacks like a duck." I've never actually seen a duck. But I knew what he meant.

"Don't forget the ribs," Dr. Wright said.

"Oh, yes," said Dr. Kohl, nodding to her. "You saw the damage to the face, but you likely missed the chest. Your victim has two severely fractured ribs, fractured near the sternum. Consistent with the same sort of straight-on impact."

"Kicked to the ground with a backward kick? And then stomped on repeatedly?"

"I'd call that the leading theory," he replied.

§

I had just gone from medical back to deck five when Sul hailed me on the feed. Could I attend a meeting later that cycle? I certainly could. Then, not five subs after disconnecting with Sul—while I was still walking to Custody—the feed chirped again. It was my new favorite person, McGregor.

"Do you enjoy aggravating ship's captains because you want us to go broke? Or is it just your natural personality?"

"Hello to you too. Clean up your own act and then we'll talk about personality. If this is the Barling captain, the one I'm holding is a murder suspect. The prime suspect in the murder of a permanent. If you have issues with Ring policy on killing a permanent, discuss the matter with the Director."

"I already did," he said. "I don't know what she sees in you, but—"

"But she supported my decision. So you got on the feed for no other reason than to call me names."

"No," he said, "To tell you that the Barling captain will be at your custody rooms in ten subs and that you'd better be there to speak with him. You stand by your decision, she stands by your decision—fine! *You* talk him down. Dispatch will not clean up your messes."

"That'll be the day. Thank you for the information. I always appreciate being informed by such a high-placed official source." He snarled and disconnected.

On the way to Custody I bought the promised big lunch. Hart probably hadn't had any breakfast before we took him in, and I didn't want the captain to think I was starving my prisoner. When I got in, I noticed that a coil of red cord was on my desk. It wasn't coiled the same way as when he wore it, so it took me a bit to realize it was Hart's silla. Rob and Don must have confiscated it. I felt some of the cord and then tugged on it. A lot stronger than it looked. Rob and Don aren't the best improvisers, but they're not stupid. I put it in the desk and brought Hart the food. I didn't bother to question him again yet, just left him alone with his meal.

The door buzzed. I admitted the Barling captain. "Where have you put him?"

"That's no way to start," I said. "First we introduce ourselves. Then you tell me who you're asking about and why. Then, maybe, if I think you have a right to know, I tell you that he's over there in that first room, having lunch. No, don't go over there. You might decide to let him out and then I'd have to get upset."

"This is too much," he said. "Once was barely tolerable. Twice—I don't know why your Ring has such a bias against us, but I've had enough of it and I'm going to see something's done about it."

"You know, you really are doing this the wrong way. You're making assumptions. I gather you and Hart both think there's some sort of history repeating here, but I don't know the history. I'm not the same security officer that was here last time. All I'm doing is confining the most likely suspect in a murder."

"You really don't know? No, I see you don't. I suppose I'm not surprised no one told you. It wasn't your Ring's finest hour."

"Why don't you tell me the story," I said, "and let me judge that."

"All right." He looked around as if searching for a place to sit—do they sit?—then decided the floor wasn't very welcoming. "The last time we were here it was for twenty-five cycles. Too long. A group of Pergati, for reasons I still don't understand, decided they disliked us and would try to make us feel as unwelcome as possible. They'd find us whatever we happened to be doing, insult us, try to start fights, any trouble they could make. We were only just beginning to make trading runs at the time—we were very concerned about making good impressions—I don't know if they knew that and were trying to get us to break, or just decided to hate us for some other reason. We held out pretty well ... I'll tell you from my own personal experience, I had to work hard a few times to keep from kicking one across a room.

"Three cycles before departure, Hart broke. This Pergat Gar leaped on top of him and tried to ride him. He got his claws into Hart's sides and Hart spent ten subs trying to buck him off. I was there. Finally he did throw Gar, straight into a wall. I hear that Gar had a bad concussion, but recovered. Meanwhile, your predecessor had Hart confined to the ship and made sure that a report was filed with the authorities on Barl. As I say, they were very sensitive to appearances then. They wouldn't listen to anyone who tried to explain the circumstances. I tried. Hart was banned from work for two years—Barl years. He was allowed to farm for his own food only. He couldn't sell his crops, couldn't work in the processing plants, couldn't go to space, anything. This has been his first trip since then ... do you understand now why we feel the way we do? What possible reason could there have been to punish Hart like that and let Gar get away with his behavior?"

I didn't know what to say. Of course there was the "no one picks on a permanent with impunity" policy, but if the captain was right, Gar had instigated it. It certainly sounded to me like Alsop had blown that one. But I wasn't sure I should admit that to the captain.

"You realize that Gar's ... well, 'widow' would be simplest ... tells a very different version of your last visit? According to her, it was Hart that had made trouble for Gar, last time."

"Yes, I wouldn't be surprised that's what Gar told her."

"And if I asked others who were here at the time, I'd get a lot of different answers and I still wouldn't know which to believe. You see my problem? I wasn't there. It's too late to sort out the truth of that. Nor is it germane. Whatever the past offenses, nothing justifies murdering Gar in the present day.

Right now it's very difficult to conceive of anyone else who had the motive, opportunity, and method. I'm still looking, because there's one issue I have to resolve. But you're going to have to face the fact that Hart may not be coming back with you. I have standing orders that the penalty for killing a permanent resident, if it can be proven, is death."

"Because your permanents are more important than anyone else's rights! See! It's just like I said—it's the same thing all over again! You only care about your own; everybody else can go to hell."

"Captain." I sighed. "For what it's worth ... I think my predecessor goofed. For all I know, he may have gone light on Gar because he didn't think he had any other option. Or maybe he was just biased. We're not always perfect. Personally, I don't like Barlings either, but I wouldn't let that get in the way of fair judgment—"

" *Why* don't you like us? What in the galaxy did we ever do to you?"

"I don't know that everyone dislikes you. My personal reasons are my own."

"I'd like to hear them."

"So you have more grounds to accuse me of bias?"

"No," he said. "So I can have at least one answer on that from someone, because it's bothered me for a long time now."

"I don't speak for anyone else," I said, "but I think you're frauds. You've built a culture just so you can pat yourself on the back for it. If you wanted to be farmers, fine, but saying, 'oh, and we're going to give ourselves horse bodies to show how committed we are' is ridiculous. Farmers use machines, even the nothing-artificial-added ones. You didn't make yourselves centaurs so you could pull your own plows; you did it so you could tell yourself how special you are.

"Not only that, but you did it in a way that guaranteed the rest of the universe would be difficult for you. If you came to us with a genuine difference, something actual and unavoidable, that'd be one thing, but yours is artificial. You can't make your own problems and then complain that no one else is cooperating with you."

He stared at me.

"Sorry you asked?" I said.

He turned around and walked out of Custody without saying a word.

I know I shouldn't have said any of it. I knew before I said it that I shouldn't have. Next he'd go to McGregor and give him more ammunition, and then there'd be a sad talk with the boss, and so on. But I'd been needing to let that out for most of a cycle by then, ever since their arrival and reading their file, and anyway he *had* asked.

§

I didn't bother talking to Hart. There was nothing I wanted to say to him at that time. I got myself some lunch, then realized I didn't have anywhere in particular to go until the back part of my brain solved the riddle of this murder, or until my meeting with Parn, whichever came first.

I wandered around aimlessly a bit, and then for no good reason went up to have another look at the room I'd found all the Mephene qov in. I was unsurprised to find it empty, even though it had been less than a cycle. If it'd been me, I'd certainly have been watching the door logs for unwanted visitors. Either they'd moved it to another room to make it harder to find, or they hadn't needed to because it had all gone out on a ship.

As I stepped back out of the room, out of the corner of my eye, I thought I caught someone disappearing into another room a few doors down the concourse. I didn't go look. Even if it hadn't been my imagination, it was such a brief glimpse that I wasn't sure what door to check. And if it wasn't my imagination, it was a confrontation I didn't need right now. I went back to my rooms to read for a while.

§

I'd been in my room maybe a period, trying to focus on my book and not having much luck, when my door buzzed. Since I didn't have a camera yet, I opened it with care. It was Brindi the Barling. I sometimes think it's too easy for visitors to find out where I live.

"As someone once said to me: What do you want?"

"I need to talk to you."

"Talk. I'm listening."

"Can I come in?"

"Why? It doesn't make any difference to you; I don't think you'd like sitting down in here."

"Are you always this much of a bitch?"

I moved in ahead of her and got the neural gun. I showed it to her. "This hurts. A lot. Now, you stay over there and I'll be over here with the gun and we'll talk." I sat at my desk chair.

"You're crazy, you know that, right?"

"No, just in a really bad mood. When I try to solve a crime I like it better if there's someone in the right and someone in the wrong. Makes me feel cleaner. Here I've got a case of an asshole killing another asshole, and that really sends me into a tailspin. What did you have to say?"

"That's the thing! Hart isn't an asshole! I've been with him for years. OK, he's not the smartest, and he used to have a bad temper, but he's a good guy! Where do you get this about him?"

"That bad temper led him to throw a Pergat into a wall."

"Because it was trying to ride him, with its claws in him! And after that, he never even came close to losing his temper again. He knew this was the only other chance for space jobs he was going to get. He'd been through hell to get here. Why would he kill that Pergat and wreck it all? He can be dumb, but he's nowhere near that dumb. Believe me."

"Maybe you underestimate his desire for revenge," I said.

"He didn't go for revenge! The meeting was Gar's idea. I was there when Gar's friend came! I heard it! It was supposed to be so Gar could apologize. Look, if Hart did kill Gar, he wouldn't have done it just for revenge. No way. I won't believe that. If he did it, it was because he had to—because Gar did something, I don't know, but I know Hart wouldn't have done it unless he had no choice. This trip was too important."

"What's this about Gar's friend?"

"Well, we don't have those things like you do, whatever it is you talk to each other on. So Gar sent a messenger. I figured he was too scared to come around a lot of us, we all still remember him—"

"Did you get this messenger's name?"

"Sure. Rot. I remember because Hart and I both were trying not to laugh—"

"A lot of Pergati have pretty funny names to us." They probably think your fake clan names are hilarious too, I didn't say. "Does anyone else besides you and Hart know Rot came to see you?"

She shook her head. "Not from us, anyway."

"Keep that to yourself."

"Okay, sure—but what about Hart?"

I sighed. "I'm trying to do what I can for Hart. I really am. But right now it looks like he did kill Gar, and there may not be much I can do."

I eventually got her out of my rooms, but it took work. I sat back in my desk chair and rubbed the bridge of my nose where the headache was beginning to form.

She'd had a point. Why was I taking this damn-them-all attitude? I didn't have any evidence Hart was a jerk, but I was certainly ready to badmouth him. Was it because I thought the whole Barl thing was idiotic? I hoped not. I hoped I was better than that. Was it because I would rather be working on the empty rooms? Again, if that was true I was really disappointed in myself.

It took me a while to get it. My mood had collapsed in on itself when I'd heard about Alsop's decision, the last time the Barlians had been here. Alsop had let me down. Had I been putting the man on that much of a pedestal? Maybe I had. Maybe I'd been thinking I'd finally found someone who didn't make any mistakes. I hate mistakes. You get told from birth that everybody makes mistakes, but what no one ever says—because they don't need to—is that none of us forgives mistakes well, that making mistakes can destroy your life. "Everyone makes mistakes" is supposed to be the consolation prize for someone who's blown it, and it's a lousy one.

I got up and went to take a shower. I had several things to do in the Pergati warrens later that cycle, and I wanted a clear head.

§

The first of my errands in the warrens was to talk to Rot. They were cagey, but not the brightest Pergat ever, and what they were trying to hide wasn't the part I was interested in. When I was finished with them, I'd determined that Brindi had been telling the truth about the message Rot delivered. Whether the invitation had been a trap, and whether Rot knew it, remained to be seen.

Talking to Rot had been just for verification, because I'd believed Brindi on that to begin with. My next errand, talking to Bis, was more important—and more painful. I realize it's bad accounting not to relate what was said, but I just can't bring myself to put it here. Especially since I had to threaten her, which doesn't reflect well on my finesse.

In case you think I'm trying to hold back info so I can look like a genius later: by the time I left Bis, I was convinced that Gar had planned something different for his meeting with Hart than he'd advertised. Bis hadn't wanted to admit it—that's where the threats became necessary—but Gar had been steaming about Hart for a long time, ever since getting thrown into a wall. Apparently Gar had never been the same since then, and he blamed Hart for ruining his life. It had apparently never occurred to Gar to question his own conduct ... it had occurred to Bis, but she'd never said a word about it.

Some people's loyalty outweighs their good sense. Would I cover up for Meridian if I knew she'd committed a murder? Didn't matter, I realized, not if half the Ring assumed I would whether I would or not. That line of thought didn't improve my mood, especially since I wasn't sure of the real answer.

My third errand was to visit the scene of the crime with my flashlight. Pergati like to build the internal subdivisions of their warrens out of wood. You probably think that's a little bizarre. It's easy to take apart and put back together and reuse; they alter their warrens a lot. It's pretty cheap—that is, it's horribly expensive on the Ring, but it's no more expensive than any other building material they'd need to ship up, and less expensive than some. It's not very tough or very durable, which is why it's not used in any of the permanent Ring walls or structures, but for their purposes, it's great. And they like the smell.

It also takes marks well. I found a groove, an impression as if something had been rasped into the wood, on the handrail at the top of the stairs, the ones I'd walked up to find the body. It was exactly where I had expected it to be.

And with that, I had solved the murder. Unfortunately, that was the easy part.

I put it all aside for now and went off to my fourth errand: Meeting Sul and Parn.

§

Parn was the first Pergat I'd had any real interaction with where the main adjective that came to mind was "old." The fur on his muzzle had long since gone gray, and he moved around the way an older human moves around, slowly and with care. I wasn't sure how Pergati ages corresponded to human ones—I wasn't even sure of their lifespan—but in my head Sul was mid-twenties, Xin Rath heading toward fifty, and by that scale Parn was nearing seventy. Which is not to say he was decrepit. His eyes missed nothing and his mind kept pace with them.

Since we were both supposed to be vouched-for to one another, I decided it would be better to get the obvious item out of the way immediately. "Did you ever get very far with what Alsop asked you to do, before he died?"

He nodded. "Catalan told you. Yes? That's good. If she trusts you, that's a good sign."

"He left a locked file. No one could guess the password but her. I want to make sure you realize where we sit. The only person he'd have to lock a file to hide it from is the Director."

He nodded again. "We talked about that. Yes, I collected data for him. It may not help you, though. The rooms that blink won't let you in because they are dangerous. That was easy to learn. The particular danger was very hard to learn. If you stepped into one of the blinking rooms, unless you remained ungrounded at all times, you would die. Those rooms that blink are carrying an electrical charge—a very strong one."

"Carrying it where? I mean, is the floor charged or—"

"The air! The air in the room itself is carrying the charge. To an extent I would not have thought possible. The room that blinks has, in a way, temporarily become a battery, a place where a great deal of power is stored. If you were to step in and create a link, say between the charge in the room and the floor outside, the power would all discharge at once. Through you."

"But what causes this charge to build up? And where does it eventually go? The rooms don't stay blinking."

"I don't know," he said. "To learn this I would have to take apart one of the rooms, or at the very least install some equipment, run wires some distance to where I could monitor it without being seen—you see why I have not risked this."

"Yes. I have reason to believe every single one of those empty rooms has its door log watched. Did you find any of the patterns Alsop was looking for?"

"He never told me what he was looking for," Parn said. "Only to collect data. I have collected much data, but if there is a pattern, I myself haven't yet found it. I will say this—there does seem to be a sawtooth. That is, there are brief times when rooms charge very quickly ... and those are the only times any rooms ever charge. Then they dissipate more slowly, losing power over time. The rate of dissipation varies."

"I don't suppose there's a safe way for me to get my hands on that data."

"I can transfer some of it to your data pad right now," he said. "Total power over time. The times and dates are given, but what is actually being measured is not said. If anyone finds it on your pad, you can make up some story. I don't recommend putting it in your file space, of course ... unless you know how to lock files like Alsop did ..."

"No, unfortunately, but I think the data pad should work. Parn-man, this doesn't seem to have anything to do with qov."

"I know," he said. "That's why I said it might not help. I have come to believe Alsop had found something he wasn't looking for. He wondered if the blinking rooms were holding qov ... but they couldn't be. If anything were in those rooms when they took a charge, it would likely have been destroyed."

"Burned. I found a room full of ashes of burned qov." I tried to put it all together, came up blank. "Are you still monitoring the power?"

"Oh yes. Never stopped. My way uses existing systems. No one knows I do it."

"Then keep doing it. If you reach a point where someone is catching on, stop. I'll try to figure out a way to enable you to get more details without risk, but I'm not going to do it unless we can do it without anyone noticing. I don't have any other ideas right now, do you?"

§

I brought Hart some late dinner, had some myself, and went back to my rooms. Meridian was asleep in my bed. I wasn't sure what it was about my bed, but if I found her in it, no matter when in the cycle, she was asleep. She had less trouble with sleep than I did. On the other hand, she was a light sleeper; it was very hard for me to sneak in without waking her. She mumbled something.

"I was thinking about you earlier," I said.

"Mrm. Anything good?"

"Thought experiment. I didn't think you'd be here this cycle, not with three ships in."

"The Pergati ship's clannish," she said. "They're partying together and then going back to the ship to play amongst themselves. This human crew's too cheap for us I think. We did get one of the horse-people in. That was a first."

"I'm ... trying to imagine how that works. I guess if you lean over a bed ... would that be high enough even then?"

"You're assuming it was a sprocket," she said, sitting up.

"Oh. But that's even harder."

"Another first; a lesbian who jumps right to sprocket-in-socket," she said. "There are other things to do, as you know perfectly well. Trixi said it was kind of sad; she said the woman mostly wanted to be hugged and touched and petted, everything else was kind of an afterthought. Trixi thought she must be very lonely. We think she went to Trixi because she thought everyone else would reject her. A lot of the humans and Pergati here don't seem to like the horse-people much."

"Hm," I said. She couldn't see my face completely from where she was sitting, but I couldn't fool her. "You don't like them."

"I think they're a little ridiculous," I said. I gave her a version of what I had said to the Barl captain.

"I guess," she said. "But, you know, some people might be stuck. If you're born to that, a couple of generations in, you didn't choose it, and maybe you hate it just as much, but you don't get a choice about it."

"That's part of my point, though," I said. "If you're born a normal human in a society or culture you disagree with, unless they physically restrain you, you can get out of it and go be something else. If you're born on Barl, you're stuck with Barl—even if you hate it, there's no real place for you anywhere else. That's a horrible thing for them to impose on their children, not giving them the choice—making a change like that for everyone without giving future kids an opt-in."

She frowned. "I don't see the difference. I was born in a colony of insane political separatists. I'm lucky to have escaped with my brain intact and I can't ever go back, not that I'd want to. Look at that woman who got away from the Tanngrevers. Look at Trixi. I don't think those handicaps are more or less than having two extra legs, not really. Maybe less. You can build a house to handle having four legs; getting rid of brainwashing's a lot harder."

I sat, staring at nothing.

"Hey," she said after a while. "I'm not mad at you."

"I know."

"What else is eating you?"

"I've solved my murder," I said, "and I'm having trouble with the dispensing-justice part."

She pushed over and snuggled against me. "Tell me," she said.

§

"I brought you some breakfast," I said to Hart.

"I wish you'd brought a cushion," he said. The custody-room floor was not meant for centaurs.

"May not be a problem much longer," I said. That got his attention. "Look, I'm not interested in hearing you fuss at everything I say, so why don't you go ahead and eat while I tell you a story. But do listen. You don't have to agree with it, just listen. At the end, we'll figure out where we stand."

He looked suspicious, but he started eating, and not with hesitation.

"First off, let's get rid of the claim that you never met up with Gar. I've checked the door logs on the outer door of the warren. Gar arrived three subs after you did, and then someone, presumably you, exited quite a while after Gar's arrival. So either you hid from Gar and snuck out later without him seeing you, which means he was killed by someone else who was already hiding in the warren—I think that's reaching too far, don't you?—or you did meet up with him, and presumably killed him.

"Second, I know the meeting was Gar's idea and that he misled you. I know he told you he wanted to apologize, and that wasn't what he actually had in mind. Now we come to the guessing part.

"I think when you were both in there, Gar tried to kill you. I think that scratch on your face is one claw from a paw swipe that just missed you. It must have been pretty hard for you to move fast when you couldn't even stand up straight, but somehow you got so he was behind you and you kicked him in the chest as hard as you could. My one objection is that if you had those padded shoes on it might have been hard to make that kind of impact. On the other hand, maybe you don't wear them very often. I haven't heard you complain about your feet after a cycle in here on this floor.

"You kicked him and knocked him down and then—what happened? Did you lose it then, a little? Maybe because you thought that by then it was already too late and you were going to be in trouble no matter what you did? I don't know. But you stomped his face, twenty times, maybe more. Then you really were in trouble. There was one thing you could do to deflect attention: you could try getting the body into a place that no one would believe you could get to.

"It threw me for a while, but I had two chances to watch your friend Brindi move around. She knew exactly where her back feet were at all times, without needing to look. So I could just barely believe that you might be able to slowly, carefully, get up a flight of stairs. And you had all kinds of time to do it. But you couldn't drag a body. You couldn't go up the stairs backward, and if you were trying to drag it while facing forward, the only way would be to drag it between your legs. On a narrow stairway? Don't think so. Over your back—maybe—if your arms were strong enough—but the low clearance would make it tricky, and going up the stairs with it on your back might be just as hard as dragging it between your legs.

"I got it when I looked at the silla Rob and Don took from you. That's some damned strong cord for something so thin. You unfastened it from your waist, got it around the corpse in a harness, went up the stairs with the loose end in your hand, and then hauled the body up over the stair railing. It would have taken a lot of force, but then, you pull a plow sometimes, don't you? And I found the marks the cord left in the railing.

"Anything material you want to add?"

He'd stopped chewing about halfway through that. I admit, the line I was expecting was, "You can't prove it," or variation. But he surprised me. He just said, "So I guess you're gonna kill me now," and started eating again.

"Depends," I said. "Why do you all wear a strong rope around your waists? Do you just like to be prepared for emergencies?"

"It means you're an adult," he said, while chewing.

"Hm. Then let's see about some adult honesty. Do you admit that the account of events I've given is true?"

He nodded, then swallowed and added, "Yeah."

"Good. I was hoping you'd know a lost cause when you heard it. Finish your breakfast and I'll escort you back to your ship."

"You serious?"

"Yes. There's got to be *some* idea of extenuating circumstances, or a permanent could get away with almost anything." No matter what my boss says. "I can't execute you for self-defense against a murderous nutcase who tried to ride you all over deck five. I'd never sleep again. But I can't let you get away without any punishment for a violent crime, so there's a condition.

"You're confined to your ship. I'm going to make sure your captain enforces that. And if you ever pass back this way, you're confined to your ship again. In short, you're never again setting foot on this Ring. I expect you to keep to that. Understood?"

He nodded. "Is this gonna get you in trouble with the bears?"

"Nice of you to think of it. Their big boss will believe me, and he'll be able to calm the others down. But all the better if you're not here reminding them."

"Thank you."

"Don't mention it. My predecessor punished the wrong person. This makes us even."

§

I have one more thing that cycle to relate.

I was walking around the Ring a few periods later, after getting Hart down into his ship, talking to the captain, cleaning up the custody room, so on. Thinking about various and sundry, feeling good about my decision while at the same time worrying if it would rebound on me later, and not really paying any attention to anything going on around me. That's how he managed to pass me, turn around in front of me, and stop me with an outstretched palm.

"Have you been following me?" I asked.

"Listen," McGregor said. "This is private. I didn't get on the feed, I didn't come to your office or your rooms, I didn't call you to mine. I'm gonna say this and be done. I know you don't like me. I don't like you either. But this isn't about that. This is a serious warning. You stop checking those rooms. You know what I mean. It's none of your business and it's not going to be good for your future if you keep doing it. That's all."

The head of Dispatch walked off without another word.

Douglas Todd

THE CASE of the WATER PHANTOM

Sometimes everything happens at once.

In the nearly two hundred fifty cycles since I'd arrived, I'd seen a number of really slow times where there was little or no ship traffic for various reasons, but this was my first Insufficient. That's what Dispatch calls it.

I don't understand the details of how the Ring punches holes in space. Someone tried to explain it to me once and I got lost about four sentences in. But they did put this much in words I could understand: draw a line through space from the Ring to wherever we're trying to make ships come out the other end of the aperture. If there's a star anywhere on that line, or close enough to it, we can't punch a hole to there.

Sometimes, even though Ring jumps aren't that huge a distance on the galactic scale, there is a star in the way of anywhere we might want to punch a hole to. We'd been fifteen cycles unable to transit to anywhere people actually wanted to go, and all I can say is, I'm glad it didn't happen very often.

We were absolutely at dock capacity. In fact we were beyond it. We had three fours and two eights docked. We had two sub-eights "shadowed," that is, they were docked *under* one of the fours, literally in their shadow. The four would have to leave before they could. Dispatch hates doing that, so you see what we'd come to. There were seven ships in near holding, and we'd already swapped out docking privileges several times so some of the ones in holding could get a turn. We were also charging for regular shuttle service back and forth to the ones in holding, and we were getting what we charged without protest. Or at least without protest that we heard about.

The crews were all getting frayed because they were running out of things to do. It doesn't take long to get your fill of our meager pleasures—drinking, dining, gambling, shopping, sexing, and A/Vs that were probably staler than what they had on their ships. My help and I were getting frayed trying to keep up with all the incidents. Most of the other Ring staff were getting frayed because we run on minimal personnel and they were getting worn out from all the business. Dispatch were frayed because they had absolutely nothing to do except keep ships from bumping into one another. In short, everyone was a bundle of nerves.

That's where we all stood (or, if you use Pergati idiom, sat) when the first body turned up.

I didn't actually see the body at the scene. I got told about it via feed as I was dragging an unconscious Cleit fumwah back to their ship to tell their captain to explain to them what "banned for life" meant when they woke up. Rob and Don were off dealing with a pack of clowns who thought it would be fun to damage some property. Sul found the body and brought it in; Sul said it had clearly been dumped where found, so seeing it in situ wouldn't have been useful anyway. I didn't catch up with the corpse until four periods later, on Dr. Kohl's autopsy table.

It wasn't pretty. The body looked like it had been whipped hard with something a couple of centimeters wide. The long welts were not only across the back and limbs but across the chest as well. The lash marks would have been red and nasty when the victim was alive. They'd bled a bit—I could see multiple tiny brown-black spots of dried blood in the wounds. Other than those spots, there was no other color anywhere in the skin. Not in the welts, not in the lips. Completely white. It took me a while to realize it wasn't just that the victim had been pale.

"Vampires," I said.

"No puncture wounds," Dr. Kohl replied, giving me a sideways look. "Nor, to return to reality, are there any sites of major blood loss. There are a lot of those tiny wounds, but collectively, to bleed out through those—it'd take many periods. And this is total. There is so little blood in this body that I was unable to get a sample."

"Maybe he couldn't get help for some reason. Maybe it was a bondage game gone bad and someone forgot he was tied up in a back room."

One of the many things I like about Dr. Kohl is that rather than rejecting my crazy ideas, he just bats them right back at me. "Then he didn't struggle. And if he was bound, it was solely by whatever created these marks. For example, I see no signs his wrists or ankles were tied. Also, you're assuming these are whip marks. I did too until I took a closer look."

"Then what are they?"

"That's the question. If these were strike marks, they'd be very hard ones, and there would be bruising or hematoma which would, I think, have been visible even after the blood loss. Conversely, if the marks were made after the blood loss—"

"There wouldn't be all the little scabs, right. So they're burns? Or abrasions? Pretty deep for abrasions."

"Up to three millimeters, some places," he agreed. "It looks like the skin has been dissolved, eaten away. Chemical burns would be my best idea, but if so, no traces of the agent were left when I swabbed."

"Doctor, you're supposed to help me clear up mysteries, not create them."

He looked cheerful. I think he likes mysteries—they keep his life interesting. "I report what I see."

My feed chirped and I answered. "Gray-woman!"

"Hello, Sul. What's the problem?"

"A fumwah is trying to destroy Corphon shop."

"Sul, I thought you could take on any fumwah in the galaxy."

"Is a truth, but fumwah has friends."

Rob and Don had finished dealing with the clown squad, but had gone right back out again to break up a bar brawl. I sighed. "I'll be right there. Stay in one piece."

§

I've already described Corphon's once before. I'd like to say he cleaned up his act after that, and I suppose he sort of did—for about five cycles. Then it had been right back to business as usual. One day I was going to hit my limit and make the case to my boss that his annoyance level outweighed his financial benefit to the Ring.

My mood didn't improve when I got there. It's hard to tell fumwah apart, but I was pretty sure this was the same one I'd dragged back to their ship earlier. Scars in the same places. They were throwing a table against a wall when I came in, and squealing something angry. When I entered, they turned to see me and shrieked. I had just enough time to think, "Oh, I guess they remember me" before they tucked their head down and charged.

The thing is, they use that opening move too much and they can't steer very well when they do it. I was ready, and got out of the way, and they collided with the door frame so hard they might actually have made a dent. In the door frame, I mean. I wasn't worried about dents in the fumwah's head. They hit so hard I wasn't sure there would be a round two. I checked around. The fumwah had three friends. Sul was atop one, astride their shoulders as they thrashed around, trying to apply the neck trick. Not having much success, but I wasn't worried because there was no way the fumwah was going to shake Sul off, and their tusks were no good against someone in that position. The second one was already down, out cold. The third one ... had come up from behind a table and just missed grabbing my arm. I ducked and rolled, and got far enough away to try to plan my dodge as they prepared to charge me. Then there was a sizzling sound, and the fumwah fell face forward onto the floor. An ahpesh stood in the doorway with a synaptic pistol.

I checked on Sul, who had just downed the last one and looked ready to handle twenty more. "We appreciate your arrival," I said to the ahpesh, "but it would have been better to have done as asked and not let this one"—I gestured to Doorframe Head—"off ship again."

"A thousand apologies," said the ahpesh, inclining their head. "Indeed we pursued as soon as we knew they had escaped." They signaled and three other ahpesh came in. Each of them took an unconscious fumwah by wrapping their tail around the torso, under the armpits, and slithered away slowly dragging the fumwah behind them, leaving Doorframe Head for the one with the gun to deal with.

"Was anyone else injured?" the ahpesh asked. I had noticed that ahpesh had become notably more polite to me since the Lu Cush incident.

"I don't know. Let's have a look. Sul, would you check the back rooms?" As Sul went into one of the back halls, Corphon oozed out of another. He has some hole he disappears into until the trouble's over. The ahpesh immediately started berating him, which was fine with me because it saved me from having to do it. I had a look around instead. The two main rooms had emptied out when the trouble started; if anyone was hurt, they'd taken their injuries out the door with them. When I'd finished my check, Corphon and the ahpesh were arguing about who would pay for damages, and I was just settling back to enjoy it when Sul tugged my arm from behind and said quietly, "You must come see, Gray-woman."

I followed Sul out the back door into the "alley" behind Corphon's. In it, sprawled atop a couple of empty crates, lay an unclothed corpse. Human. Sprocket. Dead pale, with whiplike marks all over the body with tiny dark spots in them.

"Sul, where exactly did you find the other one?"

"Four:forty-seven." Clear on the other side of the Ring. Low-traffic area, mostly maintenance and service access. "In a back hall same as this. I was passing in the concourse and smelled it."

"Smelled it? Did it smell strange in some way?"

"No, just dead human."

"We may need to take it through the bar. I'm not sure we can get a trolley around that corner."

"I will go."

Sul went to get the trolley, and I stood wondering if I should try to go back in and check on the Corphon situation. No, if by some chance I came back out and the body was gone, I'd be sorry. Let Corphon sweat. I stooped down to take a closer look at one of the wounds. As I did, there was simultaneously a bang and something whistled past very near me.

I whirled. A shadow ducked around the tight corner at the end of the alley. I ran after it, but whoever it was had too big a head start. I turned the corner, into the narrow passage connecting the back alley to the concourse, and it was empty. There were enough people circulating in the concourse that running out into it to look would have been pointless.

I had to walk all the way down to the far end of the alley to find the bullet. Our walls aren't bulletproof—hence the ban on breachables—but they're very tough. It had lodged deep in the dead-end wall, almost penetrating it. It was a little low for where my head would have been if I hadn't happened to crouch at the right time. Then again, the shooter hadn't intended it for it to travel far enough that the curvature of the hallway became a factor.

My ears felt warm; I realized my heart was pounding. I didn't know if it was fear or anger. Maybe both.

§

"Oh, good," Flanagan said when I came in. "Just the thing for a slow cycle."

"You folks are having a slow cycle while the rest of us are going crazy trying to keep up," I said. "Want to trade jobs? I'll mind the shop for you if you go fight fumwah for a while."

"No, thanks," he said. "What can I do for you?"

"May I have a rundown on what's docked?"

"Don't see why not," he said. "Let's see. The fours are cargo. Two Pergati and one mixed crew, human and Pergati. Nothing interesting in their manifests. One of them is deadhead. One of the eights is your friends the Cleit, the other is a human emigrant ship. The two sub-eights are interesting. One of them has a crew of three with one passenger. Humans. Listed as "private transport," so the passenger is either very rich or very important or both."

"Any guesses about their business?"

"If they don't raise any red flags, we don't ask, and they didn't so we didn't. They're bound for Pergati space, for what that's worth."

"What's the other sub-eight?"

"It's also private transport, but it's a tanker. A system of registry I've never heard of and I'm not sure how to pronounce."

Flanagan didn't mean a ship carrying liquid or gaseous cargo. Those were called "wet cargo," and they tended to be short-haul because there weren't many cargos of that type worth hauling through a Ring. He meant that its occupants couldn't survive in Ring atmosphere—that the ship had its own sealed environment. An aquatic species, for example, or one that lived in some other kind of gas. There's at least one species in the galaxy I know of that lives in an atmosphere that's mostly methane.

"Why are they even docked if they can't leave their ship?"

"So they can resupply. But at least one of them can leave. One of our juniors spoke to them in person to arrange power hookups and so on. Little green creature. Sometimes ships like that do keep someone of another species on as a liaison. Must be lonely. Or maybe not. This manifest is hard to read. I know there are six beings on the ship, but I can't tell whether these divisions are by species, or crew vs. passengers. Maybe they let the green one bring a friend."

"You don't sound too worried about not knowing exactly who or what is on the ship," I said.

He shrugged. "That's why we negotiated in person, so we could have a look. The one we saw, you could pick them up and break them in half, I'm told. Even if there are five of them, still no threat. And the tankers can't come out of their tank, no matter how many there are."

§

At that point—even assuming I would never be able to figure out who took a shot at me—I probably should have done more work to try to figure out the two corpses, what had made those marks, and so on. But let the truth be told: my sleep schedule had been shattered to bits by all the trouble calls over the last few cycles and I was in no condition to do procedural work, or any heavy thinking for that matter. What I needed right then was sleep, and after eating a very early dinner (for want of a better name), I went to my rooms to try to get some.

I got about three periods. Then the feed chirped. It was Rob. "What are you still running on?" I asked.

"Sorry, boss."

"Not your fault. Just trying to get what I can, when I can. What's the problem?"

"Well ... we got a weird thing here and we think maybe you'd better come see."

I couldn't get more out of him than that, and anyway if it was something that gave them pause I wanted to see it myself. I got dressed again and headed to deck five, fount of my pain.

At least it wasn't Corphon's, or I might have committed a murder myself. It was a tiny place appropriately named Pipsqueak's, which made this situation strange already, because it was a bar mostly for permanents and regulars, and its clientele were normally well-behaved. When I got there, Rob and Don were presiding over utter ruin. Most of the tables in the bar were in places they weren't supposed to be, and one of them was in pieces. The proprietor was behind the bar, looking like she was about to cry. At one side, lined up against a wall, Don was keeping watch over eight patrons who were obviously in disgrace. Several of them looked pretty beat-up. At the other side of the room, as far from the wall of shame as possible, Rob was keeping guard over a human—a very attractive human, save for the smug smile.

I've noted already that my policy on gender is to leave it blank unless someone specifically tells me otherwise, but in this human's case I wouldn't have been able to speculate on which or all or none even if I wanted to. I might have given slight odds to "male," but that was mostly because I tended to go a little too strong on the presence or absence of mammaries, especially when there were no other obvious cues. This is a bad habit.

"This one comes into the bar," Rob said, "and starts talking to that bunch over there, and then all of a sudden there's a fight. All of them doing their best to beat the hell out of the other ones. And this one's sitting in the middle of it smiling and not doing a damned thing."

"Is that a fact?" I said to the person.

"Really, what was I supposed to do?" they said. "I couldn't get out of my chair without becoming part of the fight."

"And I suppose you have no idea why your presence seems to be an incitement to riot."

"None whatsoever." But their face said they knew perfectly well, and they were pleased as hell about it.

"Rob, do we have their information?"

"Sure. One of the passengers on that emigrant ship."

"We may want to talk to you again," I said to the person. "Now get out of here. I want you back on your ship as fast as you can get there. If I find out you've gotten in any more trouble before your ship leaves, I'm going to tell your captain to ship you to your destination in a crate. Do you understand?"

"But I haven't caused any—"

"Go. Before I put you in a crate myself."

I was mostly trying to scare them into hurrying so they'd be well away before I released the combatants, but it didn't work. When they saw the instigator head for the door, two of them launched themselves, and seeing the competition get an early start, the other six followed. They nearly knocked Don over, and it takes a lot to knock Don over. The battle started again as they were trying to claw past each other to get through the door. It took another ten subs to break it up, even with three of us, and by the time we were through I was so annoyed that I snarled at Rob and Don, and I try not to do that.

I was leaving the scene and almost at the nearest ramp when someone jumped me. I'd have seen them if I'd been on a less busy deck. Or maybe I wouldn't have; I was still fuming over the business at Pipsqueak's.

They'd been waiting in a side hall. They clamped a hand over my mouth as they tried to pull me into that hall. With my peripheral vision I saw something flash in their other hand and I tried to flip them; it didn't work, but it jolted them enough that they had to adjust the hand over my mouth, and when they did, I bit it.

They yelped, and brought the knife in, but by then I had a hand loose. I pushed their knife hand away, and they moved again, and I kicked backwards and then they were off me. I spun around. They were wearing a full-face mask. They changed their grip on the knife and I knew they were going to throw it. I dodged, and I made it, but then they were gone. They'd just thrown the knife to divert me.

I didn't chase. I hadn't even gotten a good look at their clothes. As soon as they got back into the concourse, all they had to do was take off the mask to be unfindable.

I slumped down the wall. I must have sat there for a few subs. Nobody stopped, even though I was still in sight of the concourse. Nobody had had time to notice any of it. Eventually I picked myself up, claimed the knife, and walked to my rooms. Nothing happened on the way. I got to my rooms and collapsed on my bed without undressing.

§

I woke up the next cycle feeling shaky and brittle. Of course, some of it might have been blood loss. I should have tried to get patched up before sleeping. I wondered if I'd have to throw out those sheets.

I had a slash straight down the heel of my right hand, extending to the wrist. It had missed the important blood vessels. That had been where I held off the knife with my hand. What puzzled me was the one across the outside of my left shoulder. The only thing I could think of was that when they'd thrown the knife at me, it hadn't completely missed. When I tried to remove my shirt, I had to tease the fabric out of the cut and I couldn't do it without opening it back up again.

Dr. Kohl saw the condition of the bandage peeking from under my sleeve, and without a word walked over, lifted my sleeve, and pulled off the bandage. "I'm stitching that," he said. Then he saw the one on my hand and looked under that bandage as well. "That one too." He said it in a tone that left no room for discussion.

I didn't say anything as he worked on my shoulder. I felt like I'd been scolded by a parent, and of course he knew, because he misses nothing. He said, more gently, "Would you like to tell me about it?"

"Someone is trying to kill me," I said. "This is the second attempt. The one who took a shot at me behind Corphon's might have been going after whoever discovered the body we brought you; but this time he was waiting just for me."

"Any suspicions?"

"All kinds of suspicions. Nothing I can work from. I don't know if it's connected to the victims with the lash marks. I don't know anything."

"Hm," he said. "All right, let me see that hand."

He started on that one and I found I wanted to look somewhere else while he was working on it. I don't usually have a problem with needles.

"I suppose," he said, "that not doing whatever it is has provoked this response is not an option for you."

"I think it may already be too late for that," I said.

"I'd tell you to try not to reopen these," he said, focusing on the stitches, "but I know better. Your second patient was bloodless too, but you knew that. I've opened both up and taken samples. Nothing out of the ordinary, other than the blood loss. No traces of odd chemicals, nothing in the lungs or any other organs. They died because they ran out of blood. That's all I'm able to tell you."

He finished and went to wash up.

"I guess I'll go see about identifying the dead, at least." I stood up.

"Jessica." He turned from his sink. "Be very careful. I realize you may not believe me, but there isn't a crime on this entire Ring worth your dying over. I don't want to find you on my table one day." It was the first time I'd ever seen him look tired.

"Doctor," I said, "I promise I'm going to try my best not to end up there."

§

The advantage of going to a ship early in the cycle is that most visitors are aboard their ship, sleeping. I was able to get to the captain of the emigrant ship pretty easily, and by passing around images of them, it wasn't hard to find out that both corpses had been passengers on it.

The captain wasn't happy about this. At one point I thought he was going to accuse us of having a serial killer who preyed on visitors. But I think I managed to convince him that I was as upset about it as he was, and I eventually got his permission to ask around and get detailed information on the backgrounds of his passengers—all his passengers, not just the two dead ones.

The problem with an emigrant ship is that you can't usually interview friends and family. The people on this ship were travelling to start a new life in a new place, and tended to be unattached. The ones with strong home ties don't pack up and leave. Nor had they really had much chance to get to know one another on shipboard—not that they didn't try. The feed on my two corpses was that neither gent was shy and retiring—they'd each had sex with at least two other passengers, I was told, plus one wry comment that there were probably several others no one had caught on about yet. Still, not startling. It gets boring on those long trips.

You already know I didn't find any evidence saying, "This passenger used to be a homicidal maniac" or even "this passenger likes to tie people up and whip them," so I won't bother going into that.

For no particular good reason—just trying all the possibilities no matter how feeble—I went to the other docked ships. All the others but the two sub-eights were clean. Their crews were just going about their business, they all checked out, and at least one of them had been here multiple times. If any of them had reason to suddenly be a killer, I couldn't see it.

The sub-eights were complete dead ends. The first one wouldn't let me in. When I talked to them over the airlock comm and identified myself, they danced around until they got me to admit I had no real reason to enter their ship, and then shut me down cold. The tanker was no better. When I buzzed the ship, I got no reply whatsoever. I waited ten subs, and decided to try again later.

Call it a blind spot, but I had a hard time believing that the "vampire" could be a Ring resident. For one thing, wouldn't we have found other victims before this? We didn't have any especially new people, not even among the transients. If it was someone on the Ring, then why had they suddenly decided to start doing this? The crowds? We got crowds all the time—not like this, of course, but still plenty if the question was an available pool of visitors to bleed. If it was someone on the Ring, what had they been waiting for? If it was a visitor, then who and why?

Of course I had asked the human captain if there had been any unusual deaths aboard ship before they arrived, and of course he'd said no. Captains aren't always honest about things like that, though. And sometimes they don't find out.

You might wonder that I was thinking more about the vampire victims than my own personal assassin. But the former still seemed at least slightly solvable. If I thought about the other, it just made me hurt. That could be anybody—a Ring resident, a visitor, anybody. Finding a reason wouldn't help—I knew a reason already, a perfectly good one, and that didn't get me anywhere. I couldn't just walk up to X and tell him, or her, to call off his killer. Even assuming it was McGregor: No proof whatsoever. He'd call me insane.

The feed chirped. "Hey, stranger," Meridian said.

"Who's the stranger?" I said. "You've been so busy over there I'm surprised you can walk."

"Crude." But true. I hadn't seen her since the Insufficient began.

"I'm feeling very ill-mannered today, sorry. What can my crude self do for you?"

"I was thinking early dinner. I need to get out of this place for a while."

§

Meridian might have been able to walk, but she definitely wasn't at her best, and dinner was subdued. She looked like she needed rest even more than I did, and I told her so.

"And I mean rest without sex," I added.

She smiled, but it was wry. "What about you? I think you might need rest with sex. Especially after being wounded in the line of duty."

She hadn't been happy about the bandages. I talked her past it, and she was making light, but I knew she was worried. Well, come to that, I was worried too.

"I think what we both need is to get all these ships out of here ... can we help you?"

The last part was addressed to a woman—you'll understand in a moment why I jumped to that conclusion—who had come to our table and was standing there, watching us, looking like she wanted to say something. I didn't know her, but I knew I wanted to look at her.

She wasn't exceptionally beautiful, physically. She didn't look like a Venus arisen or some sort of exotic love goddess. She looked normal. But there was an attitude about her, some atmosphere, so that when you looked at her, your first thought was, "I would like to have sex with this woman," and your second thought was, "and she would like me to have sex with her." Except with a lot more urgency. As I've mentioned, I don't think I have much of a sex drive, but if she'd said, "Come with me right now and we'll do it in the back hall," I would have gone without bothering to take the time to think about whether it was a good idea. And Meridian looked ready to do it on the floor right there in the restaurant.

There was also something familiar about her, something that I had seen before, though I was sure that if I'd seen her before I would remember.

My feed chirped.

"What?" I shouted at it, and then didn't process what I heard—poor Sul had to say it a second time. Then it sank in.

Meridian said, later, how telling it was that I got up and left. She hasn't explained what she thinks it tells, but I know. The fact is, Sul's news was probably the only thing that could have pulled me away from that woman at that point—because the idea that *another* person had died in the same way before I'd been able to solve it was such a personal affront that anger kicked in and overrode every other impulse—even the feelings of jealousy because I knew Meridian was going to go off and have fun with this woman without me.

I didn't process any of that at the time. I went off to a seldom-used gantry access down on deck nine; Sul had once again been in the general area checking on who-knows-what and had smelled it. Like the other corpses, this one (a socket this time, for what it's worth) was wearing no clothing, had no identification, but there was a tattoo on their neck that was ringing memory bells, and I told Sul to get a trolley and called Rob and Don and told them to meet us at Dr. Kohl's, it was time for a council of war.

The ramps that were near there took us past deck five at a point near Custody, and I told Sul to continue on up to four, there was something I wanted to stop in Custody to check. I don't remember what it was now. I went to Custody and was just preparing to go in—I noticed something was wrong even as the door was sliding open—and I tucked and rolled and there was the big noise and then some things hit me and I blacked out.

§

I woke up. My head seemed clear. My eyes focused. I counted to twenty backwards. Not in base eight. By the time I had, I'd realized where I was.

"This is a first," I said. "I've never woken up in medical before."

"I hope you won't make a habit of it," Dr. Wright said. "I'm told it was a very small device, but I'm also told that if you hadn't reacted as you did, you'd be dead. I know you're not one for polite chat, so I'll just give you the list. You have minor lacerations all over your back, plus a few on your legs and arms. You have four major lacerations on your back which will ensure you don't enjoy moving around much for a while. Also quite a few bruises. Apart from that you have been extremely lucky. One of the fragments that hit you came within two millimeters of puncturing a lung. Another penetrated very near your spine. You have no concussion or any other damage I can find above the neck, barring insanity—probably because you were found in a tight roll with your head tucked into the rest of your body. On the whole, miraculous. Sul! You can come in. She's awake."

"If I didn't get hit on the head, why did I pass out?"

"Who knows?" she said. "Perhaps it was the stress of weathering the third attempt on your life in less than two cycles." She smiled acidly and stepped out. Sul came in as she left.

"Wright-woman is too harsh," Sul said. "She says it was all luck, but it wasn't. You rolled the right way. Bomb was set to spray the other way. Meant to slice door all into little pieces. Slice anybody standing in door into little pieces too. I had a friend look at it. Interesting work. Hard to see. Good you saw it."

"No kidding," I said, sitting up and grunting a little from the effort. She was right—moving around was not going to be fun. "Sul, was it the kind of bomb someone puts together from spare parts? Or was it something only a professional would have?"

"Mechanism could be homemade, just two sensors for when the door moved open enough. But the stuff in the door seam, explosive itself—Brun says it was special stuff, not like for mining or something."

I exhaled, then winced because exhaling hurt. "I can't keep having near misses, but it could still be anybody. I don't know what to do next, Sul."

"I suggest getting out of bed," Dr. Wright said, coming back in, "and then going to see the Director, who has asked that you go talk to her as soon as you're capable. You're capable. You won't enjoy it, but you're capable. Here." She handed me a packet of pills. "No more than one every four periods. They're painkillers. I'd give you stronger ones, but I know you wouldn't take them if you thought they'd make you loopy. These won't. I'm afraid you'll have to get back to your room in a robe; your clothes"—which she handed to me; I could see the shirt was in tatters—"aren't fit to wear. Please bring the robe back when you get a chance."

"Thank you, Doctor," I said. Her face was stern but her eyes were more concerned than anything else.

"Also, once you get through with all that, would you please go check in with Frederic? I've assured him you're fine. But he worries."

§

I hadn't been physically in a room with the boss since just before Max and Kezar died. It seemed to me that she looked more tired than the last time I'd seen her. Then again, look who was talking. I probably looked like I'd been dragged through hell and back.

"It will be several cycles before the custody area can be repaired," she said. "We simply have too much else happening right now."

"That's fine," I said.

She looked me up and down. I don't know what she was checking for.

"I've required that you act as an independent agent in the past—"

Oh, here it comes, she's going to tell me to back off.

"—and I continue to require that you do so in the future. But this is a special exception. I won't have someone trying to hunt down one of my top-level employees. If you need any assistance from me whatsoever on this matter, any sort of arrangements, tell me and don't hesitate."

I nodded.

"Do you have any at this time?"

"Not at this time, no."

"Also, I would like you to limit the amount you travel unaccompanied until you deal with this. I realize that isn't how you're accustomed to work. But consider the odds, please. At the very least, allow someone to keep track of your whereabouts closely. You're no good to anyone dead."

I nodded again. She leaned forward and made sure she had my attention. Not that she had ever lost it.

"I'm sure you realize you're not likely to be able to get him until he tries again."

I nodded a third time.

"Be ready for it. When he does, make sure you kill him. That's an order."

§

Wait for him to try to kill me again, and kill him when he does. Sure. Simplicity itself. It was easy when you were the boss.

Still, it was good to know where she stood on this. Now, the question was, was it a pack of lies? I knew she was ruthless, but could she actually have given me that speech if she had also been the person who'd set the killer on me in the first place?

I really preferred to pick McGregor, but the problem there was I couldn't decide if McGregor was that sharp. To appearances, he wasn't. For that matter, this didn't have to be about any of the various conspiracies on the Ring at all. Maybe someone had decided that I was just too much of a pest.

My head hurt, and it wasn't because of my injuries.

I was on deck two anyway, so I went back to my rooms a second time (a little nervously at the door) and grabbed both the baton and the neural gun. I had decided I wasn't going to travel without those for a while, even if the neural gun did have only one shot in it. I looked at the shredded clothes on the table and sighed. I'd really liked that shirt.

Next to the pile of shredded clothes was the knife that had cut up my hand and shoulder. It still had a stain on the blade. I went into the bedroom and got a sock to use as a makeshift sheath. I'd decided to carry that for a while too. If he jumped me again, I was going to return it to him.

I made my way down to Dr. Kohl's. "Good to see you up and about," he said, with a little more emphasis than it needed.

"Thanks. Glad to be here, believe me. Did Rob and Don get to talk to you about the third body last cycle?" I'd found out when I got out of medical that I had slept for a nice long number of periods. I wasn't complaining. I had needed the sleep.

"No. When we heard the news from Sul I turned them around and sent them home to bed. You've all been pushing yourself too hard. I hope Sul got some too, but you never can tell with that one. Dr. Wright said she had trouble getting Sul to stop standing guard over you."

"Yes. Sul went to investigate the bomb somewhere in there too. I'm not sure they sleep. You know they found all three of these bodies. I think after the first two they've been walking the ship looking for them ... what?" He was giving me a quizzical look.

"Does Sul actually prefer 'they' or have you gone all this time without knowing her gender?"

"Oh. I hate to admit it, but I really have a hard time figuring that out with Pergati. They either have to tell me or I have to learn it some other way ... she didn't volunteer it and I didn't ask."

"She is Xin Rath's daughter," he said, "from an older pairing, from before his clan formed into its current configuration. Some say she's Xin Rath's spy."

"That last part I knew. Doctor, how do you manage to know all this? There can't be more than two humans on this Ring who can keep track of Pergati relationships and all their tangles."

"And those humans are probably both in medical. It's important for doctors to keep track of the relationships between their patients, particularly in a small place like this. You know Pergati consult a geneticist before having cubs? The way they intermingle, they'd be crazy not to. At any rate, I digress. You were saying?"

"I'm pretty sure that body is one of the people who were involved in something odd at Pipsqueak's last night."

My feed chirped. "Oh, hell. Hang on, Doctor. "

"Fun's fun," Catalan's urgent voice said, "and I don't mind that she took the night off, she's entitled, but she needs to come back to work now!"

"Wait, wait—Catalan, hang on—are we talking about Meridian? She didn't spend the night with me. We were at an early dinner, but I got called away. As far as I know she planned to go back to work."

"Then where is she?"

"I don't know. I'll check on it right away." I disconnected while she was still fussing at me. I'd pay for that later. "Doctor, I know you hate the feed, but I'd really appreciate it if you'd call Rob and Don and Sul and get them here. Tell Rob and Don to bring their pry rods."

"Where are you going?"

"Arms locker." He didn't ask me whether I should be travelling alone. He didn't need to. If someone had attacked me just then, I'd have torn them to pieces with my teeth.

§

"It's like this," I said to the council of war. "I'm not going to believe this killer or killers is someone who was on the Ring already. Not when they're so hungry they've killed three people in four or five cycles. They've got to have come in on one of those ships. They seem to be human, but they're not on that emigrant ship, because that ship hasn't had any deaths like this, and also because the killers need some hiding space where they can be with their victim for a cycle or so. This is a slow kill."

"And you think Meridian is in their hands because of what happened when you were with her?"

"I do. Don't look skeptical, Doctor. You weren't there. I think the person who started the bar fight at Pipsqueak's was another. Or maybe ... no, keep that theory for later. It's enough that I think there are one or more entities who exert some sort of powerful attraction on humans. Maybe other species too. I think they can probably turn it on and off, or at least apply it selectively, because the one at Pipsqueak's wasn't interested in trying it on me, and I assume Rob and Don didn't feel any strong urges there either." I looked at them both. Don shook his head.

"They lure their victims off somewhere for fun and games, then bleed them dry. Here's a little more proof." I held up my data pad. "These are two men from the emigrant ship—corpses one and two in Dr. Kohl's drawers over there. Rob, Don, recognize either of those names?"

"Yeah," Rob said. "That's the one at Pipsqueak's. The one all the fighting was about."

"They knew that the real one was already dead. They had to give you a name, so they picked one they knew was safe to use."

All the other humans in the room exchanged looks as if trying to decide whether to believe me. Sul was leaning against a wall, appearing to barely even listen. But she was. "One of the sub-eights," she said.

"I think so too. Either the human ship or the tanker. I vote for the tanker."

"Why?" Don said.

"Let's just try the tanker first," I said. "If I told you I wouldn't be able to justify it. Humor me."

He shrugged. "You know I'm in if you say so."

"Everybody else good? I can't raid this ship alone." General consensus.

"OK. This is a needler. Rob, Don, you decide who takes it. It's not lethal unless you get a lucky hit on someone's face, but being pierced with little metal shards is a great deterrent. Use it wisely, it doesn't have much ammo. Everything else I had in the locker was too dangerous to use, except blades, and you both prefer your pry rods. Sul, I assume you prefer to use what nature gave you. I have a neural gun but it only has one shot left in it. Dr. Kohl, what are you doing?"

"Putting together a medical bag," he said.

"You don't have to come with us—"

"Don't be ridiculous," he said. "She'll need medical help." He didn't say "if she's alive." "And you don't have the time to waste arguing with me about it."

§

The dock the tanker was using was not one we used very often. I hadn't realized when I tried to talk to them before just how forbidding it was. Or maybe that was just nerves. I don't think so, though. A couple of the automatic lights weren't working, and one flickered. The whole area looked abandoned. Of course the ship had no cargo, so there were none of the usual signs of a ship that was doing active loading. The dim opening of the airway looked like a pit down to a place we really didn't want to go.

I shook it off. No time for that kind of crazy.

"I've called Dispatch. They're going to say one of their people needs to talk to ship crew about something. That should get one of them to come up. Get out of sight."

A sub or two later, a head appeared at the top of the airway, then timidly climbed all the way up. It was a small green biped with lizard-like features. I knew when I saw them that they was going to be a pushover. They walked over to me—and I grabbed them around the waist with one arm and picked them up.

It took a bit. They spoke only Bak'ti. But they were gradually given to understand that we were all going into the airlock with them, and that no harm would come to them if they cooperated. They very clearly weren't the culprit. I could have torn them in half without breaking a sweat. Also, they were scared to death.

Once through the airlock, we had to pick our way slowly, because there was barely any light. Whatever these creatures were, their vision didn't work the same way as ours. It would have been less unnerving to be able to charge in. Rob and Don didn't look happy. Sul, of course, was completely unflustered and took point.

At one corner she got down on all fours to peek around a corner at a low level— then charged around it without bothering to stand all the way up. (Pergati can run on all fours, very fast, but they usually consider it beneath their dignity.) There was some shrieking, and by the time we came around the corner, three other lizards were cringing against one wall and Sul was sitting on a fourth. The three standing looked like they wanted to make a run for it, but it was interesting—the only door they kept eyeing was the one Rob and Don were blocking, the one that led out of the ship. There was another opening they wanted nothing to do with.

"That's five," I said. "The sixth is in the tank."

"They are afraid of it," Sul said.

"Looks that way. Let's see if we can get them to say why." But we couldn't. They just kept watching the doorway to the rest of the ship when they thought we weren't looking. "I give up," I said. "They might be stalling." I moved to the inner doorway.

"Are we going down there?" Rob said.

"No choice. Which of you wants to guard these idiots?" It turned out to be moot. All five of us had clustered near the inner door, and as we did, all five of the lizards took off, running in the direction of the airlock. I heard it cycle. "How about that."

"Should we—"

"No, we'll catch them later. Come on."

The inner doorway led to a corridor which passed a crew bunkroom and a couple of other rooms and then began to descend. There was no question of going any other way; there had been no other halls. It turned a corner twice, descending all the way. After those rooms there were no other exits. Someone coming in would have to cross the crew rooms to get here; the crew knew what had been going on.

"I'm not sure what you're planning at the bottom," Dr. Kohl said. "This is a tanker. We will likely just find a sealed area we can't enter."

"No, we won't," I said.

"Why are you sure?"

"Because the victims didn't have fluid or other gases in their lungs," I said. "And because they came in using their own legs."

Near the bottom of the ramp, the light levels rose—but a strange light, an uneven purple light. When we reached the end we saw why. The ramp opened into a large, long room. There was a narrow ledge to walk on around all four walls of the room, but most of it was taken up by an enormous water tank, a swimming pool. Recessed in the walls of the tank, below the water level, were many purple lights. They shone up through the water so the water itself glowed, reflecting purple patterns onto the ceiling of the room and the walls. It was the only lighting in the huge room, but it was bright enough for us to see each other.

At the far end of the tank, the opposite end of the room, was something it took my brain a while to resolve. Gradually it came into focus. The dark lines were the tentacles of something large, amorphous, blue-black which was keeping most of its body below the waterline, which is why I couldn't quite find its edges. The white object encircled by several of these tentacles, but held so its head was above water, was Meridian.

I ran down, closer to that end. Someone behind me said to wait. I got closer— and saw Meridian move. I was sure she had moved under her own power. In fact ...

"She's alive," Dr. Kohl said behind me.

"Is she—?" I heard Don begin. Meridian's movements weren't the way someone moves in pain, or when they're tossing in their sleep, although she looked like she was asleep. She was bucking like someone who was having very vigorous sex, and was enjoying it a lot. I counted four tentacles wrapped around her. It almost looked like they were cradling her gently as she writhed.

"Don't judge," a voice said that wasn't one of us. "You have no idea what she's experiencing."

It was the woman from the restaurant, standing a little beyond us alongside the pool. "Make it let go of her," I said.

"This is complete joy. She'll never have anything like this again. You think she'll come back to you? You can't compare."

"Maybe not," I said, "but she'll be alive."

"And you think she'll thank you for it?"

I drew the neural gun and pointed it at her. "Make it let her go!"

Behind me, I heard a splash. I didn't want to take my eyes off the woman—for several reasons—but I knew I had to. Sul had dived in and was trying to tug tentacles off Meridian. The creature in the tank had started to try to wrap another tentacle around Sul and I heard Sul cry out. I dropped the gun, which probably wouldn't have worked on the creature anyway, and dove in.

I was trying to tug one of the tentacles away from Sul when I felt something around my wrist. It burned, burned horribly, and I tried to pull my wrist away but couldn't, it was wrapped around me. It was trying to pull me underwater. I pulled out the knife with my other hand and slashed at the tentacle. My wrist came away, the water was cloudy and black, and I heard someone make an angry, pained shriek. Sul had dislodged one tentacle. I cut at the other one that held her as my head came above water again. I gasped for air.

"Hurt them! Hurt them for me!"

It wasn't clear which of them the woman was pleading to, Rob, Don, or Dr. Kohl. They could have all been equally enthralled. All three were just standing there, watching her; none of them was trying to help us. But Don was the one with the needler. I saw him unfasten it from his back and get ready to fire it at me, and I knew I wouldn't be able to get out of the pool in time.

But Sul could. She was out and she rolled at Don and got under his feet and he went down, right on top of the woman, and he would have knocked her over ... except that he fell *through* her—I mean actually passed through her; she wasn't solid. He hit the deck, landing on the gun, and nearly rolled into the pool. This surprise snapped all three of the gents out of it. Sul had already dived back in, landing atop the creature in the water, and started to claw at it. I began to work at the tentacles on Meridian. The creature started moving. It was going to submerge deeper—

"Get it out of the water!" I shouted. I'm not sure who I was shouting to. "It's going to drown Meridian!"

I cut through another tentacle. It was strong, but its skin wasn't very tough. The creature was devoting all its attention to me. It had a grip on me in four places. I tried to focus on Meridian and the knife and not the burning or the pain in my back or my shoulders. All I had to do was cut off two more ...

It released both Meridian and me, completely unexpectedly. I grabbed her and tried to pull her away. I was having trouble keeping us both above water; I was having trouble just breathing. But I got her to the edge and Dr. Kohl was there, helping me lift her out. It's a sign of what I think of Dr. Kohl that as soon as Meridian was clearly in his custody, I was able to immediately switch all my attention to the creature.

It had let me and Meridian go because it was giving all its attention to Rob and Don, trying to fight them off. It had several tentacles on both of them, which was a mistake because they were using those tentacles to tug it out of the pool. Sul was still looking for things to claw. The phantom woman was shouting things at us no one was listening to. I swam over to the creature and started looking for a good place to sink a knife.

I didn't have to. Sul had abandoned the water attack and gotten up onto the edge to help pull. Between the three of them, they got it completely out of the pool just as I reached it.

It was an octopus. But not. It had squid features, octopus features, extra deformations, bumps where there weren't supposed to be bumps. I didn't want to look at it. It lay on the deck, wriggling, still fighting, trying to get back in the water. It was trying to grip the edge of the pool to pull itself back down. I cut that off. The water was completely clouded black now, and almost none of the purple light was reaching us.

In the near-dark, we watched the thing gasp and thrash. And the phantom woman started screaming. So loud I wanted to cover my ears—she kept screaming and wailing as the creature flopped around, until all at once she flickered like a light going out, and she was gone. One sub later, the creature stopped moving.

Rob and Don waited another five subs before they would let go.

§

"I need a post-mortem," Dr. Kohl said. "Pardon the phrase."

"Me too," Don said, hesitantly, surprising me.

"Where would you like to start?" I asked.

It was two cycles later. The Insufficient had ended; ships were slowly moving out. The four that had shadowed the sub-eights had left dock a period ago, and the tanker had just undocked and was in the transit queue. It hadn't been hard to round up the lizards, even as dented as we were. I'd made a deal with them: Take the ship, dispose of the body somehow, don't tell me about it, don't ever come back again. They were complicit, yes, but only because they were scared to death of it. It had probably abused them in ways I didn't want to imagine. The creature chose its crew carefully—if they'd been any stronger they'd have probably killed it long ago.

As for those dents: Meridian was stable and resting. She'd woken up several times but had been in no condition to talk much. Rob, Don, Sul and I all had tentacle burns in various places, and I'd reopened a couple of the prior wounds, so none of us were exactly in peak condition, but we were moving around.

"You knew before we went that there was only one 'human,'" Dr. Kohl said. "That was what you didn't want to explain. Also you said 'they seem human,' or something like that. Hedging. How did you know?"

"I didn't know the creature was projecting the phantom. I didn't even know they *were* a phantom. I was surprised as Don was when he fell through. I hadn't realized we'd never actually seen anything make physical contact with them. At first I just thought they were some kind of emotion-projecting being that looked like a human, and that they were the killer. Then when we found the creature in the pool, I assumed they were a go-between, luring people in for the creature to drain."

"But you knew there was only one."

"That was only a guess. In the restaurant, it struck me that there was something I'd seen before, but I couldn't tell what. The eyes, maybe, or just the general attitude. For all I know none of us were seeing the same thing at the same time. Maybe it depended on who the phantom was trying to set their lure for. I don't know. Incidentally, Sul knew it was a projection long before the rest of us—when she realized, that's when she jumped in the pool."

"You humans have the worst noses," she said. "There was no smell there and I did not see her come in. So the thing was making her."

"And lucky for us, you don't seem to be attracted to humans." She wrinkled her muzzle.

"Why didn't the phantom try to affect you, in the tank?" Dr. Kohl asked.

"I think they did. I had some trouble pointing a gun at them. But ... with Meridian there being bled to death ... I guess you could say I had other priorities."

There was a moment of discreet silence.

"How did you know to go after the tanker first?" Don asked.

"Oh. Well—that was just a wild thing, I kind of hate to admit it ... I had been thinking the marks looked like tentacles. Tentacles are usually on water creatures—in water tanks, see?"

§

Later that cycle, I was walking down deck four, thinking about whether I should go up to get some rest or down to get something to eat, when I heard Sul say, a ways behind me, "Move!" and I moved, as there was a bang and a shot whizzed past me again.

Even then I couldn't help but spare a glance at where the bullet had gone into the wall before giving chase. Damn it, breachables in a closed environment are just a really bad idea!

They hadn't expected Sul. She had insisted she be my bodyguard once it was clear that the business in the tanker had had nothing to do with the attempts on my life. The creature didn't leave its tank and the phantom could not possibly have used a gun, knife, or bomb. The lizards were beneath consideration.

Sul was already after them, and for the second time I saw her get on all fours, because the attacker was fast. They were both nearly a sector ahead of me and coming to a ramp. The attacker didn't slow down on the veer to the ramp and neither did she. Me, aching everywhere, I wasn't keeping up well, but it didn't matter because Sul was going to catch them at the bottom of the ramp anyway at the rate she was going.

When I got there, she had, and the two of them were tussling on the ground. As I caught up to them, Sul yelped, and they threw her off. I saw something glint. Of course the jerk had owned more than one knife. "Sul!" She was trying to get up and they were already getting up and getting away ... I fired the neural gun at them and they went down.

The knife had gone between Sul's ribs. It hadn't hit her heart, but it had gone into a lung; I could hear the air wheeze out of it when she tried to breathe. I got on the feed to medical and shouted for someone. Then I turned around and the assassin was a short distance down the hall.

"Go," Sul said.

I'm not saying the neural gun had been a total failure. It may just have had less charge in it than I'd hoped. They were clearly affected by it; moving, but not well and not nearly as fast as they had. That made us even. Except not quite; they had a slight lead on me and they weren't losing it.

I chased them all the way down from four to nine. When they hit lower cargo, I didn't have to count sectors to know where they were going. That other sub-eight was the only ship that hadn't left dock yet.

They had gained too much ground; I wasn't going to be able to stop them before they made it down the airway. In fact I wasn't even close ... and that saved my life. Because as I approached, two things happened—an unexpected roar and shake, which was the ship using its attitude jets to push away from the Ring; and a loud hiss and a sudden slam, which was the pressure doors at the top of the airway closing as the ship ripped away from the bottom. If I'd been in the airway at the time, I'd have been breathing vacuum.

I got on the feed. "Flanagan! The sub-eight that just kicked off unauthorized. Do *not* let it transit!"

"What?"

"Don't let it go through the Ring! The assassin is trying to escape!"

He stammered something and I hollered back at him and I disconnected and ran for Dispatch.

When I got to Dispatch, I knew immediately they hadn't listened. Flanagan was trying not to meet my eye, and McGregor was in the operations room, looming by Flanagan's desk. I could see on the big displays that the sub-eight was lining up for Ring approach.

"I told you not to let that ship transit!"

"You don't run Dispatch!" McGregor boomed. "I've warned you before! I'm not going to delay a ship just because you take some whim—"

"This is not a whim! That ship contains someone who has tried to kill me four times, not to mention has just nearly burned a hole in lower cargo, and he's trying to escape and you're going to let him because you're a thick-headed, pompous ass! I'm calling the Director."

The Ring hum was building. The ship began to advance to the aperture.

"I've already called her," McGregor said. "Did you think I wasn't going to complain about this?"

"I'm here," the boss said. Neither McGregor and I had seen her come in; we'd been too busy shouting at one another. We both startled a little, even though she had spoken very softly.

The ship was partway into the aperture now; I couldn't see all of it in the display. "Stop the ship!"

"It's too late—" McGregor said, then "Wait, what are you—"

The boss had moved to a console that sat isolated under one of the big displays and had entered a passcode. When she did, a panel had flipped up, exposing a large red button.

"Don't do that!" McGregor shouted.

She slammed her fist down on the button.

The whole Ring shook, hard enough that I nearly lost my balance. It was the usual sensation of release when the Ring shut, but *wrong* somehow, and not just because of the shaking. It was the difference between slamming shut a door, and slamming shut a door that had something caught in the way.

I saw the debris, on the display, and realized what had been caught in the way.

McGregor looked like he was about to be ill or explode or both. Most of the others in the room were staring at the display in shock. Only Flanagan looked completely unaffected.

"Send out a shuttle with an arm to clean up the mess," the boss said to Flanagan. "We don't want it damaging us." She faced McGregor.

"In the future," the boss said to him, and her voice was the coldest I'd ever heard it, "when my security officer tells you to hold a ship, *hold the ship.*"

She walked to the door and turned around. "That way, next time you won't have four deaths on your record. As you do now."

She left. I decided I had better leave too.

No, I wasn't upset about the resolution. The crew of that ship were certainly accomplices, and if four died instead of one, well, four attempts had been made on my life. Not counting nearly getting sucked into space in lower cargo. Was I going to cry for them?

But it also occurred to me that this way, no one was ever going to be able to talk to the assassin about who hired them or why, and this may have made it a satisfactory ending for someone else on the Ring as well. Including, possibly, the woman who had pressed the button.

§

Fifteen cycles later. Sul was already acting as if she'd never been injured. Custody was being mended. Everything was roses. I was sitting in my bed with Meridian. I was sitting; she was lying down, on her back. I was checking the progress of the welts, still horribly red across her pale skin.

"Desecration," I said.

"Silly," she said. "At Catalan's, it's become a joke, you know, they say 'I didn't know you were into that kind of thing.' I've seen some staff looking a lot worse and smiling about it."

"Even so."

"That's not really it, is it?"

I smiled wryly. "I suppose it isn't."

"Well?"

"Well. She—it—said you'd never want to go back. That nothing else would compare."

She got a faraway look, briefly. "She was right."

"What?"

"She was. I've never had another experience like that. Probably never will again."

"Great."

"No, you don't get it. That's true, but that's not all. That's not enough. It's not the most important part."

I looked down at her. She seemed to mean it. "I'm glad to hear it."

"I'm sorry to hear you ever doubted it."

Then she grabbed me and pulled me down to her.

THE CASE of the BIG BANG

The boss and I communicated surprisingly seldom for two people in our working relationship. (You may have noticed.) I sent regular reports, and I imagine she at least glanced at them, but she had never once made any sort of reply to any of them. Once in a while I thought about submitting some outrageous request just to see if she were paying attention, but my own sense of professionalism (I guess we can call it that) would never have let me do such a thing—which, of course, she knew perfectly well.

As for communications initiated by her, I'd long since reached the point where I considered them a bad sign. They happened so seldom that they always meant something which was going to be out of the realm of normal business. By now I was fully established; everyone on the Ring knew who to talk to when trouble happened, and I'd grown accustomed to the feed going off at all periods ... but if it was the boss on the feed, that always meant something special, and not in a good way.

Still, it was difficult for me to see how the Pergati delegation was going to be any trouble at all. To begin with, there were only three of them; and though I'd been informed by the boss that they were high muckamucks and to treat them gently, they didn't have the imperiousness I associated with big dignitaries, or with bloat-heads like McGregor for that matter. They were friendly and polite, possibly even verging on obsequious.

A cycle after their arrival, I learned why they were trying to make nice to me, when I was asked to a meeting at Xin Rath's. To my surprise, when I got there, it was just me, Xin Rath, and the three Pergati muckamucks. Actually, it seemed they weren't muckamucks: they each had only one first name that they'd admit to. Perhaps they were travelling incognito. The only one of the three who did any talking was named Tor.

"Xin Rath says you are the only human here who is to be trusted," they said.

"I would not contradict Xin Rath," I said, "but it would help to know what I'm being trusted about."

Tor gave Xin Rath a look; the latter nodded almost imperceptibly. "All right," Tor said. "We are not here on diplomatic business. We believe this station is the center of a large-scale qov smuggling operation."

"I think that is a truth," I said.

"Yet you do nothing about it—"

"Not true. Dispatch does nothing about it, but I'm not Dispatch. I'm trying to do something about it, but so far I haven't been able to find out who's responsible."

"Xin Rath has explained. How much longer do you think you would want?"

"I have no idea," I said. "It's got to be someone in Dispatch running this, and Dispatch is hard to crack, especially since the person who runs it hates me. Actually, he's a leading choice for the mastermind—but even if it is him, how do we prove it? He doesn't move the qov himself, he's not that stupid. And if we confront him, we had better have a very strong case. Even I can't get away with that without proof. He's the same rank I am. You could just end with me fired and then you lose an ally."

Tor growled. "For cycles of cycles of cycles of cycles—we cannot depend on humans, I told you this—" they said to one of the others.

"Now wait," I said. "You may have been putting up with this for that many cycles, but I've been here less than three hundred, and I was here for two hundred of those before I even realized what scale this was happening on. I don't work miracles."

"That is perhaps so," Tor said, "but there are those who will not wait much longer. Something must be done or it could be very bad."

"How bad?"

They looked at each other.

"Oh, come on," I said. "I thought we were trusting one another."

"There are people in our government," Tor said, "who already are unhappy with the Rings. You know you humans have never let Pergati become involved in their operation. The Rings make most of their money from our ships; we do all the traveling work and they sit and take from the top, is what is being said. They would be pleased to use this smuggling to show that the humans are prepared to exploit Pergati in any way possible, without conscience."

"Is this faction powerful enough to direct the action of the government as a whole? Could the pact between humans and Pergati be breached?"

"... It is possible," Tor reluctantly admitted. "The qov ban has never had strong public support, but the idea of paying less into human accounts would surely be popular. There are many Pergati who have felt all along we should be operating the Rings."

"You do realize the Ring corporation is private, not associated with any human government? Even if they let Pergati into their ranks, who's to say that would benefit other Pergati at all? It could end up still being business as usual. In fact I'd say it was likely."

"*We* know that," Xin Rath said, "but the public—"

"Right." I sighed. "Well, I don't have a mastermind to hand you. And diplomacy isn't my line. You say it isn't yours either. Why *are* you here?"

"We are inspectors," Tor said. "We are to bring back proof that qov is passed through this station in quantity. We know that five cycles ago a ship carrying qov docked here and departed empty. We have increased our patrols; we are now checking every ship that passes from this Ring, regardless of manifest. We want to find the qov taken off that ship on this station. We will mark it invisibly. When a ship containing any of it is stopped after exiting this Ring, we will know."

"And then hell will break loose. So you *want* humans and Pergati to be at each other's throats, then?"

"Do you not see," Tor almost sounded like they were pleading, "that it would be better to expose this and perhaps have a chance to settle it well, than to let it fester and be used against us? If we can say, 'yes, it is proven' and possibly stir some people into acting—"

"My worry," I said, "is that you'll spur the wrong people into acting. Dispatch doesn't care at all about qov and they don't care very much about their reputation with the Pergati. Maybe a threat of Rings being attacked and commandeered would wake them up—if you could get them to believe it. Meanwhile, not long ago someone on this Ring hired a professional assassin to come here and make four attempts on my life, because I was investigating rooms full of qov a little more than they were happy with. Are you prepared for that risk?"

I already knew what they'd answer, at least on the personal level. No Pergat will ever believe that any human could manage to get the drop on them.

"We are if you are," Tor said.

"Oh, I'm already way past that. My risk is a given. Yours is new. But have it your way. I'll be happy to show you around and let you in some rooms. If the boss throws a fit, I'll remind her that she told me to extend you every courtesy."

§

But the boss said nothing. Over the remainder of that cycle and the next two, I snuck out with the delegation at odd periods and we found qov in four rooms and marked it all. Not once did we encounter a blinking door—which was good, as I wasn't sure I wanted to explain those to the delegation, but also struck me as unusual. The stuff they used to mark the bundles with was interesting. It was a spray. They could use it while standing in the doorway and Tor assured me it would permeate all the bundles in the room.

"If they spot it somehow, they'll shut down this whole operation," I said.

"They won't," Tor replied. "Even if they did, then you would have no smuggler to worry about anymore, yes?"

Late on the third cycle, Sul contacted me, and I got out of bed to go to a secret meeting with her and Parn, our inside man in Maintenance. "Very strange data," Parn said, showing me a schematic of deck three with various numbers superimposed over certain rooms.

"This is new," I said to him. "You're tracking power levels in individual rooms now?"

"Always have," he said, "but there was nothing useful in it. But the last three cycles, this strange activity. You see here, these rooms in this sector. They were full of power—then, suddenly, not. But look!" He showed me a different chart. "While that was happening, the total amount of stored power stayed the same. Here is another set of rooms that emptied suddenly. Same thing."

"Wait." I got out my data pad, where I'd been keeping notes on which rooms I'd visited with the delegation. "These are rooms I was visiting. The power wasn't depleted; it was just rearranged. They were shuffling it out of those rooms so that I wouldn't get the blink when I investigated them. How long does the drain take?"

"Two subs perhaps. Very fast."

"So someone was following us, knew where we were going, at least in a vague way. Someone who knew why I was looking at the rooms. Thank you, Parnman. This is very useful information."

I was going to leave, then, but something about his demeanor made me stop. "Is there anything else you wanted to tell me?"

"Possible," he said. "Not sure yet." His tone was more wary than hesitant, though.

"We had decided to trust one another, remember?"

"Pergati are not big for theory," he said. "We like implementation better. We let you humans do the research. Looking around, thinking about power mystery, found something from a long time back—human named Schneider—that said space apertures might make strange things happen, at molecular level."

"Any particular kind of strange things?"

"Negative pressures and temperatures. Absolute zero, but different energy state. Eat entropy. Absorb energy from cooler things, not just hotter ones. Could make something with better than hundred percent efficiency."

"Physics isn't my strength, but isn't that supposed to be impossible?"

"Maybe," he replied.

He didn't want to commit to anything else, and I wasn't going to try to get more then and there—Sul was ample proof that you can't pry anything out of a Pergat they don't want to tell you. But I didn't disregard it. He had unearthed that information for a reason, even if he wasn't ready to tell me what the reason was yet.

§

The next cycle, I escorted the delegates down to deck nine to see them off. It was mostly for my own peace of mind. I knew now why no one had been worried about them finding blink rooms, but they *had* found qov, and whoever put the qov there knew we'd found it—if not from following us on our expeditions, then certainly by now from the door logs. I hadn't been concerned about their safety while they were deep inside the Pergati warrens, but getting them down two decks to their ship was another story. I felt a little less paranoid knowing it wasn't just me; I'd twice caught a glimpse of Sul watching our progress on the way down to deck nine (which of course meant she had allowed me to see her).

They got on board their ship without incident and I heard the thump of the kickers pushing the ship away from the Ring. I thought about going to Dispatch to see them transit, but things were still a little cold in Dispatch and I decided I had better not. I headed for Custody, not in any hurry; I was nearly at the top of a ramp to deck five when the explosion happened, and it knocked me over and I nearly fell all the way back down the ramp again.

My first thought was *That son-of-a-bitch slammed the door on them!*

Actually, no, that wasn't my first thought. My first thought was probably 'I'm falling, have to catch myself.' But once I had, then I could rewind a fraction of a sub to the whole Ring shaking and the loud doorslam bang and the lights flickering. If this had been an aperture abort, and it sure felt like it, it had been much more severe than the other one. Up on the deck five concourse (once I got back up the ramp on shaky legs) I could see into a nearby bar—people on the ground, glasses spilled—the other one hadn't done that. No one in the area looked seriously hurt, just shaken.

I started to head for Dispatch to find out if the delegate ship had really just been destroyed. If it had, we might as well just go get ready for war with the Pergati and avoid the rush. I stopped myself. If I went to Dispatch, then and there, I didn't trust myself not to rip McGregor's head off with my bare hands. Deep breaths. Get proof on the murderous jackass. Proof.

I heard a sound I had never heard before. A low tone rising to a high one, repeated. It took me a second to realize this wasn't a noise in just that area; it was some kind of siren, being sounded all over the Ring.

Then, not jarringly but very quickly, the gravity stopped.

There was some shouting and screaming. Visitors, of course—only visitors and dumb landpig security officers wouldn't know the spin-down alert when they heard it.

I got my bearings and pulled myself along by one of the concourse handrails, and I don't remember how long I spent after that going into various deck five businesses and making sure everyone was okay and getting injured to medical and so forth. Maybe a period, maybe even two. I expected my feed to go off, and it never did, so I just kept going with cleanup until I had done pretty much everything I could do. Apparently this was not a crisis for the security officer, for once.

What I really wanted to do, of course, was go to Dispatch and ask a lot of strong questions and maybe kick some asses. But right now they were all probably losing their minds anyway, and I wasn't sure showing up would be a good idea. On the other hand, it was the only place I was likely to find out what happened ... or maybe it wasn't, I realized.

Getting to Maintenance—getting anywhere—was surprisingly difficult with no spin. You'd think pulling yourself along in no gravity would be easy, but it isn't. If spin stayed down too long I was going to have biceps the size of a fumwah's.

Parn looked a little alarmed when I came in, but I knew he'd see when I shook my head very slightly. "I don't think we've met. I'm Jessica Gray. Security officer. I'm trying to get any diagnostics from this end about damage from the aperture abort."

"Oh. Yes, I see. I have no diagnostics on that, but if you go to one:forty-two you may be able to learn something from the secure maintenance team."

"Thanks very much," I replied.

It's good to have contacts.

§

I had seldom had reason to go to deck one. Neither did anyone else. The area we call the "core" is full of densely packed aperture machinery, monitoring equipment, and so on. If you needed to get to the core, you got to it from deck one, through a vast number of access tunnels and crawlways—and I do mean crawlways, where even Pergati had to move on all fours. The access infrastructure, plus the occasional maintenance storeroom or console room, was all there was to visit on deck one—and you needed very high access levels to do so. Sure, the average Ring resident could run around deck one's concourse, but that was about it.

The only door at one:forty-two led into a sort of staging area, a place where several tunnels or crawlways met. A short corridor led to an inner airlock, one of the ones which opens into the inner circumference of the Ring. A spare pressure suit and some tools and supplies indicated someone was probably outside right now doing repair work. But I was more interested in the Pergat who stood at a small table, studying what looked like a pile of metal scrap, which they were sorting out under a mesh net fastened to the table, to keep the pieces from floating away. A lot of nets like those had suddenly seen emergency service that cycle. The table, like most Ring furniture, was fastened to the floor; the Pergat had a strap loosely around their waist which was attached to a side rail, to discourage drift.

"Gray-woman!" they said, barely looking up from the pile. "Have not met. I am Brun. You may not know—"

"Sul had you look at the bomb from the custody rooms," I said. "I remember the name."

"Very pleased. That bomb was nothing, just explosive from a tube. Squeeze out, stick in trigger. This one much more interesting."

"This was a bomb? So there wasn't an aperture abort after all?"

"Sure. Abort caused by bomb. No difference to ship in wrong place. Very bad. Important people."

"Being sure it was caused by a bomb will help weather that storm, I hope." I wondered how much I should say. But I was pretty sure Sul trusted Brun. I decided it was worth the chance. "Brun, it would help a lot to be able to find whoever set the bomb. Anything you can tell me?"

"Not hard to find," it replied. "This could only have been placed with spin down. Set in a place deadly to go when spin is up, you see? So go back through times spin is down, check door logs. Very few can get in. Prit-man had to let me in to collect this."

"Oh, Prit is up here?" I hadn't seen or spoken to Prit since interviewing him with Max about the locked airshaft. All these cycles later and it still had never entirely left my mind.

"Prit-man is everywhere right now. Some maintenance only can be done when spin is down, so Prit will be trying to get people to do much while possible."

Having been invoked, Prit himself chose that moment to come into the staging room. "Gray-woman. I am surprised."

"Not very surprising," I said. "Wherever there's suspicious activity, I end up there sooner or later."

"No," he said. "Surprised because I thought of you earlier. Because of Bral-past-man."

"Does this have something to do with Bral?" My ears were beginning to feel warm. Something was forming, but I wasn't sure of its shape yet.

"That airshaft is very near. I am trying to decide whether I should order it cleaned. Very hard to clean core vent shafts with spin up." To Brun: "Have they come in yet?"

"Not long I think," Brun said. "They are running out of air."

"I must go check other things. When they come back, tell them I want their guess on how much longer spin will need to be down." He turned back to the door.

"Wait," I said. "How many people know this was caused by a bomb?"

"Myself and Brun," Prit said. "You, now. The two outside ... Brun, are there more?"

"Not from me," Brun said.

"I need a favor from all four of you. I want you not to tell anyone else about the bomb. Prit, you're going to have to make it stick with the two working outside. Do they report to you?"

"But top-big-woman is demanding this information!" Prit said. "I realize you are security officer—"

"This is important. This is about murder. Several murders. The Director may be involved."

"You ask me to risk my job!"

"If Xin Rath asked you to keep this a secret, would you do it?"

He looked startled. "Yes."

"Okay. Then talk to Xin Rath and ask him. He knows what I'm working on. He'll tell you that if I need you to keep it a secret, my reasons are the best."

"What do I tell top-big-woman?"

"Tell her you're still working on finding the cause and that repairs are in progress."

"That will not work for long."

"I'm hoping you won't have to sit on it for long. Two other questions. Just to confirm this: That vent shaft is on the way from here to where the bomb was?" He nodded. "And is there a data station I can get to on this deck?"

"There is a monitor room two doors spinward," Brun said.

§

I had been *such* a landpig. Nearly three hundred cycles and it hadn't once occurred to me. The Ring doesn't always have gravity, idiot! The bottom of a shaft is not always the bottom.

In my defense, I found as I checked logs, dropping spin was such a seldom thing that it was easy to forget that it ever happened. The last time had been about twenty-five cycles before I arrived on the Ring. Of course I didn't need to look at any of the others. It wouldn't have been more than one back because someone would have noticed Bral's death.

Bral had not been at the "bottom" of the airshaft when killed. My wild theory of him having been shot from the core end had been sound after all. I just didn't put the victim in the right place.

He'd been cleaning the airshaft during spin-down the way you can only clean it in zero gravity; push yourself up the shaft to the core end and either clean as you work your way up or clean as you go back down.

Spin being off was the common thing here, the one thing that linked it all together. The bomb could only have been placed when spin was off. The bomb wasn't meant to be used immediately, maybe wasn't meant to be used ever—it was an emergency preparation in case of just something like this, a ship that could expose the whole thing. I hadn't inspired it; I wasn't here yet. And Alsop was dead by then. Perhaps someone was worried about what the next security officer would be like. I don't know.

Bral had been on the core end at the wrong time. That was it; the only reason he had been killed. He'd seen the person setting the bomb—and that person had been ready for accidental encounters; they had "borrowed" Ferm the rat-hunter's poison speargun. The range on that was long enough to hit someone on the far side of the grate, if they were very close to it. Maybe the killer even called Bral over, got his attention, had him come to the grate for a conversation.

The spear impact would have pushed the body backwards. It definitely would have floated enough to move out of easy vision from the core end—the shaft was very dark—and probably floated all the way to the outer end, because if it had fallen any serious part of the distance once spin came back up, there would have been impact damage. It came to rest gently at the outer end, to provide an enigma for dumb security officers.

The killer was not going to be someone from Dispatch. They either had to be someone with secure maintenance credentials or me or the boss, because those were the only people who had access to most of deck one. But that wasn't a problem, because I already knew that the mastermind—call them X—hated pulling their own triggers. They'd gotten Kezar to be a triggerman, and they'd called in an assassin for me.

What I was looking for was the door logs in that part of deck one for the time period when the Ring was last in spin-down. Despite being hampered by trying to float backward every time I pushed a key, I eventually got what I wanted, matching times and all.

Korm, also works for me, Prit had said, way back when. *I think they may have never met.* And they may not ever have. Until the last minute.

I got out my feed. "Prit-man," I said to him when he answered, "You probably have them on a job—where is Korm right now?"

§

The important question then and there was: do I tell the boss any or all of what I know?

It was the question then and there because the Director's office, at two:forty, was essentially right below me, and I would pass by it on my way to Korm.

She could still be X. There was nothing that ruled out her being X. I am not a complete fool, just a landpig.

It didn't matter. I tried her door and it didn't open. It was rare to find a door that didn't open for me. I suppose I could have set my door not to open for her if I wasn't there, too. After all, we had the same level of access.

§

The Ring has things on its "inside" surface—the core mechanisms that create the aperture. It has things on its "outside" surface—the docks and gantries and kickers and so on. But it also has things on its "sides"—primarily, the jets that make the Ring spin. Access to anything that's on the "sides" of the Ring is usually on deck four. That was where I was told to find Korm, making repairs to some part of the spin system while it was turned off, and that was where I found them—floating in an access passage, face down, with their throat cut, surrounded by a red haze of blood spray that had nowhere to fall to. Not dead long. Warm.

I would have liked to have been more surprised than I was. It looked more and more like X had hoped never to actually use that bomb. Now that the existence of the bomb was known, Korm was a liability. If I'd gotten to them in time, I was sure Korm could have told me X's identity, with persuasion. Sorry about that, Korm. Not too sorry, though. I still remembered Bral's decaying, piebald fur.

§

I asked Rob and Don to deal with the body. I didn't have time for it, not with X getting desperate. Fighting a Pergat is hard for a human. Maybe Korm had some of their killer's skin under their claws. Maybe X had big scratches on their face right now. I couldn't count on any of that. For all I knew X had a tranquilizer gun.

I can't say why I chose to go to Dispatch along deck three instead of deck four, knowing that X might very well be in the area, knowing deck three was likely to be deserted. I'm really not foolhardy. Maybe I was hoping to draw X out. Maybe I was hoping to avoid X. Maybe I was just being perverse.

As I was attempting to move past a long line of rooms I knew to be (allegedly) empty, the strangest sensation began. It was Ring hum—but interrupted. It started, built up, choked off, then started again. It was oddly frustrating; you kept expecting it to get somewhere and it didn't. I realized they must be testing the aperture equipment. Repairs were almost done, then. Fine with me.

Then it hit me.

I don't know if I would have thought of it if I hadn't been on that deck, surrounded by empty rooms, at just that time. But I had it. I had solved the power riddle. Like the one piece of the jigsaw that's been holding up all your progress, all sorts of things suddenly fell into place.

Of course, it meant some of my earlier ideas were wrong. But I'd deal with that when the time came. Right now, I needed to get to Dispatch as quickly as possible.

§

"Where is the Director?"

The receptionist/bouncer looked like I was about to bite her head off. Maybe I was. "She came through looking for McGregor a few subs ago."

"I was never here," I said. "Got that?" and didn't wait for an answer as I tried as fast as I could to pull myself to McGregor's office. I still wasn't fully recovered from the bomb and the knife and the tentacles, and dragging myself all over the station by handrail was not doing me any favors.

I let myself in. McGregor was sitting behind his desk, wide-eyed, frightened and trying without success to conceal it. The boss was on the other side of the desk, her back to me. As I came in, she broke off whatever she'd been saying, and turned, and I saw she was holding a very large handgun. I hoped it didn't shoot bullets.

McGregor recovered a little bit, enough to hiss, "I see your pet snoop is here to finish the job," at the same time as the boss was saying to me, "What are you doing here?" I don't know if she was aware she was pointing the gun at me when she said it.

"Neither of you did it!" I said. "Boss, put the gun down."

"He blew up a ship," the boss said, "with a bomb which Prit says *you* told him not to inform anyone about."

"I told Prit that because I didn't want the killer to know we'd found it yet. I wasn't sure which of you it was. On the way here I realized it couldn't be either of you. Why do you think McGregor would have blown up a ship?"

"Because they were investigating—" She stopped herself.

"I'm sorry," I said. "I know you've kept it for so long. But it's got to come out, or the wrong people are going to get away with a lot. The Pergati were *not* investigating the power storage rooms. They had no idea about those. They weren't killed because of that at all. You two suspect each other of killing to protect a secret, but you're both on the wrong secret. No one else gives a damn about the power secret but you and whoever else here is in on it.

"The Pergati were blown up because of qov. They were investigating qov smuggling. A lot of people have been killed because of it—because whoever is running it, call them X, doesn't want to be found out. Bral was killed by Korm because he saw Korm setting the bomb on X's orders. Korm was killed to prevent them talking. Areese was killed because she slept with X and had stolen something that implicated them. X got Kezar to kill her, then killed Kezar when Kezar might talk, and killed Max because he was in the way. All of that, and all the attempts on me—it's all been because of qov. I know you don't care about qov, but someone here is making a whole lot of money from it, and this station is nearly provoking the Pergati to belligerence because of it."

"I know there's been some qov passing through here from time to time," she said.

"This isn't 'from time to time,'" I said. "This is a major operation. This is whole shiploads of qov being offloaded here to be shipped in past the patrols gradually. And that's why neither of you is X. Because you wouldn't put qov in potential power rooms to be burned up, as has happened several times. The main reason I became a target isn't because I was getting close to the answer, but because X thought I was burning the qov, or ordering it burned. And before that they thought Alsop was."

She lowered the gun.

"Our mastermind," I said, "is someone in Dispatch—it has to be, no one else would have the connections, not to mention who else would know the right moment to set off that bomb?—with a fair amount of seniority—but it can't be anyone who knew about the power rooms."

"That doesn't narrow it down much," McGregor said. "Aside from us, only two other people knew about the power rooms."

"There may be something else," I said. "You've probably been in a panic here. All hands on deck and so on. But whoever it was, unless they got yet another triggerman, had to leave here to go find Korm and kill them before they could talk. That wouldn't have been very long ago at all."

"We can check the door logs," he replied.

"No," the boss said. "We'll ask the front desk first."

We exited, temporary truce in effect, although the boss still had the gun out. As we tugged ourselves toward deck four (still no spin!), we had to pass the glass observation wall on deck five, looking down into the control room. Something caught McGregor's eye and he moved quickly to the glass. "Where the hell is Flanagan?" I went to look. The supervisor's desk was empty.

"Leaving his desk in the middle of all this," McGregor grumbled, as he pulled himself downramp, our other goal temporarily forgotten.

The boss watched him go. "He's not going to find Flanagan anywhere in here, is he?" she said.

"I had really hoped it would be someone else," I replied slowly.

§

Dispatch was in lockdown. No one in or out. We'd gotten up a search and determined conclusively that Flanagan wasn't in, so he had to be out. All the people important enough for Flanagan to try to ransom were safe: The boss was inside Dispatch with the other bigwigs; Xin Rath was deep in a Pergati warren with Sul on guard. That left me to get Rob and Don and search the entire rest of the Ring for a needle in a haystack, all without spin.

Actually, I didn't think I needed to search the entire Ring. Flanagan knew it was all over, that events had passed the point he could cover up. What would he do next? He'd use the time he bought fleeing Dispatch to grab some supplies, and then he'd head down to lower cargo to find a way to stow away on one of the three ships currently docked.

The boss had suggested sending some juniors to help search lower cargo, at least, but I talked her out of it. Actually, I just told her no, and she was in no condition to argue. One of them could have been in Flanagan's pay. Even if not, they weren't trained to fight and if Flanagan decided to jump them, I didn't want their death on my conscience.

Stowing away isn't easy. Almost all ships carefully control access except during periods when they're loading and unloading cargo, when they're so busy they get a little lax. Even so, there are so many people going in and out of the cargo holds at that time that it's actually very hard to get into the ship and then find a place to hide without being seen by someone. The classical method is to get whatever it is you think you're going to eat and drink, and a portable latrine, and seal yourself into a cargo crate. It isn't roomy, but it can be done if the next leg of the trip isn't too long; it's been done before.

They were still testing the aperture—hum on, hum off, over and over. I had been hoping they'd get it together by the time I got to deck nine, but it didn't look like they would. It interrupted my thinking, which wasn't any great loss because I was mostly stewing over Flanagan. Flanagan, who had been perfectly willing to tell me when a ship had a load of qov because he'd been sure I couldn't do much about it. Flanagan, who had not held up the ship with the assassin when I'd ordered him to—and had known McGregor would be all too willing to back him up. I was so angry, partly at myself, that I made it all the way down to lower cargo without being consciously aware of the journey.

While waiting for Rob and Don to come down and help, I headed toward the most likely ship. It hadn't loaded in cargo yet, and some of the crates for it were being staged out in the open—and Flanagan knew how to operate a crane; he could have easily gone down and traded one full of cargo for the one which was going to be his new home for a while.

What I had forgotten was that you can't really move cargo crates when spin is down. I know you'd think so—nice conditions for moving big heavy things!—but in practice it doesn't work out. If you slide one, you have a hard time stopping it. It still has all its mass. Put yourself on the far side of it and you'll find yourself pushed along backwards behind it and maybe getting crushed when it reaches a wall. If one crate bumps into a pile of them, it will dislodge the whole pile and send some of them floating in various directions, up to the ceiling, where they will be nearly impossible to pull down, and a hazard to life and limb when spin comes back and they fall to the deck and burst open. When spin goes down, the first thing cargo beefs do is net all their crates.

So Flanagan was waiting it out, up on a crane balcony on deck eight. When he saw me (I didn't see him), he kicked off that and launched himself at me. I found this out when he hit me in the back, and knocked me down face first and we both slid along the deck with nothing to stop us but an approaching wall.

I was seeing stars, but I also saw the wall, and I was able to twist so that he hit the wall first. He let out air explosively and dropped the knife he had in one hand, which I shoved away; it slid a long way across the floor, well out of reach. I tried to stand, but he grabbed one of my legs, and when I tried to kick his head with my other foot, I missed and kicked the wall instead, pushing me up and backward. He came with me, and went a little further than I did before running out of momentum. I tried to move but no longer had any way to, and he was in position to get his arm around my neck in a chokehold.

Fighting while floating is just about impossible. There's nothing to get purchase on. You can't flip someone or even try to dodge. I did try to kick him, backward, and made contact. He growled and strengthened his grip. The edges of my vision were blurring.

A distant sound, miles away in my throbbing eardrums. I suddenly realized what it was: the siren. I tried to get oriented. Was I on top? Yes. Good.

We were both flung outward, "out" being down to the deck. He hit it at speed, and I hit him at speed as I landed squarely on him. I got to my feet slowly. He didn't.

I took back everything I'd been saying about the repair crew for the last period. That had been the *perfect* time to bring spin back up.

I staggered away from him, still trying to clear spots out of my eyes. He was moving, damn it. I'd been hoping I'd broken his spine. I needed to get away. If he reached me, I wasn't going to be much good. Everything hurt. Where the hell were Rob and Don?

He was all the way up—not steady, not fast, but up. I ran for a dark corner. He chased me.

"I don't know why you'd want to run into a dead end," he said, having a little trouble with the words, as he stumbled toward where I was leaning against its back wall.

"Because the knife went back here," I said, jabbing it between two of his ribs at a sideways angle, into his heart.

§

Give the boss credit, she'd waited until a cycle after everything was cleaned up before calling me in. We'd both had more important things to do. We'd had to deal with a couple of messy bodies, the last of the repairs, cleanup of external debris from the destroyed ship. We'd had to put together some urgent dispatches to the Pergati government. And I'd had to ask Meridian if she'd come visit, because I didn't want to sleep alone that cycle. Meridian didn't comment on how much my hands shook.

But here I was now, sitting in the boss's office, and I was pretty sure I wasn't going to like any of the possible outcomes. That's if we ever got to any outcomes. For once she seemed at a loss for where to begin.

"Tell me the story," I finally suggested, when I couldn't stand it any longer.

"As I understand it," she said, "it was in the very early stages of Ring testing that they learned the Ring aperture defies physics—or physics as we understood it at the time. The aperture process releases more energy than it takes to generate. It takes a huge amount of power to open the portal, but when the portal closes, we get about one and one-third times that amount back.

"At first no one was sure what to do about this. Beyond the relatively modest power needs of daily Ring operation itself, what was to be done with the surplus? It wasn't worth the cost to transport it anywhere. But not long after the first Rings began operating, the Pergati standardized on engines that operated on repulsion principles, with very long operating lives on just a constant supply of raw power—largely to solve the problems of refueling over the new travel distances which were now possible. And of course when Pergati standardize on something for space travel, sooner or later everyone else adopts it too, like their timekeeping and their horrible numbers."

You're going to be amused, I know, that it took me so long to realize the numbers in base eight were because Pergati have four digits on each paw.

"Suddenly the company was in a unique position—not only were they able to make money from the transit business, but also from the power business. When ships docked to refuel, we would always have a supply of power to sell them— and their transit, which we also charged them for, would gradually recharge our supply of power for free. We equipped rooms with a variation on the same dense-storage static fields the ships themselves use to hold a large supply of power in a small space. Actually the system is built throughout the Ring. Even the occupied rooms have it. Disabled in those, of course."

"I didn't get it for the longest time," I said, "but when you shuffled power around the other cycle to prevent the investigators from finding any powered-up rooms, that was a big hint." I had another big hint—from Parn—but I was omitting that. "Then for some reason I suddenly connected that the charge built up when the Ring was used and dissipated gradually after that—as you fed it to ships. What I don't understand is why keep it such a secret? Alsop suspected you of conspiracy. Xin Rath did too. They both thought it was the *other* conspiracy, but that's not the point."

"Tell the Pergati that we've essentially been double-charging them all this time?" she said. "You're the one who pointed out that they're near revolt over some of our policies. That would just make them worse."

"I don't think so," I said, "but it depends on whether the Ring corporation is prepared to give any ground at all."

"I don't follow you," she said.

"Come clean, and lower your prices. You'll still make a lot of money. Hire some Pergati. That will be enough to convince them that you're not out to swindle them blind at all times. I know I'm an idealist but I think a little sunlight would go a long way here."

"You, an idealist?"

"Sure. I spent all those years in the Vault because I was an idealist who didn't want to have to think about the way people actually acted. And you hired me anyway."

"Your Vault experience is one of the primary reasons why I hired you," she said. "The security officer must be a person who has very few close friends, very few biases, someone who is willing even to suspect—"

"Her boss?"

"The point is," she said, not quite smiling, "someone who spent all that time in the Vault was unlikely to be scared to go it alone if necessary. And you've done well. But what do I do with you now?"

"I'm hoping for an answer that doesn't end with me going out an airlock," I said.

"No, I can't kill you. That would be a horrible waste, and I despise waste. I can swear you to secrecy, but if you were ever in a position where you felt keeping that secret was the wrong thing to do, I wouldn't trust any oath you gave me. You don't respond to bribes, and blackmail—even if I had anything to blackmail you with—would only set you against me. Have you any other ideas?"

§

I didn't have any other ideas.

Sorry; it can't always be wrapped up neatly, you know. Life doesn't work like that. We simply never did resolve it. I wasn't fired and I wasn't pushed out an airlock and I wasn't bribed (although she did raise my salary, but I think that was out of appreciation). Xin Rath and the other Pergati were satisfied by the resolution of the qov issue. Sul suspects something was swept under the rug, because Sul misses nothing. I told myself that if she ever asked, I would tell her the truth, but she never has.

The boss seemed willing to let the matter stay in stasis forever. I think she was reluctant to go to her superiors and say "Hey, I know I'm just a Ring operator, but have you considered maybe changing all your policies?" I was not. Obviously, I couldn't go over her head; I wouldn't even know how. My secret weapon was Parn. He had almost figured it out on his own even before the big bang; that's what he had been trying to tell me with the comments about the research he'd discovered. Since then, he's been the ticking clock. I've been waiting to see which would happen first: him approaching Xin Rath with what he knows; me getting impatient and *telling* him to go to Xin Rath with what he knows; or the boss convincing the corporation to come to its senses.

It looks, as I write this, as if the third choice will win. The boss did eventually make some careful suggestions, and she has informed me that my proposal has been steadily gaining traction since then. I'm hoping it won't be long before we come clean. The Ring corporation is filthy rich; it's time we cut our customers a better deal.

I never did settle whether Flanagan had been directly involved in Alsop's death. But I do know that after I told Catalan all that had happened, Meridian says she disappeared later that cycle, leaving her in charge, and didn't show up until midway through the next cycle—which Meridian says she's seen Catalan do twice before, each time because she wanted to go off and get stinking drunk in private. So I think she made peace with something, in her peculiar way.

Meridian mentioned to me the other cycle that she was pretty sure Catalan was trying to teach her how to take over the business. "She keeps talking about how the Ring isn't a good place for people her age."

"What do you think?" I said.

"I don't know. She's always had fits where she talks about where she came from and how she wants to go back some day. I don't ever want to go back to where I came from. What about you?"

I looked over at her, lying pale and naked and sensuous and utterly at ease with everything. I closed my eyes.

"I'm starting to like it here," I said.

Douglas Todd

AUTHOR'S NOTE: LANGUAGES

Writing a story which changes between several languages regularly is a tricky enough matter; writing one where none of those languages is understood by the reader is another thing entirely. I've chosen to get around this difficulty by ignoring it as often as I can.

Trade, the language humans speak in this book, is not English. In the possibly alternate future these characters inhabit, Trade is what its name implies—a trade tongue, a common language of human commerce, evolved from bits and pieces of older languages plus some new coinages. Unlike Bak'ti, it isn't a pidgin; it's a full-fledged language ... which, unfortunately, is just as unintelligible to us real-world, present-day humans as Pergati would be. In short, from our point of view, *everything* in this book has been translated.

In general the reader can assume that Jessica is speaking Trade only when talking to humans who are likely to be stubborn about it—Catalan, for example, prefers to speak Trade—and Pergati to just about everyone else, and Bak'ti only when she has to, as it's too unsophisticated to be useful for much.

Older human languages do survive, but they have become symbols of political or ethnic alliances considered somewhat regressive by other humans. For example, Meridian probably speaks some Gaelic, because she was raised in a colony of expatriate Irish radicals, who preserve Gaelic as sort of a club password. Catalan may have come from the same sort of situation. Catalonians are noted for fierce preservation of their identity, after all.

Incidentally, the poem Catalan quotes a line of is "Els Amants" (The Lovers) by Vicent Andrés Estellés.

Printed in Poland
by Amazon Fulfillment
Poland Sp. z o.o., Wrocław

53395107R00163